I0578459

One-Eyed Jack

The Deuces Wild Series
Book 3

IRISH WINTERS

One-Eyed Jack; The Deuces Wild Series, Book 3
Copyright ©2018 by Irish Winters
All rights reserved

First Edition

This is a work of fiction. Names, characters, dialogues, places, and incidents either are the product of the author's imagination or are used fictitiously. Any resemblance to actual events, locales, or persons, living or dead, is entirely coincidental. The publisher does not have any control over and does not assume responsibility for author or third-party websites or their content.

No part of this book may be reproduced, scanned, or distributed in any printed or electronic form without permission. Please do not participate in or encourage piracy of copyrighted materials in violation of the author's rights. Purchase only authorized editions.

Cover design: Letitia Hasser, Romantic Book Designs

Interior book design: Bob Houston eBook Formatting

Editor: Darcy Fairbanks

ISBN Paperback: 978-1-942895-86-2
ISBN eBook: 978-1-942895-56-5
Library of Congress Control Number: 2018935626

Irish Winter's author websites are:
http://www.irishwinters.com and irishwinters.blogspot.com

One-Eyed Jack
Deuces Wild, Book 3

You can find Irish Winters

On Facebook
https://www.facebook.com/IrishWintersAuthor/

On Twitter
https://twitter.com/irishwinters1

Sign up for Irish Winters' Newsletter at:
http://www.irishwinters.com/newsletter.html

For more information about all of Irish Winters' books, visit:
http://www.irishwinters.com.

The Dead Man's Hand

Old West lawman, gambler, gunslinger and showman, James "Wild Bill" Hickok, was murdered on August 2, 1876, while playing five-card draw at Nuttal & Mann's Saloon in Deadwood, Dakota Territory. Jack McCall, a disgruntled gambler, approached Hickok from behind and shot him at point-blank range in the back of the head, killing him instantly. McCall was later hanged for the murder, but by then, America had lost one of its premier Wild West heroes.

Legend tells us "Wild Bill" held two pair at the moment of his death, black aces and eights—the *dead man's hand*. The identity of the fifth card has been the subject of conjecture for years. For the purpose of this series, I've chosen a deuce of hearts for that card-in-the-hole, in honor of a little boy named Devlin who loved to play the violin. In honor of a father's undying love for his son.

Some players think wildcards are amateurish and juvenile. Others believe the more wildcards in the game, the greater their chance of winning. I only know that one Deuce and a pair makes three of a kind, and that sounds a lot like a family to me. You be the judge.

Deuces Wild.

Chapter One

The moment his fingertips skimmed the door handle of First National Bank on Pennsylvania Avenue Southeast, FBI Special Agent Isaiah Zaroyin felt the presence of evil. His mouth went bone-dry as the chill of mind-numbing terror from within the bank skated up his forearm, prickling every psychic nerve in his body. The man he used to be would've hesitated charging into danger, but that timid guy was gone, transformed after months of physically brutal, twenty-four-seven tactical FBI training into an officer of the law.

Shoving the heavy glass door aside, Isaiah let himself quietly into the lobby. An unattended information desk stood to his left, two glass-walled offices at his right. Three civilians, two males, one female, stood stock still in the service queue straight ahead. All four tellers, one male, three females, stood transfixed with their hands up, their wide-open eyes on some unseen person or persons around the corner to Isaiah's right.

He slowed his pace, his palm not yet on the pistol grip at his hip. Truth be told, he hated the vile weapon his job required he carry with a passion, not a typical trait for a government sponsored killer. But Isaiah wasn't *that guy*, either. More than most people, he understood how violence spawned more violence.

Staying out of sight, he called forth his true skill, and sent his powerful psychic alter ego ahead. Sure enough. *Four tangos*, as Tucker Chase, the FBI Director of the Bureau's only psychic team would say, were in the process of robbing one of the District's financial landmarks.

Greed radiated from Garrett H. Randall and his three brothers: Liam, Tank, and Robert. Tank patrolled the main floor with an open-bolt, submachine gun tucked into his chest, but Liam and Robert were already behind the teller windows, also brandishing submachine guns and forcing the employees to the floor. Garrett's brothers' minds were sketchy at best, but easy to read. They might as well have been named Curly, Larry, and Moe for the way they blindly followed big brother. Garrett was the one to watch, his mind a jumbled mess of rage, pity, and—

Isaiah cocked his head, translating the mixed signals pinging from Garrett's damaged cranium.

Street smarts, that was the underlying sensation rolling around inside that hard head, street smarts and enough anger to light a fuse without touching it. If Garrett only knew the psychic power he harbored, he wouldn't need the submachine gun in his hand. The man was deadly smart in a scary, violent way.

Isaiah sent a quick status report of all he now knew and suspected on the mental channel he shared with Tucker Chase. The perpetrators. The number of civilians on scene. The danger. Immediately, a torrent of expletives flooded the private path, all unfit for human consumption, some downright anatomically impossible.

Tucker was like that. Explosive. Passionate. Ready to fly cover for his people and the best boss a man could ask for. But a brash, former Navy SEAL who led with that big square chin of his, was no help in delicate situations that could easily morph into an armed standoff. Not today.

'Keep your ass out of sight until I get there,' Tucker blasted back at Isaiah. *'Help's on its way. Don't get yourself killed, kid. Understood?'*

Isaiah did understand, but he couldn't promise that one, so he blocked all further incoming. Tucker would've done the same. He'd follow his gut, and while he might not appreciate the blocked signal, he'd expect Isaiah to do the same.

With said gut churning, Isaiah ventured a full step into view. His heart leapt up his throat. He hadn't foreseen the fifth member of Randall's gang, the one in the too-big-for-her-petite-frame, red leather trench coat. The one hiding behind over-sized dark glasses that covered most of her face. The one with the riot of burgundy-red tangles splashing out from beneath a shabby Red Sox ball cap and tumbling down her back. The one with her arms outstretched, a snub-nosed revolver in her hands, now pointed shakily at him. How could he have missed reading her?

"D-d-don't come any closer. S-stay back," she warned, her voice tight and trembling, on the verge of hysteria. "I'll sh-sh-shoot. I m-m-mean it."

No, you don't mean it, and she certainly didn't belong on that side of the bank, but Isaiah couldn't get a solid read on her. He couldn't get past the mental wall inside her mind. That was his first clue that something was amiss with this unstable situation. Other than the obvious physical tells from the redhead. The clear signs of hyperventilation. The sweat running into her eyes. The red blotches on the slender column of her creamy neck, and the fact that she was shaking hard enough to drop the revolver—or accidentally fire it.

Despite popular misinformation floating on the web, and—let's not forget what the know-it-all film makers in Hollywood spewed as gospel truths— psychics were not mind readers. Impression readers made for a better descriptor, but aura decoders was more accurate. Psychics simply translated the mental energy produced by every living human being.

But from this woman? Nothing. So why the leather coat on a warm spring day? Did she mean to stand out in this crowd? Was this robbery about fame and glory? Notoriety? Banks had been robbed for less, but this made no sense. The gun in her hand had already achieved those things for her. Her sleeves were too long, the padded shoulders on that leather trench coat, too wide. He saw it then, the tiniest glint of silver duct tape at her wrists, forcing her hands and the revolver together. Something bulky was hidden beneath the leather. She was no robber. This was a hostage situation.

"Do what the lady says! Get your ass on the floor!" Garrett bellowed, waving his machine gun in an arc overhead. "Hand over the money or I'll shoot!" He sent Isaiah a lethal glare. "You'll die first!"

Isaiah dropped belly to the floor to appease the maniac, but kept his chin lifted, still making eye contact with the woman in the trench coat. '*Who are you?*' he asked mentally, needing her to know he was on her side and that he could help.

She never indicated she might've picked up on his covert message. Instead, her frightened gaze slid back to the teller windows where Liam and Robert now rummaged through cash drawers, where one of the female teller's mental anguish came through loud and clear. Sandra. Today was her last day at work before two months of maternity leave. She loved her husband, and she was scared to death for her unborn child. A little boy. An Invitro baby. Her last hope.

Isaiah sent Sandra a psychic wave of confidence that all would end well, then he let his unique mental powers loose to assess the real situation. Both security guards had been disabled in the lobby, one shot in the leg and bleeding, the other unconscious. The downstairs restrooms were vacant. There was no one in the safety deposit vault. The silent alarm hadn't gone off, which meant it had been disabled. No other staff was in the building. Wasn't that interesting?

Isaiah sent another heads-up to Tucker, *'Garrett has someone inside.'*

'Goddamn it, don't you dare cut me...!'

Click. Isaiah silenced what would've been another epic rant filled with testosterone. You've got to love having a tried and proven American hero on your side in a dogfight, but you don't necessarily have to like it. Or him. With Tucker for a boss, Isaiah didn't often need enemies. The guy was that good—and that abrasive.

"Make it quick, boys," Garrett ordered his brothers behind the counters. "Tank, shoot the first person who moves. Liam and Robert, load up. Take everything. Doll Face, you're with me." He clamped onto the woman's right arm, his fingers digging deep, creaking into the leather.

With no choice, Doll Face sidestepped to Garrett's side, her arms still extended and shaky, her weapon aimed too high to hit anything but the windows above and behind the teller counter. Wait. That bulk under her coat... *Damn. She's a bomb, too.*

'*I can help you,*' Isaiah projected forcibly into her mind. '*Look at me. See me. Know that I can save you.*'

Nothing. Either she was too traumatized to let him in, or she had the psychic ability to block him. It happened. That was the ultimate problem in Isaiah's very limited career field. Being psychic wasn't an omniscient, god-like trait that allowed access to everyone's thoughts. It wasn't Superman's all-knowing, all-seeing x-ray vision, either. This psychic ability worked on science. It required a sensible, semi-psychic receptor as well as a psychic transmitter, and right now, Doll Face was neither.

Isaiah's gut churned when Garrett Randall dragged Doll Face farther down the hall to the corridor branching to the right. Out of sight meant trouble for a woman. Possibly rape. But Isaiah suspected they were more likely headed for the secret basement exit only Garrett and the bank manager knew existed. *Interesting.* Garrett not only had another partner in crime, but he intended to run out on his brothers. Were he and Doll Face in on this together? Was she a decoy or a bona-fide innocent in the wrong place at the wrong time? And why leave without the bank's money?

'*The bank manager's the inside man,*' Isaiah relayed to Tucker, then shut the link down before

Tucker could get off a list of imperatives Isaiah didn't want to hear.

"You're hurting me," came a timid whimper from behind the counter. Harriet. The forty-seven-year old teller with bad knees, the one kneeling bedside Sandra. Her husband had cancer.

"Then git your scrawny legs outta my way, you wrinkled old bitch," he spat, "or I'll move 'em for you."

She cried out again as the steel tip of Liam's boot made contact, and Isaiah flattened both palms to the floor, appalled and angry. Liam was a known sadist and more lethal than Garrett. He'd no doubt shoot Harriett to prove he meant business.

Fighting an overwhelming need to strike back, Isaiah first probed Liam's brain, version 1.0 on the evolutionary scale, needing to see what the Neanderthal thought he knew. Not much. The big guy wanted cash, and was greedily stuffing all he could into a canvas bank bag he'd set on the chair by one of the teller drawers. Rapid heartbeat. Dry lips. Yet joyful. Nearly rabid with glee at what he was doing. With what he was getting away with. The only thing he'd like better would be killing every last person in the bank.

Not happening.

Isaiah shook the gruesome vision off. Being filthy rich wasn't good enough for Liam. All women in the bank were in mortal danger. Robert's greed was in lockstep with Liam's, but he lacked this brother's killer instinct. The robbery was just a game to the youngest Randall, a way to prove he was as tough as his brothers. He was here to learn.

Isaiah sent a silent push to Liam and Robert, compelling them with unimaginable need to possess every last dollar, nickel, and dime in the bank. They *had* to have it. Every. Last. Cent.

Once they were sufficiently enthralled, Isaiah turned his attention on Tank. The brute strolled the lobby, nudging the prostrate woman's hip with the toe of his boot as he went, sticking the muzzle of his weapon in the two men's faces, keeping them edgy. Toying with them like a cat with a mouse. He enjoyed terrorizing people. The customers were in damned dire straits.

A scuffle at the far end of the hall caught Isaiah's attention. What sounded like a slap. Garrett and Doll Face hadn't gone far. "B-b-but I, I can't do that," she cried, her voice verging on hysterical. "I don't know what you're talking about."

"I'm talking about the money!" Garrett's angry voice boomed. "The real money! You know where it is, I know you do!"

After another resounding slap, she crumpled to the floor, her arms still extended like sticks. Not able to catch herself, her cheek hit the polished marble floor with a crack. Isaiah winced. Blood gushed down her neck even as Garrett latched onto her coat collar and dragged her backward, the revolver trapped in her hands waving like a red flag.

The time had come. The second Garrett rounded the corner and was out of sight, Isaiah made his move. Pushing up from the floor, he took off running. Rounding the narrow service desk where customers filled out deposit slips on good days, he jumped sideways, and with one well-placed kick to Liam's throat, the sadist was down and out for the count.

But Liam got off a wild spray of gunfire before he hit the floor, raining down sheetrock and dust. The hostages cried or screamed, but by then, Isaiah had vaulted the teller counter. His boot made contact with Robert's surprised face before the guy could get to the submachine gun he had thoughtlessly dropped on the floor. Down he went, but—damn! Just as Isaiah jumped to his feet ready to take on Tank, another body hurtled the counter, this one clad in the crisp black uniform of D.C.'s finest.

A female police officer landed on her feet and—*Boom!* Tank dropped in the lobby where he stood, a bright red blossom gurgling out of the gaping hole in the center of his chest, and a shocked WTF in his eyes. Robert had come to, but hadn't seemed to notice the noise or the officer. He was still on his knees, chasing after every last bill and coin even though his brothers might be breathing their last.

Focused on rescuing Doll Face, Isaiah grasped the edge of the counter to be on his way when—

"Don't move," a razor sharp feminine voice ordered. "Hands up where I can see them, smart ass. Now!" Amazing. This female Metro police officer thought she was in control. What'd she think he'd been doing?

Isaiah did as he was told and lifted both palms, breathing hard. Talk about *Wonder Woman*. He knew this particular officer. Roxy Thurston, totally believed in herself and her shooting prowess, and she meant to put one in Isaiah's head if he so much as looked sideways. They'd run into each other before, and it always ended the same. The ballsy cop took over jurisdiction, and unless the FBI had reason to protest, Isaiah always let her.

"Shit. It's you again," she hissed, her weapon still trained on him and her eyes bright with recognition. "What are you doing here, Special Agent Zaroyin?" Officer Thurston didn't tremble or hesitate, but man, what a sight. Her chin stuck out like she already owned the place. Glossy long black hair had been pulled tight in a long ponytail at the nape of her neck. Not perky. Not cute. But all business.

A few tendrils had dared escape her control, softening the masculine set to her jaw. Laser brown eyes scoped the entire situation, flickering from Liam's prone body to Robert, still hunched over the fallen cash drawer on the floor and scrabbling for coins, then onto Tank laying in the lobby where no civilian still dared move.

"As you know, I'm FBI, ma'am," Isaiah offered, matching her calm as he lowered his hands. "You'll find my badge on my belt where it was the last time we met. There's another armed robber in the bank,

Garrett Randall. He's got a female hostage. She's armed, too, but don't hurt her. She's not with them, but she's also wired with explosives. C-4, I believe."

"We'll see about that." Thurston jerked her head toward Liam, still out cold behind the counter. "Did you kill him?"

"I might have. You're welcome to take a look. I'll wait here." *At least until you turn your back. Then I'm off to save Doll Face.*

Pressing her chin to the two-way clipped to her shoulder, Officer Thurston sent a call for immediate MPD backup. "How many did you say?" Authoritative, she demanded obedience, so Isaiah gave her that, too.

"Just the four Randall brothers, but Garrett's the only one left to worry about. He's armed with a submachine gun, and he's got inside help, the bank manager. I'm sure of it. He's taken a hostage. Long red hair. Red leather trench coat. You can't miss her."

"So you said." Tossing her cuffs, Thurston stuck her chin at Robert, still thinking she was in charge. "Secure him before he gets away, too. Do it fast." Her nose flared even as her deep brown eyes scanned Isaiah up and down in one lightning quick assessment. *Did she just lick her bottom lip?*

He did as he was told instead of watching her saucy mouth. The bumbling brother wasn't a threat, not the way he kept palming the floor for every last dollar and dime, but Isaiah gave Robert no choice but to comply. Kneeing the guy between his shoulder blades, he secured the weak-minded brother. Even cuffed with his hands behind his back, Robert lay sideways and craned his neck to grab any stray bills with his teeth.

Isaiah did borrow Thurston's cuffs to secure Liam where he'd fallen, though. He hadn't come around yet, but Isaiah didn't take chances. Tank, on the other hand, could be trouble if that injury in his chest wasn't fatal. The second eldest Randall was an ox on steroids. All brawn. No brains. Maybe dying, but... maybe not.

Officer Thurston's head canted as her dark brown eyes raked over Isaiah yet again. Her nose wrinkled, and that made her just plain—adorable—in a purely professional way. "You're really him, that mind reader dude the FBI's so proud of."

Mind reader dude? Isaiah didn't care what the FBI was proud of, but this female officer calling him a dude, like he was some freak show hiding behind a badge, bugged him. A distinct click drew his focus to the hall.

Pivoting, Thurston turned her revolver on the eldest Randall who'd just stepped into the open with his human shield, his fist knotted in Doll Face's hair, her head forced back on her shoulder. With a growl, he shoved her forward.

The poor thing's face was ruddy and sweaty, her arms still extended and her weapon angled upward. That alone made up Isaiah's mind for him. Doll Face wasn't part of this gang. She was a pawn, a woman in the wrong place at the wrong time.

"Well, well, well, if it isn't Officer Krupkey," Garrett gloated. "We meet again."

Isaiah's eyes narrowed at that off-the-wall reference to the bully cop in the musical, *West Side Story*. Those five years in the pen must have been pure enlightenment for this particular dirtbag.

"Officer Thurston to you, scumbag," Thurston shot back at him. "When'd you get out?"

His upper lip lifted in a sneer. "None of your business, pig. Now move your fat ass and no one'll get hurt." He seemed unconcerned that none of his brothers were in sight. He didn't so much as look sideways to the counter for Liam or Robert, but Tank lay there in the open. Garrett had to know he was dead. Tank's arms sprawled at his side, his fingers still on the submachine gun, but a widening pool of blood puddled beneath him, and—what the hell was wrong with Garrett Randall?

Isaiah's blood chilled. He never had a brother, but to lose three at one time... A mighty wave of empathy washed over him for all the brothers in the world. All but Garrett Randall. Why was he in this bank? What was going on?

Thurston pressed one step toward Garrett, her focus not wavering, her demeanor incredibly cool and collected considering she was the only law enforcement officer on site, and that she was in the middle of a highly explosive confrontation. "Let her go before I put a round through your left eyeball, Randall. You won't look so pretty with half your ugly head missing."

"I ain't worried 'bout no beauty contest. Hold still Doll Face." With one hand on the poor woman's neck, Garrett leveled the muzzle of his weapon over her shoulder, closed one eye and took aim at Thurston. Whimpering, Doll Face turned her cheek from the gun barrel, her arms still rigidly poised to shoot, though both of her eyes were closed and she'd aimed at the ceiling.

Good girl, Isaiah thought, certain once again that he'd tagged her motives correctly. Doll Face was the pawn. Randall was the ass. Check and double check.

"You always were an eager beaver, Thurston," Garrett snickered, "least that's what I heard in the pen. I hear you can take it in the ass better than most pretty boys."

Thurston didn't so much as blink at the ugly taunt. "You'd better believe they talk about me in the pen. Who do you think put them there?" she replied, her tone over-the-top cocky, vaguely reminding Isaiah of his boss, Tucker Chase.

But Doll Face didn't have the nerve for this situation. Her cheeks flushed even as the rest of her complexion turned a pasty shade of gray. Isaiah had to get her away from Garrett before she did something stupid, like kill someone.

Chapter Two

"Let's make this simple, Randall. Your brothers are all down. I'm pretty sure Tank's dying. You don't look like you care, but that still makes you the last asshole standing. How about you step away from the woman, and I let you live?" Roxy didn't back off for anyone. It wasn't in her training or her nature.

An ugly smile slithered over his whiskered face like a pet rattlesnake come out to play. Prison food must've agreed with him. He'd put on fifty pounds since Roxy had seen him last. The guy was butt ugly.

Garrett had just done a nickel upstate for an armed home invasion where he'd nearly bludgeoned the elderly homeowner to death. He should've gone down for assault with a deadly weapon, but the jerk had a semi-decent lawyer in the Randall family, an aunt who'd married well, and gone to college long enough to join the greedy throng of public defenders. Sylvia Delgado got him off easy. Five years was nothing.

The poor woman caught in his snare now was the problem. The redhead should faint like the damsel in distress she obviously was, but she kept waving that damned revolver like a marching baton. If she was smart, she'd drop it, but even smart people did crazy things under duress. Roxy didn't want to kill her. Didn't want to have to, but she would.

"Guess again, bitch," Randall hissed as he shoved Doll Face forward and into Roxy's line of sight.

Doll Face's arms lifted, and... *Blam! Blam! Blam!* The dumb chick fired!

All shots went high—thank God!—but between the sirens screaming outside the bank and Psychic Dude's hand on Roxy's forearm like a vise, she couldn't think clearly enough to get a shot off before the eldest Randall turned and ran back down the hall.

"Back off," she spat at Mr. FBI, ready to knock him out if he tried that stunt again. The warmth from his grip still tingled, but there wasn't time for that. "I'm working here!"

"You can't get him now. He's gone."

"You think I don't know that?" She elbowed the guy a sharp one in the ribs, pissed as hell at his steady composure as much as the fact that he was still touching her, and that—crap—she liked it. "I'm going after him. Stay here."

"No, you're not," Mr. Know-It-All barked back at her, his gaze directing her to the woman, and those damned slender fingers of his still holding her fast. Had to be the adrenaline that made her stop and listen, but the electric buzz radiating up her arm from his touch was annoying. She shrugged him off again, but didn't dare lower her piece. Not until…

The front flaps of the woman's red leather trench coat parted, revealing a much more serious problem than a bank robber on the loose. *Shit*. Psychic Dude was right. A flimsy metal harness had been fitted over her shoulders and around her chest. It held her arms rigid and raised, but worse than that revolver in her hands, Doll Face was wired with enough plastic explosives to blow Washington D.C. clear off Google maps.

"Jesus Christ," Roxy muttered. "Stand down," she sent to her fellow MPD officers lined up outside and ready to charge into the bank the first chance they could. "Don't come in, guys. I need EOD on the double. Get ready to receive all hostages but one." *The one who just might blow us all to hell.*

"Thurston," Captain Quinlan barked. "What's going on?"

She explained quickly, told him the eldest Randall had escaped through the rear exit, and the others were incapacitated. She had three bank customers, four employees coming out as soon as she could, faster if he'd get off the line. She needed EMTs to transport the two wounded security guards and the downed Randall brothers, pronto. One woman remained, still armed, and *oh, by the way,* wired to blow.

"For God's sake, get those civilians out of there!" he ordered, finally comprehending the scope of the problem.

No shit, Sherlock. "They're coming out now, Cap. Where's O'Donnell?" That would be Suzanne O'Donnell, a damned fine, ex-military explosive ordnance gal, new to D.C. Metro, but a terrific addition to the all-male MPD bomb squad.

"Suzy's suiting up now. Give her ten. What are we looking at? How much? What kind?"

"Four bricks of C-4, det cord, and a wrist watch timer," Psychic Dude replied, his voice oddly soothing. He hadn't bullied Roxy into relinquishing the scene, an unlikely cooperative change for a Bureau narc.

"You're sure of that?" Roxy couldn't get a clear look at the explosives to verify, not from this distance. How could he be certain?

"Positive." He had the temerity to walk over to the nearest teller on the floor. "Excuse me, ma'am, but all of you should leave now. Go quickly to the front entrance. The police are waiting there for you. Take it easy. Keep calm. Help each other. Officer Thurston and I have everything under control."

Quietly, Roxy relayed what Psychic Dude said about the explosives to her captain while the frightened civilians wasted no time running for their lives. "What about the three Randall brothers?" she asked Quinlan.

"They're no trouble for now," Psychic Dude answered, and Quinlan's grumpy baritone voice faded to white noise. "My name's Isaiah Zaroyin by the way, Officer Thurston, not Psychic Dude. It's good to meet you again. You can call me Isaiah. Roxy is it?"

"To my friends," she spelled that boundary out nice and clear, trying to focus on whatever Captain Quinlan was saying over her radio instead of what was coming out of the mouth of the incredibly handsome man smiling down at her. Damn, Agent Zaroyin—she refused to be on a first name basis with anyone FBI related—had sexy, dark blue eyes. This could've been one of those movie scenes that ended with the hero kissing the heroine at the end of a bank heist—enough of them had been filmed in the District—but Roxy didn't take second billing, and—newsflash! She didn't need a hero. But if she did...

"Thurston! Are you listening to me?" her boss's snarky question finally registered in the flustered female portion of her beat cop head.

She shook her distraction off. Zaroyin was trouble and the last thing she needed. "Umm, yes sir. It's noisy in here. Sorry. Say again."

Okay, so it wasn't noisy. It had gotten deathly still now that Randall and the civilians were gone. The EMTs were quietly busy with the wounded security guards, but she'd never admit that a man—this man—had distracted her. Not in a million years. Agent

Zaroyin was a Fed and she was a cop. Neither the twain shall meet and greet.

As if he'd read her mind, Agent Zaroyin shot her a secretive smile, one brow lifted, the other eyelid lowered into a devilish wink, *damn him!*

"I said I'm sending three officers in to take the Randalls into custody, so don't shoot them," Captain Quinlan all but shouted. "Can you hear me now?"

She caught the sarcasm. *Yes, I hear you now, you big blowhard.* "Understood. Over and out," she sent back meekly.

Disconnecting, she lifted her chin at Zaroyin to prove she was in charge of this crime scene. "You're the FBI's psychic." She made that a clear statement, not a question.

"I'm one of several," he replied easily. "Could you give me a hand?"

"No need. EOD's on the way. Hang tight and stand clear." She used her commanding voice that time.

But Zaroyin was already kneeling at the woman's side, one palm on her leather-covered shoulder. Her arms were still raised and trembling, the sleeves quivering. "I'm afraid that isn't an option. I need you over here."

"And I told you to back off." Didn't he realize how dangerous this situation was?

For a moment there, she thought he whispered, *'Roxy. Please This woman's scared to death. She's a victim here, and she needs a woman's touch to calm her while I defuse the bomb.'* But that would be beyond weird, right?

A shiver raced up her arms and over both shoulders, lighting the defensive side to her rough and tumble nature. Was he really a mind reader like everyone said? Could he see through her clothes? Worse, had Zaroyin just spoken to her in her mind? In her head? Damn him! Did he know she was wearing a hot pink, see-through lace bra? A black leather thong? That no answer came back to her for those questions was no help!

"What? Are you an EOD expert, too?" Roxy gulped, her Spanish/Irish up and her hackles along with it. FBI or not, this guy had his nerve to question her authority, psychically or... or whatever! And he'd better not try that mind reading thing again.

"No, but we're the only two in here at the moment. Please help me help her?"

That did it. No one said please anymore, not while looking as adorable as he did. She'd imagined that psychic—thing. Stuff like that only happened in the movies.

With one last look around, she holstered her service revolver as three officers cleared the front entrance, their weapons drawn. "You won't need those, guys. Two Randalls are down behind the teller windows, another's on the floor, there. All subdued." She walked to where Tank lay, bleeding and still unconscious, then secured his weapon and set it aside to be bagged and tagged as evidence. "Who went after Garrett?"

"Danson, Shank, and one of the rookies, I forget his name. Don't worry. We always get our man," Detective Harmon replied with a cheesy smirk and his usual swagger. "You oughta know that by now, young lady."

"Can the macho shit," she shot back at the only man on the premises in a three-piece suit, instantly riled. *Young lady, nothing, you old fart. I can kick your ass any day. And I should.*

Gray-haired and older by at least ten years, Harmon was a prick of a male chauvinist. A good cop, he always arrived with an older generation twist on what he called *just being funny* humor. He and his little posse of detectives were always making cracks about how women belonged in the kitchen like in the old days, the old cliché barefoot and pregnant, not doing man's work down at the precinct. How they looked better in short skirts than men's pants.

Get over it already. If the old days had been that good for women, there wouldn't have been a feminist movement, would there? Women weren't any different than men as far as skills, knowledge, and abilities went. They could do anything men could do, and for some duties, they were hands down better than guys. She'd certainly proved it, and she was tired of having to prove it to every asshole on the force every time she turned around.

"Officer Harmon," Zaroyin spoke up. "Please evacuate the prisoners. This bomb will detonate in less than five minutes. We don't want to take any more chances, do we?"

Roxy's heart lurched. *Five minutes?* She forgot her women's right issues and scrambled to Zaroyin's side, while Harmon and his two buddies snapped to and evacuated the prisoners. Even the EMTs dealing with Tank's lumbering body hurried.

"What do you need me to do?" she asked, her mouth dry. "Tell me. I can do anything."

"I believe you, Roxy."

Oh, so now, we're on a first name basis? Fine.

"For now, hold onto Candace's right hand and shift the weight of that weapon from her to you," Zaroyin replied calmly, his eyes locked on the woman's. "She's been holding it for more than an hour, and she's very tired. Her arms are numb. I'm afraid her trigger finger is, too."

"Candace?" *He knows this woman's name already?* Here Roxy had been bantering with Quinlan and Harmon, while Zaroyin had effectively dealt with the traumatized female hostage, learned all about her, and discovered intimate details Roxy needed for her report.

Her temper flared. This whole damned predicament ruffled her feathers, and she definitely had feathers. Spiky pinfeathers, and every last one of them was standing on end, poking at her to wrest control back from this unlikely hero. If he'd been abrasive, she'd have had no trouble, but Special Agent Zaroyin was just plain—nice. And nice people irked the shit out of Roxy.

"Candace what?" she snapped, instantly regretting her tone. None of this mess was the vic's fault, but damn. Why'd she have to look so, so innocent?

"Candace Bratton," Doll Face whispered, her voice soft and timid, but not as shaken as Roxy expected. Even with her bruised cheek and bloody lip, she looked calm despite the now less than five-minute warning. "Thanks for helping me, Officer Thurston. It's been a really bad day."

"Can you diffuse the bomb?" Roxy asked Zaroyin as she eased her capable fingers around the weapon in Candace's hand. Soothing the vic could wait. Seconds until oblivion was next to no time at all, and damned if one part of her brain hadn't already flitted home to tell her father goodbye and 'I love you, Daddy,' one last time.

"I can," Agent Zaroyin answered in the same casual and seemingly capable masculine voice. His head lowered to the exposed bricks taped to the vest covering Candace's chest. The metal contraption restraining her arms had been buckled over the vest, but damn it. Mr. FBI had gotten so close to Bratton's rather large breasts that the tips of his short hair brushed the inside of her upraised arm, and... *For hell's sake! What's he going to do? Lick her?*

Roxy stifled a grunt at the way her usually analytical mind had launched into an uncharacteristically possessive mode. She didn't care how or if Psychic Dude touched this particular hostage. Zaroyin meant nothing to her. He was just—*some guy*.

"I've never done this in person, but I've watched enough training films, and if I'm right..." He ran two fingers along the red wire between the timer and the coiled wires looped around one of the bricks, easing it away from Bratton's body. *Will you stop touching her already!*

"Wait a minute! You watched training films? You've GOT to be kidding me. And I'm supposed to trust you instead of an EOD expert?"

He never hesitated. "Cutting this should do the trick, this one right here," he said, his fingertips pointing out the wire he meant, his perfectly arched brows lifted, and those deep blue eyes, so damned—

"Ready Officer Thurston?"

"Umm, yeah. Sure." Roxy could not think! This was not the time for anything less than professional behavior, but... but... He had the most compelling eyes. She couldn't seem to tear her gaze away. Why'd he affect her like this? In the middle of a hostage situation, for hell's sake!

And where he'd come up with the multi-purpose tool now in his grip? He looked so capable and confident that she wanted to scream. This was her turf, damn it, yet he'd sneaked past her defenses like a pro, and he'd done precisely what she would've done—if she'd thought of it first. What would the guys back at the precinct say when—if—they found out?

Agent Zaroyin had barely tugged at the wire, when Roxy barked, "Stop!" before he could do anything stupid. Her heart pounded like a mother, and the top of her usually calm head felt ready to blow off. *What if he's wrong?* Candace Bratton could be a damned good actress and a suicide bomber in disguise, working a deadly misdirect while her buddy Garrett Randall got away. Okay, so that was a stretch, but still. This could all go so, so wrong, and Roxy wasn't ready to die.

"Jesus H. Christ, not so fast. You've never done this, but you're willing to take a chance and blow us to hell? Right here? Right now?" *What are you, crazy?* "Damn, I need a drink." *And a cigarette. Oh, wait. I don't smoke anymore. I'm just out of my mind for letting this sexy guy take over my crime scene!*

"Roxy," he breathed. That one word made everything perfect by the way he'd said it. Not commanding. Not cajoling. Not any of those other annoying guy-ploys men used when they wanted their way. Not one whisper of disdain, contempt, or intolerance colored that single, sweet word. Zaroyin had spoken to her as if he knew she was the coolest head in the room. As if he knew using her name would work magic on her nerves. Oddly, it did.

What is wrong with me? She blinked, not understanding how he'd filled her two-syllable name with a tender kind of trust she'd never known in all her twenty-four years. Roxy swallowed hard, looking to the victim instead of the man who just might be able to save them both. Zaroyin's gaze had suddenly become too, too—something—to risk falling into again, so she focused on the woman she should've consulted long before now.

"Are you sure about this, Candace?"

Candace nodded, her gray eyes bright with confidence Roxy didn't yet feel. But neither did she detect a shred of deceit in the woman. If anything, she radiated an eerie confidence that everything was going her way. "He's saving me, Officer Thurston. Don't you see?"

Still, Roxy hesitated. *No. I don't see, and I need to, damn it. None of this makes sense. Why should I trust both of our lives to a guy I've only met a couple times before? Why should I believe him, when I don't really know him? I'm not even sure I like him.*

"Please, Officer Thurston," Candace whispered, her big eyes brimmed with exhaustion. "My arms hurt, and I'd really like to go home to my kids."

Roxy finally had the nerve to meet Zaroyin's cool stare from where he knelt opposite her with Bratton lying between them. Rich, black lashes fringed his dark blue eyes, pulling her into their warmth and an unsettling feeling of camaraderie and that damned trust thing. Damn, she didn't know this guy, but she knew her gut. It wasn't pinching or filled with acid. Psychic Dude could be right.

"Isaiah," she said, for the first time using his name like he'd used hers, at this enormously risky pivot point, when all could go really, really bad. *Or just as good.* Where that positive thought came from, she had no clue, but once it filled her head, it seemed annoyingly spot-on. Like it belonged there. "Do it. Cut the right wire. Save the girl. Let's all go home in one piece."

Isaiah kept his gaze fastened to hers while his fingers plucked the wire away of the vest and... *SNIP.* There was no explosion. No heat or detonation. No blast and no shockwave. She'd live to serve another day.

Roxy let go of the deep breath she'd been holding. *Thank you God for the Psychic Dude.*

"You did it, Special Agent Zaroyin," Candace whimpered, snaring his head and neck inside that awkward triangle brace still under her coat.

"Wait. Hold on. Let me get you undone first," he murmured, reaching into the folds of the red leather and around her back.

Roxy nearly turned away when he lifted Bratton off the floor just enough to unbuckle the belt. Poor, innocent Candace's cheek pressed against his very fine chest. She closed her eyes. Her tears dampened his shirt, and *enough already!*

"You about finished?" Roxy bit out. *Or do you need an f-ing room, Special Agent Za-roy-in?*

"Just as I suspected." Psychic Dude didn't respond to the snark she'd leveled at him. "Randall strapped you into a double harness. He turned you into a puppet, didn't he?"

"Yes," Candace said breathily, her voice quavering along with her bottom lip.

He'd arched his neck to look down at the redhead in his arms, and damned if Bratton didn't get all misty-eyed looking up at him. But when she batted those damned gray eyes—

God, give me strength. Roxy looked to the ceiling and counted to ten, not sure why she cared if these two got it on here in the bank or afterwards in a hotel room or—*whatever!* Why her fingers had just curled into fists made no sense, either. *It's waaaaaaaay past time to get the hell out of here!*

Yet the tenderness in Zaroyin's tone tugged at Roxy's heartstrings. He seemed to know what to say to this tormented victim to calm her nerves. Candace was all but hugging him, what with her wrists still taped together, and he didn't seem to mind manhandling her, while he sliced through the duct tape, then tugged the harness and its metal supports away from her stiff arms.

"I only came here to get a home loan. Didn't think I'd end up like this." She tipped her forehead toward Zaroyin, going for waifish when Roxy wanted to knock her on her butt and tell her to *back off already!*

"Why you?" Roxy asked, her snarky cop side ready to brawl, trying to wrest control back from Zaroyin. "Why'd Randall zero in on you instead of someone else? There were plenty of folks in the bank. Why you?"

"I don't know," Candace whined as Zaroyin manfully tossed the metal frame across the floor with a clatter, but kept his hand on the middle of her back.

Roxy hadn't noticed until then, but the revolver Candace had been holding now lay tangled in the sticky duct tape at Zaroyin's knee. Like a true professional, he'd set the safety, and Roxy's heart did a funny somersault that turned into cartwheels. How had she missed that, too? She was no wet-behind-the-ears recruit. *So why didn't I think of that first?*

Oh, hell. She'd sort the details later because Zaroyin had just pulled Candace forward. Like one of those sappy Disney princesses in fairytale land where dreams came true—like, never!—she leaned into that powerful chest again. Lithe, ropey muscles rippled over well-defined pecs as he soothed her with that melt-in-your-mouth sexy male voice while she fell apart in his arms.

He told her as calmly as ever, "You're safe now. It's over."

"You s-s-saved me," she sobbed. "I... I owe you everything."

"You're okay now, ma'am, just breathe with me. Deep and slow. There you go."

Oh, give me a break! A sudden wave of righteous hostility rattled up Roxy's backbone, nipping at each vertebra and raising those edgy Spanish/Irish hackles again. That line sounded more like an invitation to sex, and her combined lineage made for a double dose of passion she didn't need at the moment.

Holy Jesus H. Christ! "She needs a medic," she declared loudly, needing to get control of herself and possibly the situation, too. "Let's get out of here. Move it guys. Now."

She wanted Zaroyin to step on it, but he was the perfect gentleman. Holding Bratton so she didn't fall. Securing one arm around her shoulders and a hand at her wrist to keep her steady. Lifting her to her feet.

"Don't just stand there," Roxy snapped, rolling her shoulders to get that annoying jealous troll to let loose. Sheesh, it felt like it had spurs on and those spurs kept stabbing the cheeks of her ass. She had no reason to be jealous of this particular redhead, and she didn't care about Zaroyin. He wasn't anyone special. He was just some guy, one of many at that. *So why the hell is he getting to me?*

"Thanks for your help, Officer Thurston," Zaroyin said when they hit the front entrance. He palmed the door open for Candace to exit, his other hand settled at the small of her back like a true gentleman.

How intimate. How irritating. You don't have to keep touching her, Zaroyin. You're no hero. Damn, get over yourself!

"No problem," Roxy shot back at him, her gaze locked on that spot between two sharp manly shoulder blades and the broad wall of a back that was to-die-for gorgeous. Wide at the top, his shoulder blades jutted when he flexed. Roxy wanted to lick her way up the column of that straight arrogant neck and bite his ear. Zaroyin radiated nothing but male confidence. Honestly. The man was drop dead gorgeous, and the rear view wasn't half bad either.

She could've slapped herself. *Rear view?* You mean the comfy looking jeans he wore or the firm globes of a taut male ass beneath those denims? Or the hollow on those athletically sculpted cheeks that showed with each step he took? Hmmm. Not a single jiggle. Possibly tanned. Definitely sexy. What woman wouldn't want to sink her nails—or her teeth—into that fine masculine backside?

Ugh! Roxy slammed her eyes shut to block her wayward thoughts of his naked ass. She wasn't looking for a man in her life. Roxy Thurston was the job and the job was Roxy Thurston. That, by hell, was all there was to it. *So stick a pin in it and get over it already!*

Shaking her out of control imaginings off, Roxy needed that drink now more than ever. Until Zaroyin came to an abrupt halt. With an indelicate, 'Ooomph!' her belly and hips collided with said manly butt, and she nearly swallowed her tongue. My hell, he was deliciously warm, and the masculine scent drifting off him oozed into her nostrils, inciting the tips of her breasts to stand up and point, demanding he take notice. How embarrassing, to be instantly hot and bothered by some FBI guy, the Psychic Dude no less, whom she hardly knew and didn't care about.

Roxy took a full step back, needing a margarita with a tequila shooter. Make that a double. *Forget the crushed ice. Just give it to me straight up.*

"What'd you stop for?" she asked, annoyed that she was, well, annoyed.

He'd just handed Bratton off into the hands of a waiting police officer, and suddenly, Roxy was lost in those sexy deep blues all over again. A shiver of vertigo slammed into her when she lifted her chin to look up at him. Not only was he fit, but he was a good twelve inches taller than her, and he was deep inside her comfort zone. She had to crane her neck to meet his gaze.

He didn't need to touch her. He had some kind of—something—that set her blood thrumming like a freight train in her veins.

"I know a place that serves a good Long Island Iced Tea, Officer Thurston. Or a margarita, if you prefer. Top shelf all the way. We could go there after this is over. Interested?" he asked. "After work, I mean."

Her mind went blank and her brain developed momentary paralysis. Her throat stopped working and she could barely swallow. His lips moved again, but processing what he said took time. Something about Long Island on a shelf and work and... Wait. What? Sex? Did he just say sex was that—*me?*

"...just to talk shop..." finally pierced the fog. One sexy masculine brow lifted, and she was utterly defenseless against his obvious psychic prowess.

"Umm, sure," she breathed, her usual tough-cop voice turned to mush.

Absolute mush.

Chapter Three

"You have to," Director Tucker Chase insisted. "Garrett Randall's still out there, and if what we suspect is true, he'll make another play for your girlfriend."

"She's not my girlfriend," Isaiah reminded his pushy boss for the umpteenth time. "Candace Bratton's a client, pure and simple, and I'm the wrong man for the job, especially if you intend on me working with Officer Thurston."

"We don't have clients, nimrod. We're FBI. We have victims. Suspects. CIs." As in confidential informants.

Isaiah stared the former Navy SEAL down. Tucker could get under anyone's skin with his perpetual innuendos, name-calling, and insinuations. Unfortunately, he'd also been on scene immediately after the hostage situation. He'd seen Isaiah exiting the bank with his arm securely around Candace Bratton's shoulders, comforting her. But that didn't make her his girlfriend.

A single mother with two kids: Kitty, twelve years old, and Darrin, ten, Candace was caught between a rock and a hard place. Between her ex-husband, Bob Bratton, who hadn't been in her life since Darrin's birth, and her former father-in-law, one headline-making Chester Bratton, known up and down the East Coast for his safe-cracking talent, she couldn't seem to win. But that wasn't the worst of it.

Seven years back, Chester had partnered with Garrett Randall and his three brothers to rob an armored car in D.C. Oddly, that heist went down at the same bank the Randalls had attempted to rob this morning. They'd gotten away with five million in large bills back then, and were on the lamb for two years. The problem to their perfect plan was that Chester Bratton retained the five mil, not Garrett Randall or his brothers. They were supposed to meet up later to split the goods. That never happened.

Garrett got antsy. Then the unfortunate altercation with Mr. Whidbey occurred. Out of the blue, the kindly old gentleman bought Chester's rented house out from under him, as well as the five properties surrounding it for a real estate investment to fund his retirement. When Garrett caught wind of the quick sale, he went looking for his cut, but ended up being charged with assault with a deadly weapon after he'd bludgeoned the elderly homeowner, who, by the way, knew nothing about the robbery or the five mil.

By then, Chester had skipped town. To this day, the FBI suspected Garrett had offed him, but couldn't prove it. It seemed Garrett's problem was the same as the Bureau's and Candace Bratton's. No one knew where Chester or the money was. Not even his son. Bob Bratton had an airtight alibi and the motel receipts to prove it. He'd been in Boston at the time of the heist.

"Where is she now?" Isaiah asked, tired of the continuous power struggle with his boss. If Tucker toned down that alpha personality of his, he'd make more friends and influence fewer enemies. But that was Tucker for you. An obnoxious Navy SEAL at heart and proud of it until the day he died.

"Taking a lie detector test." Tucker cocked his head, squinting, giving Isaiah the evil eye. "Don't give me that look. She volunteered, said she'd pee in a cup and take a drug test, too, but we don't need her to do that."

"But you don't believe her." Isaiah made it a fact. "You think she knows where Chester and the five million are."

"I don't trust anyone, you know that. But tell me this. Why can't you get a read on her?"

And there it was, one of those puzzling psychic anomalies Isaiah had no answer for. He'd encountered very few people able to block his mental probes, but Candace Bratton was one of them. He'd sensed her resistance to his gentle touch immediately in the bank. While she'd projected a certain level of fear, there was also a calculating side to her, which explained why she'd kept her weapon raised despite the metal framework inside the trench coat.

Until Tucker asked, Isaiah felt almost certain she'd been honest as far as the hostage situation went, ninety-nine percent sure, but that annoying one percent bugged Isaiah. Candace was an intelligent woman, and Isaiah hadn't been able to get a decent read on her, not once during the attempted robbery. He'd bet his last dollar the polygraph wouldn't be any more conclusive.

"Being psychic does not make me God," he told his boss patiently.

"You were right about the insider though. The TSA folks at Dulles intercepted First National Bank's manager, one Clint Janeway. Guess he thought he could live happily ever after in Samoa with his share of the robbery."

Isaiah shrugged. Janeway should've made it his business to understand the difference between diplomatic relations and extradition treaties. Some countries were only too happy to work with US law enforcement. All they asked for was an offer of reciprocity should they need a similar favor of extradition in the future. Proof, yet again, that most criminals, bankers included, were not the smartest people. "I checked his work history. Janeway's worked for First National over eleven years. Want to bet he was involved in the original heist?"

"Already working that angle, but he's lawyered up. It'll take time to prove."

"Garrett planned to betray his brothers," Isaiah informed his boss. "It didn't bother him when Tank went down. He barely noticed." *How does a man do that?*

Tucker leaned into the conversation, his brow furrowed and eyes gone darker than usual. "No shit?"

Isaiah nodded, perpetually tired of the world of deceitful, conniving men.

"You want to know why I named this team like I did?"

That question came out of nowhere, but Isaiah already knew the answer. Tucker's love for his son ran deep, and the thirteen year old's name was Deuce. There was a heart-stopping time when Tucker had thought he'd lost this boy, back when Tucker's ex-wife had fled the country and ended up in Vietnam. He'd gone into Hell to get Deuce back on United States soil. But that was another story.

Suffice it to say that with Tucker Chase at the helm, the Deuces Wild Team lived up to its name. They had a reputation for getting the hard jobs done while stretching the limits of the law, much like the Texas Rangers of Old West notoriety. Only there were no laws on the books that governed psychic energy— yet. That didn't mean Tucker didn't see himself as Wyatt Earp. Yeah. He thought he was a legend, too.

When Tucker didn't proceed to dazzle Isaiah with his customary bullshit, Isaiah asked, "I give. Why?"

Eying Isaiah with something akin to tenderness, Tucker produced a set of playing cards, shuffled them like a dealer in Vegas, then turned five cards over, revealing a royal flush, all hearts, as well as one Joker.

Isaiah straightened, wondering how Tucker drew those specific cards from a shuffled deck. Was this a trick?

Tucker set the ace aside and tapped one finger to the king of hearts. "That's me. I run this show. I'm king over my team. No one else has a say. Not even Director Strong."

Yeah, yeah, yeah. King, Ace, what was the difference? They both spelled ego, which Tucker had just demonstrated in—aces. Isaiah stifled a smirk.

Tucker tapped the queen next. *Has to be Eden. She's the heart of this—*

"Not Eden. Melissa," Tucker corrected.

Whoa. That was new. Tucker had just read him as well as those cards. Isaiah sat up a little straighter.

"She might not work for me, but she's part of this team. So yeah, she's my queen. Always has been, always will be." Tucker fingered the jack next. "And this guy..."

The jack of hearts showed his profile instead of his entire face. One-half hidden, one-half visible. Had to be Tucker's son.

"Not Deuce." Tucker stared at Isaiah through lowered brows, his eyes more black than brown, and Isaiah was sure. His boss's psychic skills were growing stronger.

"Me?"

Tucker's gaze lowered to the card almost as if he were looking beyond it. "To be called a one-eyed jack's usually a slur. It means you're a liar and a charlatan, a guy who presents himself as a gentleman while he knifes you in the gut. But you..."

"Wait. You think I'm a liar?" That hurt. Of all Tucker's team members, Isaiah preferred to stay in the background. He was support staff, nothing more, but he was no liar.

"No. Never. Hear me out. I had a spotter when I was in Pakistan a few years back. Played a game on our downtime called One-Eyed Jack. In the rules, all jacks were wild, so if you were dealt one, you protected it. Jacks were a bonus card that no one else knew you had. They entitled the holder to one free mark on the game board, but the one-eyed jack of hearts, well, he was different. With that card in your hand" —Tucker tapped the card again— "you couldn't lose. The one-eyed jack of hearts was the only card in the game that could kill your opponent, and if you played it right, win the game."

Soooooooooo not what Isaiah expected. "I don't kill people, Boss. Please get that straight once and for all. I hate that side of my job, and if there's another way, I'll always find it."

Tucker nodded. "I know that about you and I respect it. But besides Melissa, you're the one I trust the most, Isaiah. You taught me all I know, and you're honest and straight with me, and..." Tucker lifted the jack of hearts, flipping it between his fingers like a dealer would. "To be honest, you're the real power behind this crazy team. Don't take this wrong, but you're... you're..."

I'm what? Isaiah held his breath. He'd never seen this side of his boss before.

"You're like a little brother to me," Tucker breathed. "And yeah, I know who you are. I see the intellectual who thinks he can save the world without resorting to warfare, but know this, Isaiah. The day will come that you have to become that liar and charlatan to save lives. You'll have to be deceitful and double-dealing. You may have to kill."

Isaiah shook his head even as he recognized the truth. He just couldn't imagine a scenario he couldn't control, either mentally or psychically. It just wasn't in the—cards.

Tucker finally looked Isaiah in the eye, and the tender moment—or whatever it was—vanished. Masterfully, he returned the cards to his drawer, tipped back in his chair, and thumped one monster-sized boot onto his desk. "But this is the way this thing's got to go down, kid."

Caught off-balance by Tucker's revelation, Isaiah found himself staring at the waffle tread of his boss's boots, waiting for Tucker to vocalize what Isaiah now knew was coming. *Wait for it...*

"Office Thurston's on her way over. Meet her at ground level once she clears security, then the two of you..."

"No, Boss. I'm not working with Officer Thurston to guard and protect anyone."

"...will escort Mrs. Bratton and her kids to the..."

"You're not listening, Tuck."

"...FBI safe house on Embassy Row and you'll stay there with her until this thing blows over."

Isaiah stood, the vertebrae in his spine cracking as he did. A man and a woman, especially this particular woman, shouldn't work together, not if they'd be alone for any extended time. He'd never admit it to his boss, and he'd kept a psychic lid on it, so Tucker wouldn't pick up on any stray vibes, but Isaiah had definite feelings for the sassy MPD officer. He'd had them since the first time they'd met. Too bad none of them were professional. "Trust me on this. You don't want me and Thurston working this case or any other case together."

"Why not?" Tucker lounged, his hands behind his head, and his big hard head totally missing the point.

Isaiah paused. This Tucker he understood. The man was a brash, bare knuckles kind of guy, one you definitely wanted on your side in a brawl. But when it came to sensitive topics like romance and relationships, hell, the entire feminine gender for that matter, Tucker usually hit a solid three on the sensitivity scale of zero to ten. How his new wife, the very independent Melissa McCormack of McCormack Industries fame, had ever fallen for a man of his obnoxious, take-charge caliber baffled Isaiah. But now he wondered. Tucker's psychic abilities were definitely growing stronger. It was a reach, but might he also be growing more—sensitive?

As if he'd never strayed from his take-all-comers Navy SEAL persona, Tucker added insult to injury. "Look at it as the Bureau doing a favor for the local yocals. Besides, Thurston asked for you specifically."

Great. She'd gone over Isaiah's head and straight to his boss for this cozy assignment. What was that about? "I'll take care of it," Isaiah said, resigned. There was no sense arguing.

"And kid..." Tucker tossed a set of keys over his desk at Isaiah. "Lock up the safe house when you're done. It's a beaut."

Isaiah snagged the keys hurtling at his head. "Does Miss Bratton know we're relocating her family today?"

"Not until you tell her, she doesn't. Let me know when you're in for the night, will you?"

"Yes, sir." That ought to be a treat, informing an already distraught woman that the FBI planned to uproot and transplant her family into the very busy Northwestern portion of the District. Isaiah stuck the keys in his pocket and left his boss behind.

He hadn't had time to run home and change clothes yet, and he needed a shower. Hell, he hadn't planned on entering the bank, either. It was merely on the route he took every day, and the sensation that something was terribly wrong inside was the only reason he'd stopped. There were times he truly hated his psychic gift, but the relief he'd sensed from those poor tellers once he took Liam and Robert down, made the day worthwhile.

Isaiah still had an unpleasant task ahead, but telling Candace about this drastic change in her current life didn't compare to rubbing elbows with Officer Thurston on a day-to-day basis. Not by a long shot. Candace, as far as Isaiah could tell, was manageable, but Roxy? Working with her would be akin to playing with unexploded ordnance for the fun of it.

It wasn't that Isaiah didn't like Roxy. He did. Too much. The passion for her job that the saucy Hispanic radiated, astounded Isaiah. But for the life of him, he couldn't explain why the image of her in leather pants and a tight, wet, tiny T-shirt that amplified her already lush assets, blasted his psychic nerves every time he'd dared tiptoe through her colorfully explicit aura. Roxy held nothing back, and oh yes, she slept in the nude.

Isaiah scrubbed a hand over his face, annoyed he'd lost control over his psychic gift where she was concerned. But honestly, every memory in her head declared Roxy held nothing back. Her after-hours were just as energy charged. She dominated the neighborhood where she lived with her father, where she also taught self-defense classes at the local community center. On her time off, she delivered meals for senior citizens in the same neighborhood. They loved her. Heck, everyone loved her.

Single and a practicing Catholic, she still lived in her father's home. Despite her multiple responsibilities, Roxy seemed on top of the world and able to kick ass any day of the week. Energetic and over-confident, she resembled Tucker Chase with her rock 'em sock 'em, ask forgiveness later style. Talk about a live wire. And trouble.

Isaiah had first met her on another joint Metro/FBI task, this one involving a porn shop with known connections to the sex trade. That was when those first erotic images of her showed up in his head. Working with her had done things to him. The sight of her, the way her hips swung from side to side, and the pleasantly overwhelming scent of coconut in her wake, had aroused a side Isaiah hadn't realized he'd possessed until then.

Working so closely with her had made him want to do things to her, and with her, that until then he'd never dreamed of doing, much less looked forward to. Like night after night of steamy, sweaty sex. Like marathon days of taking her every which way he could. Like Total. Complete. Abandonment.

Yeah. Not happening, and precisely why this joint op was a bad idea. Isaiah rolled his neck from the stress that came simply by thinking of Roxy's silky olive-toned skin. At least it looked silky to him. He had yet to lay a finger on her, but the swish of all that jet-black hair and the way it hung down her back when she walked... The way that ponytail flipped side-to-side off her shoulders when she ran... The way the tips of it slapped the taut cheeks of her sexy ass...

His tongue ran a single lap over his bottom lip, wondering what she'd taste like. Sweet? Salty? The woman was enticing as all get out. And so not happening.

Isaiah had built his life on the bedrock principal of utter control. At the beginning of every day, he knew precisely what the next twenty-four hours held. From sun-up to sundown, and from his morning shower until the second his head hit his pillow at night, he planned, executed, and adhered to well thought out, meticulously planned daily schedules. Impulsive decisions weren't solid, nor could proper conclusions be drawn in the thick of battle.

Tucker and Roxy might shoot from the hip. Not Isaiah. He preferred thinking his way out of difficult situations. Like today. He'd had everything in control until Roxy showed up. From that second on, his blood had fled south and it seemed his mental talents went with it. It couldn't—shouldn't—positively wouldn't— happen again.

Since the spectacular debacle of his father, Abraham Zaroyin's fall from grace and this subsequent, and very much publicized twenty-years- to-life sentence for treason, Isaiah prided himself on his iron self-control. The lack of it was what had driven the once highly esteemed Dr. Zaroyin to the poor judgment that had ultimately cost dozens of FBI agents' lives.

Isaiah refused to be the son who followed in his father's footsteps. His mother had trusted his dad. Look how that turned out.

Only now... Isaiah stiffened his chin. He had two women to deal with, Officer Thurston and Candace Bratton, neither of which he wanted to rely on. Hoping to intercept Officer Thurston before she barged in on Bratton's polygraph like the rowdy maverick she was, Isaiah turned sharp at the next corner, and...*Oomph!*

He ran face first into said Metro PD officer.

Chapter Four

"You jerk! You spilled my coffee!" Tugging what was once a crisply ironed shirt away from her now dripping wet chest, Roxy bit back what she would've said if one of the guys in her office had done what Special Agent Zaroyin just did. The idiot! The cups of her hot-pink bra were now hot-damned-ruined by black coffee that—*Shit!*—oozed southward, trickling past her belly and into her pants. A shiver coursed up her spine, making her wiggle.

"Man, I didn't see you. Sorry." Dumbfounded was a good look on Zaroyin. He seemed torn between eyeballing her soaking wet pockets and looking her in the eye. But that blush creeping up his scruffy cheeks like a fever? The flustered glint in his eyes? Simply adorable.

"Jesus," she hissed, maintaining her bitchy-chick persona just to torment the smart assed federal agent who everyone said could see through walls, but apparently wasn't good with corners.

Sure enough, the coward ducked into the nearest office and returned posthaste, sputtering and waving a handful of oversized paper towels. Everything got more interesting then. At the precise point of contact, where most guys would've dabbed at her shirt *'pockets'* or outright copped a feel, Agent Zaroyin's big, manly hand froze in midair. His fingers crunched those paper towels. His mouth opened and closed like he'd turned into a fish out of water. His Adam's apple bobbed, and the big guy seemed to have trouble swallowing—or breathing. But did he touch her? *Uh-uh.*

"You're... you're wet," he murmured, his eyes gone black and hazy, and the blue nearly gone. "D-did the coffee b-burn you? Are you hurt? Was it very hot?"

I'm wet all right. The urge to be daring—make that naughty—to arch her breasts into those capable hands tripped into her mind and quirked the corners of her lips like the trollop she normally wasn't. It'd be worth it just to watch him unravel, though. It'd make this boring day in FBI Land more interesting.

Roxy opted for snark instead. "It was coffee! What do you think?" *You moron.* "You know anyone who likes hot beverages dumped down their shirt?" *Stand there and suffer, Mr. Psychic Dude.*

Uptight and tense, that was Zaroyin. A pompous ass and a big time jerk if she'd ever seen one. After the incident at the bank, he'd asked her out for a Long Island Iced Tea, but did he deliver on that alleged date? Did she get an apologetic phone call or an, *'I'm sorry, but something came up,'* lame excuse during this long, damned day?

Hell no, and there'd been plenty of time to make a call. Federal agents took breaks, lots of them. She knew they did. But, no. What she'd gotten was stood up, which she was stupid not to have seen coming. After all, guys from the high and mighty Bureau thought they were better than the local police. They were *'the Feds'*, and because they were, everyone else was a lesser life form.

For a moment there in First National, she'd truly thought he was different than other guys. She'd thought he had honor. Kick that stupid notion to the curb. Honor was as rare a commodity these days as chivalry and honesty. It wasn't often she was wrong about a guy, but hey. It happened.

Agent Zaroyin's lips twitched. *How interesting.* His brow pinched over dark blues that had grown bigger. And blacker. He didn't seem to know what to do next. He cleared his throat and—

BAM! Roxy found her butt pushed backward until she was up against the wall of what she now knew was a janitor's utility closet, complete with shelves full of cleaning supplies, a utility sink, an opened box of those over-sized paper towels, and one hot as hell Alpha male.

At least that was what Roxy thought she saw right before Zaroyin's mouth landed on hers in a warm, wet *'hello there!'* Her eyes slammed shut at that point. The lights went out, and she lost her ever-loving mind. Everything faded to black as the slick, frantic tangle of their tongues dancing together lit her up like fireworks on the Fourth of July.

Clutching her biceps, he plundered her mouth in greedy sweeps she didn't think twice about returning. This man tasted like—starlight. A heady mix of wind and night. Of something she couldn't make sense of, not here. Not now.

She'd never known intangible things like midnight came with flavoring, but—*oh, my hell*—they did. This man was the epitome of a beautiful aching song rising up from her soul, and damn, Roxy craved another taste of the heaven that came with his kiss.

Snaking both hands around the strong column of his neck, she pulled him in close, wondering where her mashed paper coffee cup went. Her backside ended up on the counter. Had Zaroyin closed the door behind him? Must have. The only light in this stuffy, overheated closet came from somewhere below. But where had the elastic she'd bound her hair with this morning gone? Why were his hands cupping her jaw like he needed to hold her still to kiss her? *And why, oh why does he smell so good that I want to eat him up?*

Thrilled at the mingled fragrances of midnight, clean linen, starch, and manly deodorant in her nose, Roxy's lips and tongue took another delicious tour of his mouth, hungry for whatever this was. She'd never—NEVER—gone from zero-to-sixty this easily, but her motor revved hot and ready for the finish line now. Lust for another taste of his potent lips, for the scrub of his five o'clock shadow on her chin, roared through her veins like a stiff shot of bourbon. No ice, just a pyroclastic, out-of-control spark that rendered her pliable, and apparently, flammable. Everything he did made her so damned hot.

Frantic for the touch of more skin on skin, her fingertips skimmed over his shirt and slid easily into the front of his jeans. He accommodated the forbidden foray by clenching his stomach muscles and offering more room to maneuver. Bravely, she took hold of him.

Oh God, oh God, oh God. The man went commando, tripping her circuits once again. She licked her lips. Zaroyin was as hard as steel, damned thick, and ready. Every last feminine muscle contracted in anticipation. She'd barely rocked against his hips when a firm, masculine hand settled at the small of her back, pressing her firmly where he wanted her to go.

Roxy hadn't been involved with any guy, much less been this horny, in a long time. Yet here she was, on the verge of detonating from just the taste of his wicked tongue, and how he'd taken charge of her body without asking. Why had she let him? This hadn't ever happened before, but having her hands on him, giving back as good as she got? There was no way she'd put the brakes on now. Together, they were high-octane fuel on the verge of blowing this concrete building in the middle of the District sky high.

Growling now because she couldn't wait one more second to get this show on the road, Roxy trembled. "Please," she whispered, her voice ragged and needy, so unlike her. If this was going to happen, it had better happen fast. Now. Before she changed her mind.

Zaroyin growled back, her breasts flattened against a very muscular chest. Easing away from her mouth, he bowed his forehead to hers, panting in her face even as she gripped his cock.

"Shirt off. Now," he rasped, sliding one palm from her back, past her belt, and into her pants. Her shirttail ended up by her shoulder blades, when, without asking, he shoved her bra up with his free hand. He inhaled deeply as his nose skimmed over the plump swells of her girls while he squeezed her ass. "So sweet. So damned sweet. Coconut lotion, huh?"

"Y-yeah, yesssssssssss," she sputtered despite her sex-crazed haze. For some unfathomable reason, it pleased her that he'd noticed. Just as quickly, his breath whispered over her feverish skin, fanning the flame in her blood, and she lost her mind again.

With a groan, Roxy tipped her head back at the pleasure zinging between her nipples and her core. But when he drew one aching tip into his fiery mouth... When he suckled and nibbled... When he moaned as if he'd just inhaled a box of chocolates instead of her sensitive flesh...

The burgeoning fireball at her core sizzled into blinding fireworks, and she was a goner. Roxy wrapped her legs around his hips and ground herself against him, and...

The most intense orgasm screamed up her spine, shattering every last personal boundary she'd ever set in her life, and her best intentions along with them. She hung on tight while her world shattered around her, blowing itself outward, then, just as quickly, pulling itself back in with one crazy reverse fireworks show.

Like a gentleman, Zaroyin swallowed the scream that breached her lips, but *h-h-holy hell.* A tsunami of aftershocks roared through her. Clenching her. Gripping him. He groaned like a big cat. A sleek, powerful cat. As she settled back to earth, his lips peppered her chin and neck with melt-in-your-mouth kisses, grounding her. Man, could he kiss. Soooooooo good. Maybe too good to be true.

She still had her pants on, but he hadn't yet undone her belt. Tears sprang to her eyes. The tenderness of his mouth roving over her sweaty skin made her cry, and that was a first, but wow. If he could do that to her with just his mouth, what would the throbbing beast in her hand do? Did she dare find out?

Breathing as hard as she was, Zaroyin cupped her ass in his large capable hands. Drawing back to release her death grip on his manhood, she pulled her hand out of his pants and snuggled into the crook of his neck, content to breathe the musky warmth of him into her soul. Yet she couldn't sit still. Her fingers tunneled through his hair, and that was another sensual discovery. He'd cut it short since she'd first met him, bristly short. The prickles parted as she stroked and petted, her poor heart pounding from the quickness of her most excellent orgasm ever.

I don't know how you did that to me, wow, oh wow, oh wow. Let's do it again.

All the while, Agent Zaroyin held her carefully, almost reverently. For as big as he was, the man was uncommonly gentle. Refined. Almost timid. After the way he'd dragged her into this closet, she'd expected to be naked, her clothes hanging off the rafters, and on her knees by now. Instead, she was mostly, still dressed. The tender, semi-polite way he handled her made her feel—precious. Delicate. As if she were fragile, which Roxy Thurston most certainly was not.

But she was grateful for his strength at the moment. With her heart hammering like it was, she couldn't have stood on her own two legs if her life depended on it. She wanted to stay where she felt— safe.

Roxy swallowed hard, her throat gone dry and her morals shredded. Never before had she done anything like this. Why'd Zaroyin affect her like he did? Why this man? This wasn't just a make-out session. This was mind-blowing sex in a closet.

It all started when he'd wrested control from her back in the bank. Had he used his psychic powers on her then? Was he now? Was that all this was, him influencing her mind just to have sex with him? Was he that powerful or was this some kind of dark magic?

Okay, erase that stupid thought. Her hands slid over his shirt and down his warm back. For sure this wasn't just sex, and it wasn't magic. She'd enjoyed it enough to know Zaroyin wasn't a jerk that used women. She'd seen him with Bratton, and Isaiah had been the perfect gentleman in every sense of the word. Kind and caring, he'd taken care of everyone with courtesy and consideration, two traits not normally displayed during bank robberies. Diffusing bombs. Stuff like that.

Yet something was happening, and it had to stop. Roxy wasn't stupid. She recognized the signs. Somehow in this closet, he'd become *Isaiah*, not just Psychic Dude, Dumbass, or Mr. FBI. If that meant what she thought it did, this could be very, very bad.

Special Agent Isaiah Zaroyin might be... Just. That. Good.

Chapter Five

Never, as in never ever, had Isaiah done what he'd just done with Officer Thurston. Never! But damn. She'd kept mouthing off at him, egging him on until he'd lost control and reacted. And double damn, the lady could kiss. The first taste of her coffee-flavored lips drove him over the edge of insanity, and that audacious tongue of hers was as pushy as she was. And her hair...

He could barely make his throat muscles work to swallow. The second those sleek black curls had escaped her hair tie, he lost it. The sensual glide of all that silk through his fingers made him hard as a spike, and those soft, plump breasts smashed against his chest certainly hadn't told him 'no'.

Isaiah knew it then. He might be one of damned few, powerful Level Ten psychics in the world, but Roxy Thurston was dangerous.

Shifting his hands from her backside to under her thighs, he straightened enough to keep her balanced. While the countertop was clean enough, Isaiah had no intention of letting Roxy go. Not yet. Not when he still had to face her and admit he'd stepped way out of line with an officer of the law. The consequences would be career ending. This moment was so not his style. Remorse crept up his throat, and yet he knew he'd do it again. In a New York minute.

"That was damned nice," she murmured against his neck, her warm, slick lips tracing up his jaw to nibble his earlobe instead of biting it off, which he'd half expected.

"It was," he agreed, his legs weak with what he still wanted to do to her. With her. Roxy was as sexually responsive as she was passionate, a tough combination for any man to deny. And at the end of the day, Isaiah was just a man. A very lonely man. He swallowed hard. "I'm afraid I owe you an apology though. I lost my head."

"Me too," she whispered. The crazy woman giggled, and he hadn't seen that very feminine reaction coming, either. He'd expected a fight or a caustic comeback. Roxy Thurston was certainly capable of either, but snuggling with him in a janitor's closet after they'd gone crazy on each other? Not so much.

"We shouldn't be doing this," he told her.

"You're right. We're derelict in our duties."

"Both of us could get fired."

"Fraternization will get you every time."

"We really should stop."

"At least, be smart. Someone might catch us."

"Professionals. We're professionals—"

"Stop it," she hissed, her fingers tapping at his collarbones to get his attention. "Stop beating yourself up, Isaiah. I couldn't stop this fire between us any more than you could, so don't regret what we did here."

He smiled at the sound of his name—his real name—on her lips. She was right. The chemistry between them was a mind-blowing flash fire, one that still simmered and could easily snap back to life if he wasn't careful. "I still should've asked. A gentleman always—"

"Takes care of his lady first," she finished for him, wiggling her sexy body against his raging hard-on. "And you certainly took good care of me."

My lady? Good care? Damned if that didn't fill Isaiah's chest with a fierce rush of male pride. "I did?" he asked, easing back to see her in the dim light creeping under the door.

Luminous dark eyes sparkled up at him, changing her from a pack of red-hot firecrackers to rays of pure sunshine. He was pretty sure she was blushing, the way she bit her lip and lifted one shoulder.

"Yes, you did, and I've, umm, never done anything like this before, either." Her brows knitted like a guilty little girl who'd been caught with her fingers in the cookie jar. "Honest. I don't date. Much."

"Me neither. I'm not even sure how we got in here," he told her, racking his brain to remember precisely what happened after he'd claimed that first kiss in the hall. "Do you?"

She cocked her head, her eyes gone sultry dark as her gaze zeroed in on his lips. "It started like this," she said as she tugged him down to her level and covered his mouth with hers, her fingers holding him in place.

Kiss self-control goodbye. Isaiah slipped one hand beneath her shirt and palmed a lush warm breast, the tip still wet from his mouth. For one brief second, he debated the wisdom of sex in a closet on government property. It plain wasn't smart. But that tender peak had just pebbled into a hard knot under the pad of this thumb. With the sultry scent of Roxy and coffee in his nose, Isaiah succumbed to temptation. Thinking was way over-rated anyway.

Shoving her shirt up and out of his way, he had that tender nub between his lips and teeth in a hurry. Nibbling and suckling, lathing and moaning, he drew her breast into his mouth until she jerked against him and mewled, "More!"

Her mews sounded as sweet as a kitten's and the decision was made. "Not here," he told her, fighting the storm rising between them while she continued thrusting her hips into him, making him harder than steel and just as dumb. That randy thing in his pants seemed to think it was in charge, and maybe it was. When had everything gotten so out of control?

"Not now. Damn it," he hissed, struggling to dominate the caveman instinct to mate and do it now.

"Yesssssssss, now," she hissed back at him, matching his thrusts every inch of the way. "I don't want to wait. I can't. Hurry."

Isaiah lost it. Bending to her will, he undid her belt and unzipped her pants. Fumbling with urgency, he dropped his jeans to his knees. With his back to the door so nobody could see Roxy if they were interrupted, he lifted her plump ass off the counter and fastened her to his hips where she fit like she was made for him. The scrap of a leather thong she wore didn't stand a prayer of coming between them, but wasn't that an interesting piece of the Officer Thurston puzzle. This woman was one helluva challenge.

He tugged it aside. "Hold onto me, babe. That's the way. I won't let you fall."

With one arm hooked over his neck, she directed him inside her warm, wet body with her free hand. Damn, she was a strong little thing, built of muscle, passion, and a helluva lot of determination. Isaiah growled at the heat and the squeeze radiating off those exquisite female muscles.

"I think I'm on fire," he growled. But what a slick, sweet fire she was. So fine...

"Fire and gasoline, baby," she moaned, her voice gone breathy and low. She wiggled until there was no more of him to give. "That's you and me. Burn baby. Burnnnnnnnnn."

Filled to the hilt, he eased her up and down until those feminine muscles tightened, squeezing the life out of him—or into him. He'd read somewhere that an orgasm was comparable to a mini-death, but Damn...What a way to die.

With an unladylike grunt, her head tipped back. He covered her mouth with his as again, he swallowed her scream of release. The heady vibration of it coursed over his tongue and into his throat. The way she bit his lip while panting into his open mouth, triggered his release. At the pinnacle of another thrust, the most delectable fire roared up his spine and through him, wiping out every intelligent, well-thought out reason not to be doing this incredibly insane, intimate, heavenly act with this once in a lifetime lady. Thrusting instinctively, he filled her physically as she filled him. Emotionally. Spiritually. Eternally...

No other woman had ever touched him at the levels Roxy had just reached. Make that breached. Whether she knew it or not, she'd gotten into his soul with that bossy act of hers. And there he was, one of America's most intelligent professional FBI agents, a Level Ten psychic for hell's sake!—having out of control sex with a hot-blooded, passionate woman in a janitor's closet, without a single thought of protection—for his heart or for the baby they might've just made. It was possible. He knew biology, just not how to control it.

Sweaty now and reluctant to face reality, he let his damp forehead drop to her shoulder. "Condom," he whispered with regret, still breathing hard. "Damn. I should've thought to suit up before we—"

"That makes two of us," she huffed, her cheeks pulled back in the smile he felt on his neck. "Don't worry, Isaiah. I got carried away, too, but I've got us covered. I've been on birth control since, ah, since I was seventeen."

He wanted to ask what kind, pills or that long term shot, but he shook his head against her, instead, still sick at heart that he'd lost control. That he'd been thoughtless. That he should've been a gentleman instead of a rutting pig. She deserved so much more. "Next time will be different. I promise. I'll make it good for you," he murmured between heavy breaths.

"Next time?" Roxy tipped back then, her dark brown brows arched and her black eyes sparkling in the dark. Her palms landed flat on his chest, and he knew he'd said the wrong thing. "What? You think this is more than just sex in a broom closet? You think us banging each other like a couple dogs in heat makes us a couple or something? You think we're more than just fuck buddies?"

Ouch. He winced at her vulgar rampage of what, for him, had been the most beautiful act he'd ever participated in. That word. He used it on occasion, but it sounded so much more crass rolling off her lips.

For the first time, he pushed into her mind and past her mental defenses. Damn. She had a wall of them. Prickly. Wiry. Snarky defenses. But the scared little girl he sensed on the other side of that wall, the one with two little fists up and tears glistening in her big, brown eyes, that person was not the same face Roxy showed the world.

Holy shit. This was downright tragic. A long time ago, someone had hurt this defiant woman, bad enough she no longer trusted people. Hence the snark and the tough career she'd chosen. Hence the badassed cop veneer. The self-defense classes and the need to stick close to her neighborhood. To give back. Somewhere along the line, Roxy'd made up her mind she'd never be weak again. *Holy shit, indeed.*

Swallowing hard, Isaiah eased back. Some things were worth fighting for, but there were better ways to fight than confrontation and dominance. Pulling all of his compassion into play, he went for broke. "I think what you and I did here definitely makes us more than just buddies," he said calmly. Letting his gaze roll past her mussed shirt to the juncture of their still very connected bodies, he allowed a small smile at the lovely sight. They weren't dogs in heat. If anything, this was a once in a lifetime 'his and hers' moment to be celebrated, not denigrated or reduced to something less, with crude street slang. "Not that I'm hearing church bells or anything, but you still owe me a date."

"I owe *you*?" she asked as she settled her backside more firmly on the counter. Twisting to the side, she grabbed a handful of tissues from the same box he'd pilfered earlier. With one palm in his chest, she shoved him back, breaking their connection.

A whine nearly slipped from his lips. He missed her heat and her warmth, and no, they weren't the same thing. One came from her succulent core, the other from the heart she hid so skillfully from the world.

"Give me a minute, will ya?" she snapped as she cleaned herself and straightened her clothes. Down went her bra and shirt. Up went her pants. Damned if that didn't change everything. Isaiah pulled himself together, too.

"The way I remember it, Bozo," Roxy quipped when she was done, "I don't owe you anything. You stood me up."

So now I'm Bozo. That should've hurt, but now that he knew the real Roxy, Isaiah could've stood there in the dark and listened to her the rest of his life. She was all woman, and the dim light creeping under the door gave him just enough view of her that he knew he wanted more. She hadn't looked at him since she'd shoved off. An elastic appeared out of nowhere. She secured all those tangles and curls back into a rigid, tight ponytail before she finally met his eyes.

Taking a chance with his life, Isaiah ran a fingertip up her arm, past her neck, and over the silky smoothness of her hair, content to have shared something priceless despite what she'd said. Resistant at first, she finally mellowed and asked, "What?"

"I didn't stand you up, Roxy," he told her firmly. "I couldn't get away until now, and you know it."

She huffed. "Not even for a break? We get those down at the precinct, you know. Bet you FBI jocks do, too."

Isaiah suppressed a smile. She must've really been looking forward to that drink. "After giving her statement, Candace volunteered to take a polygraph, and because of who her ex-father-in-law is, questioning took longer than expected. You know how complicated these cases can be. Nothing's easy in our line of work. What time is it, anyway?"

"Eight o'clock, moron. At night." Roxy tossed the tissues into the waste can under the counter. Without a second's hesitation, she dropped off the counter and melted into him, her cheek against his chest. Her hands snaked around his waist, coming to rest at the small of his back. *Will surprises never end?*

Isaiah stooped to wrap his arms around her much smaller, shorter frame. Bowing his chin to the top of her head, he realized he was content for the first time in years. What a forbidden delight it was to hold this delightful bully girl close enough to feel the beats of her strong, proud heart. Whatever had happened in her past to make her so defensive now, Isaiah wanted her to trust him enough to tell him about it. Someday.

He stilled when it dawned on him that her heart beat in sync with his. That anomaly brought an odd sense of joy he hadn't expected to find in the dark of a janitor's broom closet. Sinking his nose into the fragrant tendrils of her sleek black hair, he took a deep breath of the exotic combination of coconut shampoo and their forbidden sex, mixed with a healthy dose of the janitor's lemon cleaner.

"Too bad. I won't be free 'til this thing with Garrett Randall's settled," she said, her fingertips fluttering over his pecs. Soothing him. Making him believe the fire between them could forge these last few forbidden minutes into something lasting. "He's still on the run, but I'll be the one who nails his ass."

'I'd rather nail yours,' sprang to Isaiah's normally very-much-in-control mind, but he caught himself before it breached his lips, and he said, "Haven't you heard? We're partners now. I'll be working with you until Randall's behind bars."

She tipped back from Isaiah then, her keen Metro PD eyes razor sharp and her beat cop chin up. "You're kidding. Your boss fell for the line of BS I told him?"

Isaiah grinned like he hadn't in years. Ah, he knew it now. He was in for a wild ride these next few days, weeks, or months. "Director Chase is a guy, not a saint. Of course he fell for it." *Just like I'm falling for you.*

The identical grin cracking her face was the best answer she could've given.

Pulling her back into his embrace, Isaiah tipped her chin up and branded her with a slow kiss. Somehow, this one felt better than the others he'd rained all over her face and mouth minutes ago. This one was different. It was pure and deliberate, and there was nothing out of control about it. If anything, it was simple and sweet and tender. Just the way he'd planned it.

Chapter Six

"I can't believe this is happening to me," Candace Bratton murmured as Roxy drove her home.

"It's a tough break," Roxy agreed, "but it's over and you're a survivor. Focus on that."

"Ha," Bratton breathed. "Surviving's not all it's cracked up to be, Officer Thurston. Trust me. Me and my kids know."

Roxy glanced sideways at her passenger. "What's that supposed to mean?"

Bratton lifted her chin and faced straight ahead, a definite tell she was hiding something. Could be her pride or it could be a defensive reaction to the disastrous day she'd had. But it could be a lot of other things, too. "Are you married?" she asked, her face to the window and a tone of yearning in her voice.

Roxy shook her head as she maneuvered her unmarked sedan around a double-parked white utility van on East Capitol Street Southeast. Bratton and her kids lived on 11th Street, north of the Navy Yard at the mouth of the Anacostia River. She didn't yet know that she and her little family would soon be relocated to an FBI safe house across the District. Roxy left that dirty job up to Isaiah.

At the thought of his name, a tiny flame sparked pleasantly to life in her gut, warming the blood in her veins and making her mouth water. Man, the chemistry between them was off the charts crazy, and those amazing eyes of his…

A coy smile curled Roxy's usually snarky lips, just thinking about how quickly she'd fallen apart in his very capable hands. The man was a nice package of sizzling eye candy with just the right touch of humility and charm. She still answered Bratton with a definite, "Nope." *Not only no, but hell no.* Marriage took commitment Roxy didn't need in her already jammed-packed life. Pure and simple, Isaiah was a red-hot distraction she had no time for. He had to go.

"Why not?" Candace asked. "You're young and gorgeous. I mean, look at you. I'm sure *you* have no trouble getting dates." The way she'd emphasized 'you' made it sound as if Bratton had trouble dating. *Stick a pin in that interesting info byte.*

Annnnnnnnnnnd… it was past time to set some ground rules. Roxy cranked the wheel and took a sharp turn onto Eleventh. "Let's get one thing straight, Mrs. Bratton. I'm not your girlfriend, and this is not a cozy sleepover with Special Agent Zaroyin and me. Our business with Garrett Randall is deadly serious, and trust me, he will come after you again. You don't think he'll hesitate to use deadly force when he does? Guess again. You got off easy today. Randall will kill to get what he wants, and you and your kids are just in his way. Do I make myself clear?"

"Crystal," Bratton replied to the city flying by her window. "The only reason I asked is because there has to be more to life than just surviving, know what I mean? That's all I've done for years. I go to work and the kids go to school. We work hard, but at the end of every day, I've still got bills I can't pay and more crap to do than I'll ever have time for. Working at the diner sucks, but it's not like I have much choice, do I? I can't quit work to take night classes to better myself because I'm the only thing standing between my kids and foster care. Life shouldn't have to be so hard for a single woman."

By the time she'd finished that rant, Roxy was certain Bratton was crying. The quick dash of her hand across her face confirmed it. Roxy took a second look at the side of Bratton's face, now hidden beneath a curtain of messy, red tangled hair. The woman was a neurotic mess, but know it or not, she'd just given Roxy one helluva motive. She could very well be stringing everyone along while working with Garrett Randall to make that better, easier life.

"Yeah, I know what you mean, but surely there's something you get out of this, like your family, right? Kids make it all worthwhile, don't they?" That's what some of her married friends said, when they weren't complaining about the high cost of healthcare, childcare, and the messy rooms of the spoiled brats they'd spawned.

A deep sigh answered. "I don't know what I'd do without them," Bratton murmured as she straightened in her seat and looked out the windshield. "What are the police doing at my house?"

Excellent question. Roxy parked behind the cruiser, its blue and red lights still flashing over the front of a shabby colonial townhouse. Unsnapping her seatbelt, Bratton had one foot out the door before Roxy grabbed her elbow and jerked her back to her seat. "Shut your door and stay down."

"But my kids are in there!" Bratton cried, tugging to get away.

Roxy dug her fingernails into Bratton's bicep, determined to hold her in place until Roxy knew what had happened. "No, you'll stay here until I know what's going on."

Thank God, a black SUV rolled to the opposite curb. Agent Zaroyin unfolded his long legs from the vehicle and climbed to his feet. Unexpectedly thrilled to see him again, Roxy rolled her window down, hoping he knew something. "What's going on?" she asked, her throat gone dry at the mouthwatering sight of him. Isaiah made that black suit he'd changed into look good. Tall, dark, and wickedly handsome, the man was sex on two long, lean legs.

"Break in," he replied easily, his gaze warm enough to make her blush. "Stay here and keep your ears on. I'll tell you when it's safe to go inside."

"My kids!" Bratton screamed from the passenger seat, blasting Roxy's eardrums with her panic. "Were they home when this happened?"

Superman's brows creased to a sharp V. "Not as far as I know, but I'll make sure for you, ma'am. You stay here with Officer Thurston, Candy. I'll be right back." With long strides, he ate up the sidewalk, ducked and disappeared beyond the yellow police tape.

Oh, so now it's Candy. Roxy rolled her neck at the sudden stranglehold of the green-eyed monster within her.

Just as quickly as he'd ducked inside, Isaiah leaned back out and waved for her to bring Bratton in.

"I want you to open your door and walk straight into your house," Roxy told Bratton. "Don't look around and don't dawdle. I'll cover you."

"Whatever," Bratton said as she bolted. Roxy scrambled to keep up, her weapon drawn and her eyes raking the surroundings.

Not one of the District's affluent neighborhoods, Candace Bratton's home showed its age. The gate to the fenced-in backyard sagged open at an angle, indicating a malfunctioning hinge. Silver duct tape stretched across one corner of the cracked front window. No spring flowers brightened the weedy flowerbed under the same window, and if these homes had been built ten feet closer to each other, they could've been row houses. With postage stamp-sized yards, they all needed paint. Overall, the entire area spoke of lean, hard times. No wonder Bratton knew the difference between surviving and living.

At the door, Roxy greeted two patrol officers, Humphrey and White. The place had been ransacked, pictures torn off the walls, their frames smashed and broken glass all over the floors. Overturned furniture littered the front room, kitchen, and down the hall. No spray paint though, which teenagers would've done out of sheer stupidity. They always seemed to need to tag their work, like it made them somebody when it didn't. But who'd ever broken into this place had taken time to open every CD case in the black plastic tower, now broken into several pieces on the floor. Whoever did this was looking for something.

"What's going on, guys?" she asked, holstering her piece to survey the damage.

"Neighbor called in a B and E."

"Did that neighbor get a plate? Can he or she make a positive ID?" That'd sure as hell be a nice change.

"Running it now," Officer White replied. Tall, dark, and black, his surname made as much sense as hers. Most people probably didn't expect a black man to respond when they were told Officer White was coming to their aid. Many didn't expect a Hispanic female officer named Thurston when she showed up at crime scenes, either, but hey. If there was one thing Daddy Thurston got right in his life, it was marrying and loving Maria del Rosa Thurston the way he did. *If only Mama could see me now.*

By then, Isaiah had righted the couch and straightened the cushions. He'd also assured Bratton her children weren't home at the time of the break-in. "Do you know where they might be?" he asked her.

"Phones," Bratton muttered, scratching her hands over her scalp as she tossed a handful of her red hair over her shoulder. "They both have cell phones, but that creep in the bank took my purse, and I don't... and I..."

Roxy's ears perked up. Weren't the kids a little young to be trusted with cell phones? How could the beleaguered Candy afford extravagances like that when she was struggling to make ends meet? Or so she'd said.

"Give me the numbers," Isaiah said smoothly. "I'll make the call, so you can talk to them."

"Oh, yes," she cried, her eyes glistening. "I'm losing my mind. Of course, call them. Please hurry." She rattled off two numbers that Isaiah deftly entered into his cell. In a second, he handed it over, and Bratton sank to the ratty couch crying, the phone to her ear. "Kitty. Hi, it's Mom. Where are you, honey?" She nodded, wiping her eyes at whatever Kitty was saying. "Um, yes, you can stay another half hour, but please don't walk home."

"Tell her to stay put. I'll pick her up," Isaiah said.

Bratton's eyes welled as she mouthed, "Thank you," and Roxy couldn't stomach the scenery any longer. She turned away. Something was very off-putting about Candace Bratton. Roxy damned well knew it. She just couldn't put her itchy finger on precisely what that something was.

"A friend of mine will come get you, honey. Stay inside. Yes, you can trust him. He's an FBI agent and..."

"Send her my photo," Isaiah said as he thumbed through his phone. "Here. Send this. That way she'll know who to expect."

"Yes, okay. I'm sending you a picture of the gentleman who'll be there. Yes, I'll tell you all about it when you get home, but please, baby. Do as I tell you and don't go anywhere else, okay? What? You want to come home now?"

Isaiah nodded. "I'm on my way. Tell her to watch for a black SUV with FBI on the side doors, but to stay inside. I'll give her the code word *'homework'* when I get there. She's not to go with anyone who can't give her that code."

Bratton relayed those instructions and finished the call. She gave him directions to Kitty's choir director's home while he forwarded his picture to Kitty's number. "I hope you don't mind, but she's worried."

"Not a problem. I'll get Darrin, too. Where's he?"

"Probably playing with his friend, Jimmy. Let me check." Bratton dialed another number, the cords in her throat tight as she waited. "Jimmy? Hi, it's Darrin's mom. Is he there with you?" she asked, her eyes bright with relief again. "Good, hey, listen. Something happened today, and I need you to come home. No, Jimmy can't sleep over tonight, so listen to me, okay? A good friend of mine's coming to pick you up right after he gets Kitty. No, baby. I'm not hurt. I'm okay, promise, just...."

She closed her eyes, her lower lip quivering. "Please stay inside until he gets there. His name is Isaiah Zaroyin and he's a really good guy. You can trust him, and when he gets there, he'll give you the code word *'homework.'* Don't go with anyone who can't give you that secret code, okay? I need you here with me, Darrin. Understand?"

Bratton seemed anxious by the end of that conversation, but overall, it went smoother than Roxy anticipated. Most kids would've pitched a fit at being pulled away from their friends. Maybe she was wrong about Bratton.

"Are you sure you don't mind?" Bratton asked Isaiah, her eyes translucent with unshed tears as she gave his phone back.

Resting his hand on her shoulder, he ducked to her level and peered into her eyes. "This is what we do, ma'am. Try not to worry while I'm gone. Officer

Thurston?" he asked as he lifted to his feet and directed her to the front door with a quick nod.

Like a new recruit, she'd just stood there watching him handle Bratton instead of questioning the investigating officers. How unprofessional. "Yes?"

"My money's on Randall for this B and E," Isaiah said quietly, his sharp gaze back on Bratton. "He knew where she lived and he's trying to intimidate her."

"Or he thinks the money's here and she's in on it with him," Roxy bit back. For a psychic, Isaiah sure couldn't see the forest for the trees. This act of Bratton's could be just that, an act, and her kids might be in on it for all Roxy knew. Yeah, Bratton did seem truly worried, but Roxy had seen a lot in her time with MPD, and she didn't trust anyone. Not even Isaiah. Yet.

He stared her down. "You may be right." Well, at least he gave her that. "Don't let her out of your sight while I'm gone."

Roxy bristled, feeling like a yo-yo caught between Isaiah and the sad lady who seemed to have his undivided attention the way his eyes kept straying back to her. "You think I don't know my job? Get over yourself, Zaroyin."

Damn, there was that handsome smile again, lighting her insides like a flash bang, then gone before she knew it, leaving behind only the shockwave she'd tasted in the broom closet.

"On the contrary, Officer Thurston. I think you know more than I do about a lot of things." His lips pursed for one split second as if he wanted to kiss her goodbye. Talk about unprofessional.

Roxy took a deliberate step back. "Make it quick," she hissed, using her best cop voice to keep him in his place—and to keep her hands off him. Now was not the time for play. "We've got work to do."

"Yes, ma'am," he said as he turned on his heel and left.

One second later her cell rang with an incoming. She checked her caller ID. Damn Zaroyin. He had her number and now she had his. Sneaky, but effective.

Roxy strode back to the couch and knelt at Bratton's knee. "How about you and I go through your apartment to see if anything's missing?"

Bratton raked another handful of hair behind her ear. "That's a good idea."

"Officer Thurston? Ma'am?"

Roxy pushed off the floor to face Officer White. "Yes?"

"We've got a name to go with the plate Mrs. Bratton's neighbor gave us."

Thank the Lord for nosy neighbors. "Who does it belong to? Who did this?"

"A known felon. Garrett Randall."

Damned if Isaiah wasn't right again. Roxy placed a call to him.

He answered at one ring. "FBI Special Agent Zaroyin."

The deep baritone pitch in his voice caught her by surprise. "You were spot on," she told him quietly, her hand cupping her mouth so as not to panic Bratton, who stood now with Officer Humphrey. "Randall busted up this place. Don't come back. Get those kids to the safe house after you pick them up. I'll meet you there with Bratton."

"Understood," he clipped. "Be careful."

"Always," she replied, for some reason touched that he'd said what he'd said. That he might care. "See you soon."

Didn't that sound cozy and a little too damned familiar? Shrugging away from the slippery slope of feelings she seemed to be tumbling headlong down, Roxy turned on Mrs. Bratton. "I want you to get up and pack bags for yourself and your kids. Do it quickly. We're leaving in ten."

"Why should I?" she asked, her gaze darting over the mess in her home. "This is my house."

'Because I told you to,' nearly snapped out of Roxy's mouth, but she said, "We're relocating you and your children to a safe house in the Northwest District. Step on it."

Bratton chose that moment to make a stand. "No," she declared, tossing her head and making that red mane of hers tumble like a crimson waterfall over her shoulders. Want to bet she used that ploy to get her way when she was a kid, too? Wasn't working on Roxy. "I've worked too hard to make this house a home. Okay, it's not much, but if whoever did this comes back—"

"Don't you get it? There is no if. Randall did this." Roxy gave it to her straight. "And he did it in broad daylight with your neighbors watching. He's not afraid of you. And another thing..." Roxy took a firm step into Bratton's comfort zone. "You want to tell me how he knew where you lived? How he knew which bank you'd be at this morning?"

"He... he was here?" Bratton blinked those big gray eyes like she was processing the cold, hard facts. Or planning her next ruse. Or coming up with another useless, feminine trick. *How stupid could this chick be? Flirting doesn't work on female cops, only dumb jocks.*

"Things don't happen by coincidence, ma'am. Of course he was here. Now do as I asked, because we're leaving whether you're ready or not." Nodding to the officers, Roxy asked them to, "Help her pack."

"But Officer Thurston," Bratton whined.

Did she just stamp her foot at me? Roxy wanted to roll her eyes.

"I can't leave without Nugget."

Annoyed that she didn't know who Nugget was by now, Roxy cocked her head at her annoying charge. "Without who?" This Nugget Dude had better be a gerbil.

"My kids' dog." Bratton turned to look down the hall. "I can't leave him behind. It'll break Darrin's heart."

Shit! Roxy glared at this new bit of info, and the time it had taken Bratton to suddenly worry about her son's pet. Fur babies were right up there with children as far as Roxy was concerned. If anything ever happened to her longhaired Siamese, Toy, she'd be a wreck for months. But why had Bratton suddenly pulled the sympathy card out of her sleeve? Why not a helluva lot sooner if Nugget was so important to her kid? Not that it mattered. Roxy'd never leave a man behind, not even the four-legged kind.

"Then pack some kibble," she told Bratton. "The dog's coming with us."

It took Humphrey and White five long minutes of calling, searching, and canvassing the backyard to come up with Roxy's next problem of the day-from-hell that... Would. Not. End. Not only was Nugget a ginormous golden retriever with more hair than an *Ewok*, he was gone.

Chapter Seven

Roxy was late, and Isaiah had one of his feelings. Standing at the drawn blinds behind bulletproof windows at the safe house one block off Embassy Row, he made small talk with Kitty and Darrin Bratton while the seconds ticked into minutes. Then half an hour.

Still no Roxy.

"So you've got a dog?" he asked Darrin as he kept one eye on the busy street.

The boy was a miniature Candace while his sister must look more like her father, Bob Bratton. Darrin's hair was coppery- red, but not as bright as Candy's. His skin as creamy white with a healthy dose of cinnamon freckles sprinkled over his nose and cheeks, and his lips were as full. He had his mother's gray eyes. A boyish cowlick topped his forehead, turning the peak of his buzz cut into a tiny whirlpool that must have been a bear to tame on school picture day.

He'd brought a rubber ball with him, his dog's ball. After the first hundred or two bounces, Isaiah had persuaded him to put it in his pocket so it wouldn't get lost—or tossed far, far over the fence. The kid knew how to irritate his sister. Isaiah too.

Kitty, on the other hand, was a pre-teen who sported long and straight dark brown hair and a healthy tan. Thick black lashes fanned her cheeks and accentuated her chocolate brown eyes. Candy had better get ready for trouble. The day would surely come when her daughter would be a heartbreaker boys couldn't resist.

"Did they find him yet?" Darrin asked, his eyes glimmering. The poor kid hadn't stopped fidgeting since Isaiah retrieved him from his friend's front door. "They gotta find him. He'll be scared, and he's a big baby when it's raining and it thunders, and…" He took a shuddering breath, smoothing his fingers over the lump that was the dog's ball deep in his pocket. "They gotta find him, Mister."

"They will," Isaiah assured him again. "Trust me, those police officers know their job. They'll bring Nugget with them." *I hope.* "So tell me why you named him Nugget. Is he as heavy as gold?"

A timid smile curled the corners of Darrin's mouth. "No, sir. It's because—"

"He's the color of gold, dummy," Kitty said with a roll of her eyes. "Duh."

"I was gonna say that," Darrin cried, elbowing his sister in the ribs.

"Ouch, you little worm," she said. "That hurt. I'll tell Mom."

"Kids," Isaiah said softly. "I know you're worried, but let's keep our heads, okay? Your mom will be here soon and she'll be hungry. Let's surprise her with a nice, hot dinner."

Kitty's nose wrinkled. "Us? Fix dinner?"

He winked at her. "Sure. This place is stocked with everything you can imagine. What'll it be? Spaghetti and meatballs? Grilled chicken? Soup and salad?"

"I prefer shrimp Alfredo," Kitty said loftily, her nose in the air like a typical teenager.

Of course you do. "Do you know how to make it?" Isaiah asked, because he sure didn't.

Her shoulders lifted. "Sorry. Cooking's not my thing. Isn't that your job?"

"I'm a guy, remember." Isaiah chuckled on his way to the spacious kitchen, complete with a gourmet selection of cookware, appliances, and ingredients. It'd sure be nice to find a couple pouches of frozen shrimp Alfredo in that side-by-side freezer. He jerked the freezer door open. Damn. No such luck. But that big bag of pre-cooked frozen shrimp could prove useful. "I know a few things. Come help. Many hands make dinner taste better."

The kids followed. Darrin scrambled onto the nearest high stool at the breakfast bar, bouncing the ball again.

Isaiah rolled his neck at the tweaked nerve the noise from the ball incited. "So why the dog's ball? Is it like a good luck charm or something? Do you carry it everywhere?"

"Nah, but me and Nugget were playing before school and I forgot I stuck it in my pocket. I'm not hungry."

"Awww, poor widdle Darrin's too worried about his widdle fuzzy hairball to eat," Kitty teased as she took the stool beside her brother. "Big baby."

"Am not," Darrin said, leaning into her with another shoulder shove. "You are."

"Oh, boo hoo. I'm not the one crying when Nugget doesn't come home, am I?"

"So? I'm not the one who broke the back gate, Missy Kitty!"

"Don't call me that, Staring Darrin," she shot back, sticking her tongue out.

Isaiah caught Darrin's hand in midair before it made contact with the side of his sister's face. Just as quickly, he lifted the ball from the boy's other hand and set it high on top the refrigerator. "There. It can wait for Nugget just fine right up there. Kids, you've got to stop picking at each other. I know you're worried, but—"

"I'm not worried," Kitty informed him haughtily. "I'm immune to the emotion. I've never worried about a thing in my life. Ever. What's gonna happen's gonna happen, and there's nothing you or I can do about it!" She'd ended on a shrill note that declared the opposite of every word she'd just spoken. The girl was a puzzle.

Isaiah held onto Darrin's much smaller hand, surprised when the boy curled his fingers into his palm. Both kids were rattled. He got that, but something else was going on here. No twelve-year-old girl should have such a fatalistic outlook on life, and that speech? Where had she heard that line of nonsense? "Don't worry, I'll fix your backyard gate," he told Darrin to calm his nerves. "And yeah. I'm a guy, but I'm still a teensy bit worried," he told Kitty.

Her eyes widened. "You are?"

"Sure. It's been a hard day and hard days make it difficult to relax at night. Things tend to stick in my mind, and sometimes I can't get my brain to shut up and let me eat dinner in peace." Extricating his fingers from Darrin's, he gave the boy a manly shoulder bump with the flat of his fist. "I'll bet Nugget's the same way. He gets an idea in his head, and, bam, he takes off, and he forgets it's time for dinner, huh?"

Darrin's head bobbed. "He likes to chase Mrs. McCarthy's white cat."

"And the paperboy, the mailman, kids who ride by on bikes, and..." Kitty ticked off a list with her fingers, doing that eye roll thing again. The girl was all about drama. Was that normal for kids her age? For that matter, were twelve-year-olds teenagers? The world of kids baffled Isaiah.

"Agent Zaroyin," Darrin asked, his lower lip quivering. "What if Nugget doesn't come home this time? What if your police friends can't find him or they scare him? What if—"

Kitty grabbed hold of Darrin's neck and pulled him into her arms. "Will you stop it?" she asked, her eyes suddenly as misty as his, but her voice had gone soft and tender. "Nugget always comes back. He's too dumb to stay away for long. He likes to eat, remember?"

"But I'm not there, and he doesn't know any of the police guys," Darrin whined as he buried his face in his sister's neck. His little shoulders shook. "Kitty, he'll be scared and 'sides, Mom gets mad and locks him outside sometimes and... and he might not want to come home this time."

Isaiah placed his palm in the center of the boy's back. The second he did, his mind flooded with the love this little man had for his faithful companion. And just that fast, Isaiah knew where Nugget was. "Does Nugget like hamburgers?" he asked the kids calmly.

Darrin's tear-streaked face came up. "Nugget loves any food, why?"

Isaiah narrowed his eyes. "Isn't there a Burger Bar two or three blocks from your house? Does a Mr. Giovanni work there, and do you know him?"

Darrin's eyes turned into tiny saucers they got so wide. "Yessssss," he hissed. "Mr. G's a really good guy and he gives Nugget hamburgers that get dropped or ones he accidentally burns. How'd you know all that stuff?"

"Because I know how to think like a dog," Isaiah said slyly, "and you can, too. Dogs have the best noses in the universe, and Mr. Giovanni makes the best burgers, sooooo..." He drew that last word out to let Darrin arrive at the same conclusion.

"Nugget's at Mr. G's!" he crowed.

Palming his cell phone, Isaiah dialed his new partner to tell her where to look for Darrin's dog. "Yeah, Mr. G's is on the east side of Kingman Park. You can't miss it. See you soon." Ending the call, he pocketed his phone just in time to catch an armful of boy.

"Thanks Mister," Darrin said, his sweaty little cheek pressed against Isaiah's and his heart pounding so hard. "I know he's just a big dumb dog to most people, but he's the best friend I got, and I... and I..." A hiccup lurched out of the kid's throat. "I'm gonna pay you back for being so nice to me, I promise. Someday. Honest. I promise."

If that didn't melt Isaiah's heart, nothing could. Winding one arm around Darrin's little boy body, he returned the hug, keeping it manly. "'S okay, Darrin. Us dog lovers need to stick together, don't we?"

"Ah-huh, we do." Easing back, Darrin blinked up at Isaiah, his eyes filled with awe. "Wanna play ball,

Agent Zaroyin? I don't have my mitt, but I know how to catch a fly ball without it. Can we, please? I'll let you pitch."

This kid. Isaiah ruffled the buzz cut that bristled the top of Darrin's head. "As soon as we get finished making dinner, you bet. Whose your team?"

"The Nats, of course," Darrin giggled, his good nature restored. "Who's yours?"

"Um..." Isaiah didn't have a clue who the Nats were or what answer to give this charming boy. He'd never played baseball in his life, but if Darrin liked the Nats... "I like the Nats, too." *Least, I do now.*

A big grin cracked Darrin's face, scrunching his nose and revealing teeth that were white, but a little crooked and would need braces one day. "Then let's get dinner fixed. I'll help. Come on."

And just like that, crisis averted. Isaiah pulled a fairly easy recipe for shrimp Alfredo off his cell. Kitty defrosted the bag of shrimp Isaiah found in the freezer, while he made the creamy sauce and boiled water for the pasta. Humming to himself, Darrin set the table for six, just in case, he said, that Nugget got to sit with them, which he also said would never happen.

"My mom doesn't like dog hair in the kitchen, so he has to stay in my bedroom when we're eating dinner, even if it's just pizza and we're eating on the floor in front of the TV." Darrin chuckled to himself. "But I sneak him food, and someday, you'll see. Mom'll let him sit beside me. She will."

The kid sounded so hopeful. For a moment, it seemed time stopped and hit rewind. There were no bad men like Garrett Randall afoot in the world, only hairy golden dogs and optimistic little boys. There was no mad scientist who'd gone to prison for turning honorable FBI agents into living drones. There was only a fat, lazy Siamese cat named Hoi Toi and a motherless twelve-year-old named—Isaiah.

Chapter Eight

Holy Christ! Roxy cursed under her breath as she sped Northwest to Embassy Row, pissed at the delay that could've ended Mrs. Bratton's life, not to mention Humphrey's and White's lives. Her stalwart brothers-in-arms followed in their cruisers in case Garrett Randall was just that smart. Plus, they had Nugget with them, a bigger than a small horse, ball of excited, fluffy, gold fur that had nearly torn the house apart once he'd finally come home. He'd been crazy happy to see her, even ran circles like an out of control idiot.

Shit! Could an undercover protective detail get any more screwed up? Sure didn't seem like it. At least Bratton's dog was accounted for, but damn, the thing was a hairy beast. Roxy was a cat person. Hair and drool? *Uh-uh. No. Thank. You.*

Too late she remembered the late night Navy Concert-on the-Mall taking place tonight. No wonder there was so much foot traffic. District streets were always a bear to maneuver, but special events made them ten times the nightmare. Pedestrians, especially tourists, tended to think they owned the right-of-way, even when they skipped crosswalks and dodged into traffic.

Then there were the delivery guys. Gunning her vehicle's engine, she skirted yet another double-parked van in her lane. Man. Didn't anyone in this city know it was illegal to double park—even for deliveries?—which she doubted the driver of the van was making at this late hour, but still. Traffic cops needed to write more parking tickets and people needed to pay bigger fines. This was ridiculous!

"Thanks for waiting until Nugget came home," Bratton said quietly from the passenger seat on this desperate night. That was the ultimate irony. While Humphrey and White had scoured the neighborhood, the mammoth dog had simply strolled home like a good boy who'd been out for a walk.

Roxy mumbled a quick, "No worries." None of this was Bratton's fault, but Roxy couldn't deny that the woman bugged her. It might be due to that green-eyed monster that had perched like a troll on Roxy's shoulder since Isaiah came into the picture, though. In fact, the more she thought about it, that was precisely what was wrong. Jealousy. Yeah. That explained a lot. Too bad it didn't explain everything.

Finally, she cranked the wheel of her unmarked sedan a hard right off Massachusetts Avenue NW, and onto Florida Ave NW. Tucked between Florida Avenue NW and New Hampshire Avenue NW stood a bungalow no one would suspect the FBI used to stash high-value targets. Most homes in this elite part of the District maintained the same high security, iron gates and bars on the windows. The safe house on Swann Street fit right in.

Roxy rolled up to the twelve-foot high, wrought iron gate at the end of an elaborately laid brick driveway. Stretching her left arm through the driver's side window, she tapped the call button.

"You're late," Isaiah answered cheerfully.

"Let me in," she replied. He knew why she was late. She'd certainly called him enough with updates on Nugget's progress over the last couple hours.

Slowly, the gate opened inward and cleared the driveway while ten short concrete posts known as bollards lifted out of the ground behind her vehicle to prevent a second car from entry. Activating the radio at her collar, Roxy informed her traveling companions they'd have to wait their turn. The cruiser parallel parked, blocking said driveway, but damn. She could hear Nugget barking all the way up the driveway to the eight-columned portico stretched over the grand entry. Poor Officers Humphrey and White. Wasn't that just great? Not.

"So this is it," Bratton said. "Nice."

Before shifting into park, Roxy turned to her charge. "Are you okay?"

Bratton nodded. "I wasn't expecting... this. It makes my house look like a dump." The home was extraordinarily large for a federal safe house, but that's the way things were on Embassy Row. Nothing was too big or too ornate, and Roxy'd bet a month's pay this was the confiscated home of one Bernie Koldewyn, the District's own ponzi scheme artist who'd bilked millions from unsuspecting investors, friends, and family.

The massive, wooden, double entry doors split as two children ran to the car. "Mom!" the red-haired little boy yelled, but the dark-haired girl trailed behind him, shrugging her shoulders like it was no big deal to be uprooted in the middle of the day and stashed in an FBI safe house.

Isaiah followed, his attention on the cruiser beyond the gate. "Welcome to your home away from home, Candy."

Roxy rolled out of her vehicle with her hand on her pistol grip, instantly on edge, and not because Isaiah looked happy to see *Candy*. "You want to let my escort in?" she asked, nodding at the kids. "They've got a suspect these two need to interrogate." *A big hairy suspect.*

In minutes, Humphrey and White rolled to a stop beside Roxy's sedan and Bratton's son squealed, "Nugget!"

"Sorry about that, guys," Roxy told her fellow officers as they handed the leash on Nugget's collar off to the anxious boy. "Let me know whose fingerprints were all over Bratton's place, will you?"

"You bet," White replied. "Good luck, Officer Thurston. Call if you need anything?"

"Will do. Same to you."

That earned her a raised brow as if Officer White didn't think he'd ever need her help. Isaiah interrupted the snarky retort forming on Roxy's lips with a hurried, "Let's take this party inside, folks."

By then, Bratton's son had Nugget inside with Bratton and her daughter following, while Roxy and Isaiah took up the rear. "Any problems finding this place?" he asked, his palm in the middle of her back, not pushing, just lightly herding her along with the others like she needed his superior male presence.

Roxy shrugged out from under him. "What? You think just because I'm late that I don't know my own backyard?" Instantly, she regretted snapping his head off. It was a fair question, but why her hackles were up, she didn't know. They just were, damn it.

"No, Officer Thurston, but traffic's heavy when there's entertainment in the capital. Have you eaten yet today? Are you hungry?"

Ha. He thought her snarky attitude came from her empty belly. *Well, guess again, Mr. FBI.* Security details always turned her into an alpha bitch protecting her litter. The waves of warmth radiating from that wide, firm palm were deliciously distracting, though. All at once, every atom in her body seemed to be leaning toward him for a—hug.

Inside the mansion now, because this place was a freaking mansion—Roxy stepped away from Zaroyin and took in the high vaulted ceilings and the marble floor of the entry with an aggravated glance.

"Christ, couldn't you guys get something easier to secure?" she bit out to get her mind off the delicious way he smelled. "This place is a nightmare. How can we possibly defend it against Randall? The man's got explosives, damn it. What were you thinking?"

"Do you honestly think he knows where we are?" Isaiah replied, his tone light and downright cheerful as he pointed to the crystal chandelier overhead. "Security cameras, Roxy. Smile. You're on someone's TV right now, and that someone's as sharp as you are. They already know your weight, height, and what you ate for breakfast."

Grunting, she told him what she thought of that stupid FBI comment. As if she wasn't already plenty distracted, now Roxy had to deal with the loss of that warm hand on her back. The chemistry, or whatever this thing zinging between them was, annoyed and tantalized her like nothing before. Randall had better make his move soon because Roxy could feel her control slipping whenever Zaroyin came around.

He went on as if he had no idea what his proximity did to her. "This place is under twenty-four-seven video surveillance, inside and outside. Once I activate the system..." He took one step behind the entry door, lifted what looked like an oil painting but was actually a hinged door to a control panel, and tapped over the numeric keypad. "There. We are officially secure in one of the safest, safe houses in the District. Candy and her children will be under armed guard—that's you and me—until this thing is over. Two more agents are outside in an unmarked car, so yes. I think we've got the upper hand where Randall's concerned. Don't you?"

He'd just answered all her questions, but did she want to admit the Bureau might just know what they were doing? Not so much. "Are they your men or mine?" she asked in a civil tone. "Those two in the unmarked?"

"FBI, but we're willing to work with MPD in any capacity you'd like. Are there officers in particular you'd recommend for this detail?" He cocked his head, his dark eyes hooded. Yeah. He could feel the energy crackling between them like the lightning in a plasma globe the same as she could. His tongue made a quick swipe over his bottom lip as if he were thinking the same thing she was. *Sex on the floor. Now. Hurry. Fast!*

"Umm, no," Roxy said, her voice gone hoarse again, damn it. How'd he do that to her? "Excuse me but I've got to check in."

"As do I," he replied, his cell in his hand, but not at his ear.

Roxy placed her call to Captain Quinlan and advised him that she was in for the night. All the while, she kept one eye on Isaiah. He hadn't lifted his cell to make his call, yet his eyes had darkened, and he nodded as if he were speaking with someone. Interesting. The man must have some kind of psychic link with his boss. She couldn't help wondering if he could turn it on and off like a phone. Was it only mind-speak or was there a mental video upload that came with it? Could Isaiah project pictures to his boss or just conversation? Was there a limit to the distance he could reach? Better yet, could he teach her to do that mind-speak thing, too?

When he winked, she blinked, embarrassed he'd caught her staring. She cut him off. "Let's go eat, Zaroyin. What'd you fix? It better be good."

Cranking her neck to break eye contact, she turned her back on him and headed for the room where Nugget's big bark had just come from. Had to be the kitchen or dining room judging by the smells emanating from that direction.

"Your favorite," Isaiah murmured as he stepped to her six.

Again, his palm hit the small of her back, but she had an arsenal, too, and snark was her weapon of choice. "Ha. You don't have a clue what my favorite foods..." *Oh, my hell. Maybe you do. What's all this?*

Roxy came to a full stop at the lavish banquet table where Bratton now sat cheerfully between her kids, a feast laid before them. Someone certainly knew how to set a formal table setting. Shrimp Alfredo. Cold, peeled shrimp. Cocktail sauce in cute little ceramic dipping cups. A crisp green salad full of cucumbers, black olives, tomatoes, and some kind of white cheese. Goblets full of what had better be water, not white wine, stood near elegant white china plates and bright shiny silverware.

The dining room looked utterly resplendent, like nothing Roxy had ever seen before in a safe house. She shot Isaiah an appreciative look even as her belly growled, giving her away.

"Have a seat, Officer Thurston," he offered gallantly, his hand at his side instead of on her back, where she would've preferred it. But this was just a job. Nothing more. The mistake she'd made in the broom closet wouldn't happen again.

"Hi guys," she offered to the kids. "I'm Metro Police Officer Roxy Thurston, but from now on you can call me Roxy, got it?"

The girl rolled her big, brown eyes. *Okay, message received. You think you're tougher than me. I can deal with that, especially since you're just a teenager.* "You must be Kitty."

"Wow, and you must be a rocket scientist," Kitty drawled.

That earned the girl Roxy's most sincere smile. Snark, she understood. "I think I'm going to like you." Turning to the boy and his dog, she asked, "Darrin, right?"

His head bobbed. "And this here's Nugget. Thanks for finding him for me, Officer, umm, Roxy."

Her shoulders lifted. "I couldn't leave him behind, could I?" she said as she ruffled said dog's pointed, hard head. The crazy mutt seemed to like her. He'd come to her knee at the sound of his name as if she'd intentionally called him. As if she liked dogs. "Are you a good boy?" she asked.

"Woof!" Nugget answered. The goofy guy dropped to his butt, lifted his sleek gold muzzle and told her again, "Woof, woof!" in his great big outdoor voice.

"He likes you!" Darrin squealed. "Look Mom! Nugget likes Officer Thurs... ah, I mean Roxy!"

A frown tweaked Roxy's lips at this new development. She didn't like dogs, per se. She was a cat person, the adoring staff to the feline goddess that shared her father's home with her. Not dogs. Well, okay. Maybe this one dog had a few redeeming qualities. Now that he wasn't running loose, he was an obedient sort of fellow and he did have big brown eyes that seemed to draw her in. She took a knee and gave him another pat and a long stroke down his fluffy neck.

"Down," Isaiah said quietly behind her. His palm was flat and his fingers were spread forward as he talked to the dog like he knew what he was doing. Damned if Nugget didn't drop to his belly, his gaze bright on Isaiah.

Roxy cupped his head and smoothed both hands over his ears. The dog's fur was sleek and smooth, nothing like Toy's soft and cuddly fur, but it was more pleasant than Roxy expected.

"This bad boy's had obedience training, hasn't he, Candy?" Isaiah asked.

She'd changed from a nervous woman into a happy mother, her gray eyes bright with relief instead of clouded with worry. "It cost me an arm and a leg, but he grew so big and so fast his first year, so yes. I sent him and Darrin to puppy obedience school. I didn't need Nugget tearing my house apart."

"Wanna see the tricks he can do?" Darrin asked.

"How about we save that show for after dinner?" Isaiah replied smoothly.

Kitty's brow lifted in typical teenage annoyance, but Darrin's eyes sparkled. "You got it, Agent Zaroyin." The hero worship glittering in his eyes was hard to miss. Wow. Isaiah had certainly imbedded himself quickly within this little family. The cozy scene looked good and normal at first glance, but getting friendly with the clients could go wrong on so many levels. This was still a security detail, yet Isaiah didn't seem worried at all. If anything, he looked at home.

Annoyed, Roxy lifted to her feet, wondering which of the several doors in the two hallways that branched off the dining room led to the nearest bathroom. She needed a moment to catch her balance. The troll sitting on her shoulder had too easily roiled her jealous side into attack mode, and so had Isaiah's apparent friendship with every Bratton sitting around the table. Even the snarky teenager Roxy'd felt an instant kinship with.

"Through that door, first room on the right," he said. "If you're looking for some place to wash your hands, that is."

Roxy leveled a shrewd eye at him. Had he just read her mind? Embarrassed at the notion and what else he might've psychically deduced, she smoothed her palms down her thighs. There was no way he could see through her clothes, but not knowing that for certain kept her self-conscious and off-balance.

"Umm, thanks," she murmured, as flustered as she'd ever been. "Be right back."

Roxy made a quick get away as the banter between Isaiah, Darrin, Kitty, and Candy followed her down the hall. Once behind the closed door of an equally opulent washroom that made her feel even more out of place, maybe out of her league, she pressed her hand to her breastbone to calm her wildly beating heart.

She was the job, damn it, and the job was her. That's all there was to it, and this was nothing But. A. Job. So why'd she feel like she didn't belong at that dining table? This was the District, for hell's sake. *My District. My turf.* She knew every street and every back alley, and more than anyone else, she belonged, damn it.

Swallowing hard, she took a quick look in the ornate, gold-framed mirror that stretched the entire wall over multiple sinks that looked like china bowls lined up on the expensive marble counter. *Damn, how many sinks do rich people need to wash their hands and powder their faces? Apparently six.*

Roxy could've cried. After her service on the force, after all of the men and women she'd arrested, tackled to the ground when they thought they could run from her, after all her arrests, bookings, and testifying in court—the dark eyes staring back at her from the mirror were still the same.

She forced another swallow past the tightness clamping her throat. This time she couldn't run home to Mama. That escape route was forever closed to her, but the first free moment she got, she meant to call her father.

Isaiah Zaroyin had better watch his step, damn him. He might've had his way with her once, but it wouldn't happen again. Mama and Daddy had taught Roxy well, and Roxy Thurston was tough. She didn't need a man in her life. That was who'd made her weak in the first place. It wouldn't happen again.

Chapter Nine

After Isaiah showed Candy and her children to their rooms, he returned to clear the dining room table and start dishes. Cleanliness may not be next to godliness, but an orderly house made everything else run smoother. When he got there, the table was not only cleared, but wiped clean. The sound of Roxy's authoritative voice led him into the kitchen where Nugget sat in apt attention at her knee.

"Who's a good boy?" she asked him in an adorable babyish voice that made Isaiah grin. Of course, Nugget's bright brown eyes followed her as she bent at the waist, talking to him like he was a kid. "Can you shake hands with me, too?"

Nugget wiggled his fluffy butt before his right paw landed in her upturned palm.

"Good boy!" She all but squealed. Tossing a dog biscuit from the opened bag on the counter, she told him, "Roll over."

No sooner asked than accomplished. Nugget couldn't seem to obey this delightful woman quickly enough, and Isaiah knew how he felt. Clawing back to his feet, the other 'good boy' in the room, resumed sitting with his ears perked forward and his attention riveted on his new friend, or at least on the treats in her hand.

Folding his arms over his chest, Isaiah leaned against the door jamb, content to watch the show. What a sight. Officer Thurston seemed to enjoy this four-legged Bratton more than the others. Roxy's uniform, the one he'd nearly torn off her in his one and only out of control moment in the broom closet back at FBI HQ, wrinkled at the waist and smoothed over her backside as she bent over again. Oddly, he wasn't as embarrassed by that observation as he thought he'd be. Normally not one to ogle the ladies, he knew he'd tear her clothes off again if she didn't turn around and notice him pretty soon. Nugget wasn't the only hound dog in the house.

The long ponytail down her back flipped from side to side while she ran Nugget through several more easy tricks. Sit. Beg. Lay. Over. "One more, big guy," she told him, the treat in her hand now held high over his head. Her enthusiasm ranked right up there with Darrin's. "Take it."

He looked up. Then, as gingerly as Tinker Bell landing on a flower petal, Nugget stretched to his back feet, and, without touching Roxy's fingers, he snagged the end of that biscuit and carefully eased it out of her grip.

She dropped to her knees, hugging the shaggy fellow once he was back on all fours. "You're such a good boy," she crooned, her fingertips dancing over his snout and cradling his face even as he chewed. Some dogs red-zoned when anyone came too near their food, but not Nugget. He seemed as gentle as a lamb. A big, golden lamb.

"Tell him to hold," Isaiah said quietly, not wanting to startle Roxy or the dog.

Her brows lifted as she cast a quick glance over her shoulder. "How long have you been standing there?"

Isaiah shrugged. "A minute or two."

Lifting to her feet, she dropped one hand to her hip and cocked a saucy eye at him. "What's that mean? Hold?"

Isaiah egged her on. "Just tell him. If he's as smart as I think he is, you'll see."

"Fine." Roxy turned her back on Isaiah and told Nugget to," Hold."

The dog never hesitated. In one lightning fast leap, he launched his big furry body at Roxy, knocked her to the floor, and placed his slobbery alligator jaws over her throat. Roxy let out an unladylike, "Ugh," when she hit. One big paw hit the center of her chest, mashing her breasts, but holding her where she'd fallen.

Worried she'd hurt her head, Isaiah ran to her side. "Are you hurt?"

Angry brown eyes locked on him even as she ran her fingers over Nugget's big head. "Damn you, Zaroyin," she hissed. "This isn't funny. You knew he'd do this, didn't you? Now tell me what to say to get him off."

He breathed a sigh of relief. "Just tell him, off."

She lay there running her fingers over Nugget's grinning face for a second longer before she muttered, "Okay, off, you big hairy mutt. Get. Off."

A silly grin stretched his black lips as Nugget promptly did as she'd commanded, but not until his tongue took a healthy swipe over her chin and mouth, covering her in drool.

"Ugh! Stop it! Eww. Dog slobber. Eww!"

Chuckling, Isaiah gave her a hand up, and there it was again. The sizzle. The fire. That overwhelming, inner-caveman need to shelter her, to serve and protect this hot-blooded woman. It happened every time he came too close. The second he touched her skin, his body hardened into a knuckle-dragging Neanderthal while his overly-intelligent, twenty-first century, gentlemanly resolve melted like chalk dust on a hot summer sidewalk in the rain.

Automatically, his nostrils flared to draw in more of the sweet, sultry fragrance that came along with Roxy. He couldn't quite come up with the exact name for the scent. A cross between coconut, flowers, and sex, he found it deliciously erotic. Enough to make a man drool. The fire in his blood spiked the need in his pants.

Releasing her, he took a step back, but he was no better than Nugget when it came to wanting—very much—to please Officer Thurston. A better man would've done a quick about face and retreated to higher, safer ground, but apparently, Isaiah's better days were behind him. In two quick steps, he had her in his arms before he knew how it happened. It just did.

Like the last time, she didn't resist, not even for a second. Instead, her sharp fingernails dug into his biceps and her lush mouth opened to receive him. This was so, so wrong, but damned if Isaiah knew how to stop what kept happening between them.

"Not here," she murmured even as her tongue tangled with his.

"I know a place," he growled, his palms smoothly cupping her ass, lifting her off her feet as he took decisive action. Her holster rubbed against his thigh and she had to be feeling his underarm holster and his pistol, but he could do this quick. Couldn't he?

There were five points of egress from the kitchen: one to the main dining room behind him, the one at the right to the smaller, staff dining room where separate bedrooms waited for him and Roxy, one to the left hall where the Brattons now—hopefully—slept in their two bedroom suite. The single door directly across from Isaiah led outside to the covered patio at the rear of the home, and the last exit next to the door to the staff quarters went downstairs to the wine cellar in the basement.

Five points of escape from the house—or intrusion into it—that Isaiah had thoroughly vetted prior to Roxy's arrival to be certain they were defendable. With the security system now activated, all exits were secure.

He had yet to tell her that most of the house was barricaded from their use. Tucker did that to ensure their living portion was defensible. That consisted of the massive front entry, the formal dining room, kitchen, and just enough rooms to house Candace Bratton's family and her security entourage. Isaiah certainly didn't plan to update Roxy now, not with his hand on her smoking hot ass, and not with what he had in mind for the rest of her. Something out of character, outright dangerous, and downright dirty.

Palming the first door in the hall past the staff's dining room open, he set Roxy to the edge of the queen-sized bed to his right. He didn't need lights for what would happen next.

Groaning, she sank beneath him, her hand clamped around the back of his neck, taking him down with her. Gingerly, he took a knee at her side to keep from crushing her with his full weight. Skimming his palms up her arms, he ended at her jaw. Cradling her face, his thumbs memorized the contours of her high cheekbones and mapped every nuance of her chin, absorbing the satin touch of her skin as he kissed, tasted, and nibbled.

"Hold that thought," he growled as he eased his holster off and set it on the nightstand within reach.

Hurriedly, she unbuckled her belt and did the same, securing her revolvers on the opposite nightstand. From that moment on, everything happened in fast motion. Her fingernails raked over the shirt on his back until they met his belt. A growl percolated against his lips when she wrestled with the buckle.

"Damn," she complained.

"I can do that for you if you'd like," he breathed into her mouth.

"Then do it," she ordered, arching her hips against his belly, setting him on fire.

This is so wrong. Yet so, so right. Frantically, Isaiah divested himself of his clothes while Roxy peeled out of hers. All knees, legs, and nothing between them but the dark, they slammed back together in a frenzied flash fire that threw sparks to the ceiling. He couldn't get at her fast enough.

"Someone should be standing guard," she breathed even as her fingers wrapped around the base of his aching manhood, gently squeezing more flames into his throbbing veins while her warm, wet tongue licked his hungry lips.

Gasping at the depth of need her touch incited, he managed a rugged, "I know." *Damn, how I know.* The blaze crackling in his veins ramped into a cat-o-nine-tails, scouring up his spine with the desire and need to deliver one helluva good time to this woman. Organized thinking took a back seat to passion.

But everything was happening too fast. Whether she knew it or not, pumping him was the worst thing she could do. "Stop moving your hand," he ordered, "or this will be over before it begins."

That earned him a throaty mewl. "But I thought you'd like it," she purred.

Instantly, his heart launched into a set of jumping jacks like a teenage boy who'd made third base on his first date might have done.

"That's the problem. I like it a lot, only now..." He pressed himself into the entrance of her core, testing to be certain she wanted this as much as he did. "I can stop if you'd rather not," he offered, not exactly lying, but burning to hear her breathy 'yes, yes, yes!' again. For the first time in his life, he understood the fierce drive to procreate. His brain felt like a damned racehorse pounding toward the finish line.

When she thrust her hips forward and growled, "Just do it already," Roxy closed the gap between them so quickly that he jerked with the relief, thrilled at the slick feminine heat encasing his length and working him like a glove. Velvet and steel, they were a match made in heaven. In just seconds, Roxy came apart in his hands, and when she did, her muscles clamped down on him. Squeezing him. Pushing him to the point of no return.

Closing his eyes, Isaiah punched deeper into the warmest heaven on earth he'd ever known, his dreams of what paradise felt, tasted, and smelled like now complete. Lowering his nose to her forehead, he inhaled all that was right with his crazy, over-controlled world. The scent of her delicate sweat. Her coconut shampoo. Whatever flowery scented cream she'd applied over her beautiful cheeks and forehead. All of it. He took in every last epithelial wafting off her warmed-up body and made them his world. His universe.

A tear welled at one corner of his eye when he sensed Roxy seemed to need the same thing he did, that she was just as amazed at the attraction between them as he was. That maybe, just maybe, she was just as hungry for him as he was for her. Yet he'd plundered her like a pirate in town for one night, mauling the first wench in sight.

The need to regroup and reconsider his obvious lack of finesse tweaked Isaiah's conscience. Maybe this—this thing—could grow into more than the slam, bam, thank you ma'am he'd reduced it to. Maybe he could make this right.

Her palms still rested on his shoulder blades, keeping him in place as aftershocks vibrated her core, clenching him as if she needed him to keep her from falling apart. That he could do. Dropping his nose into the warm crook of her neck, Isaiah buried his face amidst the tangles of black silk and satin skin. Strands of her hair tugged at the day's growth on his chin, and right or wrong, there was nowhere else he'd rather be than tangled up with Roxy Thurston.

She grunted against his cheek, an oddly indelicate female sound that made him smile. "Wow. That was fast."

"We do seem to come in a rush," he agreed, his heart still pounding out an exquisitely fierce set of push-ups in his chest and throat. Swallowing hard, he licked his lips and prepared to get back to the business of standing guard. Somehow.

"You think?" The hint of snark in her voice seemed gentler here in the dark.

Still trying not to crush her, he met resistance when he eased up. "No. Stay," she grumbled, her arms once more tight around him and her heart pounding as hard as his. The gentle rhythm of it melted into his steady thump, thump, thump until all he felt was the harmony of—their heartbeat. It felt so right lying in her arms. A man could almost believe this was that something more that Tucker had found with Melissa. That this could be what his fellow psychics, Ky and Eden, had. What Agent Tate Higgins and his new wife Winslow had. What everyone else seemed to have except the kid who yearned for it most.

"Damn it, Zaroyin," Roxy said, her fingers rubbing circles over his shoulder blades. "I don't know which end's up when I'm around you."

That earned her a smile. "I could show you which end is—"

She bit his earlobe. "You know what I meant, smartass."

"I do," he admitted, grinning at her not so gentle play. He'd never been with a woman as physically strong nor as tomboyish as Roxy. Hell, he'd never been with many women at all. He'd been that stupid little good boy who colored within the lines. Look at all he'd missed.

"I don't seem to have much control around you, either." *And I don't like it. Well, okay, maybe I do like it, but I don't know why I'm drawn like a magnet to you, of all people. It's weird and it's wrong to be doing this on duty, and... I want to do it again.*

As if she'd read his mind, her body lifted against his hips, inciting round two. "I could show you a thing or two about contr—"

Isaiah swallowed her reply. Her, teaching him sex, was the last thing he needed. From out of nowhere had come a need to possess her, so strong that it compromised his control and his heart. The fierce magnetic attraction worried him. This wasn't love. It couldn't be. Love was a deal breaker for his kind of psychic. If anyone in the universe had to be in control of his surroundings every minute of every day, it was Isaiah Zaroyin.

He was that guy, one of very few Level Ten psychics in the world, who could influence others without them knowing it. His was a powerful gift and along with great power came... You got it. A responsibility so overwhelming that at times, it weighed on him like an anchor and a curse.

The consequences of owning a mental gift like his had already wreaked havoc in his life. He refused to ever be naïve again. Yet here he was, out of his ever-loving mind and breaking all the rules. Again. Twice in the same freakin' day! This kind of lust could get somebody killed. It had to stop. Soon…

Roxy's hand slid down his bare belly, trailing smoldering brimstone in its wake. "Come on, Isaiah. I want your lips. Kiss me again."

Chapter Ten

What made Isaiah too tempting to resist? That sexy mouth of his, for one. The taste of his lips was wine in Roxy's mouth and she was drunk, head over heels, out of her mind, sloshed. How could he do that? With just one kiss, she'd fallen like a tramp on two-bit street, trolling for a quickie. How could this have happened? To her, an MPD officer of the law? And how could she stop the storm of emotions he'd set loose?

Whether he knew it or not, he'd incited a craving for all things Isaiah in her gut and in her heart. Worse. Because of him, she'd just tossed her reputation and her badge to the wind for the second time in one day. If Captain Quinlan ever found out...

A nip at her bottom lip stole every last worry and fear of what Captain What's-His-Name might think.

She was thoroughly, utterly lost to the power of the hot-as-hell man storming her senses. Her brain and body focused on the finely muscled, masculine body pressing her into the mattress of a bed she had yet to lay eyes on. If not for the dim light from the hall, she wouldn't have seen the tempting glimmer in his dark eyes that drew her like an addled moth to a delicious flame.

Oh, who was she kidding? Roxy clung to Isaiah like a life raft in a hurricane while he entered her again, and she did it because she wanted to, damn it. She wanted every last inch of this sexy beast and she wanted him now.

Inhaling deeply, she breathed his breath, loving the taste and scent of every molecule and atom of him. She wanted his body and every last chamber of his heart, as if this thing between them had anything to do with their hearts. For now, it was nothing more than chemistry, a flame she couldn't put out because—she didn't want to.

"More," she demanded, and Isaiah complied, filling her to the hilt, going deeper and going stronger, working her into a fever pitch. Before she could count to ten, it happened again. She hung on to his massive forearms as he took her higher and sent her on a whirlwind into the stars. Like the pleasurable escalation of a sneeze, she came apart too, too fast. A sensation like that ought to last more than a few seconds. Shuddering waves of warmth oozed down to her toes like the fiery trails of fireworks, these more delicious than the first. And she was—oddly—complete.

Something about this man made her feel incredibly healed, yet still, so incredibly broken at the same time. Roxy pressed her face into the hollow of his neck, worried what he'd see if he looked too closely. Suddenly, the room wasn't dark enough.

Surging one last time, his release followed hers with a grumbly purr that made her want to pet him. Her fingertips itched to stroke every bit of his bare skin. To drive him wild. Isaiah was that untamed panther of the pampas, taking her by surprise and pouring himself into her with passion and some kind of erotic power she had no defenses against. Maybe even—loving her. For that was what this felt like, the kind of true love she'd read about in fairytales. The kind of love her mother had with her father. The way Isaiah held her with so much tenderness and care, it couldn't be anything less, could it?

Even as Roxy banished the thought, for the first time in her life, thoughts about motherhood and babies came to mind. Maybe just one baby. A little boy with dark eyes and dark hair. With this guy. If he stayed. Couldn't this, please, just this once, be her fairy tale come true? Or would he end up being just as cavalier and thoughtless as every other guy?

Greedily, Roxy held on tighter, ashamed at the depth of her neediness, but not ready to let him go. Not yet. If this was all a lie, she'd deal with it later, but if—*please, oh please*—this feeling with Isaiah was true and real, she wanted to hang onto it a few minutes longer.

A deep masculine rumble in his chest vibrated straight to her heart and feminine pride surged through her. She knew it to her soul. Isaiah was happy, and she was the one who'd given that to him. She could feel it radiating off him. This one stolen moment was like a comforter she wanted to pull over their heads and hide from the world. If only.

Yet he didn't push back. Instead his arms went slack, and collapsing his weight against her, he pressed her pleasantly into the mattress. Holding her, his palms still cupping her ass, and her legs still embracing him.

Roxy held him as tenderly as he held her, stroking his muscled back. The man was elegantly fit, not thick-necked and muscle bound like so many guys at the gym she frequented. He had the grace and body of a runner, lean and lithe, yet solid. His abs were washboard hard and tight, the rest of him was the same.

Their connection both warmed and chilled Roxy. This wasn't love, and she was a fool to have thought it could be. At the most, Isaiah was just temptation in the wrong place at the wrong time. He and she were simply horny. That was all. She squeezed her eyes tight against the heartbreak sure to follow.

"I want a date," he growled into her ticklish ear. "A real date. Soon, damn it. No more skulking around in the dark."

"Ha," she snorted, doubting his sincerity. Wasn't this what all jocks did, schmooze their way out of your bed so they didn't have to look you in the eye in the morning? Make you feel special and unique, as if you were their one and only, right before they...

"I'm not dumping you, Roxy. The minute this joint operation's finished, I want dinner and dancing," he added huskily. "Maybe more."

Yeah, right. And I'm dumb enough to believe in princesses and dragons. Roxy pressed the heels of her palms to the front of his massive shoulders, but she couldn't move Isaiah an inch. If anything, he seemed to relax more, weighing her down, fastening her to the mattress. He seemed too happy for his own damned good, but no man invaded her privacy like this.

"Not fair. You can read my mind," she accused, "but I can't read yours."

"Ah, so *you* were thinking of dumping me."

She could feel his grin wrinkle at her neck. "No, I... Hey, do you have x-ray vision?" blurted out of her before she could control her big mouth.

Easing his bare chest away from her still throbbing breasts, Isaiah peered down at her in the dark. One hand slid over her hip and up her ribcage until it ended at her cheek. She blinked, not able to see him clearly. But man, he had big warm hands. Like a fool, she leaned into his palm, relishing the scent of their sex on his fingers and the tenderness he seemed willing to share.

"I'm not Superman," he told her, his voice unusually rough, "and no, I can't see through walls. I don't fly over tall buildings, and I can't read your mind. But you do lead with your chin, and I'm a pretty good judge of body language. You're always on the defensive. I'm not sure why that is or what happened in your past to make you that way, but I'll never invade your privacy to find out. Although…" His forehead dropped to hers as he thrust his hips into hers. "I do seem to have breached your defenses twice today."

She heard the question in his tone. He wasn't sure about what he'd done—what they'd done—yet. He was concerned she might think he'd done her wrong. Roxy solved that with a quick peck on the end of his nose. "Guess thinking you could see my underwear made me defensive," she admitted, though she knew he was right. There was more to her story, but trust was not her strong suit. There might come a day she shared that sad tale, but there might not.

Isaiah trailed the pad of his thumb over her cheek as if he were wiping tears away, which he most certainly was not. Roxy didn't cry. "Would you tell me if I go too far?"

She nodded, thrusting forward to get him moving, but failing. Isaiah obviously wasn't going anywhere until he was ready. Oddly, the dominance he wielded so easily didn't threaten her like it did when others pushed her around. With Isaiah it was—nice. Make that steamy. "I think we've already gone too far, big guy."

He smoothed one hand over her head, threading his fingers into her hair as he tilted his chin and kissed her forehead. "About that date..."

Crunch time. He seemed sincere, but she'd been burned before, and trust was always an issue. He'd been right about her leading with her chin. Dusting guys off before they got in too deep had always worked in the past. She nearly snorted at that thought. Hell, Isaiah was already in—deep—and warm. He wasn't going anywhere soon, but he probably didn't want a real date. This was all fast talk after a damned hot tumble. Nothing more. "We'll see."

He matched his forehead to hers, his nose to her nose. "That's not an answer, but I'll take it," he said huskily. "When you're ready, Roxy, I want to be the one you come to."

That earned him a well-deserved grunt. "Think I've already come enough for one day."

"That's not what I meant and you know it." His mouth descended in the dark, his lips perfectly aligned with hers, and damned if she could resist... One. More. Taste.

What was I saying? Going to do? She couldn't think around this guy!

"I'm sorry, but I have to leave," he whispered, breaking the kiss and a tiny piece of her heart, leaving her breathless and dazed and wondering why she had to let him go.

Lifting to his knees, he let his fingertips trace her centerline, between her breasts, and down her stomach ending at her bellybutton. He leaned over and swirled his tongue into her belly button, sending shivers up her body and pebbling her tender, aching nipples. One touch. That was all it would take to ignite her all over again.

"A date, Roxy," he breathed over her wet navel, curling her toes but not going any farther down her body. "With lights and music and enough time to do this..." Another warm breath skated up her belly to her wet nipples. "...right. Satin sheets would be nice. Dinner. Wine. Maybe a can of whipped cream."

"Ah-huh," she agreed because right then, she'd agree to anything if he'd only kiss her again. Instead, he disappeared into the dark and left her wanting that elusive more.

Standing there in the hall, Isaiah took a quick minute to zip his pants and buckle his belt. He'd doffed his suit jacket in the dining room earlier, but he'd just left his dress shirt in Roxy's room. At least, he'd thought to grab his holster and weapon before he'd made his exit. But a bare-chested FBI agent on the loose while on duty? *Not cool, man.*

He made a hasty exit to retrieve the duffel he'd brought with him and left behind in the entryway. Unzipping it, he made quick work of easing into a black polo with the FBI logo high on his chest. Isaiah made it a rule to always dress the part. That way, there'd be no doubt as to who he was and why he was here. He left the duffel behind the door. For now.

Thank goodness, the Brattons were still in their suite and hadn't caught him sneaking out of Roxy's room like a dog in the night. It had taken all Isaiah's control to leave her, but there'd been no choice. Roxy was something else and he was just a man. A very stupid man who kept making the same mistake. Only it felt like so much more.

Swallowing hard, he checked his pistol and adjusted his underarm holster. Would he do it again, make love with Roxy? In a heartbeat. Was it smart? No. Not by any definition of the word. Was she irresistible? Oh, hell yes.

Lifting his fingers to his nose, Isaiah closed his eyes, savoring the alluring scent that held him spellbound and kept him going back for more. Whatever this thing between them was, he intended to keep at it until he knew for certain if it were fools gold or the real thing.

Another hard swallow. Roxy'd caught his eye the first time they'd met, and he was damned if that feeling in his gut had only grown stronger since then. No woman had ever sneaked past his psychic defenses the way she had, yet her psychic skills were minimal, nearly non-existent. On the psychic scale that ended with Level Tens, she was a solid three. A normal. Except she wasn't normal. Not really. Roxy had instincts and courage, and she'd learned early to trust her gut and her intuition until they were finely honed tools in her MPD arsenal. Did the image of her in her uniform still make him as hard as a spike? *Damn straight.*

Pivoting, Isaiah looked behind him, through the perfectly aligned kitchen doors between where he stood and the dimly lit hall to the Brattons' suite. He could easily sense Darrin, Kitty, and Nugget in there. All were asleep and content now that they were together again. But when he pushed for some indication from Candy, the same blank wall came back to him. He couldn't detect an aura, a shadow, not even the hint of a breath that she might be sleeping in close proximity to her children, or that he might've mistaken her signal for theirs. All he got was dead air.

Disconcerting to say the least. Backtracking down the hall in his stocking feet, Isaiah stopped at the Bratton's bedroom door and pressed his ear and his palm to the flat wooden surface. In all his years spent honing his own peculiar psychic gift, he'd come across very few individuals who were naturally able to block him. Usually highly intelligent, most had no idea the riddle they posed to a Level Ten.

Wise old Mother Nature made the human mind a master deceiver, and no two brains on the planet functioned quite the same. Psychics, even Level Tens, were unique from each other, and none that Isaiah had met so far in his life were mind readers. Neither did they have x-ray vision as sweet Roxy had innocently thought.

Isaiah's lips curved at her dismay when she'd blurted that question out loud, but it was one he'd heard before. Non-psychics were similar to *Muggles* in the popular *"Harry Potter"* series of J. K. Rowling fame. They thought they were alone in the world, when oftentimes, they were pawns caught in a matching of wits between psychics and those who thought to use psychics for the three Gs: gain, glory, and greed.

That was what had snared Isaiah's father and why he served time in a federal penitentiary now: the glory of saving American military lives at the cost of their free will. In the end, Doctor Zaroyin realized the threat he'd posed by taking away the right to choose, but by then, his error in judgment had nearly cost his only child's life.

Desperate for funding, Dr. Zaroyin had turned to the unscrupulous Senator Bick, who was likewise on the fast track to all three Gs. When the congressional mastermind couldn't get the elder Zaroyin to fall in line with his plan for global domination, Senator Bick and his evil wife abducted Isaiah and forced him to track other psychics with the intent to breed him with another Level Ten, to build a super race.

Sound familiar? Not unlike Hitler, they'd eagerly sacrificed the scores of FBI agents who'd innocently volunteered for the surgery that implanted Dr. Zaroyin's computer chips directly into their brains. By the time Isaiah's father realized the flaws to his innovative invention, the damage was done. His only son lay restrained in a secret bunker near Boston while the Bicks tortured him to search out other psychics to serve their ignoble end. And too many good men and women died in the line of duty. Some actually ran themselves to death after receiving the command to locate another Level Ten, Eden Stark Winchester.

That was where Director Tucker Chase, FBI Special Agent Ky Winchester, and Isaiah's best friend, Special Agent Tate Higgins came into the picture. All psychically gifted in one way or another, these agents along with Eden, now comprised the one of a kind, psychic arm of the Federal Bureau of Investigation.

Ky and his wife were the ones who'd rescued Isaiah and ended Senator Bick's life in the process. Then Ky, Tate, and Tucker rescued Eden after Cassandra Bick and her lover stole Eden from Ky's home in the middle of the night. By morning, they'd smuggled her out of the country and all the way to Sierra Leone, Africa, intending to use her as breeding stock the same way they'd done with Isaiah. By the end of that mess, Eden was back in Ky's arms, while Mrs. Bick, her lover, and dozens of deluded FBI agents ended up in the morgue wearing toe tags. Talk about a nightmare.

So yeah. The three Gs weren't all they were cracked up to be.

Is she in there or not? Isaiah wondered at Candy's bedroom door. *Do I dare open the door and check?*

After what his father had done, Isaiah hated invading anyone's privacy. Yet quietly, he did just that. On protective details like this, privacy took a backseat to safety. It had to.

And there Candy was, sound asleep on the king-sized bed between her children, her arm around Kitty, and her red hair tied back in a ponytail. Darrin lay with his back to his mother and sister, his arms around Nugget's neck. It made for a happy picture, and after the kind of day Candy had just survived, she deserved it.

Isaiah let the door ease shut, satisfied all was well for the night. As many precautions as he and Roxy had taken, this should be what his former Navy SEAL boss called an '*easy day*.' But what did Tucker always say after that? Oh, yeah. '*The only easy day was yesterday…*'

A sense of foreboding settled over Isaiah's shoulders like an invisible wet blanket as he settled onto a kitchen chair. From there he could see both halls, to his left the one where the Bratton family slept, to his right the hall that led to Roxy. It hadn't eluded him that Nugget wasn't in the kitchen where Isaiah had left him when he'd gotten caught up with

Roxy. But more disconcerting? That Candy slept with her back to her son while she'd snuggled her daughter.

Perhaps the size of the bed was the reason for the distance between mother and son. Perhaps Nugget had simply scratched at Candy's bedroom door until someone let him in. Perhaps not...

Chapter Eleven

Roxy jolted upright. Shots. Two very distinct shots had just interrupted an erotic dream about her favorite janitor's closet. Scrambling to her feet, she strapped her holster on her hips, checked her weapon, and exited her room. Rounding the corner from hallway to kitchen, she tucked her shirt into her pants, which were plenty wrinkled after the way they'd hit the floor earlier. Where was Isaiah?

"I'm in here," he called quietly from where he stood at the narrow window alongside the front entry doors.

Damn, he's reading my mind again. "What's going on?" she asked as she took in the sight of him standing at the window. How could he look cool, calm, and collected when she probably looked like some whore after a three-day drunk? Self-consciously, she smoothed her hair away from her mouth and swept it behind her ear, wondering where her elastic was when she needed it most.

Isaiah's sharp gaze rocketed over her breasts to her feet and back up again. "I can't raise Agents Gibson and Torrence."

"Your undercover guys?"

He nodded one curt nod before he surveyed the street and front yard again. "You stay here while—"

"While I what? Bake cookies and let you walk into trouble by yourself?" she bit out. "Not happening, Zaroyin. In case you haven't noticed, I'm not *Suzy Homemaker*."

"And I'm not asking." He didn't break eye contact with whatever or whoever he was watching. "Be right back." With a twist of the elegant door handle, Isaiah left her, which made sense. Someone needed to stand guard over the Brattons, but damn. Roxy'd rather be out there beating the shit out of the bad guys than babysitting.

Checking the door behind Isaiah to make certain it had locked behind him, she swept through the entry headed for the Bratton's suite. Without knocking, she entered the cozy room.

"What' wrong?" Candy asked, blinking as if she'd been disturbed.

"Nothing. Go back to sleep," Roxy ordered, then thought twice about what she was doing. Her client deserved a better, more courteous answer. "What I meant is, Agent Zaroyin's outside checking our perimeter. I just wanted to make sure everything was good with you. Need anything?"

Bratton nodded, her red ponytail bobbing down her back. "Just one thing. I wish you'd call me Candace or Candy. Bratton sounds so cold, like you hate me, or something. Have I offended you? I'm sorry if I did. I just don't remember."

Well, shit. "Sorry," Roxy offered lamely. "It's the job, not you. Stay here. Keep your kids company until Agent Zaroyin gets back inside. If you need anything, let me know, umm, Candy." *Argh! Why, oh why, does that name have to irk the hell out of me?*

Stepping back, she made a hasty retreat instead of chatting with her new BFF, thankful Isaiah hadn't witnessed her comeuppance. It was just possible *Candy's* intentions were legit. She certainly looked the part of a damsel in distress at the bank. It was also possible that these, these—these feelings—might stem from the green-eyed troll planted firmly on Roxy's shoulder, the one that squeezed her jugular with a vengeance every time Isaiah so much as glanced in *Candy's* direction.

Rolling her neck to dislodge that troll's grip, she inhaled a deep breath, breathing in, breathing out as she forced her self-control to re-engage. She'd never been the jealous type before, mostly because she avoided men, so there was nothing to be jealous over. She simply didn't need the drama they wreaked in her life and the lives of those she loved. But then along came Isaiah, and suddenly, she wanted to kill another woman just because he'd looked twice at her. What was up with that? Roxy didn't care if Isaiah and Candace got it on. Let them. That'd save her the inevitable grief of an affair ending before it got started.

Just the thought of him with another woman left Roxy edgy. Stiffening her spine as well as her resolve to end this thing, Roxy strolled back to the entry, studiously scanning her path as she went to be certain the house was still secure. *Where the hell's Isaiah? What's taking him so long?*

Once again at the window, she parted the sheer panels and peered outside, careful to peek quickly instead of making herself a target. The manicured lawn stretched quietly to the security fence. The driveway was clear since she and Isaiah had moved their vehicles into the four-car garage after dinner. Nothing looked out of place. *So yeah. Where is he?*

She'd just thought that something had to be wrong for him to be gone so long, when, out of the corner of her eye, she caught a shadow standing alongside one of the eight columns to the covered portico. Actually, it was just the shadow of an elbow as if some guy had just raised a pistol skyward. A gasp stole her breath. Isaiah was in trouble!

"I'm safe," he murmured behind her, scaring the holy bejesus out of her.

Pivoting, she had him in her sights without intending to aim at him, shaken that he'd snuck up on her. "Where have you been?" she hissed, lowering her weapon but not holstering it. Not yet. If he could sneak up on her, someone else could, too.

He had the nerve to put a finger to his lips and tell her to, "Shush. My men are outside. That's my buddy you saw just now. Agent Higgins will be spending the night up on the roof, so stand down. You're okay."

"I'm not worried about me," she snapped. "I want answers. Where the hell did you just come from?"

He nodded to the east side of the house, lifting a shiny gold key ring to her view. "Rear exit through the kitchen, remember?"

"Then why didn't the alarm go off?"

Isaiah's big shoulders lifted. "It would've if I hadn't disabled it in time. Don't worry, it's activated again."

She could've spit nails at his nonchalance and lack of being forthright. "I'm not worried! I'm mad. Why's Higgins here? Where'd those shots come from? What's going on?"

The smirk in his eyes faded to black. "Someone murdered Gibson and Torrence in their car tonight. Execution style. They'd seen something and had already called for reinforcements, but my guys couldn't get here fast enough."

"Randall," Roxy breathed. "How'd he know we were here?"

"That's what I—I mean we—need to find out. Did you check on Candy and her kids?"

Roxy wished she couldn't smell him. She nodded, remembering their last encounter and how he'd ended it with one scorching kiss. Her lips still burned from the stubble on his chin. From his teeth. "I woke her up, but they're fine."

"And you were certain she was sound asleep when you checked?"

"You suspect her?"

"I suspect everyone."

Good to know. Roxy could've hugged him for that. "Yeah, I'm sure."

"Then we sit tight. My team's out there. If this was Randall—"

"Who else could it be?"

"Ever heard of innocent until proven guilty?"

"Not when two men die on stake-out. Randall did this, you know he did."

Isaiah blew out a deep sigh. "I do, but we need evidence to prove that, and we needed more protection. That's where my team comes in. They'll set up a post outside while we cover things inside. Now let's check on the Brattons again."

He led while Roxy followed. Just like before, Candy startled at the sight of them entering her room without knocking. "Something's wrong, isn't it?"

Isaiah told her bluntly. "Two federal agents were murdered while they kept watch in their vehicle. We suspect Garrett Randall. Do you know how he tracked you here?"

Lifting to her elbows, Candy tugged the blanket up to her chin and shook her head. "He's... he's here?" she asked, her lower lip quivering.

Roxy narrowed her eyes, trying to see what it was that lent an air of deceit to Bratton's innocent act. Did Isaiah feel it too? The woman was lying, but damn. Her body language gave nothing away.

"Mom?" Darrin asked, sleepily reaching for Nugget, who strangely hadn't sounded any alarm. "What's the matter?"

Isaiah must've zeroed in on that peculiar lack of response as well. "Darrin, everything's okay. But can you tell me where you got Nugget? A pet shop maybe?"

"From a guy," he mumbled as he rubbed a fist into his eye, "at Wal-Mart. He was selling puppies and Mom said it was okay if I got one."

"What'd the guy look like?"

"For heaven's sake," Candy whispered. "That was a long time ago. How's he supposed to remember something like that?"

Isaiah waited on the ten-year-old's answer. Kids tended to be truthful.

"I know he was bigger than me and he smelled like he'd been drinking, but the puppies were so cute."

"Right. Puppies are cute, but did this guy have brown hair, brown eyes, and did he walk with a limp?"

Roxy nodded at Isaiah's quick thinking. Years before the armored car heist, Randall had sustained a broken leg that hadn't healed properly during another run-in with the law. A kid might remember something like that.

Darrin scraped a hand over his head. "I don't remember, but he let me have my pick of the litter. Why? Is something wrong with Nugget?" At the mention of his name, Nugget's tail set to thumping.

"No, Darrin. Nugget's fine now that he's with you." Isaiah ran a hand over the dog's head, ending at his smiling snout. "How'd you earn the money to buy his new collar? I'll bet you had to work extra hard for that one, huh"?

Roxy cocked her head. She hadn't noticed the dog's collar until now. *Good call, Zaroyin.*

Darrin tipped up on one elbow. "I didn't buy him a new collar. Mom? Did you?"

Candy was already nodding. "What's the big deal? I bought him a collar last time I went to the grocery store. The last one was dirty. So what?"

"Might be nothing, but..." Isaiah fingered the smooth brown leather circling Nugget's neck. "If it's okay with you, I'd like to borrow it," he told Darrin with a wink. "Don't let this bad boy out of your sight, okay?"

"Sure, Agent Zaroyin." Hero worship gleamed in Darrin's sleepy eyes as he hugged Nugget again. "He always sleeps with me anyway. He'll be fine until he's got to go outside tomorrow morning and do his business. You'll have it back by then, right? I don't want to let him run anymore."

"You bet, buddy," Isaiah replied, then to Candy he said, "If I find anything, I'll let you know, but please stay inside with your children. Don't go outside and don't let them out of your sight."

She gathered Darrin against her hip. "Of course. I'll be right here."

Outside the bedroom door, Roxy asked, "I knew it. It's bugged, isn't it?"

Isaiah shook his head. "No, but it's got a tracking device implanted along the side. Feel this?"

He shouldn't have made contact with her satiny skin when he handed Roxy the collar. But he did...

Chapter Twelve

"We can't keep doing this," Isaiah muttered as he dragged his mouth away from Roxy's, his blood on fire at the mere touch of her skin on his. The woman was his heroin, and he'd become a hopeless addict with no sense and less restraint. Worse, this addiction was growing. Just knowing she was in the same house with him had him on edge.

Pressed against the wall just outside Bratton's room, she answered a breathy, "I know," into Isaiah's open mouth. Totally smitten and about to lose his mind, Isaiah allowed her to stand, but he didn't release her forearms. For a woman, Roxy was built. Lean muscle mass met his fingers everywhere they wandered. And they liked to wander. Even now, when he had hard evidence in his hand that someone had tracked them to the safe house, Isaiah wanted nothing more than to bend Roxy over the nearest table and make her scream for more.

Fighting his shaky control, he drew in a breath and took that all-important step back from temptation. It was hard to swallow. Harder to breathe. His entire body was... Just. Damned. *Hard.*

"Check out the third rivet from the buckle," he said gruffly. "It's removable." *And so is your shirt.*

Roxy looked at the collar in her hand, dazed as if she couldn't think straight, either. Thumbing the rivet, it popped off and fell to the carpet. Isaiah knelt at the same time she did, and damn. The carpet would do just fine.

Roxy trembled. "I think one of us should ask to be reassigned."

"I already refused this assignment once," Isaiah told her even as he tilted forward on his knees, intent on her lips.

She never even tried to stop him, just melted under his mouth with a delightful whimper. They both would've ended in each other's arms if Candy hadn't jerked her bedroom door open and nearly stumbled over them. "Help!" she cried. "It's Kitty! Asthma. Quick! She can't breathe!"

Mortified at what he'd done outside a client's door—for Christ sake!—Isaiah pushed off the floor. "Since when?" he barked—as if he'd never lost control. "She was fine a minute ago."

"It just started," Candy yelled over her shoulder as she flew back to her gasping daughter on the bed. "I left home so fast, I never thought to bring her inhaler, and the one in her backpack's empty. Quick! We have to go to the ER right now!"

Already out of his pajamas and dressed in jeans and t-shirt, Darrin's eyes flooded. "Hurry, hurry," he cried. "She can't breathe! We gotta go!"

Taking command, Isaiah shook his head. "No, buddy. You stay here with Officer Thurston and Nugget, while I take your mom and Kitty to the hospital. I need a man in the house, okay?" He'd already scooped Kitty into his arms, keeping the blanket wrapped tightly around her.

"But I wanna go," Darrin cried, fighting tears. "She's my sister. You gotta let me go with you." A hiccup wrenched out of him, melting Isaiah's heart. Pesky little brother or not, this little guy loved Kitty fiercely.

Roxy intervened, laying a firm hand on his shoulder. "Isaiah's a good guy. Everything will be okay. He won't let anything happen to Kitty. You'll see."

Darrin turned into her and wrapped his arms around her waist. "'Kay," he said. "I trust you guys, but hurry. Isaiah has to hurry!"

Isaiah gave Roxy what he hoped was a look of appreciation while he angled Kitty out the door, her mother fast on his six. "I'll be in touch," he called over his shoulder on his way to the garage.

"Copy that," Roxy replied evenly, her hands on that little guy's shoulders like any good mom. Where that thought came from, Isaiah didn't know, but he liked it. Roxy would make a good mother.

In seconds, he and Candy were at the security gate. Driving behind bullet proof, tinted windows lent a feeling of safety to the surreal moment, but knowing that Tucker Chase and Tate Higgins were on the premises cinched the deal. Those two were men of war. Both had seen their fair share and both had come out stronger and meaner for it. If Randall wanted a fight, he had one helluva beat-down coming.

Driving like a bat out of hell with two MPD cruisers on his butt, Isaiah made it to the Georgetown University Hospital in less than seven minutes. Once inside an ER exam cubicle, the attending physician had Kitty on her back and attached to a nebulizer in seconds. Only then, did Isaiah allow a deep breath. This was his fault. He should've noticed the girl's pallor when he'd been interrogating her brother and her mother. What was he thinking? Of Roxy and how to get her out of her pants, no doubt. It had to stop. At least, it had to slow down.

Fighting for composure, he stepped out of the cubicle to collect his thoughts. Kitty could've died and that was on him. *'Shit!'* as Tucker would say if he'd been any good at getting into Isaiah's mind. *'Pull your head out of your ass, Zaroyin.'* Of course, he would've added a few more earthy descriptors, and he would've been right. This joint assignment was a mistake, had been from the beginning.

For the first time since that night long ago when he'd found his mother murdered in his room, Isaiah doubted his gift and his sanity. He was no hero, not if he couldn't ensure the safety of a twelve-year-old girl, and certainly not if he couldn't keep his hands off Roxy. *What the fuck was I thinking!* Another Tucker Chase euphemism.

Shit, now he wasn't even making sense, and that had to stop. Isaiah stiffened his moral fiber, gave his addled brain a good shake like he'd give a dirty rug, and settled his butt to one of the molded plastic chairs outside Kitty's examination room. He could hear her struggling to breathe from where he sat.

Gradually she calmed down. The medicine must have worked. It took a few minutes, but gradually, his breathing evened out as well. Isaiah swallowed. He drew in a deep, cleansing breath and swore he'd forget Roxy until this thing was over. Kitty deserved the best he had to give, and so far, she hadn't had that. Well, no more.

Hands on his knees, he pushed up and bucked up. Only when he re-entered the cubicle, Candy was gone. "Where's Mrs. Bratton?" he asked the emergency room doctor.

Dr. Duggan shrugged. "She left right after you did. Didn't you see her?"

"No, I didn't." *And I should have.* Isaiah took one step outside the exam room, looked both directions, then ducked back in. "Promise you'll stay with this girl," he ordered Dr. Duggan, flashing his FBI badge to prove he meant business.

The wide-eyed man nodded. "Sure. I can't leave until I'm sure the medication's working anyway. Go. Find her mom."

"Trust me," Isaiah hissed, mad at himself for ever trusting Candace Bratton. "I will."

Roxy dragged Darrin out of bed and into the kitchen. She knew how to fix a mean cup of hot chocolate, and while she guarded him, that was what she intended to do. Cheer him up as best she knew how. All boys liked hot cocoa, didn't they?

Nugget dropped to the floor under the table in the kitchen with a growly groan that mimicked Darrin's when he dropped his forehead to his arm on the table. "I know I tell her I hate her guts sometimes, but I really don't, you know?" he asked tearfully.

"Stop beating yourself up, kid. That's just something brothers and sisters tell each other. You didn't mean it." Roxy poured three cups of milk into a copper saucepan, added a cup of heavy cream, and doused that with a teaspoon of vanilla and a cup of the cocoa mix she'd found earlier when she'd done dishes. Stirring while the concoction heated, she resolved to be a better mentor to the Bratton children. And their dog.

"It's just that she used to be my best friend, but now she's like someone I don't know." He dragged a finger under his nose. "She acts like I bug her all the time, and she's mean to me, and she's meaner to Nugget. She calls him a pig, and she screams at him cuz she hates his hair cuz it gets on her clothes. But a dog's got hair and he can't help it if it gets all over the place, can he?"

Roxy winced that what she and Kitty had in common might be a mean streak. "Sure, I understand. You're her kid brother. Of course you bug her. And I'll bet you like bugging her, don't you?"

"Sometimes," he admitted sorrowfully. "All I have to do is wake up in the morning and breathe to bug her." Darrin sighed as dramatically as only a ten-year-old boy could. By then his arm stretched across the table and his chin rested on his bicep. His eyes drooped. The boy was tired and way too serious for a kid his age.

Roxy snorted. "Trust me. She's just being a typical teen girl. If you think she's bad now, wait until she starts dating."

"But why?" he asked, his tears on the rise again. "She used to be nice. She'd take me to the park, and we'd ride the merry-go-round together, and we'd laugh and play, and we'd feed the baby goats in the petting zoo. Now all she wants to do is paint her fingernails and play games on her cell. She never laughs and we don't go to the zoo anymore."

Darrin yawned and just in time, the hot cocoa was warm enough. Roxy poured two mugs and set one under his nose. "You want marshmallows or whipped cream with that?"

That woke him up. "Whipped cream!"

"The fluffy stuff it is," she said with a chuckle. Isaiah had promised her a night full of dinner, wine, and the creamy concoction in the spray can she found on the top shelf in the refrigerator. Filling Darrin's cup to the brim with a spiraling mountain of fluff, she topped hers off with just a dab, smiling at the thought of her and Isaiah getting it on with a can—or two—of whipped cream.

Darrin came up from his mug with a creamy white moustache, his eyes bright again. "This is good."

How well Roxy knew. "It's my mom's recipe. She used to make it for me when I was your age." It was one of her best memories, sitting at another kitchen table in the dark of an early morning, sharing cups of hot cocoa made the old fashioned way, in a saucepan, before Mama went off to clean houses for rich folks. There'd been no fancy spray whipped cream back then. Roxy's parents couldn't afford many extras, but Roxy had never known that.

Until she went to school and learned how cruel children could be—mostly because they'd repeated on the playground what they'd heard at home—Roxy had honestly thought all children lived in a small but clean house with two sets of aged grandparents. She'd thought all mothers and fathers worked two jobs to make ends meet, and she'd thought all parents adored their children. It seemed life had a mean streak, too.

"You got any sisters?" Darrin asked, his chin still on the table and his cup tilted so he could slurp without much effort.

Roxy reached over to scrub her hand over his head. What a cute kid. "Nope. I'm an only child."

That earned her a grunt. "Then you're lucky. I wish I was an only kid. Maybe Mom would like me better."

Excuse me? Roxy cocked her head. "Your mother loves you, Darrin. I know she does. You should've seen how worried she was when she sent Agent Zaroyin to go get you."

Another grunt. "I like Agent Zaroyin. He's my friend."

He seemed to be everyone's friend. "Where's your dad?" Roxy asked, glad for the change of subject. Bob Bratton hadn't been in his kids' lives since Darrin was born, but she didn't know much more than that.

Darrin shrugged. "Don't know. Guess he never wanted kids screwing up his life, so he only stayed until I was born."

"She told you that?" What a lot of adult garbage to dump on a little kid.

Darrin tilted his mug and took a long slurp. "It's no big deal. Kitty's just like me. A bastard."

That ugly word raised Roxy's ire. "Who told you that? The kids at school?"

He shook his head. "No. My Mom. It's true. I looked it up. I got no dad, and that's what bastards are, kids with no dads."

Darrin said it so matter-of-factly that Roxy cringed. For once she wished she had ESP, so she could forward that disturbing bit of intel on to Isaiah. What would he think about his precious *Candy* now if he knew she referred to her kids as bastards, and that they accepted the moniker like it was nothing? Explaining playground bullying was one thing, but to tell them up front that their dad hadn't wanted them seemed unusually blunt and cruel.

Something about Mrs. Bratton gnawed at Roxy's gentle nature, and yes, she had one. Folks might not believe it, but she could be downright nice when—if— she wanted to.

"You're not a bastard, Darrin," Roxy said quietly, her eyes on what was left of her now cooled cocoa, "and neither is Kitty. But you are children who've been deserted by their father. So what if your dad wasn't man enough to stay? That doesn't change the fact that you're still a good boy. Did you leave him? Uh-uh. You can't drive, can you? He's the adult. He's the idiot who did the driving away. Bob Bratton's the loser, not you." She'd gotten more riled as she'd talked, but damn it. Roxy would never understand absentee fathers if she lived to be an old maid. Darrin was one in a million and a real charmer. *How stupid was his father that he couldn't see that, huh?*

Another shrug. "It don't matter." Darrin took one last slurp and righted his cup with a satisfied gleam in his eyes. "Agent Zaroyin likes me. I can tell. Maybe he'll play catch with me in the morning."

Roxy had no doubt Isaiah would do just that. "Hit the road, Jack," she said as she lifted to her feet and took the mugs to the sink.

"M-m-my name's not Jack."

Roxy glanced over her shoulder to find big tears shimmering in Darrin's eyes. She flew to his side. "Hey, what's this about?" she asked, smoothing a hand over his trembling shoulder.

The poor kid sobbed. "I'm Darrin," he said hoarsely. "Don't you remember? We just had cocoa, and you gave me whipped cream, and we talked like we're friends. I'm Darrin, not Jack."

Why he needed to be called by his right name struck Roxy's heart like a hammer. She'd done this to him, scared him into thinking she'd forgotten him when there was no way she could. "I know who you are, baby," she soothed as she tugged him off his chair and into her arms. "Trust me. I'll never call you Jack again, Darrin. From now on, you're Darrin the giant killer."

He tipped his head into her shoulder, trembling. Like her mother did when Roxy came home crying after her first bully enlightened her with the lie that she was a lazy Mexican, Roxy sat there on the kitchen floor and rocked the little boy who'd stolen her heart. Being called *Jack* was nothing compared to the ugly slurs she'd endured, but what had happened in this little guy's ten years that he'd reacted so strongly to being called Jack?

Roxy intended to find out.

Chapter Thirteen

Isaiah combed the hallways leading from the emergency room, desperate to locate Candace. Only when he passed the chapel, did he get that feeling again. Someone was in mental anguish, but that person wasn't her. Palming the door open, he peered inside the reverent space.

Muted spotlights bathed the large wooden crucifix at the front of the room. Six rows of padded wooden pews lined the way forward. Candace was on the second row near the front, sitting at the end with her head bowed. A hefty man in a dark hoody sat behind her. He lifted to his feet when Isaiah approached, but kept his head down, the hood concealing his features.

Isaiah stopped him with a hand to his wrist. "Sir?" he asked, sensing the man's utter despair. "Is there anything you need? Can I ... help?"

Red-rimmed eyes stared back at him from beneath a shock of shadowed auburn hair. "Can you turn back time and give me my boy back?" the man asked, his voice ragged and filled with pain.

Ah. A dying child. That was the one thing Isaiah wished he could do, bring the special person he'd loved back to life. "I'm sorry," he offered, ashamed he'd suspected this grieving father of being mixed up with the likes of Garrett Randall.

The man pulled away. "Then leave me the hell alone," he bit out.

Isaiah watched him go. The poor guy's shoulders slumped. He shuffled like an old man with no reason to live. For a moment, Isaiah worried if he should follow him to make sure he wasn't headed to any number of the bridges on the Potomac to do himself in. A man without hope was one of God's cruelest tragedies.

But at the chapel door, the big guy turned, tipped his index finger to the rim of his hood and nodded once at the alter as if he'd reached an understanding with the Lord. Maybe he had. Isaiah surely hadn't, not for the sweet life taken from him when he was Kitty's age. What he wouldn't give for one more day with his mom.

A hand in the middle of his back brought Isaiah around. "I'm sorry I ran away," Candace whimpered, tears brimming her eyes, "but I can't take it when she struggles to breathe. I feel like it's happening to me, as if I'm suffocating right along with her. I had... I had to…" She flung herself into his arms. He barely caught her before she snuggled under his chin.

"I hate asthma. It takes everything. My peace of mind. My calm center. And someday, maybe even my daughter," she cried. "How does anyone survive that?"

From breasts to hips, she pressed her warm body into him. One hand circled his neck, the other slithered inside his suit jacket and ended nestled at his hip, a little too warm, given their body guard/client roles. Yet he read nothing into it, just did his best to comfort Kitty's mother without leading her on. Sometimes people needed a hug.

"When I left, Kitty looked and was doing better. Her cheeks had more color. She was breathing easier. Let's go back, so you can see with your own eyes."

Her head bobbed, bumping his chin, but she made no effort to extricate her limbs. She sniffed. "She's so little and frail."

He nodded like the big dumb jock that he morphed into at tender times like this. Women were not his strong suit, and Isaiah, the top Level Ten psychic in the country, honestly didn't know where to put his hands. Firmly and without moving his palm or fingers in any comforting gesture that might be mistaken for a sexual come on, he placed one palm lightly on just the top of her shoulder.

Not her arm, where a man's touch could be mistaken for right or possession, and not her neck, the single most telling grip a man could exert on a woman. A woman's neck was a fragile thing, a puzzle of bones that could be stroked or just as easily snapped. To hold the nape of a woman's neck implied trust and intimacy. The only nape Isaiah wanted in his hands belonged to a spitfire Hispanic with blood in her eye were she to catch him like this, almost—but not really—embracing the woman Roxy thoroughly distrusted.

Hands down, Isaiah trusted Roxy more than Candace. No matter how much empathy he'd extended to this woman, he kept coming up with zero. She never gave his psychic probes more than a smooth flat surface to bounce off of. She was the echo that never came back to him, the void in the mirror where her reflection ought to be. Even now, in what surely had to be one of the worst moments in her life, Isaiah sensed no emotions from Candace Bratton. Despite her display of affection for Kitty and Darrin, he sensed no depth to her. No real concern. No hint of motherly love.

Interestingly, Roxy had stirred the deepest depths of his soul with just one touch. But Candace? She'd thrown her entire body at him., and he didn't feel a thing.

When Candace snuggled in closer, his nose filled with the fragrance of strawberries from her shampoo, and Isaiah's mind flew back to the safe house and Roxy. She always smelled of coconuts and sunshine, as if she'd just come in from the outdoors, as if she loved every minute of her rowdy, cop-on-the-beat life, and couldn't wait to get back to it.

Her coy smile, the one she hadn't known she'd shared with him, now reminded Isaiah that he had his hands on someone else—and that Candace's hair was unbound instead of secured like it had been back in the ER. *When did that happen?*

He dropped his arms to his sides. "Time to go," he said sternly. He was not a love-the-one-you're-with kind of guy. "Dr. Duggan's with Kitty, but she'll be upset and wondering where you are." *Wouldn't any kid who'd nearly died want their mom to be there with them?*

Candace shook her head, her long mane flouncing from side to side. "Uh-uh. She's been here enough times. She knows I can't handle seeing her like that. She'll be fine. Stop worrying."

"But she's your daughter." How could a mother not want to be with her panicked child when said child could barely breathe? When that child's lips had been blue when she'd been brought in? When she might die? Kitty's condition had frightened Isaiah, and he wasn't ashamed to admit it. He'd thought he'd arrived too late to save her just like he had with— *Mom.*

When a sigh shuddered through Candace, Isaiah thought she'd come to her senses, that she'd do right by her child and go running back to the ER. Instead, she asked, "Can we sit for a while longer and just talk? It's been a really bad day."

He closed his eyes, fighting a growing sense of urgency to be somewhere—anywhere—else. His sense of duty had changed. In the bank, he'd honestly thought she was a woman fighting for her life. Now he didn't know who she was, and he was tired of her mixed signals. They did need to talk.

Very carefully, he took hold of her biceps and extricated her from his proximity. Without another word, he gripped her elbow and directed her to the rear bench nearest the chapel exit. "I'm FBI, ma'am. I'm here to protect you and your children," he told her sternly in case she'd gotten the wrong idea. Women tended to crush on the guy who came to their rescue. He didn't want to be on the receiving end of any infatuation. "So talk."

That brought a coy smile to her lips, not what he was going for. Smoothing her hands over her hips, she sat at the end of the bench, forcing Isaiah to step around her. He took the seat a respectable three feet to her left, turned and lifted his knee to the bench as a barrier between them. This was not one of those cozy moments. "What's so important you can't talk about it back at the house?"

"Oh, nothing," she said, her eyes on her fingertips now fluttering on her knees. "It's just been a crazy day, and I guess I needed adult conversation instead of all the drama for a change."

He waited. Gradually it came out. She'd been born the fourth daughter of parents who liked their booze more than their kids. Her childhood was no picnic, but on rare days, her mother and father tried to be fit parents. They'd camped out a lot, and because of those excursions, she loved the forest near Roanoke, and she adored Williamsburg with its colonial atmosphere. She'd never planned on having children, but now she had two, and she couldn't be happier. She worked hard, and she meant to be better off than her parents someday. Sooner than later, she hoped.

Candace ended with, "A girl can dream, Special Agent Zaroyin. What about you? What was it like to be you when you were growing up?"

He'd hooked one elbow over the bench back and interlocked his fingers over his stomach, listening and asking a question or two as her story had unfolded. But he hadn't expected that question, and he should have. Isaiah had certainly heard it enough.

The tiny hairs up the back of his neck prickled upright. Strange that one simple question seemed so much bigger than it was, but surely she knew the infamous story about his father's misdeeds and his mother's horrific demise. They'd both made national headlines. If Candace didn't know who Isaiah Zaroyin was by now, she had to be the only one on the East Coast who didn't.

Ever since the arrest and sensational sentencing of his dad, he'd fought the ensuing self-serving demands of every greedy news outlet, magazine and talk show host, to 'follow-up' with the son who'd lost everything. He'd been stalked by reporters and paparazzi, all wanting to wring every last anecdote, salacious bit of gossip, and minute of his past life out of him. To twist his words until they turned into sensational, eye-grabbing fodder for all those *enquiring minds* out there in John-Q-Public land. Tragedy, rumor, and outright lies now tainted the once noble Zaroyin name. Worse—treason. How could she not know?

Yet her question seemed innocent enough. Like every other time he'd probed her mind, he could detect nothing past the obvious question. She was no spy for any media outlet. He had only face value to rely on and she seemed genuinely interested.

That alone cinched his decision not to share. *'Seemed'* relied solely on appearances, not facts and certainly not truth. Until he found his way past whatever self-defense mechanism she'd mentally constructed to block his probes, all Isaiah had to go on was her projected *appearance* of being a good mom. Her *appearance* of being a hostage. Not good enough.

Until he could validate what he suspected were facades between him and the real Candace Bratton— whoever she was—he erred on the stuffy side of polite, FBI propriety and said, "I grew up in a home with two good parents. Went to school. Studied hard. Typical boring life for the average kid, I guess."

She cocked her head and blinked at him. "You were an only child?"

"Yes."

"Any pets?"

He let her have that one. "Hoi Toi, a longhaired Siamese with chocolate brown toes. Big blue eyes." *And my only friend for a long damned time after Mom died.*

"Aww…" she breathed, batting soft gray eyes that were an open invitation for trouble. Candace certainly gave off all the right vibes of an innocent caught up in something bigger than she was… until her hand came to rest on his thigh.

He looked down at her sensible womanly fingers. Clean cuticles. Real nails, not acrylic fakes. Tapping. Just tapping. Light as a feather on the inside of his thigh. They looked almost childlike. Almost innocent.

If he were any other man, it'd be easy to capitalize on this tender moment and turn it into something sexual. It'd be easy to take that seemingly sweet gesture as an invitation, lean in and pull her under his arm. Comfort her. Kiss her. Lie to her and tell her everything would be okay while he stroked the luscious red hair spilling over her shoulders and dripping down her back like a ruddy waterfall. It was obvious she was looking for a friend with benefits.

But Roxy waited back at the mansion…

Candace's long slender fingers kept tapping. She chewed at the inside of her cheek while Isaiah held his breath, hoping she had something more to say. If ever there was a moment to come clean, this was it. He could be that much of a friend, simply someone to confide in, to share the burden with, so to speak. Needing her to open up, Isaiah rested one hand over hers to stop the incessant tapping that had no chance of leading him into temptation. "You've had a tough break," he said quietly. "What can I do to help that I'm not doing now?"

Impossibly, the chapel grew quieter. Stiller. Colder.

It seemed time stood still. She stared sideways at him, her chin quivering just the slightest bit, her body language easy to read. She couldn't decide what to do, but what that decision involved, Isaiah had no clue.

At last her lashes fell. She tugged her fingers from between his hand and his thigh, and the moment for truth was lost.

"I can't help you if you don't trust me," he told her firmly, intertwining his now free hand with his other once more, both back on his chest where they belonged.

She faced the cross, tipped her chin up, and sniffed. "Let's go see if my girl's finally ready to go. I am."

Isaiah nodded, though she didn't see it. The wall between them remained unbreachable, and the woman's mind was locked up tighter than a castle's keep. Politely, he followed Candace back to her daughter's side.

Kitty looked pinker but still pale and wrung out. Her eyes were feverishly bright. Still, she offered a limp wave when Isaiah ducked into the room. "You came back," she said breathlessly—to him, interestingly. Not to her mother.

"Of course, I came back for you, kiddo." He stepped to one side of her bed while Candace took the other. "How are you feeling?" he asked as he fist bumped Kitty's shoulder.

"Better," she whispered. "Man, that was a close call, huh?"

He dipped his head to her ear and stage-whispered. "I'll tell you a secret if you promise not to tell anyone. You scared the crap out of me, young lady, and I'm a big FBI guy. I don't scare easy. Don't let my boss know, okay?"

Kitty let loose a weak, wheezing rasp of a giggle. "Ha. Don't... make me laugh. I scared me, too."

"So what brought this attack on? You were asleep. Does that happen often at night?" he asked as he straightened the warm blanket covering her and tucked it under her chin. The poor thing still shook, no doubt from the adrenaline still in her system.

"It's hard to say," Candace answered, her gaze on her daughter and her lips thin. The calculating look in her eye caught him up short. "Sometimes stress will do it. We've certainly had enough of that today, haven't we?" she asked her daughter brusquely.

Kitty nodded, her eyes drowsy. "Love you, Mom," she whispered.

Isaiah stepped back, taking it all in. Candace certainly acted like a loving mother. And that was what bothered him. It was all an act. He knew it the moment she didn't tell the daughter who could've died in her arms tonight, *'I love you, too.'*

Chapter Fourteen

Roxy stood guard over Darrin and Nugget while they slept. They'd gone back to the Brattons' room, which gave her the chance to do a little detective work on the sly. Kitty's asthma attack had certainly come on quickly, yet checking around Brattons' bed, under it, and between the covers revealed nothing suspicious. The suitcases they'd brought with them were opened in wild disarray, piles of clothing and shoes scattered on the floor. Two cosmetic bags, both opened and a myriad of tiny jars, tubes, and bottles decorated the dresser top.

Roxy did a quick search of said suitcase and bags. She peeked into the dresser drawers and the walk-in closet, but all were empty. Apparently Candy didn't plan to stay long enough to unpack. Roxy gave the end of the bed one last pat on her way out the door.

Just as well. No mother would intentionally induce an asthma attack in her child, would she? Nah, she might be a floozy, but she loved her kids. Roxy was one hundred percent certain of that. Almost...

Back in the kitchen, she washed the saucepan and mugs, tidied the kitchen and wiped the table. That little guy of Bratton's had gotten under her skin. What a good kid Darrin was, Kitty too, the poor thing. Roxy had never had asthma, but she could relate to the helpless feeling that came along with suffocation. Damned if her hand didn't automatically circle her neck in a reflexive response from something that happened long ago.

The memory rose as vividly as if it were yesterday. Mario Forsythe. Hawthorne High. The ever-so-handsome quarterback who thought he was a dandy with the ladies. The girl's restroom across from the gym. Homecoming dance. Balloons and confetti.

She'd only dated him once, the night of the homecoming dance, but that was enough. Hawthorne High had just cinched a crucial game. They were on their way to state, and Mario was the hero of the hour. Collegiate football scouts were in the house that night, and they'd talked with him and his coach. He was going somewhere. He thought he was hot. So hot that she'd give it up to him when he snapped his fingers. *Like hell.*

The jerk followed Roxy and her girlfriend into the restroom, and Roxy learned the meaning behind the saying, *'if looks could kill.'*

"Don't tease," he'd growled at her after she'd resisted his crude advances and he'd slapped her to the floor. "Every other bitch in this school spreads her legs for me. You're better than they are? Come on. Get up off the floor and bend over like the slut you are." He'd snapped his fingers at her like the entitled jock he was and clutched his junk. "Give it up. I ain't got all night."

"I said no," she'd told him as she'd climbed to her feet, trembling so hard she could barely think. Her dress was torn by then, the bodice hanging by a strap, and her very practical white cotton bra exposed. The *friend* she'd come into the restroom with had long since run for her life. *Her* life, not Roxy's. Julie hadn't gone for help. No, she'd deserted Roxy like a cockroach fleeing a sinking ship.

But Mama had always said it was okay to hit a bully if they hit you first. Roxy curled her fingers into a fist, her thumb up tight against the side of her index finger so it wouldn't get broken. She meant to give Mario something all right.

He'd lunged then. Before she could punch his solar plexus, he had her by the neck, lifted her against the sink, and choked her with his thick, dirty fingers. His muscled knees had no trouble parting her flailing legs, not in that stupid dress she'd worn.

Darkness swarmed at her peripheral. She couldn't catch her balance, and no matter how hard she'd tried, she couldn't get a grip on the porcelain sink behind her. Up went his hand under her dress. He tore past the elastic of her panties, and rubbed her where no boy had ever touched before. Grunting like the pig he was, he stuck his fingers into her virginal body while she gasped for air and the lights dimmed.

Roxy knew then that Mario was high on something. With one repugnant sweep of his mouth, he'd licked her face as if she were a sucker. Slick, slick, slick went his nasty tongue and nose over her cheeks, chin, and lips. His breath stunk of poor dental hygiene and cheap beer, while his whiskers scraped everywhere he touched until she was chafed and raw. He poked and prodded at her virginity until she saw red.

When he jerked his belt off with his free hand and snapped the air with it, lightning struck in that women's restroom. But it had nothing to do with the measly piece of leather he'd been so prickishly proud of, nor what he'd intended to do to her with it.

Oh, no. Roxy couldn't remember precisely what happened next. Until she'd heard the pop of that belt, she'd simply been fighting for her life. But then— instead of being the helpless rape victim and crying for him to *'oh, please, stop!'*—she got mad. And then she got even.

Where her courage or her strength came from, she had no idea, but by the end of the violent encounter, blood puddled on the floor beneath the sinks in the girls' restroom, and none of it was hers.

Roxy walked away from the confrontation half-naked with handfuls of Mario's sleek black hair in her fist, but proud of herself because she could walk away, and because now, that sick freak knew. She wouldn't go quietly.

Her good girl reputation was still intact, but she was pissed at the whole damned world for letting that happen! To her! To any girl entrusted to the school board's care! She was just as angry with the chicken shit teachers who had to have known the pervert that their star quarterback was! How could they not?

Instead of a walk of shame, and despite her ragged state of undress, she'd lifted her chin in defiance to the crowd that had gathered like a bunch of cheerleaders outside the restroom doors. The cowards! They had to have heard him bellowing at her, and she knew damned well they'd heard her screams. But had anyone thought to intervene? To stop him? To save her?

Even her supposed girlfriend was there, clapping like Roxy had simply won a wrestling match instead of a fight for her life. God, she'd hated every single one of them that night. Still did.

Someone must've called the police, most likely the principal. He had the most to lose once this bullshit went public, well, besides Roxy. But that was the night she knew she'd become a female police officer. More than anything, she would learn how to better protect herself and others from good-looking punks like Mario. From that night on, she vowed to be tougher than everyone else and to never—NEVER—let any man do that to her again.

After the kindly male officers had covered her with a blanket and cordoned off the restroom, the EMTs showed. They took care of Mario first because he'd made the most noise. No wonder. As the EMTs passed by with him strapped to a gurney, the crowd stilled. Guess bawl baby Mario had a gushing broken nose, a severely scratched face, mashed fingers, and some seriously swollen testicles. *Boo-hoo-hoo.*

Roxy had watched in silence, staring at the bastard, but not once had he looked her in the eye. Funny thing. Every last one of those first responders who'd showed, the police officers, EMTs, and the firemen, had nothing but good things to say to her. Good things like, "You go, girl!" and "Guess you showed him, Roxy," and "Good for you!" and "I wish every girl had your brand of guts." She'd glowed that night, even after enduring the humiliation of a rape kit later at the emergency room—just to be sure. Her mom and dad were shocked and angry when they'd arrived at the hospital, but Roxy had reassured them she was okay, that she'd never given in. That he'd never walk straight again.

She never returned to Hawthorne High.

Lost in remembering the ensuing PTSD that lingered after that night, Roxy rubbed her fingertips over her trachea where once an asshole had left an ugly collar of bruises. But that was then, and this was now. Mario Forsythe couldn't get to her anymore, because bullies were cowards at heart. Every last one of them. They didn't go after chicks who could beat their asses. Besides, he'd moved out of state shortly after spending two years on home confinement for the assault.

Hawthorne High lost state that year, and to her knowledge, hadn't recovered their once stellar reputation. But Roxy Thurston had. She'd overcome Hawthorne and Mario because she was born to be a survivor, never a victim. She taught other young men and women self-defense now, so they'd never know fear and humiliation by a bully. Because Mario might be gone, but there were plenty of others in the District.

Turning off the kitchen lights, Roxy said goodbye to her past one more time. With her hand on her revolver grip, she rechecked the windows and doors, making certain they were secure, at least the ones she could. Interestingly, Brattons' hall ended at a massive locked double door for which Roxy had no key, and she wanted one. How could she do her job with most of the mansion off-limits? *Mental note to self: badger Isaiah until he tells me everything about this house.*

She smiled to herself. No doubt he would've done just that if they'd been able to keep their hands to themselves.

Satisfied that all things were locked up, she dragged a chair from the kitchen table and set it near the middle of the room. From there, she could watch three of the five exits to the room: the doorway to the formal dining room straight ahead, the hallway that led to staff quarters at her left, as well as the one at her right to the Brattons' suite. It irked her that the cellar and patio exits were at her back, but what else could she do? She'd made certain both were secure before she sat down.

And just because she meant what she said, her revolver, now cocked and ready, rested with one in the chamber in her holster. Isaiah wouldn't sneak up on her again, the dog. Not that she'd shoot him if he did, but if Randall came calling? Him, she'd shoot in a heartbeat.

For the next hour Roxy watched, waited. She made certain Darrin slept soundly and she patrolled her kingdom every half-hour with revolver in hand. Precisely at midnight, her cell vibrated on her hip. She didn't recognize the number on her caller ID, but the FBI logo attached to it quickened her response. "Officer Thurston."

"Hey, Roxy," an affable, baritone voice replied. "This is Director Chase, Isaiah's boss. You can stand down for an hour or three if you're tired. Go ahead. Get some shuteye. You might as well. It's quiet out here and we're not going anywhere."

"Thank you, sir, but I'm not tired," she told him in no uncertain terms, her weapon once more holstered. "And I don't sleep on the job. Not until Isaiah, umm, Agent Zaroyin returns." She rolled her eyes at that less than brilliant comeback that made her sound like she planned to sleep with Isaiah once he got back. Not a bad idea, but so not happening.

Director Chase had the nerve to chuckle. "Figured you'd say that. This place is a jewel, isn't it? All the comforts of home, plus."

"Comfort, nothing. It's an eyesore and a nightmare," she shot back at him. "MPD would never use a monstrosity like this for a safe house. What were you guys thinking? The grounds are too big and the home itself is an invitation for trouble with all these rooms. I can't even check most of this place. Why the hell not?"

Another manly chuckle resonated over the line as if Director Chase had just dismissed her angst. *How dare he?* "That's what my wife says, too. You'd like her. She's smart, like you."

Not if she married you, Roxy thought, but she said, "If you say so. But I mean it. I want a key to check the rest of this place. Have you heard from Isaiah... er, umm," *Damn it, I mean...* "Agent Zaroyin yet? Will he be back with Bratton and her daughter anytime soon? Is Kitty okay?"

"Mrs. Bratton and her daughter are doing fine, but Isaiah's got his hands full from what I heard. Guess he met some guy in the hospital's chapel that gave him an odd vibe. We're running the perp's description through our database to see who we come up with."

"Not Garrett Randall?"

"No. Isaiah would've recognized him on sight."

"Not Chester Bratton?" With five million at stake, Candy's ex-father-in-law had to be hanging around nearby, waiting for his chance at the money.

"Negatory," Director Chase drawled.

Roxy nearly snorted. Who'd he think he was, a trucker on the interstate? "Then who else knows about the five mil?" she asked him point blank. "Who else wants Mrs. Bratton dead?" Randall's brothers were either dead or incapacitated. Who was left?

"All good questions for which I have no immediate answers," he offered what sounded like a canned FBI answer. "Mind if I come in for a spell?"

Roxy stalled. Tucker Chase was FBI and a former Navy SEAL. Isaiah trusted him. That meant something, right? Besides, how much trouble could he be? "Sure. I'll unlock the rear exit. Do you know where that is?"

Knock. Knock. Knock.

Roxy spun around to the banging on the door at her rear. Her weapon sprang instantly to her palm, ready to fire, and—damn him! It was Chase, and like Isaiah, he'd scared the bejesus out of her. The red-laser dot from her piece now danced over his smug face, right between his eyes. This arrogant guy had no idea what he'd just done, or how close he came to being dead. He didn't look like he was worried about it, either. His black brows waggled beneath a black ball cap turned brim backwards. This clown was a director? Damn, the Bureau was desperate if they'd hired him.

With her heart pounding in her chest, Roxy holstered her revolver before she turned the deadbolt and let Isaiah's cocky boss inside, then relocked the door behind him. By then, her fingers were trembling and the alarm blinked its ten-second countdown before it notified the police—which was her.

Swallowing hard, she forced a deep breath and keyed in the proper code to cancel the notification and reactivate the alarm. Thankful that Isaiah had at least revealed that before he'd taken off, Roxy was unnerved that she'd drawn on his boss. That she could've killed him if she'd been a green recruit. What is it with these FBI guys that they thought they could sneak up on her like they both had? Was that some kind of training or was it all a game to them? SEALs could be arrogant, but Isaiah wasn't former military. Were they—dumb? Egotistical? This kitchen had too many points of egress, damn it!

Turning on Chase, she caught sight of his broad back just as he headed down Brattons' hallway. She followed, as he passed the bedroom where Darrin and Nugget slept and went straight to the door for which Roxy had no key.

Interestingly, Nugget scratched at the other side of Darrin's closed bedroom door now. He growled, which made Roxy feel better, but why hadn't he reacted to the previous sounds of gunfire? Silly dog wasn't much of a guard dog.

Roxy stored that away for further scrutiny. Right then, she had a rogue FBI director in her safe house, and he had the key for that closed double door in his hand. What the hell?

"Stop," she ordered, pissed again at what Isaiah hadn't shared with her and should have. "Where do you think you're going?"

"Hopefully, nowhere," Chase said as he opened the door, flipped a switch to his left, and peered into the great unknown. A wave of cool air filled the hallway as if the rest of the home was unheated, which made sense. "You can come with me or you can stay put and guard Darrin Bratton. Your choice, but I'm checking the rest of this place. You're right. It's too damned big."

Roxy swallowed hard, but leave Darrin alone? Not on your life. "Tell me what you find when you get back," she told Chase, "but I want the key to that door before you leave."

He nodded, his short stock rifle up and snug against his chest in a comfortable hold. The man moved like a professional, at ease with his weapon and unafraid to go it alone. Still not looking at her, he stepped into the room beyond, scanned to the left and then to the right. Tossing her the key, he muttered, "Now be a good girl and lock up behind me, will ya?"

With pleasure. The door swung inward and closed behind Chase with a firm click. Roxy locked it and stepped back, her hackles up at that last remark. For a director, he sure had no problem talking down to her. A man could get fired for what he'd just said. *Good girl? My ass.*

While he was gone, she made another sweep through the portion of the mansion she did control, wondering what other intel Isaiah had neglected to share. The FBI had a rep for steamrolling its partners in law enforcement on joint operations. Was that why he hadn't shared what he knew, because he thought he was superior to the local police like his boss obviously thought? The notion settled like a wet blanket over what she'd hoped was a decent—make that great—working relationship. With Isaiah. Not Chase.

Antsy now that she had a Fed prowling around her mansion, Roxy couldn't sit still. One more time, she checked Darrin, then, just for good measure, let Nugget loose in the hall. One armed guard could only watch so many doors, windows and hall. She wished she'd thought to use Nugget as a resource before. Dogs made the best partners.

Even now, he'd beelined to the door at the end of the hall. Sniffing and growling, he dropped to his belly, his nose pressed tight against the crack of light under the door as if he could smell something he didn't like. Had to be Chase.

"Feel free to bite him when he comes back," Roxy encouraged. *I would if I were you, but that'd make me a bitch, and, oh wait. I am a bitch!* She rolled her eyes again at her warped sense of humor. She wasn't opposed to being the alpha bitch when circumstances called for it.

Shrugging to alleviate the tight knot under her right shoulder blade that had plagued her since Chase showed, she tapped the toes of her right boot and waited with Nugget. How long could it take to search empty rooms? Unless they weren't empty. Glancing up at the ceiling, she crossed her arms over her chest, anticipating the sounds of a struggle, at least footsteps. But nothing came back to her.

Okay, it was just possible that Chase was good at his job, the silent but deadly type of operator. Another smile curved her lips. That made him sound like a fart, which, in a way, he was.

Nugget's ears perked forward just as Chase knocked again.

"Who is it?" Roxy asked just to be a smartass. He was the one who'd gone looking for something—or someone—hadn't he? Why should she just open up without making sure he was who he was supposed to be?

"Chase," his big voice boomed.

Nugget was on his feet by then, the ridge of hair up his spine lifted and his posture tense. Something was definitely up with this dog. Was it Chase? Nah, couldn't be. He was a good guy.

"How do I know it's really you?" Roxy teased. She had Chase there, didn't she?

The key turning in the lock proved otherwise, when Chase let himself back into the inhabited portion of the mansion with a big grin on his face. "Funny girl," he said.

The man was handsome in a dark, intimidating way. And big. Broad, like a wall. His boots had to be size thirteens, and you know what they say about men with big feet. They had bigger egos. If he let his hair grow, it might curl at the ends. Rugged. That was the word for this macho guy. Chase was an alpha if ever she'd seen one. No wonder she found him abrasive. They were two of a kind. *Alpha bitch meet alpha prick.*

Roxy took a step back to let him pass, but he just stood there, blocking the way with his hand on the door behind him and the butt of his short stock rifle under his chin. Jerking his head back toward the supposedly vacant part of the mansion, he said, "All clear."

She covered her relief with her best snark. "Good to know since coming to this monstrosity of a safe house was all *your* idea."

He grinned then, a truly beautiful grin—for a man. The glint in his dark eyes from the overhead light snapped at her attention. "No wonder the kid likes you."

Don't even go there. "What's Darrin Bratton got to do with anything?"

Chase winked, his big brown eyes full of mischief. "Not that kid. Isaiah. That kid."

Oh. Him. Roxy choked, taken by surprise, but a little bit pleased at the observation. "He... he does?" *Who turned the thermostat up?*

Chase's brows dipped together in amusement. "Yeah. He does, but don't tell him. He'll kick my butt if he finds out I talked."

I'd like to see that. "You're wrong," Roxy said firmly, her nose in the air. "We're just two professionals who are—"

"Doing a bang up job." Again the man chuckled. *Did he mean bang up as in banging each other?* Her face heated at the insinuation. *Crap. How much did Chase suspect?* "Trust me. I know a few things about women, and he's got his eye on you. Oh, shit..." Chase tapped his index finger to his right temple. "I forgot. He can hear me," he whispered.

"How?" Roxy demanded to know. Isaiah was miles away.

"He and I have a link. Up here." Chase tapped the tip of his gloved index fingers to his forehead. "Don't ask me how it works. He listens in on me any time he wants, but I'm not as sharp as he is. It's rare that I can reach out, and, you know, touch him, so to speak. Yeah, yeah, I hear you," he muttered. Apparently, Isaiah had reached out and touched his boss, Roxy hoped with a good hard smack. "When are you getting back? Your lady's worried."

Chase said that with a smile that made her head spin. Was he pulling her leg or was he really speaking with Isaiah? Mentally, for hell's sake.

"I'm not his lady," she set him straight.

Chase nodded, winking again. For two cents she'd poke that big brown eye of his the next time it winked. He looked so damned smug, and that shit-eating grin didn't help.

When he ended the mind-speak with Isaiah, he pointed his weapon to the floor. Nugget still hadn't moved his nose from the closed doorway and that alarmed Roxy. Chase noticed, too. Palming the door open once more, he told the dog to, "Kill."

"Kill?" Roxy all but screeched when Nugget took off like a freight train, his nails clattering across the hardwood floor and his voice lifted in an eerie howl. "What if there are kids in there? Stupid college kids just having fun and a kegger?"

Chases' eyes narrowed as Nugget's howl turned into a barking snarl. "Then they'd better be faster than he is. I didn't see anyone, but it sounds like he did. Here, boy!" Chase called out, his rifle stock snug to his chest again and one foot through the door. "Here, boy!"

Holy shit. Who could've been in this mansion all this time? Just some idiot college kids out to have a good time? Vagrants? Nah, Chase would've seen them when he'd scouted the place. He was smart. Annoying maybe, but no one to be trifled with.

Roxy shut the door behind him and locked it, her nerves on edge and her throat gone dry. Could Nugget have gone after Randall?

Panicked now, she ran to Darrin, needing to touch him to make sure he was safe. Randall was just as smart as Chase. She wouldn't put it past him to have planned a diversion to draw her away from Darrin. Not happening, damn it. If Randall thought he could get past her, he was in for a fight.

Chapter Fifteen

Isaiah encountered not one, but three MPD cruisers on the drive back to the mansion. *'Hey, Tuck,'* he sent to his boss over their private mental channel. *'I've got heavy police presence on my tail. What's up?'*

Tucker replied instantly. *'Nugget's missing.'*

'How'd he get loose?'

'Jumped through a plate glass window on the second floor. He saw something outside the mansion he didn't like. Went crazy and took off like a shot. Haven't seen him since.'

"Great," Isaiah muttered out loud. How could he tell Darrin his dog was lost again? Or Kitty, who was asleep with her head on her mom's shoulder?

"What's wrong?" Candace asked. After that awkward moment in the chapel, she'd settled back into motherly mode, but Isaiah had glimpsed a different side to her tonight. His confidence in her had dwindled.

"While we've been busy at the hospital," Isaiah whispered, wondering about the wild goose chase that might've actually been a well planned misdirect, "Nugget jumped through a window and took off. Has he ever done that before?"

"He's never even growled much before today. Why would he?"

"Not sure," Isaiah replied thoughtfully, but dogs pulled some amazing stunts while protecting their families. "Maybe he saw someone he didn't like."

"Did he get hurt?" Kitty asked what her mother apparently wasn't worried about.

Isaiah passed the question along to his boss. *'If he did, I'm not seeing any bloody tracks,'* Tucker replied. *'Your ETA?'*

'Be there in five," Isaiah replied, but to Kitty he said, "Nugget's got a hard head. He'll be okay." *I hope.*

'We'll be waiting.'

'Copy that.' Isaiah drew in a deep breath of frustration. Roxy was right. The mansion posed more problems than it was worth. It was time to relocate. He queried his boss with that option.

'Possibly,' Tucker shot back at him, *'but tonight, we stay put. Get that girl and her mother inside. We'll re-evaluate come daybreak.'*

'Do me a favor. Cut the exterior lighting until we're inside.'

'Can do.'

'See you soon, Boss.'

'Count on it.'

Isaiah cut his ETA by two minutes, then opened his window, and waved to the officers in the three cruisers as he glided through the gates and into the darkened garage. "Stay inside until the garage door's secure, ladies," he told his passengers. Once the doublewide door rolled to the concrete floor, he breathed a sigh of relief. "Okay, now let's get you inside."

Candace seemed more obedient—or something—as she hurried past him with her arm around Kitty's shoulders. The garage stood separate from the mansion, so they headed straight for the rear exit that would put them in the kitchen. Kitty stuck to her mother's side while Isaiah followed closely, keeping an eye out and shielding the women from whoever was out there watching in the dark.

For the first time in a long time, his pistol was snug in his hand. With the thoroughness of a man who could actually sense others in the dark, he scanned every dark shadow, every void, and everything that so much as hinted at movement. At the door, he reached around Candace for the handle, his hand in the middle of her back if push came to shove.

A twig cracked at his right as Tucker Chase came into view. "Tate has the high ground," he advised, meaning the Bureau's best sniper, Agent Tate Higgins, was on the roof with his rifle.

"Good to know," Isaiah replied as he blocked the doorway now that the women had gone inside.

Tucker lifted one boot to the railing that surrounded the Trex walkway running from garage to patio. "How's the girl?"

"They treated her there, then sent her home with a new inhaler," Isaiah answered. "She'll be okay once she gets some rest."

Tucker scratched his chin. "Seems odd, an asthma attack in the middle of the night. They know what set it off?"

"Could've been stress. She's just a kid and it's been a tough day. You have a name for that guy in the chapel yet?"

Tucker stared past Isaiah into the dark. The man went scary quiet sometimes. Like now. Icy fingers tap-danced up Isaiah's spine, yet he held his position, glad his boss had his back. Until Tate bellowed in Isaiah's head, *'Son-of-a-bitch is hurting him!'* at the same moment that Tucker yelled, "Duck!"

A shot rang out, the round splintering the doorjamb just beyond Isaiah. Slivers and chunks of fragmented wood sliced through the air, nicking his forehead. "Shit," he hissed as he slammed the door, then dropped to his haunches, craning to see whatever Tucker and Tate had seen that he hadn't.

Tuck stood unflinching as he fired one, two shots over Isaiah's position and into the night.

Blood ran down Isaiah's face and into his eyes, screwing with his vision even as he cast his inner eye, the one that could see and influence most people, into the dark streets beyond the safe house. Like a high-powered scope, it narrowed on the broad back of an angry man hurrying at a fast clip due south. His aura swirled around him in a blurred blend of blacks and reds and—enough pain that Isaiah could taste it. Blood. Isaiah saw blood on the man's hands and in his heart. This attack wasn't about the money. It was about revenge.

Tucker stopped shooting, his pistol still lifted, his shoulders squared. "Bastard dropped a package over the gate before he fired on us. Two of your MPD buddies took after him."

'He's bleeding!' Tate supplied from the rooftop. *'Get your asses moving!'*

Oh, shit, shit, shit. Isaiah knew precisely what the shooter had dumped over the fence and who was bleeding. Wiping a hand over his bloody brow to clear his sight, he ran with Tucker on his six. There in the dark of a day that wouldn't end, he found Nugget, the golden fur on his ribs glistening with blood.

"What the fuck?" Tucker bit out as he dropped to his knees beside Isaiah. "Dispatch," he snapped into the two-way clipped to his collar. "I need emergency services at our safe house on Embassy Row. Make that a veterinarian. Stat!"

Isaiah smoothed his fingers over Nugget's big head, down his neck, and over his ribs to locate the precise source of all that blood. Jumping through glass should've sliced his snout, maybe his muzzle, but Nugget face wasn't injured. The poor guy lifted his head, looked past Isaiah and whined again.

Tate was suddenly there, his rifle slung over his back as he elbowed Tucker out of the way. "I've got you, big fella. You're not dying on my watch. Just breath. Help's on its way."

Isaiah leaned back on his heels. If anyone could get through to Nugget, it was this guy. Tate had an in with animals, a psychic link. If Isaiah had been a practicing Catholic, he'd think Tate was Saint Francis of Assisi reincarnated.

Tate worked methodically over the dog's chest with big, gentle hands, searching for the elusive wound Isaiah hadn't yet found.

"You feeling anything besides blood and fur?" Isaiah asked. Damn, there was so much of it, and all of it slick, warm, and deceitful. He'd never forgive himself if Nugget bled out this close to safety and the boy he adored.

Tate grunted, his eyes focused, his lips set in a thin line. "He's been stabbed under his arm. Here, see?"

"Shit," Tucker hissed when Tate lifted Nugget's front leg and blood spurted onto Tucker's hands. "What kind of asshole stabs a dog, then dumps him like this?"

Neither Isaiah nor Tate answered the rhetorical question.

"How bad is it?" Isaiah asked, even as he looked down the street across from the gate. Was this attack just another distraction to keep him and his people running in circles? That didn't feel right, not as viciously as this dog had been hurt. This attack seemed more—personal.

"Two fingers deep," Tate replied grimly. No wonder Nugget shuddered and groaned. Tate had obviously stuck two thick fingertips into the wound. "Hold him steady," he ordered. Reaching into one of his many jacket pockets, he pulled out what Isaiah now knew every Marine and SEAL carried—his blow out kit. And in that blowout kit? Two packs of *Quik Clot*, a powdered clotting agent used in combat to slow blood loss from bullet wounds and—stuff. *Thank God.*

Tate tore the foil packet open with his teeth, spat, then lifted Nugget's front leg and doused the gushing wound with the powdery clotting agent. "Steady," he told the dog as he wadded a handful of cotton packing and compressed the wound. "This is gonna sting."

Damned if Nugget didn't calm as if he'd understood the husky Alaskan hunched over him was there to help. Why wouldn't he? Isaiah had no doubt Tate was keeping up some kind of a mental link with the dog.

Isaiah bowed his chin to his chest, so damned thankful for warriors who knew how to save other warriors, even the furry kind. There weren't enough men like Tate and Tuck in the world, and every day

Isaiah strived to be more like them and less like his father. They stood for what they believed in, and they believed in noble things worth dying for, like liberty, freedom, and covering your brother's asses. Even your four-legged brother's asses.

"Hey," Tate snapped, jarring Isaiah out of his reverie. "Are you okay?"

Isaiah nodded, concerned what Tate might've seen in his eyes. "I am now. Thanks guys. Thanks for... for everything."

Tate stuck a bloody hand on Isaiah's shoulder, instantly diffusing the ragged emotions swirling in his head. He'd never be tough enough or mean enough to be a Marine, but if he could be half the man Tate was, well... That was good enough for him.

At last he looked his buddy in the eye. Big mistake. Tate didn't use a lot of words and tonight was no different. He grunted once, then gave Isaiah a quick nod that plainly said, *'I've got your six, brother.'*

Isaiah swallowed hard. He'd never had a brother until he'd joined this ragtag team of psychic misfits, who, even now, were learning more about their psychic powers than any scientist in a lab could ever teach them. Tucker and Tate, Ky and his sweet wife, Eden—family didn't get any better than this.

"Let's move him inside," Tucker said quietly. Even he seemed to be touched by the tenderness taking place on this very different battlefield.

Isaiah looked over his shoulder to where one of the three MPD cruisers was still parked. An EMT wagon had just skipped the curb alongside them, its red and blues flashing. Damned if it wasn't Harley Mortimer, one of Alex Stewart's men, now working his part-time job, the graveyard shift for the emergency animal clinic in the District, unfolding his long legs from the driver's seat.

Alex owned one of the best covert surveillance teams on the East Coast, possibly in all the USA. He'd successfully competed for jobs that normally fell under the FBI's charter, but when he'd proved he could do their job better, cheaper, and with considerably less loss of civilian life, he'd indirectly challenged the Bureau to rethink their burdensome procedures. And they had. Finally, the FBI was back in the business of serving America instead of covering its ass with reams of bureaucratic procedure. Harley was one of Alex's best, God bless him.

Tucker tagged Roxy to, "Open the gate. Harley Mortimer's here. We're coming in."

Roxy had to be tense being out of the loop like she was. The gate opened just barely enough for Harley to squeeze through before it closed again. "What have we got here?" he asked as he joined the huddle around the downed animal. The medical kit swinging from his hand belied the concern glistening in his eyes.

Isaiah could barely speak. Turned out he didn't have to. A little boy's voice shattered the muffled silence of the night. "Nugget!"

Damn. Darrin knew. "I've got to go," Isaiah told Harley, his voice as hoarse as shit. "This is Nugget. He's Darrin's dog, and Darrin's just ten, so please..." *Damn, this was hard.* "Please don't let Nugget die."

The sweet dog lifted his head, the whites of his eyes wild as he searched for his boy. Harley settled the animal with one word, "Stay," and to Isaiah he whispered, "This dog is *not* going to die. I won't let him. Go tell that little boy I said so."

Isaiah pushed to his feet, wiping his eyes so he could be the man Darrin needed to see by the time he made it to the front door. Before he knew it, he was inside where Roxy stood with Darrin. The boy had crumpled to a heap, sobbing his eyes out, his shoulders heaving and his heart broken. Yeah. Old Yeller had nothing on reality.

Without saying anything, Isaiah sank to his knees and instantly, Darrin climbed into his lap. "I wanna see my dog," he cried, his whole body sweaty and shaking. "Nugget," he called out again. "I wanna be there right now! He... he needs me!"

'Tell him Nugget's alive,' Tucker whispered on their private link. *'Lie to the kid, damn it. At least until we know if Harley can work miracles like he thinks he can.'*

"He's alive," Isaiah said softly, his chest tight and hurting. Harley was a good soul, a kind soul like no other. Maybe he was a miracle worker, too.

"But..." Roxy murmured from the window where she watched the goings on, and Isaiah looked up into her teary face. "We saw that guy dump him over the fence and what if—?"

Isaiah shook his head at her. Darrin needed to believe, so Isaiah told him the same lie every combat medic in the field told the wounded men and women he'd served. "He's going to be okay, Darrin. Nugget will be okay."

Chapter Sixteen

Tucker led the way, bringing the stretcher with Nugget inside the home. They were worried about more shooters, and this vet Isaiah called Harley couldn't operate in the dark. Agent Higgins must've gone back up to the roof since he didn't come in, and that was encouraging. As quickly as he'd bolted off the roof to get to Nugget's side, Roxy had a feeling if he thought he could leave the dog in Harley's care, then everything would be okay. She clung to that feeling because, well. She wasn't so sure.

Roxy watched the sad procession pass by her with a beautiful golden dog that looked to be sound asleep, his long pink tongue lolled out of his mouth, and his chest heaving as he panted for his life. She'd watched Isaiah kneel, and she'd seen how eagerly he'd gathered Darrin into his arms. She saw his beautiful blue eyes fill with tears and she saw his hands enfold a tender little soul against his great big heart.

Then she was on the floor with him, holding them both and fighting her tears. Unexpectedly, Tucker Chase knelt with them. Not her favorite guy, but so be it.

"Knock it off," he murmured gruffly. "For God's sake, the dog's not bleeding anymore, and Harley's ready to do some quick surgery. Nugget'll be back to normal before you know it."

But Roxy recognized a fatherly lie when she heard one.

Darrin lifted his tear stained face from where he clenched the front of Isaiah's shirt. "Can I see him, Mister? Can I, huh, please?"

Tucker stalled. His gaze softened as he studied Darrin, and damned if the gentleness in his eyes didn't boost him up a notch in Roxy's esteem. "Would you mind if we clean him up first? He's a little bloody." *What an understatement.*

"But I wanna see him, in case..." A hiccup wrenched out of Darrin. "In case... you know... in case he—"

Tucker skimmed his big manly finger under Darrin's quivering chin. "Hey, tough guy. Nugget's not going to die, you understand? Now let me go see if Doc Mortimer says you can see Nugget. Wait here. I'll be right back."

"'Kay," Darrin murmured, his throat muscles working as he swallowed his tears. "I can wait, but

Mister…" He lunged out of Isaiah's lap and into Tucker's arms, and hung on as only a desperate little boy could, his head against Tucker's massive chest. "Would you please tell him I love him more than anything in the whole, entire world? Would you tell him I'm waiting for him, and I promise I'll play ball with him every single day for the rest of my life and I'll brush him and walk him and I'll let him sleep in my bed too?"

"You bet," Tucker replied, his voice gone gruff and low. When his palm cupped the back of Darrin's head and tears shimmered in Tucker's dark eyes… *Ah, shit.* Roxy couldn't take anymore. The shadow darkening this tough guy's face was so damned sorrowful, she turned away to keep from bawling. There was more to this alpha male than she'd given him credit for, and like it or not, Tucker seemed to know precisely what Darrin needed to hear. But when he enfolded Darrin under his chin with his nose in the kid's hair like he did? She lost it.

Lifting to her feet, Roxy stepped away and put her back to the wall, automatically in self-defense mode. Damn these guys! They were breaking her heart, and that just didn't happen. It couldn't. They were supposed to be tougher than her, not a bunch of *Stay-Puft* Marshmallows in disguise. Scrubbing her hand over her face, she swallowed her tears and her pride.

It was a good thing Candy and her daughter weren't there, probably because Kitty wasn't feeling well enough to be on her feet. They might not even know this drama was unfolding. But still...

Roxy looked through the kitchen and down the hall. Candace sure had a knack for not being around when her kids needed her.

By the time she'd gotten control, Tucker had eased Darrin back onto Isaiah's lap. "You stay here with Officer Thurston and Agent Zaroyin. Be right back, kid." Pushing of the floor, he made a hasty retreat, but he came back just as quickly. Holding out his hand, he fluttered his fingers for Darrin to join him. "Come on, kid. Get your butt in here."

Darrin scrambled to follow, as did Roxy and Isaiah, but she hung back at the door. It was enough to watch whatever unfolded next from a safe distance. Be it sorrow or joy, she didn't need to be in the middle of it.

Tiptoeing to where Harley stood over the prone animal now laid on the formal dining room table, Darrin peered up at the man with the lopsided grin. Harley stood a good six feet, three or four inches tall. Sandy-haired and one of those gregarious types, he stuck his hand out, and thankfully, it wasn't encased in a bloody glove. "Hey, little buddy. Are you the proud owner of this knucklehead?"

"Ah-huh," Darrin said, tiptoeing another step closer, his neck stretched to see past the equipment on the table to his dog. "His name's Nugget and he's my bestest friend in the whole world."

"Well, isn't that a coincidence? He's one of my best friends, too! Come on up." Harley lifted Darrin into his arms, high enough he looked down at the unconscious dog. Harley pointed at Nugget's mouth. "See that tube I taped between his teeth? That one right there?"

Darrin nodded, wide-eyed, taking it all in. Nugget panted like a beast, his ribcage already cleaned and shaved. Where Harley had gotten the medical equipment now positioned around the dog, Roxy didn't know. She was just grateful that each of these men treated Darrin like he was important instead of just a kid in their way.

"Well, that's in there because I had to intubate good old Nugget so he wouldn't swallow his tongue or anything else while I'm stitching him up," Harley explained, his voice kind and gentle. "You know, like spit or his teeth. You know what intubate means?"

Darrin shook his head.

"It means I was real careful, when I placed something called an endotracheal tube, an ET, down Nugget's throat so he can breathe while I operate. Medical doctors do that with people sometimes, too."

"They do? Well, then...'kay."

Harley definitely had a way with kids. "Want to help me?"

Darrin's eyes grew wider. "Can I?"

"Why sure! You're the man he listens to, aren't you? Who else do you think he wants at his side while I fix him up good as new?"

The little boy in Harley's big arms wiggled, this time with a measure of excitement instead of grief. "Okay, but you have to tell me what to do cuz I never done this before." He said that so seriously that Roxy's heart clenched again.

"I can do that." Harley grinned a beautiful lopsided grin, and it was easy to see that he truly loved saving dogs and the little boys who loved them. "Well, all righty then. Let's get to work and save this best buddy of ours, shall we?"

It took patience and around ninety minutes, but finally, Harley finished, and by the looks of it, he had a new partner in the veterinary business. Darrin all but glowed. When the last stitch was nipped close to Nugget's shaved ribcage, Harley offered Darrin a knuckle bump that brought more tears to Roxy's eyes. "I think we're done here, Pardner. Nugget needs to sleep for a while, but in a day or two, he'll be ready to play ball. Now how 'bout we hop on over to the local saloon and swallow a couple pints of root beer while we wait for this fellow to wake up?" Harley leveled a stern eye at Tucker Chase. "You do have root beer here, don'tcha, Sheriff? Maybe a bag of barbecue chips to go with it? A fellow gets mighty hungry when he's saving lives and busting broncs."

Oh, God. Roxy wiped a finger under her leakiest eye. This gentle giant cracked her up.

With a chuckle, Tucker rolled off the chair he'd taken residence on while watching the surgery. "If we don't, I'll go get some. How's our patient?"

"He's gonna be just fine," Darrin announced with a genuine smile from the chair beside Harley. He'd stood and watched every incision and every stitch, and not once had he cried or winced while Harley did what he had to do. He'd dabbed Harley's forehead with a tissue when Harley asked him to. He'd even stuck a bottle of water with a straw in it—courtesy of fast-thinking Tucker Chase—in Harley's face when he'd said he was thirsty.

After Tucker left to *rustle up* some root beer, Isaiah sidled next to Roxy. Tugging her backside away from the wall, he stepped in behind her, circled his arms around her waist and dipped his chin to her shoulder. "Thank you," he whispered in her ear, "for being here. For trusting me."

Of all things, she got goosebumps just from the sound of his voice. "I do trust you," she admitted quietly. "More than you know." *And way more than I ever expected.*

He nipped at her ear just before he whispered, "Harley found a note rolled inside Nugget's collar when he prepped him for surgery."

Roxy leaned back to look up into Isaiah's eyes. "What now?"

"A warning." He stuck his hand in his back pocket and pulled an evidence bag up for Roxy to see. The hand scrawled paper was bloody, but the caps were clear.

I CAN GET TO YOU AND YOUR KIDS, DOLL FACE. ANYWHERE. ANYTIME.

Chapter Seventeen

"Was that the same collar you took off of him earlier?" Tucker asked.

Now that Nugget rested comfortable and warm in the padded crate Harley'd brought with him, Harley had left. He'd left instructions, a plastic vial of pain meds, and his bill, which Tucker had promptly folded and stashed in his rear pocket. Nugget's crate was now situated just inside the formal dining room where they could all keep an eye on him.

Darrin was back in his room sleeping with his mother and sister. Isaiah had tucked him in—one last time—for the night that wouldn't seem to end.

Isaiah was beyond exhausted, not having slept since the night before. Roxy looked as bleary-eyed as he felt. They were both in need of some serious downtime. Unfortunately, that didn't seem to be in their near future when Tucker called an earlier-than-shit, three in the morning meeting. The only man not present, Tate Higgins, remained topside, poised to shoot the next person who came within walking distance of the front gate.

Whoever'd built this house had installed electric wrought iron fencing around the entire yard, all except for the front stretch. What were they thinking? Even now, Tucker had a MICAP, a *Mission Impossible Capability Awaiting Parts* purchase order into the higher ups at FBI Headquarters to solve that critical issue first thing in the morning. If approved for funding, workmen were scheduled to arrive at eight in the morning, and wouldn't that just make guarding the Brattons a whole lot easier? Hell, no.

Isaiah didn't relish the reality of more people traipsing through what had become an impossible assignment. Easy day, nothing. Whoever'd come up with that phrase was a moron. Must've been a Navy SEAL. Probably Tucker.

"No, Boss. It's not the same collar at all." He shook his head as he produced Nugget's other collar from his pants pocket. "This is the one someone wired to track Nugget's whereabouts. Somebody out there's using this dog, and I think I know where he's been all this time. Mr. G's, the hamburger joint on the east side of Kingman Park. Nugget's been known to wander off there. Now I know why." *Just wish I knew who that person was.*

He'd intended a more thorough examination of the altered original collar, but Kitty's asthma attack had precluded his good intentions. Honestly, so much had happened in the last twenty-four hours, he'd completely forgotten the collar. Was Randall using Nugget or was that guy in the chapel responsible? Or—perish the thought—was Mrs. Bratton involved? And with which man? Both of them?

Roxy nodded, and for an instant, Isaiah wasn't sure she hadn't honed in on his inner questions. "That explains why Nugget didn't bark when he heard the shots that killed your agents earlier. He knew who was out there."

"It also explains why he charged the plate glass," Tucker agreed. "Randall probably signaled him."

"If it was Randall," Isaiah interjected. "We don't know anything for certain, yet."

"Son-of-a-bitch." Tucker's fist hit the tabletop. "Gibson's wife delivered a nine-pound baby boy last Monday. Their sixth son. We know that much. Now what?"

Now those boys grow up without their dad, Isaiah thought, sick at heart all over again. The rhetorical question hung like a dark cloud over the three of them. Gibson and Torrance were the agents who'd been murdered in their car just hours earlier. All the eulogies in the world could never adequately describe the loss of a father to his sons. Isaiah hated the human cost of fighting crime.

Pushing past his own memories, he tossed the evidence bag with the collar and note to Tuck. "Forensics needs to work their magic on this, and they need to do it tonight. Harley found it wired to Nugget's new collar. We need hard evidence to nail whoever's behind this before he strikes again."

"To the wall," Roxy murmured. "The sooner, the better." She'd gotten quieter as the day—and night—had dragged on.

"You kids look like shit," Tucker muttered, his dark eyes unusually sharp and alert. The man was a damned fighting machine. Close encounters like tonight's seemed to energize him. "Go to bed. Tate and I will stand guard until noon, then you're up" He stuck one palm in Isaiah's face before he could protest. "I said beat it, Zaroyin. Take off. Now."

Weary of the world of men and sick of Garrett Randall in particular, Isaiah pushed away from the table. "G'night then. Night, Roxy."

She didn't answer and she didn't move. He was glad for the stall tactic, if that was what it was. With Tucker inside the mansion for the rest of the night, they'd be wise to sleep in separate beds, not like they'd done much sleeping when they'd been together so far, but it could happen.

Isaiah retrieved his duffel from the front entry. After closing his bedroom door, the room one door down from Roxy's, he dropped his butt to the end of his bed, more tired then he'd ever been. Fumbling through the bag at his feet, he pulled out a pair of navy blue boxers and his shaving kit. A shower before bed helped him sleep better, and man, he needed that tonight, er, this morning.

Lightheaded and fighting a migraine in the front left quadrant of his brain, Isaiah stumbled into the mega-sized bathroom, his eyes half-closed. Pastel blue marble tiles with veins of what looked to be real gold lined the floor and extended halfway up the wall to delicate one-quarter coving. Crystal cups in golden sconces over the sink provided blinding visibility that Isaiah promptly turned off. His retinas couldn't take it. Not tomor-r-r—*this morning*.

Cranking the shower faucet to hot, he stripped out of his clothes and folded them neatly on the counter. Folded clothing fit his duffel better. A man needed organization and order in his life, and Isaiah was all about that kind of self-control. Okay, so he hadn't done so well in the self-control department as far as Roxy was concerned today, but tomorrow, that would change. It had to. Mostly because tomorrow was already here, and he wasn't kidding anyone.

If it hadn't been for him being distracted, Nugget wouldn't have gotten hurt. If he hadn't had his mind on Roxy, the day would've gone smoother. The kids would've been safer. It could've ended up being one of those *easy days*. He would've tuned into Randall's Neanderthal brainwaves sooner, and known the man's plans before anything happened. No doubt he would've unlocked Mrs. Bratton's mental block too, maybe identified the mystery man in the chapel.

Yeah. Things had to change and they had to change now. Before anyone else got hurt.

Pressing his forearm to the tiled wall beneath the showerhead, Isaiah leaned his forehead to his arm. Hot water streamed down his back, and he let his mind wander. Damned if the thing didn't wander straight through the wall to his favorite distraction. Roxy.

Licking at the rivulets running over his lips, he growled at himself. This was the first time in his life that he couldn't explain why he couldn't control himself. Just one look, one touch—hell, all Roxy had to do was breathe, and his brain disconnected from the mission. From sunup to sundown, he wanted her in his arms and in his bed, preferably naked and sweaty beneath him. Groaning with pleasure. Screaming his name. Bucking against him as he feasted on her lush body. Raking her nails down his back when she came and came.... and came.

But they'd been playing with fire, and the flames had finally raged out of control, bringing consequences Isaiah would blame himself for the rest of his life. A boy had been hurt today and his dog had nearly died. Two agents were dead, and the weight of all that loss sat like a stone in Isaiah's gut.

As the lead agent in charge of this mess, everything that went wrong was his fault. He hadn't been himself since Roxy burst into the bank in all her tough-chick glory, wresting control from him at the bank with just one lift of that cocky chin. One toss of her ponytail. One take-no-quarter spark in the sexy, brown eyes that told him to back off, she was in control. That she owned him.

Damned if she wasn't right. From that moment on, his psychic depths had gone shallow. He couldn't get through to Bratton and he had no game—other than to get into Roxy's panties, which he had. Like Samson in the Bible, Isaiah now knew his greatest weakness. It seemed he couldn't have both, his psychic power and the woman of his heart at the same time. There was just one thing to do. He had to tell Roxy this thing between them was over. Done. It had to be. For everyone's sake. Tomorrow.

A little flirtation was one thing, but this had gone way past flirting. Volcanic was more like it, catastrophically, exquisitely explosive in a Krakatoa, blow an island off the face of the map, kind of way. Just like that heard around the world explosion, she'd blown his sedate, well-organized mind clean off the planet. And he'd been lost in space ever since.

It had to stop. Isaiah stood there staring at the gold-veined tile, wondering how to tell the woman he cared for more than himself, that he couldn't risk the lives of everyone involved just to satisfy his craving for her. They had to stop meeting. He wouldn't choose her over them. His job came first. She'd understand, wouldn't she? She was a professional. She had to know they were both *screwing the pooch*, as Tucker would say.

Isaiah knew the precise second she entered the bathroom. The glass shower door opened behind him, and she was there. "Roxy," he murmured, needing her so damned bad even as he wanted her to leave him alone.

Two slender arms slid around his waist. Her long hair draped over his backside as she laid her cheek against the waterfall sluicing over his shoulder blades. "I'm so sorry," she whispered. "What happened today is my fault."

"No," he hissed as he turned around to face her. He'd never seen such a glorious sight. She was naked. Her black hair now hung in wet ringlets over her shoulders, cupping her nipples, both lovely shades of pink perfection in the centers of two lush, kissable breasts. "None of this is your fault," he said as his gaze wandered to the sight of her tempting feminine parts below, and his randy cock sprang to attention.

"Yes, yes it is." She looked up at him, blinking into the shower spray splattering off his shoulders, missing the stand-up show happening below his waistline. "If I hadn't been preoccupied... If I'd kept closer watch on Darrin and his dog..." She stomped one bare foot. "Ah, forget the excuses. If I'd been better at my job, none of this would've happened, and you know it, too. I can see it in your eyes. We're not good together."

Isaiah squared his shoulders to keep the spray from hitting her sad face. "No, baby, no. If anyone's to blame, it's me. I'm the Psychic Dude, remember? I should've known what Randall was up to. I should've seen everything." *I just can't seem to see anything, when I'm near you.*

He licked his lips, his mind suddenly more intent on savoring the steady streams running in wild abandon over her satiny skin than in solving the mystery of why his psychic sight wasn't up to its usual clarity. The water dripped off her lips and ran down her chin to her neck to the plump cushion of her waiting breasts. His cock had proudly noticed the way her nipples hardened into tight little diamonds. His hand lifted to cup her breast, but first...

He should step away. And he would have, but Roxy beat him to it. Her chin came up. Her wet, succulent lips parted, and she said, "Don't touch me, Isaiah. I can't control myself when you do, and that's why I'm leaving first thing in the morning after I request to be removed from this case. You need a detective on your side, not someone like me."

There went the last of Isaiah's good intentions. "No," he ground out. "You can't do that." Even though he knew she should. "We can make this work. I don't need some big-mouthed detective like Harmon in my face. I need you. We're good together, Roxy. Damned good, and you know it."

Biting her bottom lip, she shook her head. "Y-yes, I can leave, and I will, Isaiah. My mind's made up. I've been thinking about it since Nugget got loose. It's the right thing to do. Mrs. Bratton and her kids need the best protection they can get, and I'm not it." With a quick hand, she swiped her hair out of her eyes, and he knew how hard saying that was for her because Roxy Thurston, the toughest beat cop on the District's streets, was crying. "It'll be for the best," she said, her voice bereft of the customary snark he'd grown to love. "You'll see."

Aw, hell. Isaiah couldn't take the sight of her standing alone, her hair gleaming wet and teardrops beaded on her lashes. She'd always been his dream come true, and he couldn't give her up. Not now and not tomorrow. Tugging her gently into his arms, he held on tightly to the only woman he'd loved—*yes, loved*—in a long time. He was done denying it.

Genuine warmth infused his entire body with her inside his arms, a raging fire that knew no bounds and that filled him. Only this fire was different. It was more about her and less about him. It was pure. Feral, maybe, but utterly—pure. He wasn't falling, yet he was dizzy, and he couldn't catch a breath. He wasn't a caveman, yet his muscles flexed with a fierce primal need to protect her. To shelter her. His blood burned, not with testosterone to ravage her lush, sweet body, but to claim her with devotion and—his soul.

So this is love, he thought, even as, "Don't go," blurted out of his heart. Thinking fast so as not to say too much, too soon, he added, "Why should you leave now when we've got Randall right where we want him?"

"We, we do?" she asked, rubbing her cheek over his left pec like a cat marking her territory—or a woman savoring her last moment with her man before she left him forever.

The pesky guy below sagged to half-mast at that very real possibility.

"Of course, we do," Isaiah went on, making things up as fast as he could. "Randall thinks he's got the upper hand. He thinks we're scared of him, well, are we? Are you?" Isaiah didn't mean to call her out like that, but desperate times called for desperate tactics, and Isaiah was as desperate as he'd ever been.

As expected, her brows clashed and her chin lifted. Lifting her head, she stuck a fingernail in his pec, her tough chick back in the fight. "I'm not scared of anybody. Not even you, Buster."

Buster? Me? Great! Isaiah's need for Roxy in his life took control of his brain. "Then tomorrow, we prove Randall wrong. If he wants the money from that armored car robbery so bad he'll kill for it, let's give him what he wants. The Bureau's got a couple million on hand for cases like this. I say we leak the word—somehow that—"

"That we found it? Good plan." Hope sparked back to life in Roxy's eyes. "Maybe Tucker could hold a press conference to get the word out?"

Isaiah nodded, his hands smoothing over her shoulder blades and down her sleek back to her sweet, plump bottom. He couldn't get enough of this woman, not if he lived to be an old—but horny—old man. "That's my girl. Tucker's got just the big mouth for the job."

Roxy quirked a tiny smile. "I didn't like him at first, but he kind of grows on you, doesn't he?"

"Like a fungus," Isaiah admitted with a grin. "Tucker's fighting his own demons, but he's one of the best men I know."

Roxy's slender fingers fluttered over Isaiah's chest, and there went his heart. *Ker-thump. Ker-thump. Ker-splat.* Right at her feet.

"Stay," he begged, his heart so damned full of love for her that it might burst before he was brave enough to tell her. "Darrin and Kitty need you here. Believe it or not, Mrs. Bratton needs you, and..." He swallowed hard, struggling with the truth storming in his heart. "I need you, Roxy."

Chapter Eighteen

Bratton didn't need her. The kids might, but their mother? That was a laugh. Roxy wasn't falling for that line. But Isaiah shouldn't have said he needed her, and he shouldn't have looked into her soul like he did. The second she felt him pouring his heart into her, Roxy's resolve to remove herself from this case went up in smoke. Tipping to her toes, she planted a kiss on his lips that should've curled his toes. It surely curled hers.

He took over then, his powerful arm sweeping her off her feet as he ducked out of the shower and took her to his bed. Every last reason she had for leaving melted in the tender way he anointed her mouth, chin, cheeks, and eyelids. It seemed he couldn't get enough of her. How well she knew the feeling.

She'd seen the fine lines of scars running up his arms and over his chest. Someone had done despicable things to this man's body, but the sight of them spiked an internal trigger she hadn't realized she possessed. She longed to soothe Isaiah in ways no one else could. She'd give anything to crawl inside of him and heal him from the inside out. She wanted to be the one he came home to at the end of a hard day, the only one he laid down with at night. Every night.

Desperate for the searing connection they'd shared before, her naked body arched into his of its own accord, stamping the contours of his hips on her inner thighs, and that luscious six-pack of his on her belly. More, more, more...

His fingers touched everywhere, smoothing and probing, pinching and urging the ragged edges of her heart into the fray. Combustible. Roxy was frantic for his body and on the verge of flying, if she didn't burst into flames first.

At last his skillful fingers trailed down her belly, while his tongue made soft sweet love to her mouth. Hunger spurred her on as he probed her most feminine secrets. So many sensations! Everywhere! She couldn't keep up.

"You're wet," he murmured into her mouth. "So freakin' tight."

"For you," she answered, her voice tight and so, so needy. "Stop playing. Now, Isaiah. I want you inside of me now."

The man lived to serve. Entering her body with one ardent thrust, his teeth clamped down on her shoulder at the same time. Her pleasure spiked. Like a damned rocket.

Groaning, he amped up the action below while she matched him thrust for thrust, crazy with needing him. Not one to wait until he got it right, she showed him what she needed and where she needed it, stroking him until at last... at last...

"Coming," she cried as the pleasure built to a screaming crescendo, climbing up her back and thighs and her core and... "God, oh God. Now. Now. Now!"

Her body bowed in sweet surrender to the man filling her to the hilt with heat and passion and—love. Yes. She knew it now. This was love, purely and simply the most exquisite branding of one soul to another. Committed to the intimate privacy between a man and a woman who cared more for the other than they did for themselves.

"More," she mewled, her snarky MPD personality thoroughly subdued and smitten with this darling, charming alpha male in the palms of her hands. Submission. That was what this was, only this kind of submission made her smile. It was good and wonderful, and she wanted to go again.

He hadn't climaxed yet, so she dragged her fingernails down his back to his buttocks. If he thought he was getting away with being that unselfish, he had another *think*—yes, *think*—coming.

Thinking too hard was always his problem. The man was too cerebral. He needed to let go and live for a change.

Digging her fingernails into the muscles of his taut backside, she quickly got what she wanted. With one last pounding beat, he stretched her to the point of the most delicious pain. When he shuddered, growled and roared her name, she knew he was the only man in the world for her. And oh, yes, her man was happy, and she'd given him that release from the demons that haunted him.

Roxy purred like a cat, still shuddering with waves of her own aftershocks. The perfection of this moment knew no bounds. Could anything be sweeter than lying in his arms and loving this man? Her man?

Drained of all energy, Isaiah sagged into her arms, his head heavy in the crook of her sweaty neck. She tugged her hair out of his way so he could breathe, and she let her fingers skim up the back of his neck and into his damp hair. Threading her fingers through the short lengths of it, she cupped him to her. Tears came to her eyes, but they were tears of joy. No one had ever given her a gift like this before.

"It's been a helluva day," she whispered, like he didn't know that?

His head bobbed and he murmured, "It has," into her neck, but he didn't move.

Satisfied for the moment, Roxy held onto her man. This was what she wanted more than anything, a good man who looked out for her and who put her needs before his. A man who loved children and dogs and his country. A man she could respect and love—yes, love—for the rest of her life. God hadn't made many like Isaiah, and she wanted him with every last passionate beat of her heart.

Softly, she hummed a lullaby that her mom had once hummed to her. It took seconds before Isaiah's breathing grew even and steady. A smile curved her lips. He'd fallen asleep in her arms, pinning her to his bed. Right where she wanted to be.

"Sit!" Tucker's voice rang out sharp and stern.

"What now?" *Oh, oh, this can't be good*, Isaiah thought to himself as he straightened his tie and took a seat at the formal dining table in what had become FBI Central now that Tucker was on the job.

Isaiah picked at an invisible piece of lint on his jacket cuff just to enforce the calm he meant to project. After waking up with Roxy's delectable warm ass pressed against his very horny body, they'd made love like a couple rabbits, showered together, and even brushed their teeth with the same toothbrush—his.

He had nothing to be ashamed of and there was nothing to tell. He loved Roxy and he meant to tell her. Soon. So there. *Let it rain.*

Roxy took a seat one chair away from him. She folded her hands like a prim old-fashioned school marm. "What's up?" she asked, her brown eyes clear and her chin stuck out. For a female officer, she had the street-wise, nail-eating machismo of a beat cop, down pat. She also made that uniform look good. Especially the pockets. *Damned good.*

Isaiah dropped his gaze before it rolled over her chest, feigning disinterest when he really wanted to tear that meticulously pressed garment out of his way and drag her back to his room for a little game with the cuffs she'd snapped on her belt this morning.

"Explain." Tucker slapped two eight-by-eleven glossies across the table. Like trained little tattletales, they slid under Isaiah's nose. He leaned nonchalantly forward to peruse the evidence, which he already knew was against Roxy and him.

Shit. One showed him in all of his black-and-white glory entering Roxy's bedroom with the lady in question in his arms. Time stamped five fifty-three pm. Yesterday. Yep. That was about right.

The other showed Roxy at his bedroom door, looking like a thief—or a lover—as she entered without knocking. Time stamped in the wee hours of this morning, right before she'd joined him in his shower. Again, spot on. Whoever back at FBI Headquarters had supplied Tucker with these photos was just doing their job, and damn it, Isaiah knew there were cameras throughout the mansion, but did he care? Not anymore.

His feelings for Officer Thurston weren't negotiable. If Tucker threatened to fire him, so be it. But he doubted Tucker would go that far. As bullheaded as his boss could be, Isaiah sensed mischief stashed up Tucker's rolled-up sleeves along with his hairy arms, not discipline. Certainly not politics. He just wasn't that guy.

"Well?" Tucker asked, one brow spiked in that bossy way he projected when he chose intimidation.

Isaiah shrugged without batting an eyelash. "Well, what? Looks like someone caught us on our way to a strategy meeting."

"Strategy meeting, my ass." Tucker leaned his big chest over his clenched fists on the table and grunted. "You always carry your co-workers to strategy meetings, Zaroyin?"

Roxy led with a grunt of her own. "We were just goofing off. So what?"

"On duty?"

She lifted her shoulders. "Shit happens."

"What's that on your neck?"

Isaiah let his gaze roll across the table to where Roxy sat. Damn. He'd marked her with a raspberry in more places than just her neck, but just the one showed. A wave of pure lust smacked him upside his hard head. He wouldn't have done that if she hadn't tasted so unbelievably sweet, but once he started, well, he could no more stop branding her than he could cease breathing. She'd become part of his soul. And now she was his.

The woman handled the nosy question with ease. Instead of nervously fingering her collar, which Tucker had obviously expected her to do judging by the disappointment that flitted across his face when she didn't, the MPD Officer intertwined her fingers and leaned into Tucker's direct line of attack. "I cut myself shaving. So sue me."

Tucker kicked one booted foot under the table, amusement glimmering in his eyes. "You're a woman," he bit out. "Please tell me you don't really shave."

"What if I do?" Her chin came up, and Isaiah could've laughed out loud when Tuck's icy veneer crumbled.

A genuine smile curved the former SEALs lips that time. The man had laugh lines deeply etched at the corners of his eyes, and at the moment, they glowed like a sunrise off the Atlantic on the first day of summer. It was no wonder women swooned when he walked by, not that he noticed. As good looking as he was, Isaiah also knew Tucker was not the brightest bulb on the Christmas tree when it came to understanding the intricate workings of the female mind.

Yet he seemed to be enjoying this game of cat-and-mouse with Roxy. Reaching across the table, he brushed the glossies back into his possession. With his sharp eyes trained on his subordinates like the famous sniper he was, Tuck tore the photographic evidence against them into halves. Then fourths.

Finally eighths before he tossed them aside and growled, "Get the hell out of here."

Shoving back from the table, Isaiah lifted to his feet, but before he could make a break for it, Tucker rapped his knuckles to the table. "You do know CCTV is everywhere but in the bathrooms and bedrooms, don't you?" Closed Circuit Television.

"It's too damned bad we aren't using them to locate Randall instead of wasting time on..." Isaiah sniffed. "...stuff like this." He would've held Roxy's chair for her, but she was already halfway out the door.

"See you later, Boss," she shot over her shoulder.

Tucker's gaze followed her even as he motioned Isaiah to sit back down. "We need to talk."

Chapter Nineteen

"What are you doing down here?" Roxy asked the magnificent male specimen seated at the table in the kitchen wolfing down a humongous bowl of oatmeal sprinkled with walnuts, brown sugar, and drowning in what looked to be heavy cream and enough cholesterol to gag a moose. "Who's on the roof?"

Tall, dark, and built like a bear, he glared at her from beneath dark, bushy brows, whether in disgust or amusement, she couldn't quite tell. This FBI agent dwarfed the elegant wooden table, and he held that spoon in his fist more like a weapon than an eating utensil. Instead of a reply, she got a grunt, his piercing dark brown eyes devoid of humor as his spoon hit the bowl under his chin once more and ladled a hefty portion into his mouth.

When he failed to reply, she soldiered on. "You must be Special Agent Tate Higgins."

"And you're Officer Thurston," he mumbled around the mush in his mouth. "Glad we got introductions out of the way." And just like that, he'd dismissed her.

We'll see about that.

Not one to accept a brush-off, Roxy flipped the chair across from him around, straddled it, and folded her arms across the wooden back. "That was a decent thing you did last night, doctoring Darrin's dog until the vet got here. Where'd you learn that?"

One burly shoulder lifted. He grunted and kept on eating.

She tried again. "So which FBI deadeye's up on the roof if you're down here stuffing your face?"

It'd sure be nice if he made eye contact when he was spoken to. Might make her heart go pitter pat—on a good day. But this was not that day. Agent Higgins ladled another spoonful into his mouth and swallowed, ignoring her.

Intent on rattling his stalwart composure or to die trying, she lifted her butt up from the seat, leaned forward and stuck her hand in his face. "Sure nice to finally meet you, Special Agent Higgins. Any guy who'll put his life on the line to save a dog he doesn't know, is a friend of mine."

Scowling like a bastard, this formidable Special Agent wiped the back of his hand across his mouth and set his spoon to the table beside the bowl. He picked up the napkin she hadn't noticed he'd wrinkled in his other hand, and he wiped his mouth before he folded it into a neat rectangle and set it across his empty bowl. A quart carton of milk stood at the upper right of his bowl, and somehow, Roxy knew he'd drained it dry straight out of the carton.

"I like dogs," he said, his upper lip twitching with definite male attitude, and his unspoken words—*more than I like people*—clear.

Roxy gave one curt nod of acknowledgment. Of course he liked dogs. He was one of those sheep dogs standing guard over his flock. One of the few. The brave. The best.

As if he agreed with her assessment, very deliberately he reached across the table and shook her hand, his massive grip swallowing her fingers. *Day-am!* With one touch, he'd turned her fingers into pretzels. This was a man to watch out for. The more he gripped, the harder she squeezed back, totally ignoring the pain in her fingers and glimmering teardrop building at the corner of her eye.

He cocked his head. She did him one better and stuck her chin out in defiance. *I may be a woman, but no man bests me with just a handshake.* If he wanted to play good cop, bad cop, she meant to be the baddest cop he'd ever met.

And just like that, it was over. He let go, and she didn't whine or flex her knuckles like a silly woman when he did, either. "You like dogs more than people." She made it a statement, sure to keep her throbbing fingers in sight so he'd know that she'd won, not him.

He gave her his chin, his lips pursed tight. Yep, she was right about Tate Higgins. He'd rather be anywhere else than sitting here talking with a woman—or anyone else for that matter. She got his drift. Most days she didn't like people, either. Like clowns in a circus, they chased after fads, rainbows, unicorns, and their own asses.

"You want a beer to wash that oatmeal down?" she asked, egging him on. Funny. Here sat one of the hardest FBI agents to crack, and he'd breakfasted on oats instead of raw meat, which Roxy could so see him doing.

With another grunt, Special Agent Higgins pressed both palms flat to the table beside the empty bowl and lifted up from his chair. Roxy found herself craning her neck just to maintain eye contact. She jumped to her feet. A massive wall of coiled muscle strained the shirt at his chest, his biceps, and his shoulders. Tate Higgins was built like the *Hulk*, and a tiny part of her wanted him to sit back down so her fight-or-flight reflex would back off and calm the hell down.

"Morning, ma'am," he said, his voice rumbly and rough like a grumpy bear fresh out of hibernation.

"Name's Roxy," she told him, not blinking.

Tapping two straight fingers to his forehead, he shot her a half salute, and because she was who she was, Roxy turned her back on Higgins and walked away first. The encounter put a definite spring in her step. *Damn, that was fun.*

"Hey, Tate," Isaiah said as he pulled up a seat at the kitchen table. It turned out Tucker's concern echoed Isaiah's. This safe house's cover was blown. He wanted the Bratton's moved as early as possible, but he also wanted Tate in on Isaiah's scheme of luring Randall. "What's up?"

Tate stood with his hands on his hips, looking down the hall toward the Brattons' suite where Roxy had gone. "I like her."

"Who? Roxy?" Tucker asked. He hadn't taken a seat, but watched from the opposite doorway where he could see straight down the hall to the Brattons' suite. His gaze followed Tate's. "She's a spitfire, that's for damned sure."

"She's... different," Tate said thoughtfully.

Isaiah looked up at that odd remark from the man who rarely shared his opinions on women, not even his wife. Roxy ought to be proud. The big guy didn't have much of a feminine side to get in touch with, and he didn't like most people. To openly admit he liked her was an honor.

From the wild state of Alaska, he'd lost his parents early in life. After a couple tours of duty, he'd come home uptight and reclusive, preferring the wild outdoors to the hectic civilian life of the city. Then along came Winslow Parrish, the little woman who'd turned him on his ear and won his heart. He hadn't been the same man since. A good woman will do that.

Isaiah rapped a loose spoon on the table so both these testosterone-amped Neanderthals would stop staring down the hall, damn it. There'd be no ogling his woman, well, unless he was doing it. "Question. Who's on patrol outside?"

Tucker blinked, shook his head, and Isaiah wanted to smack him for whatever he'd been thinking. No man got that dazed look in his eye unless it had to do with a woman, and Tucker'd better not be thinking of her like that, damn his big, square head.

The random thought made Isaiah smile. He hadn't had a possessive bone in his body until she'd come along, now he sported one in his pants all day long. Yet he'd only known her, truly known her, for twenty-four hours. What had happened to his highly evolved brain? Seemed his little brain was in charge.

Rubbing a hand over his face, he hoped he'd masked his own delicious and terribly wicked thoughts of that woman, but damn. He was a goner. "Brattons still in their suite?" he asked to get his mind out of the gutter.

"Last I checked they were asleep," Tate said, sitting down again. He pushed his cereal bowl out of his way and crossed his beefy arms, his elbows on the table and his fingers interlocked.

Just because he could, Isaiah sent a gentle probe Roxy's way. Her mind was on what they'd done last night. In the shower and in his bed. She positively glowed, and didn't that send a shot of pure lust to his groin? The lady was killing him and she didn't even know it.

"MPD sent a couple cruisers over early this morning," Tucker replied, finally dropping his butt into the chair next to Tate. He shoved back from the table and dropped both elbows to his knees. Staring up at Isaiah through his brows, he looked like the deadly sniper he was. "I figured the more the merrier. Plus, we need the assist when we move the Brattons, so I've got extra patrols in the area. Don't worry. If Randall makes another move, we'll get the son-of-a-bitch."

That was what every good officer of the law said. "Tucker and I have been talking," Isaiah informed Tate. "What if we mix things up a bit instead of sitting here waiting for him?"

Tate grunted. "Go on."

"He's got to be close, right? I can sense him, can't you?"

Tate slung one arm over the back of his chair. His upper lip twitched with the insolence he did so well. "Yeah, but I'd just as soon let him come to me now that I know he's been using a good dog like Nugget to do his dirty work. Shitty trick, hurting a dog. Men like Bratton need a come to Jesus meeting, and I want to arrange it."

"I know what you mean," Isaiah said as he turned to his boss. "How much cash can you get your hands on? As in millions. I'm not talking pocket change. I want Bratton to think we've located the armored car cache in Bratton's old house, and I need him to see us taking it. I want him so hungry for it that he makes a mistake."

Tucker ran a hand over his big chin. "I can request a million without much hassle. Any more will take longer, and it'll be harder to justify, but he doesn't need to know that. Did you know she never divorced Chester Bratton's son?"

Isaiah froze. "She's still married to Bob? You don't think he's in league with Randall again, do you?"

Tate growled. "Five mil's a lot of margaritas south of the border. Of course Bob Bratton's working with Randall. Why wouldn't he be?"

"Because I can read what's going on in Randall's head" —*when I'm not distracted by Roxy*— "but I haven't picked up a single vibe on Bob Bratton. Besides, I don't think Randall's in a sharing mood with Chester Bratton, not since his brother died at the bank."

"Tank had it coming," Tucker said. "I went to bat for Roxy over that one, else she'd still be on mandatory leave pending an MPD IA review right now."

Wasn't that the truth? Internal Affairs always said they were there to help, but the truth was, they often got in the way of good police work. Isaiah understood the need for checks and balances behind the rule of mandatory downtime that followed an officer-involved shooting, but if not for Roxy, there'd be a smoking crater in the District right now. Did IA take that into consideration?

Isaiah rolled his shoulder, irked that his possessive streak had now overlapped into Roxy's official business. *Good hell, Zaroyin. Get a grip.* "Anyway," he started again. "It's time we take the fight to—"

"Now hold on a minute," Tucker growled, his palms forward to placate Isaiah. "I've already got agents staked out all over this city looking for the bastard, and your job" —he stabbed a finger in Isaiah's face— "is to sit tight and keep our little family safe. Yeah, I'll consider baiting Randall with a cover story about finding the stash, but you won't be involved. I'll handle it, all of it. Who's to say that'll end this showdown anyway? You're guarding Bob's wife, not his ex, who by the way, Randall believes knows more about the five mil than she's telling us. And furthermore—"

"So do I," Tate muttered.

"You what?" Tucker asked, his brows up. The man liked to monologue more than he liked to remind everyone he'd been a SEAL.

"She knows something about the five mil. I can feel it," Tate said, his jaw set in that stubborn way he had. "Can't you?" he asked his boss pointedly.

Tucker huffed. "No, damn it. I can't get a sense of where Randall's at, and I can't pick up any vibes from Mrs. Bratton. That's your job."

"Wait a second." Isaiah waved for his boss to shush. He leaned into Tate, looking closer at the man with the expressionless face. "Can *you* read Candace Bratton?"

Tate shrugged. "Not exactly."

"Then how do you know she knows where the five million is?"

"Because her dog doesn't like her and she's mean to Darrin." Tate grunted like it was obvious. "Have you ever looked at those two kids? Why's Darrin got red hair like she does, but Kitty's hair is dark like mine?"

"Because the kids' dad was brunette and their mom's a redhead, moron," Tucker sniped, tipped back on the rear legs of his chair. "It's all about genetics, but that has nothing to do with the armored car heist. Jesus! Get with the program, Higgins."

What Tucker said was correct, but Isaiah's quick mind still tripped over what he thought he knew about genetics, recessive genes, and heredity in two seconds flat. It wasn't much, just enough to know that it took two people with the same recessive gene to produce redheaded offspring. Two people with red hair in their genetic backgrounds. Somewhere. Generations ago, maybe. Or a redheaded woman who'd seduced a redheaded man. Like Candace and that hopeless man back at the chapel. He had red hair, and come to think of it, the coppery color was a lot like Darrin's. Isaiah was almost sure. It hadn't struck him as unusual at the time. But combined with his inability to read Candace, it did now.

"It's him," he muttered to himself as his synapses fired back to life and his Roxy-befuddled brain rapidly connected facts to motive. "His son isn't dying. That's not what he meant. He isn't allowed to see his kid. That's what he was talking about. He's lost custody or something, and shit. She's holding something over his—"

"What are you talking about?" Tucker snapped.

Isaiah sucked in a deep breath, certain he was on the right track. It made scary, logical sense. "That man in the chapel. The one I asked you to have FBI forensics identify."

His psychic power ramped into overdrive, searching back for a replay of the desperate vibes that had shuddered off the man in the chapel last night. The death of a son would surely produce that depth of misery, but what if it was a different kind of death, the kind where the kid wasn't physically dead, but where the father was denied access to the boy he loved? Or—*oh, my hell.* A universe of what-ifs crackled to life in Isaiah's head. What if that man's son was in danger, and he couldn't do anything to help him?

Plink, plink, plink went the dominoes. "That guy. He was sitting behind Candace in the chapel when I caught up with her, but he left when I arrived," Isaiah said, more to himself than to Tucker or Tate. "They'd been talking. Her hair was undone. I'd interrupted something that devastated him, but Candace..." *Damn, I wish I could get past that woman's defenses!* Yet even with her daughter in the ER, she hadn't seemed anxious or worried. She hadn't acted like much of a mother at all, more like a woman who had all the time in the world. More like a calculating woman who'd let her hair down to tease an already tormented man. With what? Sex? While her daughter could've been breathing her last? When all he truly wanted was his child?

A chill shivered up Isaiah's spine at the she-devil in disguise that he'd been dealing with and believing, all this time.

"So?" Tucker asked, once again interrupting Isaiah's pinging thoughts.

"He has red hair," Isaiah blurted out. "Not bright red, but... auburn. Coppery. Just like Darrin's. And he has the same fair complexion. The same freckles. But Bob Bratton's hair is brown, dark brown. Too dark. And his eyes are just like Kitty's."

That's who he is!

Isaiah turned on his boss. "You want to bet Darrin's not Bob Bratton's son? That guy in the chapel is, but Candace won't let him see his kid. That's what he meant when he asked, *'Can you turn back time?'* He wasn't asking to go back to before his child got sick. No, he wants to go back to undo the worst mistake of his life. With Candace. He's not just sad, he's mad as hell, and..." Isaiah wanted to smack his hard head for not seeing this sooner. "It's him. I know it's him, Boss. Bob Bratton isn't Darrin's father. I don't know the guy in the chapel's name yet, but I'm positive that he's Darrin's biological father. Whoever he is, he loves his son, and he wishes he'd never met Candace."

More dots lined up. *I am so dumb!* "That's why Bob Bratton left Candace. She cheated on him and got pregnant by another man, and..." The image of Candace snuggled in bed last night with Kitty in her arms and her back to Darrin flashed into Isaiah's head. The motherly show of affection was another lie. That had to be when she'd induced Kitty's asthma attack. She hadn't hugged Kitty because she'd loved her more than Darrin. She didn't love either of them.

Tucker's brows crashed to a dark thunder line over his already stormy eyes. "You think we've got a third player in this party?"

Tate offered his customary grunt. "Five, Boss." He ticked them off his fingers. "Garrett Randall, Chester Bratton and his son, Bob. That makes three. Whoever this redheaded mystery guy is and..." He tipped back to look down the hall. "The bitch in the bedroom down the hall."

That was a strong word for Tate, but the descriptor fit.

Isaiah raked a hand over his head as the stars lined up. Only one thing sprang to mind that Candace could hold over a man, forcing him to stay away from his child. Make that five millions things. She knew where the money was.

All the unanswered questions turned his brain into an out of control pinball game, complete with flashing lights. Did a record exist somewhere to give Isaiah the mystery man's name? A motel receipt? A marriage certificate? A divorce decree? Or had they been just lovers? Were they ever newlyweds? Those details would take time to locate, but what had Darrin's real father done to alienate Candace?

Shit, shit. Shit. Isaiah swallowed hard past the dread climbing up his throat. Was this even about the money or was something else, something more diabolical going on? Candace Bratton had proved elusive at every turn. Was this simply a ploy to torment the two men unlucky enough to have fallen in love with her? Was she one of those black widows, willing to hurt her children to get back at their fathers? And how the hell did Garrett Randall fit into her scheme? Was this love triangle really a four-way nightmare between her, Bob, Randall, and the mystery guy?

A noisy grunt from Tucker zeroed Isaiah's focus back to the kitchen. "And again I ask, so what? We *think* we know who *some guy* in the hospital chapel *might* be. Big deal. How's he related to Randall, and what's his stake in the five mil? That's what I want to know. Answers. I want real answers, not hypothetical guesses."

Isaiah stared past his boss, his mind tuned like a sniper's scope back on the precise moment he'd touched the man in the chapel's wrist. Isaiah had gotten an instant psychic jolt as if he'd recognized the man at a scary intimate level. It hadn't been simple grief staring back at him. Not pain or anger, either, but raw, utter desolation. It was like looking into a mirror and seeing the reflection of the twelve-year-old boy he'd been the night he found his dying mother on his bedroom floor. The night when Isaiah fully understood there were ugly, evil predators in the world—the human kind.

He shoved to his feet, his mouth gone dry with remembering. Along with it came the angst of a father who adored his son, but had never seen him. Could never play baseball with him or listen to Darrin talk about this favorite team, the Nats. Could never hold him in his arms and tell him that he was a good boy.

Isaiah's mouth went dry. "I've got to talk to Candace."

Tucker stopped him cold. "Not until we talk to Roxy first. Get her back here. She's a woman. I want her take on this."

Isaiah canted his head, not sure who his boss was at that moment. Looked like Tucker. Sure didn't act like him though, not if he'd just included Roxy in FBI decision making. Tucker had definite rules about working with the locals. Could his sweet, intelligent wife, Melissa, have finally gotten through that thick, hard skull of his and turned him sensitive? *Nah.*

Off the subject sidetracks like this tended to rattle Isaiah's overly controlled brain, but in this one minute reprieve from the monumental tasks at hand, one helluva insight blinded him now.

"Boss," he said before he lost the thought. "We may have one more suspect."

Tucker stared at him like the devil, but Isaiah kept going. "I got a good read on the guy who dumped Nugget over the gate. He wasn't Garrett Randall. I sensed no greed for the missing money. He wasn't the man in the chapel, either. No, that guy was filled with rage, not grief. The guy who hurt Nugget..." Isaiah cast his mind back to the swirling aura that had all but carried the man from the safe house. "He wants revenge, not money. He stabbed Nugget to get back at Candace Bratton."

"Just what I need," Tucker roared. "One more damned player."

With long strides, Isaiah left his fuming boss behind and walked swiftly toward the Brattons' suite. He needed time to focus, but that didn't seem possible in this multi-level operation.

Tapping softly at the closed door that Roxy had only moments before entered, he'd no more than cocked his head to listen for her reply, when Tate bellowed, "The redhead's gone! Get to the kids! Now!"

Chapter Twenty

Roxy couldn't believe her eyes. From the emergency room to this! Poor Kitty lay stretched on one side of the bed, pale and as still as death, barely breathing, the sun from the open blinds streaming over her.

Darren knelt on the bed beside her, crying and tugging at her arm. "Come on, Kitty. You gotta wake up or Mom's gonna be mad when she's done taking her shower."

Roxy leapt to his aid. "What happened?" she asked Darrin before she screamed at the closed bathroom door, "Goddamnit, Bratton get your ass out here!"

Roxy's training kicked in. Quickly checking the girl's throat for obstructions and finding none, she began CPR, starting with emergency ventilation. The poor kid was warm. That much was good. Switching adeptly to chest compressions, she told Darrin to, "Get your mother out here."

He ran to the bathroom door and pounded. "Mom! Mom! Kitty's dying! You gotta come help now!"

Roxy didn't have time to wait for Bratton to show. "Come take my two-way," she ordered Darrin. Beads of sweaty panic dripped into her eyes, but she was pissed as hell at the woman taking a leisurely shower while her daughter struggled for life. Weren't moms supposed to have some kind of a sixth sense to know when their kids were in trouble? *I'm no mom, but I'm here. Why the hell aren't you!*

Darrin scrambled back to his sister's side, his eyes wide but focused as he gingerly unclipped the radio from Roxy's collar. The poor kid was on the verge of hyperventilating.

"Good, now hold the button on the side, and yell, 10-33," Roxy ordered. Police code for emergency. Send immediate assistance.

He nodded, pressed the call button and very distinctly said in a polite little boy, inside voice, "Ten-thirty-three."

"No, no, no!" Roxy blew out a burst of frustration, sending the tangles in her eyes flying. "Louder, Darrin. Scream it. We need help! Do it!"

What a mess. The poor kid was shaking, but that time he put his heart into it and bellowed out a strong, "Ten-thirty-three!" to be proud of.

"Now give them this address," she ordered, giving him the safe house location.

Just as he did, Isaiah burst into the room and right on his heels, Tucker. "You go after Mrs. Bratton," Isaiah ordered his boss. "I've got this."

Sirens already screamed in the distance, but why had Tucker left? "She's in the shower, dumbass!" Roxy called after his disappearing butt.

"No, she isn't. She's outside, headed for the fence," Isaiah informed, his voice as calm as a summer day even as he stepped between Roxy and Kitty to take over compressions. "Hey, buddy," he said to Darrin, "You did real good calling for backup. I'm proud of you. Now let's save your sister, okay?"

He'd taken the words out of Roxy's mouth, but the way he was always so damned steady and gentle... Roxy would've cried if she hadn't been breathing for Bratton's daughter.

Poor Darrin huddled into Isaiah's side and Roxy didn't blame him for choosing Isaiah over her. She'd come on too strong and she wasn't the motherly type anyway, but Kitty's unresponsiveness rattled her to the core.

Damn that woman! Bratton had no business having children. As quickly as she cursed their mother, she sent a prayer to the universe. *Cut these kids a goddamned break!*

Between Isaiah's steady chest compressions and the mouth-to-mouth Roxy studiously supplied, they kept Kitty breathing until the EMTs arrived and took over. By then Roxy was exhausted and fit to be tied. For a safe house, this mansion had seen more traffic in the last twenty-four hours than a freakin' hotel.

"We're coming with you," Isaiah told the EMTs as they prepared Kitty for transport. "I'll follow in my car." He got that far off look in his eye, and Roxy knew he was either mind-speaking to his boss or Tate Higgins. These three were the oddest FBI agents she'd ever worked with. Downright spooky at times and she was tired of being out of the loop.

Isaiah turned his gaze on Roxy then, his eyes bright and sharp. "Tate'll take care of Nugget until we get back. Tucker's watching over Mrs. Bratton."

It should've meant something that he'd switched from calling her Candy to Mrs. Bratton, but the shattered look on Darrin's face did Roxy in. He'd been so brave during Kitty's first attack and Nugget's injury. *Good mothers just don't do this!* Kitty and Darrin deserved more, damn it. "What do you mean he's watching her, Isaiah? What's she doing?" *And where the fuck is she going?*

He pursed his lips and nodded in Darrin's direction. Okay. Message received. *Tone it down.* Roxy nodded back. The poor kid didn't need more stress, but she wasn't so sure Isaiah hadn't heard that last expletive, the one she'd only thought.

'*Can you read my mind?*' she projected mentally at him.

"For now, he's tailing her, watching to see who she links up with and where she's going," he replied evenly, no hint that he'd heard the question in his eyes or his reaction. "Due east at the moment."

Okay, that was stupid. Of course, he can't read my mind. He's not Superman, remember?

Roxy let out a measured sigh. She got the message loud and clear. Isaiah still wanted her to control her mouth. For Darrin's sake, she could, but she also wanted some of that mind-speak ability, and she wanted it right now.

For the first time in a long time Roxy hadn't been as tough as she needed to be. Bratton had deliberately hurt these kids. Not only were they good kids and vulnerable, they'd gotten to Roxy in a way she hadn't expected. Something inside of her recognized the unconditional love they had for their mother, not that Bratton deserved it, but that was the way kids were. They never stopped loving their moms.

"She know he's onto her?" Roxy asked evenly.

Very deliberately, Isaiah shook his head as if there were more he wanted to say, but couldn't. Placing a hand on Darrin's shoulder, he said, "You're with me. Let's follow the EMTs to the hospital." On the way out the door with the boy, he asked Roxy, "Would you please gather some of Kitty and Darrin's things while we go talk to Nugget before we leave?"

She heard what he hadn't said. He planned to move Darrin and Kitty, if she lived, out of their mother's reach. It was about time. *Thank you, Jesus.* "Sure thing," she answered. "Tell the big guy hi for me."

Roxy hurried, fighting her own overdose of adrenaline as she stuffed little boy clothes and teenage girl things into one bag. Funny. They didn't have much, and most of it was ratty and threadbare.

Mrs. Bratton on the other hand, had much nicer things, every item folded with care in her suitcase. Expensive perfumes. Plenty of satin underwear. Bras. Nightgowns. Sling-back sandals. An open-toed pair of stiletto heels. You'd have thought she'd packed for a party instead of federal protection.

Oh, my hell, no. An eight-inch purple vibrator slipped out from under that jumbled stack of panties. Seriously? She'd brought something like this? Here? What'd she plan to do, take the edge off while her children slept next to her? *Argh! What a bitch!*

But wouldn't you know? She had taken her coat. Must've stashed that in the bathroom before she'd deserted her children. Damn her! Astounded and angry all over again, Roxy left Bratton's things behind. The detectives from MPD could bag it and tag it for evidence when they showed. Harmon would have a field day.

Hurrying, she cleared the suite in time to see Darrin wiping his eyes while Isaiah escorted him out of the formal dining room to the rear exit. "Don't worry. This isn't goodbye," he reassured the boy. "As soon as we know Kitty's okay, we'll come back and get him. And if we can't, Special Agent Higgins will bring him to us, okay?"

"Oh... k-kay," Darrin sputtered, his lower lip quivering as another tear rolled down his nose and hit the front of his already dampened t-shirt. He peered behind him even though Nugget was no longer in his line of sight. "Don't forget to tell Agent Higgins to bring his food, too."

"You bet," Isaiah answered. "Officer Thurston, how about we let this tough guy ride shotgun with me. He's had a hard morning."

"You got it," she replied, her mind made up. Conniving Mrs. Bratton was in league with the treacherous Garrett Randall. They were both going down.

"How are you feeling, honey?" Isaiah asked a sleepy-eyed Kitty Bratton. He hadn't left her side since she'd suffered an intensely severe asthma attack, which Isaiah now knew her mother had induced before she'd disappeared over the security fence. Damned conniving, that woman. Pre-meditated murder, if Kitty had died.

Praise the Lord for first responders. Those EMTs had had her breathing on her own before they'd hit the University Hospital for the second time in less than eight hours.

"Tired," Kitty murmured around the nasal cannula tucked under her nose. Pale and weak, her frail body seemed plastered to the bed instead of lying on it.

"Do you remember what happened?" Isaiah probed gently. These kids needed a safe place to land. It certainly wasn't with their mother, and the safe house just plain sucked.

Kitty yawned and shook her head. Her lashes drooped. "Later," she sighed.

He stood over her, watching her sleep and noticing things he hadn't before. She had rich brown hair and a perky nose that turned up at the end. A light sprinkling of brown freckles dotted her cheeks, not the cinnamon freckles her brother had. Where his fine bone structure took after his mother's, Kitty was larger boned, her musculature, dense and tomboyish. Like Roxy's.

Kitty was athletic material, yet she didn't play sports. Isaiah knew that for certain. He'd delved into her mind when he'd thought he'd lost her, when he'd mentally encouraged her to '*Live, Kitty. Help me out here. Roxy's breathing for you, but you've got to want to live or nothing we do matters. Don't give up. Darrin needs you.*'

Thank God, she seemed to have listened. Isaiah's greatest worry was that he'd have to tell Darrin he'd lost his mother and his sister. After what went down with Nugget, the poor kid couldn't take much more.

Roxy sat in one of the many waiting rooms down the hall with him at the moment, but Isaiah had one thing to do before he left Kitty's side. Pulling a device out of his inner suit jacket pocket, he scanned the kids' suitcase, something he wished he'd thought to do earlier.

Sure as shit, he hissed when he found another transmitter tucked deep inside an inner zippered compartment. It was no wonder Randall had found them so quickly. Between the device installed in Nugget's collar and this clever little transmitter, Randall knew right where to look.

Using one of the evidence bags he always carried in his back pocket as a glove, Isaiah removed the transmitter, turned the bag inside right, and secured it until he could pass it to another agent for transfer to the FBI lab for analysis. Maybe they'd get lucky and find a print.

So why'd that other guy hurt the kids' dog? Just to prove he could? It made sense on a sadistic level. Hurt the kids to get at their mother. Panic Candace. Make her think she had to do something—anything— to stop the madness. Force her hand.

Yet that wasn't what happened, was it? Candace had not only drawn expert FBI resources away from the safe house at the same time she'd tried to kill her daughter, but she'd done it with cold-blooded intent. No child should have to suffer what Kitty and Darrin had gone through tonight.

Yet Isaiah read other motives into the strategy Candace had adeptly executed. She'd certainly played the damsel in distress card before. Who's to say this wasn't another ploy to make her look desperate enough to do something as crazy as induce an asthma attack that would surely draw those same FBI resources into play to save Kitty? She'd played it damned close to the wire, but she'd also known she had highly-trained support close at hand who'd jump to the rescue. She'd already tested those waters, hadn't she?

The real question was, who was the spider and who was the fly? Isaiah felt certain she knew where the money was, maybe Randall, too. But did she know the man who'd nearly killed Nugget? Had she made so many enemies she no longer knew who was who?

No matter how Isaiah spun it, it all seemed to come back to that damned stolen money. The only thing he knew for certain was that Candace Bratton was a threat to her children. He'd already filed a protective order. Family Services was on their way. But how to tell Kitty and Darrin...

Reaching for his cell, he tagged his partner. "How's it going out there?"

"He's asleep," Roxy replied, her tone soft as if she'd been dozing, too. "How about you? Kitty's okay?"

Pleased at the tense note of hope in her voice, he nodded though Roxy couldn't see him. "She's breathing easier. The doctor gave her something to help her sleep. You need to know that I'm taking these kids home to my place. They can't go into the system. They need protection. It's the only way."

An audible sigh of relief breathed over the line. "I was hoping you'd come up with something."

For the first time since Kitty's attack, Isaiah smiled. Whether she knew it or not, Roxy had the maternal instincts of a mama bear. "I still have to get a judge's approval, but I'm not worried." Getting Family Services to agree could be the sticky wicket, but Isaiah intended to use every last one of his persuasive powers to get it done. Kitty and Darrin didn't need the stress of foster care on top of everything else they were going through.

"You'll come with me?" he asked.

That earned him an indelicate snort. "What'd you think, moron? That I'd leave you with two kids by yourself? I've got news for you, Zaroyin, I'm no quitter."

"Good answer," he murmured, loving the fire in her quick retort and the sound of his surname on her lips. She made Zaroyin sound good and honorable again. He didn't even mind that she'd called him moron in the same breath. Working with Tucker, he was used to the name-calling, and Isaiah understood where it came from. Roxy wasn't talking down to him. It was her tough-girl way of handing out endearments. God bless the day she called him sweetheart. He'd be in real trouble then.

Chapter Twenty-One

Later that night, Roxy helped Isaiah transfer the Bratton children from the safety of the hospital to Isaiah's FBI SUV in the lower terrace of the parking garage. He'd passed the evidence he'd found in the kids' suitcase to an FBI agent at the scene. Both signed the required chain of evidence forms, but didn't it figure? Bratton and Randall were in on this together.

Roxy found it hard to believe Bratton would've agreed to get herself blown to hell just to get on Randall's good side, though. That didn't make sense. No. Something had to have happened between then and now. Maybe she'd opted to hook up with Randall now that she knew he had a hard-on for her. Maybe she was using him like she seemed capable of doing with every other male who came too close to her web. She'd certainly played Isaiah.

That notion pissed Roxy off. And to think she'd fallen for that whole damsel in distress act back at the bank. If she knew then what she knew now, Roxy would plant a fist in that woman's lying face.

MPD stood on guard, blocking the entrances and exits until the kids were once more out of sight. With blacked-out, bullet proof windows, and reinforced plating that turned the vehicle into a fortress, Isaiah rolled out of the underground parking lot, dropped south to Interstate sixty-six, crossed the Potomac, and headed west with an escort of four MPD cruisers. In an hour, he pulled off the freeway, angled southward through a forested area, sparse with houses, before coming to a stop. Tall evergreens guarded the ten-foot wrought iron fence enclosing the gated community.

"Hey, Sweeny," Isaiah said to the silver-haired gentleman who'd ambled out of the guard shack. "Quiet night?"

Roxy peered past Isaiah to take stock of the guard who'd tipped the brim of what looked to be an Irish cap to Isaiah. Tufts of bristly white hair stuck out around the brim. "Aye, 'tis quiet for sure. I've been missing you, young man. Are you home to stay this time?"

"For a while," Isaiah answered.

Sweeny smiled past him to Roxy. "Ah, I see you've brought a lady friend. Hello there."

"Nice to meet you," she said. He seemed harmless enough.

Sweeny flipped a lever inside his four-by-eight shack and the barred gate lifted. "A good evening to you both."

"Same to you," Isaiah replied.

Roxy kept one eye on Sweeny in her side mirror as Isaiah drove through the gate. The gate lowered, and the older gentleman ambled back inside his shack. "What a boring life. Can you imagine sitting all day and night in a shack, waiting for someone to show up?"

Isaiah chuckled. "He's not as bored as you might think. Before he built these townhouses, Sweeny owned this land. Since his wife passed, I imagine this little job gives him a reason to get out of bed every morning. He gets to chat with people as they come and go. It keeps him from being lonely."

That made sense. "What's his first name or does everyone just call him Sweeny?"

"Leonard, but yeah, he goes by Sweeny."

"So where are we?"

"Over the river and through the woods," he teased. "I still own my parent's place in Bethesda, but I live in Riverwood now. It's far enough from work, but not too far from everything else."

That explained the rural setting. "You heard from Tucker again?"

Isaiah grimaced as he shook his head. "I'm blocking him at the moment. He's still cursing a storm for losing Bratton. I can only take so much profanity."

"You turned him off?" she asked, incredulous that his psychic skills were that powerful.

"More like I turned the volume down. I know where he is. That's enough for now."

Speaking of turning the volume down... "My dad used to spend all day watching television after Mom died," Roxy said quietly. "He kept it on and loud, twenty-four-seven. I think he was trying to drown out the world. Noise can do that, you know. It gives you less to think about. Then one Sunday he went to early Mass at Saint Pat's. Father Diego talked with him and he hasn't been the same since. He made peace with what happened. Now he helps at the church almost every day."

"What's your father's name?"

"Hayden. Hayden Thurston." Roxy kept her gaze out the window as the tall evergreens yielded to manicured lawns, private cobbled drives, and whitewashed horse corrals. How would it be to own so much property that you couldn't see your neighbors' homes?

Darrin and Kitty had both fallen asleep in the back seat. With every mile the District fell behind, and Roxy relaxed. Neither Bratton nor Randall could get at these children now.

Isaiah's hand found hers in the dark. "I'm sorry for your loss," he said kindly as his fingers interlocked with hers over the console between them.

And suddenly she wanted to talk.

"She thought she could save the world." Roxy squeezed back, just enough to let him know she appreciated the connection. The silence stretched, but when Isaiah didn't prod for more, she filled in the blanks. "Mama used to bring friends home." A grunt came out of nowhere, but in respect for her mother, Roxy didn't go there. Her mother had a good heart. Even after what happened, that counted most.

"But sometimes," she cleared her throat, "her *friends* were people she'd just met. Some were down on their luck. Runaway kids, streetwalkers, vagrants, you know the types. She'd talk to anyone who looked like they needed a hand up, and she had an instinct for them, too. Daddy always said if she looked for trouble long enough, she'd find it."

And she had. Roxy drew in a deep breath, not sure she could tell this story again. It dredged up feelings she'd fought hard to bury, at least to control. Right on cue, Isaiah squeezed her fingers, letting her know he was still listening. That helped.

"Anyway…" She huffed, blowing the pesky strands of loose hair out of her eyes. "One Saturday night after Mass, a punk named Ritchie Gardner ran into her in the church parking lot. She'd stayed late to clean the kitchen after cider and donuts. Saint Pat's always holds a little get together after Saturday night Mass, you know, for newcomers and old-timers. People like to linger and chat, especially if Father Tom's there."

Roxy stole a sideways glance at Isaiah. His eyes were on the winding road as the SUV maneuvered around rolling ranches, long lines of fences and stables. Sitting there with one hand on the wheel, the other snug over hers, and with the streetlights flickering over his face, the man was debonair to a delicious fault. Not at all what she'd expected in a G-man. He reeked of class and privilege, and why he couldn't seem to keep his hands off of her warmed her to her soul.

Kitty and Darrin slept as her story continued. "Ritchie grabbed Mama when she went to unlock her car. He didn't want money or drugs. He just wanted to kill someone. Said he needed to *feel alive.*'"

Roxy stopped then, her stomach churning at the senseless loss and pain that never went away. Like reruns of Leonardo DiCaprio slipping into the frigid Atlantic after the Titanic sank, this story always ended the same. There was no happy ending. No cavalry showed up at the last moment. No rescue boats. No saviors. Mama was still gone. What Roxy wouldn't give to have just one more day with the woman who'd loved her unconditionally.

"Ritchie stabbed Mama thirteen times for the *fun'* of it," Roxy said evenly, willing her self-control to get a grip. "My Mama, Maria del Rosa Thurston, bled out on the cold asphalt of Saint Pat's parking lot before anyone noticed her car was still there. Daddy didn't know until the emergency room called him, but by then..."

Isaiah's fingers gripped tighter.

Roxy tried again, her control slipping. "By then, she was gone," she said, her voice no more than a whisper. "The court could've treated Gardner as an adult, but because he was only sixteen and *'confused'* at the time he committed the murder..." How she hated timid, confused people who justified their cowardice and got away with it. "He got off easy. He'll spend the rest of his teenage years in a juvenile detention facility. When he turns twenty-one, he'll face prison as an adult."

But none of that mattered. Maria del Rosa Thurston was still gone, and Daddy Thurston and Roxy were left to suffer in silence. Ritchie Gardner could never serve enough time to make up for murdering her mother. Worse, the sniveling bastard would be out on the streets again in three-to-five with good behavior. She truly wished he would *clean up his act*, get *saved by Jesus*, and all that liberal bullshit. It'd make her job easier. The minute he hit the streets, she meant to be there, waiting for him. Laying for him.

Daddy deserved the peace of mind of knowing his wife's killer could never hurt another person. Yeah. Roxy had a plan, and she knew just how she'd do him. Thirteen times, only he'd never see her coming. She was just that good.

"Mom died the only time I sneaked out to go talk to a friend," Isaiah said breaking the silence. "I was twelve. I found her when I climbed back in my bedroom window. There was a lot of blood. I slipped in it, and fell on her and..."

That brought Roxy around. "No," hissed out of her. "Tell me her name."

He nodded, still staring ahead, his left hand fisted, clutching the wheel. The cords in his neck hardened, when he struggled to say, "Francesca. Frannie. Dad was working in Chechnya when they met. Mom was a foreign aid worker from Austria. They... they fell in love and moved to America before I was born. Both naturalized, but..." He swiped a hand over his face, his eyes on the road. "Anyway, they never found the guy who murdered her, but I know who he was, and who paid him to kill her."

"Christ, who?" Roxy wanted to know. She'd add those sons-of-bitches to her list and get peace of mind for Isaiah, too.

The fingers on her hand tightened, his thumb tapping a gentle beat on the back of her hand. "It doesn't matter now, Roxy. They're both dead. My mother's murderer died in prison, and my buddy Ky Winchester took care of the man who hired him. Remember Senator Douglas Bick?"

Ah, yes, Bick. "The sleazy dirtbag who married that freakazoid woman from Hollywood?"

He nodded, and Roxy had to look twice. Something glimmered at the rim of his eyes, but it wasn't revenge. It was the same sadness that welled up from the bitter hole in her heart.

Isaiah spared her a quick glance. "My dad got mixed up with Bick and his wife. He needed funding for his project. You knew that, right?"

She nodded. Everyone knew Abraham Zaroyin, the immigrant from Chechnya, the scientist responsible for the deaths of hundreds of FBI agents, all to prove some harebrained idea that would've turned U.S. military members into mindless robots during combat. Some of the Bureau's finest had volunteered to beta-test Dr. Zaroyin's *Wonder Chip*, as the press had tagged it. Drones, he'd called them, once he'd implanted that chip into their brainstems. But the judge who'd sentenced him called the people who'd ultimately died at his hand—husbands and wives. Mothers and fathers. Sons and daughters.

At the end of the day, he said they'd died in the line of duty to their country. They were the heroes. Dr. Abraham Zaroyin was just another mad scientist out to rule the world. The press called him Dr. Abraham *Frankenstein*. They said a lot of other ugly things, too.

Endless talk show hosts compared his work to the medical experiments performed at the Dachau, Natzweiler, Buchenwald, and Ravensbrueck concentration camps during World War II. They went after the CIA and the Bureau for their lack of oversight. Then they went after Isaiah just because he was the madman's son. They said '*like father, like son*'. They said other horribly sensational crap, too.

Roxy remembered the front-page pictures of a younger Isaiah dodging reporters and cameramen, his hands up to ward them off and his head down. How hard that had to have been for a young man alone in the world. She knew firsthand how cruel people could be. How quickly friends turned on you.

Flipping her palm face up, Roxy clenched Isaiah's hand and held on tight. There it was again, the same buzz she always felt when they were skin to skin. This time, it ran deeper than lust, vibrating from his skin to hers and up her arm like the spark from defibrillator paddles, trailing unidentifiable emotions with it. Her heart swelled with compassion for the gentle warrior at her side. He'd already hit every last high mark in her book as far as looks and sincerity went. Now they had something else in common. They'd survived monsters.

"I'm sorry," she told him, more aware of his true charms than ever before.

Like the class act that he was, Isaiah merely shrugged, as if what he'd been through was no big deal. But it was.

"At the time, we didn't know Bick had also ordered the hit on Mom. He did it to keep Dad in line, but by then..."

Roxy slid out of her seatbelt and knelt on her seat, needing to touch more than just his hand.

"What are you doing?"

"This," she told him as she pressed a kiss to his cheek, which of course he dodged, so it ended on his lips. The SUV slowed to a crawl as the kiss deepened. Tears breached Roxy's eyes for all Isaiah had suffered. He should be the bitter one, mad at the world, and kicking against the pricks. Out for revenge. But he wasn't, was he? Somehow, he'd risen above the legacy he'd inherited. He'd proven he wasn't anything like his father, and that all by itself was an unbearably sad accomplishment. What son didn't want to be like his dad? Roxy'd give anything to be as kind and loving as Daddy Thurston. Abraham Zaroyin was a fool.

The teardrops on her lashes framed Isaiah's face in sparkles when she opened her eyes.

"What was that about?" he breathed.

She could barely speak, so she merely said, "Nothing. I just wanted to."

His gaze narrowed, and yeah, he probably saw right through that lie, but she couldn't tell him how much he meant to her, not yet. He'd think she pitied him, and she didn't. Not for a second. There was nothing to pity about overcoming adversity the way he had.

"It has been a tough day. Are you going to be okay?" That was Isaiah, through and through. Always thinking of others. Always looking out for the weary and the weak. Like her.

She nodded, slid back to her seat and buckled up. The SUV rolled on.

Isaiah took a slow right and turned onto a cul-de-sac with a single home at the center of the turnaround. "What's he do?"

"Who?" she asked, her mind on the gorgeous house he'd just parked at. Entirely in red brick, the quaint colonial presented two striking columns to the street, a pair of hunter green doors between them. It looked too big for one guy, and it irritated her that she didn't know if this was his parents' home or if he owned it, free and clear. How rich was he? Or was he? Those were important details to most women. Why hadn't that been important to her until now?

"Your dad. You said he helps Father Diego at Saint Pat's. I was just wondering what he does there. Is he a deacon? A janitor?"

She understood then. Isaiah needed to distract her from his loss. Survivors were like that, either they wallowed in their grief and never moved on, or they focused on others, and grew stronger. Oddly, she had to admit that she hadn't moved on as well as Isaiah. She still planned on offing Ritchie Gardener, and some days, she obsessed how she'd do it.

"Nah, nothing like that," she told Isaiah, playing along. "Mostly he keeps the place clean. Does small maintenance jobs. Repairs things that get broke. Windows. Kitchen and bathroom faucets and toilets. Stuff like that. You live here alone?" she asked to get the spotlight off her.

"Not anymore," he replied with a sly grin as one of two garage doors slid upward to let him pass. "Don't get out until I'm sure we're secure. Then we'll wake the kids and go inside."

"I'm awake," Darrin said sleepily.

Isaiah shot Roxy a look. "How long have you been listening?" he asked, his eyes on the boy in the rearview.

"A few minutes," Darrin admitted. "Sounds like me and Kitty aren't the only ones."

Roxy flung an arm over the seat back to face him. "The only ones who what?"

Darrin turned his face to the view inside Isaiah's immaculate garage. The poor kid's expression was desolate in the fluorescent lighting. "The only ones nobody wants," he said softly. "I don't even have a dad, and my mom... my mom..."

A sob hiccupped out of him, and Roxy couldn't take it any longer. She snagged his wrist, then his hand, holding tight to a little boy who believed he was nothing. "Don't even think that, not for one minute, Darrin," she told him in no uncertain terms. "You're a good boy, and you'll grow up to be a great man. Trust me. I know from experience. Bad things happen to good people all the time, but that doesn't make you anything like Ritchie Gardner, does it? You heard me telling Isaiah about that Bozo, didn't you?"

His eyes shimmered when he met her gaze. "Even if I'm not that guy, it still don't make me nobody."

This kid was breaking her heart. Roxy clung to him until the garage door came down and Isaiah gave her the go ahead. Intent on proving Darrin wrong, she flew out of the SUV, then dropped to one knee as he slid out of the vehicle. "Now you listen here, Mister Darrin Bratton," she said as she took hold of his bony shoulders. "Don't you dare believe what other people say about you, not ever. You're a great kid, and you've got a big heart. You love dogs and your sister. You love your mom too, and maybe she isn't smart enough to see it, but it's clear as a bell to me. I see it, don't you, Isaiah?"

Isaiah's palms clamped onto her shoulders as he leaned over her back. "Listen to Officer Thurston, Darrin," he said, his voice warm and gentle. "She teaches kids your age self-defense. Want to learn a few survival techniques while you're stuck here with us? I'm sure she'd be glad to show you."

That broke the dam Darrin seemed to be holding back. His eyes brimmed, and before she knew it, he threw himself into Roxy's arms, his little boy body shuddering with sobs as he ground his face into the crook of her neck. Damn, this poor kid was one big heartbreak. She closed her eyes, swallowed hard, and vowed she'd find a way to make him smile again.

"Mom tried to kill Kitty," he sobbed, "and now, she ran away, and she left me and Kitty, and what's gonna happen to us? I want Nugget!"

"I want Nugget too, baby," Roxy soothed, her eyes plenty misty. She had no experience with kids, but this little guy and his sister had gotten under her skin from the get-go. She peered up at Isaiah, but the sappy smile on his elegant face was no help.

The handsome guy winked and cupped her elbow, tugging her to her feet with Darrin still in her arms. "Come on, Darrin," he said in a gruff man-to-man voice that made her look twice. Were those tears glimmering in the corners of his eyes, too? "How about if you take care of Officer Thurston while I carry Kitty inside. Let's find the best place for Nugget's bed. I'm thinking he should stay with you in your room. Sound good?"

Darrin's head bobbed. "Yes, Agent Zaroyin," he said as he grabbed Roxy's hand extra tight. "And Kitty can sleep in my room, too, cuz she might need someone to watch over her and keep her from almost dying in the middle of the night again."

Isaiah scooped Kitty easily into his arms. Still asleep, she snuggled into his chest. "I've got a better idea. How about you, me, and Nugget bunk together so Officer Thurston and Kitty can have their own room and some privacy? You know how girls are." He said that with a mischievous roll of his eyes. "That way us guys can snore if we want to."

Darrin shot Isaiah a look of pure adoration. "'Kay," he replied, swiping the last of his tears away. "And maybe we can tell jokes and scary stories and stay up late?"

"Now you're talking," Isaiah said as he marched his new little family into a very clean mudroom, then to the kitchen of every woman's dreams. Marble countertops. Travertine floor tiles. A fancy chef's island complete with a gleaming array of copper pots and pans suspended on a massive rack over it. Muted lighting that sprang to life beneath the cupboards as they approached. A side-by-side refrigerator/freezer combo in black, not that annoying stainless aluminum that showed every last fingerprint.

The woman inside Roxy nearly drooled. *Tomatillo enchiladas anyone? Fresh off the griddle tortillas? Homemade salsa with just enough zing to water your eyes and make you beg for more? Her all time favorite, the hominy filled and very spicy posole, just the way Mama used to make it.*

That there were no frilly feminine touches, no magnets on the fridge, no cutesy salt and pepper shakers, and no sign that any woman had prepared breakfast for Isaiah in this very masculine kitchen, helped. But damn. Roxy stopped crushing on the culinary treats she could whip up for a midnight snack. How could she and Isaiah ever get together again with two kids in the house?

Chapter Twenty-Two

They didn't tell a single joke or scary story. Instead, Darrin fell asleep on his back with one arm thrown over his forehead and his mouth wide open. Snoring. For a little guy, he made a lot of noise.

Since he couldn't sleep, Isaiah lay listening to Tucker's latest rant in his head. He'd posted extra agents and pulled video surveillance footage from every metro stop in DC trying to track Bratton, but without success. Isaiah was tired of the gratuitous F-bombs with every failed lead.

Tate on the other hand was in transit to Isaiah's house with Nugget, as well as with Isaiah's and Roxy's duffels from the safe house. Isaiah didn't need his as much as Roxy needed hers. It was early morning, and Isaiah could've engaged his co-worker in psychic conversation, but didn't. The quiet man would be here soon enough.

After he grabbed a quick shower, Isaiah opted for a light gray polo over jeans instead of anything remotely related to FBI standard issue. This job had become an undercover mission of the highest priority. No one needed to know he was working from home.

On his way to the kitchen, Isaiah backtracked down the hall to peek into his spare guest room. Letting just the barest sliver from hallway light breach the darkness, he checked on Roxy and Kitty. The sight that met his eyes was worth the risk of Roxy catching him and telling him to shut the damn door.

Dressed in one of his old white T-shirts from the closet, she lay with her back to him facing Kitty. Her knees were bent, and sometime during the night, she'd interlocked fingers with Kitty. For now, they both slept soundly. Roxy's glossy hair had pooled in an ebony cascade on her pillow. Even in sleep, her chin tilted with attitude, but for once, her brows weren't furrowed and her lips weren't pressed tight and thin. She looked more like a loving mother who couldn't bear to be separated from her daughter. Isaiah eased the door shut without a sound. He'd just seen heaven in his fortress of isolation, and it was glorious.

Padding back into his kitchen in his stocking feet, he started breakfast for his friend. One three-egg omelet, heavy on the sausage, bacon, ham and cheddar cheese later, Tate arrived. Isaiah had been watching for him and opened the secure garage when he'd pulled into the cul-de-sac, then closed it just as quickly once Tate was inside.

After surviving brutal torture at the hands of Senator and Mrs. Bick, Isaiah took no chances. He'd been abducted out of his parent's home in Bethesda, right off their front step when he'd answered the bell. Hence, he'd added additional security to his place to ensure he'd never be kidnapped again. Call him anal, paranoid, or obsessive compulsive, he didn't care, but his own top-of-the-line security cameras now recorded every square inch of his five-acre lot of land.

For now, there were only two ways into his home: the main garage door Tate had just driven through and another door at the rear of the garage that opened to his backyard. At one time Isaiah entertained the notion of adding another exit off his kitchen. It'd make access to his patio easier, but then he'd recall how Bick's thugs had gotten to him. So yeah. No. More. Doors.

A trusted security company monitored the place. Any breach would trigger an alarm and the local authorities would be here in seconds. Motion-activated lasers that could blind a man at one hundred yards when engaged, lay low along the foundation where most intruders wouldn't think to look for them. Hidden cameras watched the only two exits to his home. And just because accidents still happened, he maintained an ironclad panic room in the hall off his living room. As many as four adults could live comfortably in there for a week should intruders ever gain the upper hand.

To top it off, he'd established a personal psychic link with the FBI, via Tucker Chase's hard, but honorable head. Isaiah hadn't intended that extreme security measure when he'd accepted his first job with Tucker a couple years back, but he was glad every day since, for the way it had worked out.

And now Isaiah had a watchdog in his house, although Nugget was one subdued puppy as he shuffled into the house at Tate's side, his head down and his tail limp. "Morning," Isaiah offered as he set the platter of bacon on the table. "Where's his crate?"

Tate grunted a surly, "Humph," took a seat and asked, "How's the kids?" instead of answering. That was Tate for you, stoic, surly and inclined to ignore common niceties as a waste of time. Nugget's crate didn't matter anyway. The gentle guy had already turned himself into a fluffy, gold rug curled at Tate's feet.

Isaiah poured himself a cup of coffee as he let his acute psychic senses flare through his home to answer Tate's question. He took a seat opposite Tate at the table. As a rule, he didn't tamper with other people's energies or brain patterns. Years back, the Bicks had tortured him, forced him to do vile things to others to achieve their end game of world domination. Isaiah never forgave himself for the pain he'd caused others, including his friends.

Since then, he didn't invade anyone's mental privacy unless they were on the wrong side of the law. Until last night when he'd deliberately coaxed sensations of peace and comfort into Kitty's and Darrin's exhausted minds to get them to sleep. He'd filled their heads with simple visions of better times, of ferris wheels and carnival rides, of picnics and family dinners around a kitchen table. He'd whispered and told them to sleep deeply and to dream. It'd been easy. They both craved those things.

But Roxy was something else. The woman hadn't relaxed enough to be influenced until a couple hours ago. Her headstrong heart had all but glowed through the guest room walls, set foremost on guarding Kitty; secondly, on planting her fist in the middle of Bratton's lying face—her thoughts, not Isaiah's—the next time they met.

But he'd uncovered something else in that gentle contact with the real Roxy Thurston. The little girl he'd sensed earlier, the angry one with her hands knotted into fists, was still very much there, but this time her secret stood out like an ugly slash through her aura.

Roxy harbored a death wish.

She meant to end the life of the man who'd killed her mother, even if it cost her life in the process. She'd fixated on a noble but bullshit justification for that plan: revenge. Then she'd justified it with her deep-seated loyalty to her father, and she'd excused it away because she loved her dad. More bullshit. It was never love that murdered another in cold blood, unless that distorted emotion came from the valiant heart of a grieving child, who'd gone off the deep end because she adored the man she called *Daddy*.

Tate rapped his knuckles on the table, drawing Isaiah back into the kitchen. "You're zoning out on me, brother."

Isaiah honestly couldn't recall the question he'd meant to answer.

From beneath lowered brows, Tate muttered, "Stop it. Whatever you're doing, knock it off."

Isaiah nodded, not denying his breach of psychic etiquette or that he should cease and desist. The first rule of their office was: *Stay out of each other's heads.* Roxy deserved the same respect, and yet... he couldn't leave her with that awful weight in her heart. As a child in a similar situation, he'd learned the hard way. You could tame the raging beast called grief if you stroked it often and fed it enough. Roxy had certainly nurtured the grief she'd carried until it walked beside her like a massive black lion on a leash, licking its lips and hungry for blood. Until she'd tamed it into a man killer.

Closing his eyes, Isaiah took a deep cleansing breath even as Tate huffed in annoyance. Isaiah had no more power to predetermine a person's decision than the man in the moon did, but he could do what he'd always done. He could plant a seed. This wouldn't take long.

Isaiah planted a mental image inside Roxy's mind of her father standing over another grave—hers. In the image, James Thurston stood alone in a cemetery with tears coursing down his face, crushed infinitely more by the loss of his only child than he'd been by his wife's murder. Isaiah painted the day behind him full of dark clouds, rain, and wind, desolation and a father's despair.

He tucked this very compelling, fatherly reaction between two happy memories: the one of her in her pretty white dress on her First Communion day, when she'd made her parents proud; the second of her parents' last wedding anniversary when she'd treated them to their favorite restaurant.

Isaiah left the suggestion to blossom at her acceptance, or to wither with her denial. As before, Roxy held her future in her hands. He withdrew from her, and let that one seed be enough. Brushing a hand over his eyes to clear the vision, Isaiah faced his scowling friend.

Tate's long fingers drummed the tabletop. One brow spiked like the devil. "You gonna tell me what you're up to?"

"Gardening."

That earned him another grunt. "If you're a gardener, I'm the Pope."

"Your Excellency," Isaiah murmured, tipping his coffee cup. "To answer your original question, the kids are fine. Kitty's breathing evenly, her air passageways are clear, and Darrin snores as loud as you do. We know where Candace might be headed yet?”

Tate didn't bat an eye. “To hell.”

“Probably.” Isaiah drained his cup and set it aside. Tate's plate was empty. “Seconds?”

“No thanks,” Tate replied as he leaned in. “I double checked her ex's alibi from the day of the heist. Bob Bratton said he was out of town. Said he had a job interview in Boston. Said he wanted no part of his dad's mistakes, so he'd left before everything went down, only the name of this prospective employer he supposedly saw didn't pan out. There is no Jack Fillion in Boston who owns a boat company. Only some guy by the same name who owns a pub on Mercy Street. He and his wife of eleven years run the place.”

“Still sounds like Bob had prior knowledge, but he also had receipts. Either he got out of town to cover his ass or—”

“Or he had business in Boston directly related to the heist. He's hiding his old man or the money.”

“Or he's telling the truth. Sons don't always follow in their father's footsteps.” Isaiah tapped his index finger to his lower lip. The name Fillion meant something. He sensed that much. He just wished he knew what. “No one checked Bob's alibi back then?”

Tate shrugged. “Guess not, but I'm headed north to meet the guy he claims he talked to.”

“Why?”

Tate's dark eyes turned black like a predator's. His nostrils flared. “Because I know a liar when I smell one.”

Chapter Twenty-Three

Roxy tossed and turned. She dreamed of white dresses and spring mornings. Her nose twitched at the scents of freshly mowed lawns and spring flowers. May flowers. One perfect Sunday morning when she was Mama and Daddy's pride and joy. The day of her First Communion. Her lips curled at those tender memories. She was that innocent girl again. *Mama and Daddy love me.*

'*They still do,*' some handsome guy with deep blue eyes murmured.

Jerking awake, Roxy ran a quick hand over her tousled hair. Sitting up in the bed, she struggled to recall the dream, but as usual, ended up with fleeting fragments of feelings she couldn't quite catch. Reaching for the hair tie on her nightstand, she let the dream go and left the warm bed behind. Time to get moving.

Showered and redressed in the uniform she'd worn the day before, Roxy wished for her duffel and the clothes in it. Clean underwear would certainly feel good. So would one of the clean T-shirts she'd packed, but her things were back at the safe house.

Instead of complaining, she took a deep breath and faced the darkened bedroom. Kitty hadn't moved and she didn't say anything, but something had changed. She wasn't asleep.

"How are you feeling?" Roxy asked.

Until Bratton and her cohorts were behind bars, she meant to stay close to this girl. There'd be no more mysterious asthma attacks, not unless Candace suffered one after Roxy caught up with her and punched her in the throat. Wait. That wouldn't be an asthma attack. It'd be a busted trachea. *Too damned bad.*

Kitty drew in an even breath, and the sound of it brought a sigh of relief to Roxy. Never again would she take breathing for granted. Filled with inexplicable emotion, she sat at the edge of the bed and brushed the tangled curls away from the girl's eyes. "I know you're awake."

Stretching, Kitty stifled a yawn. "Where's Darrin?"

"He bunked with Agent Zaroyin last night. Feel like getting up or would you rather eat breakfast in bed? I make a mean egg and cheese omelet."

"I want to see my brother."

"Shower first?" Roxy coaxed.

"Uh-uh. I wanna see Darrin. He's little and he's scared and..." The girl's eyes brimmed.

'And you need a hug,' Roxy thought, but she said, "Let me see if he's awake. I'll be right back." She left Kitty leaning up on her elbows and trying not to cry, while Roxy hurried to Isaiah's bedroom.

With Isaiah's and Tate's lowered voices coming from the kitchen, Roxy felt okay opening Isaiah's bedroom door. She'd no more than peered inside when a big fluffy dog brushed past and ambled to the bed where Darrin lay sleeping. Despite his stitches, Nugget climbed up beside Darrin, put his big fluffy butt at his sleeping boy's back, and collapsed with a groan.

"You probably shouldn't have done that, big guy," she whispered to him, "but now that you're there, keep Darrin company, okay?"

Nugget groaned as if he'd understood, so Roxy shut the door and left the guys alone. Hurrying back to Kitty's room, she told her that Darrin now had Nugget with him.

"Oh, good," Kitty breathed. Yet a tear glimmered at the edge of her eye.

Roxy sank to the bed, wanting this young woman to know she'd be safe from now on. "Want to talk?"

The girl shook her head, and Roxy knew this was serious. "No one can get to you here," she said. "I don't even know where we are." That was semi-true. All Roxy knew was that Isaiah's home was in the middle of horse country west of the District, in the upper-class neighborhood of Estelle Estates, so named after the grandfatherly guard at the gate's deceased wife. But she trusted Isaiah. Kitty could, too.

Kitty grunted one of those teenage girl grunts that managed to sound uncouth and sarcastic at the same time. "The story of my life."

"What's that mean?" Roxy asked softly. When Kitty's lips thinned, she said, "If you'd rather talk to Isaiah—"

"I don't want to talk to anyone," whined out of the girl, but Roxy knew better. Kitty had something to say; she just didn't know how to say it. Sure enough. Once she pushed her butt against the pillow and headboard, it poured out on another whine. "I really do love him. He can be a pain in the ass, but... he's the only brother I've got."

Okay, that was promising. "Darrin is a good boy," Roxy agreed to get things rolling.

Kitty stretched her fingers into the blanket on her lap, clenched, and fisted the fabric. "And now, because of everything my stupid mom's done, we'll end up in foster care, and I'll never see him again, will I?"

Ah, that. Roxy swallowed hard, needing to be straightforward without breaking this fragile girl's heart. If Roxy had her way, she'd adopt these kids herself and get them forever out of their mother's influence.

Whoa, whoa, whoa! Just plain, back that crazy-train up a few hundred miles. Where the hell that outrageous thought came from, Roxy had no clue. But this was Kitty and Darrin, not some strange kids she'd plucked off the streets. She knew these two, and—*I like them,* she admitted hesitantly, as if she needed to try it on for size. *Yeah, I... I do. I like them enough to want them in my life, and... Maybe I can talk Dad into letting them live with him while I work, and maybe...*

She groaned at the wild ideas taking her common sense by storm. Cops didn't take at-risk kids home with them. They just didn't. That was what Family Services did. That was their mandate. Hers was to serve and protect, not to house every cast off kid that came along. Rather than opening her suddenly unpredictable mouth and inserting both feet, Roxy opted to listen.

Kitty's head tilted back as she stared at the ceiling. "They're going to find out everything."

"Like what?"

Fat alligator tears welled in Kitty's sad eyes. Her chin came up. Her lips pinched. "Nobody knows this, and you have to promise not to tell. Swear it. You can't even tell your boyfriend out there," she said with a head jerk at the closed bedroom door.

Roxy said what she could. "I can't promise anything, Kitty, but I can be your friend if you let me, and friends always have each other's backs, don't they? They take care of each other and they don't lie to each other, either."

Kitty's eyes narrowed to slits and for a moment, Roxy thought she'd lost her confidence. Until she murmured, "Darrin's not my brother. He's my half-brother. We have different dads. Only..."

Roxy hid her surprise. "Only what?"

The poor girl bit her lip and the deep brown of her eyes turned liquid. "Only he doesn't know it, but... but..." Another whine eked out of her. "But his dad's a really nice guy and he loves him. I know he does, and he'll fight for Darrin. He'll make sure Darrin goes home with him, but my dad won't fight for me. He hasn't been around since Darrin was born. I don't even remember what he looks like."

Of course not. You were two years old when he deserted you. "Have you met Darrin's father?"

"Yeah, once. He came to our house, but Darrin was playing with his friend, and Mom wouldn't let him in."

"So he's never seen his dad? He doesn't know anything about him?"

"Uh-uh. But that's not the worst. Don't you get it? It's me no one wants, because... because..." She sucked in a deep sigh and blurted, "Because I'm as bad as my mom!"

Roxy'd had enough. Jumping to her feet, she rounded the bed and had Kitty in her arms in seconds. Threading her fingers through Kitty's hair, she pressed her chin to the girl's forehead and told her, "Shush, baby. Just shush and don't you dare cry. That's not true. You're bright and you're beautiful, Kitty Bratton, and you're nothing like your mom. Somehow this mess will work out, just you wait and see."

"No, it won't." Her entire body trembled against Roxy. "I know what'll happen. I'm too old to get adopted, and I'll get jerked around by Family Services, and I'll have to live with people I don't know or like, and..." her chest hollowed with another shuddering breath. "Worst of all, I'll never see Darrin again, and he'll never forgive me for all the mean things I did to him and said to him and... and..." Kitty buried her nose in Roxy's shirt and cried, "I hate my mom! This is all her fault. She did this to me and Darrin. I'll never forgive her!"

A better person's first impulse was always to deny that kind of a statement from a kid, but Roxy let it ride. She hated Candace Bratton, too. What the woman had done to her kids was unforgiveable. Children should be treasured, not used and abused by their parents. *Damn her.*

Roxy opted to tread softly. "I think we need to tell this to Isaiah. He'll believe you and he'll understand, trust me. Maybe we can come up with an option besides foster care. Come on. If you're up to it, let's go find him. I think Agent Higgins is here, too. He's the one who brought Nugget. They need to know."

Kitty's fingers dug into Roxy's shoulders even as she lifted a hand and combed her fingers through her hair. "I c-can't talk to them like this. Look at me. I'm a mess."

Roxy eased back to look down at the young woman. Because of her mother's cold-blooded actions, red splotches covered Kitty's neck and tear-stained cheeks. Her normally tan complexion was pale. Black shadows rimmed her eyes, but she was also a fighter, and that said a lot. Kitty reminded Roxy of another young woman who'd once thought she was a loser and a mess, too. *Look how that turned out.*

She tugged Kitty back into her arms. "Let me tell you a secret," she whispered against the girl's sweaty head. "When I was in high school, some of the other kids picked on me because of my skin color. They called me wetback and greaser. Yes, I had a few good friends, but others said I was a lazy Mexican. They didn't care that my dad's a full-blooded Irishman from County Waterford. They bullied me and didn't invite me to their birthday parties or dances because of stuff they'd heard in their homes. That was the real problem, the lies their moms and dads believed."

She blew out a big huff, squared her shoulders, and kept on keeping on. "The only time I got invited to the homecoming dance, I was a senior in high school. I thought the guy who asked me cared about me, that he was different." Another sigh. "He was different all right. He tried to, umm, take advantage of me in the girls restroom during the dance."

Kitty stilled. "He tried to rape you?"

"Yes, but that's not a nice story, and besides, it's not important anymore. I'm over it, and I'm stronger because of it. In the end, he got what he had coming to him, and me?" Roxy pressed a kiss to Kitty's forehead. "I got smart and I got even. He didn't get what he wanted that night. Instead he ended up with a broken nose and some nice deep scars he'll have to look at every time he shaves."

"You got him good?" Kitty asked.

"Oh, yeah. And then some." *Just wish I could remember how I did what I did to the jerk.*

Kitty's grip loosened, and Roxy thought maybe her heart rate had evened out.

"The point is that you're nobody's victim, Kitty Bratton, not even your mother's. She'll pay for what she did and the lies she told you, but you're better than she is. Trust me. I know a good person when I see one, and you're the real deal."

"I like you," Kitty whispered, and Roxy knew what she needed to do.

"And I like you," she said fervently. "Be brave, Kitty. Everything's going to work out the way it should. Now let's go enlighten Agents Zaroyin and Higgins about Darrin's father. And who knows? Maybe one of them will make us girls breakfast. We deserve to be queens for the day, don't we?"

That made Kitty smile. "Ah-huh," she said as she lifted her head and peered up at Roxy. "But I need a shower and a hairbrush first. I want to look my best. Do you think Agent Zaroyin likes me?"

Now it was Roxy's turn to grin. "Absolutely."

Chapter Twenty-Four

"What's he look like?" Isaiah asked casually, needing Kitty to confirm what he already knew about Darrin's father.

For now, Tate sat at the table watching, his arms folded over his chest while Isaiah transferred French toast stuffed with cream cheese and drizzled with chocolate syrup, a favorite from his childhood days, to Kitty's plate. Still in the flannel pajamas Roxy had hurriedly packed for her the night before, Kitty had taken a stool at the breakfast bar. Thrilled that Tate brought her duffel, Roxy'd already stashed it in her room. Darrin and Nugget hadn't made an appearance yet, and that was just as well. The boy needed his rest.

Kitty's eyes lit up when Roxy topped the toast off with a puff of whipped cream and said, "There. Now it's perfect. Eat up."

Roxy took a seat at the table with Tate and a second cup of coffee, obviously pleased with herself for this break in the case. Isaiah hadn't the heart to tell her that he, Tate, and Tucker had already figured out who Darrin's real father was. There'd been so much happening that he hadn't had time to bring her up to speed, and he wouldn't now. With Family Services in the kid's immediate future, Roxy needed this reprieve as much as he did.

Kitty folded a large piece of the gooey toast into her mouth and moaned, "This is so, so good." After another succulent mouthful, her head bobbed. "Oh yeah. Sorry, I almost forgot. Darrin's dad's skinny. Tall. Kind of boring looking."

"My dad?" a bewildered, sleepy voice asked at the doorway. "You found him?"

Ah, shit. Isaiah closed his eyes at the hope in those five words. Shell shocked. Stunned. Darrin seemed frozen where he stood, so Isaiah went to him. "Come sit down with Kitty. I've got breakfast for you, and yes, there are some things you need to know."

Blinking like a deer caught in the headlights of the eighteen-wheeler of truth barreling down on him, the boy let himself be led to the bar stool beside his sister. Isaiah stood beside him and took hold of the little guy's hand. "I'm sorry you heard that, but it's time you know the truth. Bob Bratton isn't your real dad. That's why he never stayed in touch with you. He didn't leave because he didn't love you. He left because he was very mad at your mom for lying to him."

"But Mom..." Darrin gulped. He licked his lips. "Mom said Dad took one look at me when I was born and left because I was... because I..."

"Your mother lied to you, too, kid," Tate inserted gently. "You're not any uglier than the rest of us."

"'S right," Kitty whispered, her tone soft and low. "I seen him one day, Dare. Your dad came to the house, but Mom wouldn't let him inside. She made him stand on the porch and she told him to go and never come back, that she'd do worse things than keeping him from seeing you. She said a lot of other mean things, but all he kept saying was he had a right to see the kid he loved."

"He... he loves me?" Darrin asked.

Kitty's head bobbed. "That's what he said. I was there. I heard him."

"Where was I?" The poor kid was breaking Isaiah's heart.

Kitty shrugged. "Playing over at Jimmy's. Where else?"

Isaiah blew a breath through his pursed lips, striving for patience at the brutal lies Candace had fed her children. They might have different fathers, but they were her flesh and blood. Why hurt them like this?

Tipping into Darrin, Kitty put her arm around her brother's shoulder and tugged him into her side. "We both got different dads," she told him quietly, her breakfast forgotten. "I'm sorry I never told you, but Mom made me promise not to."

"Does he look like me? Maybe just a little?" Darrin asked his sister, his eyes bigger. Brighter. Too damned hopeful for a little guy who'd known more bitter disappointment than any kid should.

Kitty's snarky side seemed to have vanished along with her mother. Canting her head to the left, she looked her little brother over and nodded. "Now that I think about it, yeah. You do look like him." She cocked her head to the left as if she'd never seen him before "You've got the same freckles and the same color hair as him, only his eyes are—"

"Green," Isaiah whispered.

Her head bobbed. "Yeah. I think. I didn't really get a good look at him cuz Mom never let him come in, and she didn't know I was watching, but yeah. I remember thinking they reminded me of emeralds."

Darrin turned to Isaiah. "But I got gray eyes, so maybe he's not—"

"He is your father," Isaiah interrupted as he took hold of the boy's cold fingers. "Trust me, Darrin. That man is your father." *And he's dying to meet you.*

"What's his name?" Tate asked Kitty.

Isaiah sent an appreciative nod to his buddy for that revealing question. Darrin needed Kitty to confirm what Isaiah already knew.

Her delicate brows narrowed. Her tongue slid over her bottom lip in earnest concentration before she finally said, "Jack something or other."

"Jack Fillion?" Tate asked, his voice uncommonly gentle considering the storm clouds in his eyes.

"Yeah. You know him?" she asked.

"Not yet," Tate answered.

"But I've met him," Isaiah whispered to Darrin "At the hospital the night your sister had her first asthma attack. He was there in the chapel sitting in the pew behind your mother." *And her hair was undone as if she'd tried to seduce him.*

How Fillion knew Candace would be there at that specific time made no sense. Not unless he'd been stalking her, or he was in on it—whatever *it* was—with her. Not unless she'd contacted him somehow and told him to meet her there. Not unless she'd used her daughter's asthma attack to meet up with her ex-lover.

But that didn't gel with the emotions Isaiah had picked up from Fillion that night. He'd exuded all the fear and desperation of a man losing his child, not deceit nor subterfuge. At that time and in that specific place, Isaiah had honestly assumed that Fillion's child was dying, which in a way, he was—if Fillion had no way to reach out to Darrin. But using Darrin to get back at Jack proved Candace's treachery. To borrow from Tucker's rich stockpile of expletives... *What a flaming bitch.*

"B-but Mom says calling someone Jack's the same as calling them an, umm, an..." The poor kid swallowed as if he didn't want to say the next word.

His lovely cinnamon lashes fell like curled butterfly wings to his cheeks. Finally, he whispered, "An ass."

"Is that why you were upset when I called you Jack?" Roxy asked, her dark eyes wide. "Oh, baby. Darrin. I didn't know. I'm so sorry I hurt your feelings." She shot a quick glance to Isaiah. "I just told him to hit the road, Jack. It's a saying. That's all."

She took a step toward Darrin's stool, but Isaiah intercepted her and knelt at the boy's knee. That forced Darrin to look down at him, but it also gave this abused child the position of power for possibly the first time in his life.

And time stopped. Isaiah glanced up at Roxy. Over these past days, she'd transformed into the kind of mother these kids needed, one wiling to fight for them. Right now, it was all she could do to not take Darrin in her arms and rock him like the lost little boy he was. Isaiah sensed the ferocity rolling off the mother bear at his six, precisely what he wanted back in his life. His mother used to stand her ground. She'd thrown her heart and soul into everything she'd done, too. That was why she'd been in his bedroom that night. She hadn't run to him for protection. No. She'd run there to save him.

Only he hadn't been there.

But he was here now with Roxy and two kids who needed saving as much as he did. For a moment, he felt his mom smiling down at him. Isaiah took a deep breath, aware how great the gift of a mother's love was to a child. To a man. Humbling. So. Damned. Humbling.

Isaiah could barely speak. "Darrin," he breathed. *I know just how you feel, you poor damned kid.*

Tears had spiked Darrin's glistening lashes into points. He licked his lips and swallowed hard, and Isaiah would've done anything to erase the humiliation dimming this little warrior's countenance. Instead of sharing Tucker's one-eyed jack theory, Isaiah opted for the blue collar approach. "Jack is a proud name, Darrin. It's a good name. Have you ever heard someone called the jack-of-all-trades?"

Darrin shrugged, shaking his head like he didn't care. The boy's gaze dropped. He was ashamed, and that just wasn't acceptable, was it?

Isaiah tried again. "A jack-of-all-trades is a man who's good with his hands, Darrin. He's a man who fixes what's broken because he's not afraid to work hard for what he wants, like knocking on your door and facing your mom even when she lies to him."

Darrin sniffed, still not meeting Isaiah's eyes, but definitely breaking Isaiah's heart.

"Jack Fillion's looking for you," Isaiah promised. "Your real dad cares about you and he wants you in his life. He loves you. Trust me. I know that much about him."

"Then why'd he leave me?" Darrin finally whined. One tear tracked down his ashen cheek. "All my life I been waiting for my dad to come back home, and...

and..." Before Isaiah knew what happened, Darrin lurched off the stool and into his arms, burrowing his face into Isaiah's shirt. "I want you to be my dad. Please."

Well, damn. That didn't go as expected. Isaiah bowed his head, mashing his cheek to the side of Darrin's sweaty head as he sank to the floor and gathered Darrin onto his lap. Like one lost boy to another. Like a father to his son. *Mission accomplished, Zaroyin. Only you're not the right dad.*

"Just you wait," Isaiah whispered. "The second you meet Jack Fillion, you'll know he loves you. You'll see it in his eyes and you'll hear it in his voice."

Darrin's chest hollowed with a shuddering sigh. "But you'll still be here, won'tcha?"

Isaiah couldn't lie, so he gave the boy what he could, a pitiful answer at best. "If I'm not, I'll always be just a phone call away."

'*I'm not going to Boston,*' Tate sent psychically to Isaiah.

'*I can't believe Jack Fillion would ever hurt a child like Bratton's hurting these kids. The man I saw in the chapel isn't made that way. Fillion wouldn't have hurt Nugget, either. That had to have been Randall. I looked into Jack's eyes, Tate. He's suffering as much as his kid is.*'

Ever so slowly, Darrin lifted his teary face and faced Isaiah. The desolation in his eyes had been replaced by years of practiced, thoughtful consideration. He swallowed hard. His forehead wrinkled as if he was considering the truth in Isaiah's promise. At last he sighed, no doubt like he had hundreds of times before, when forced to deal with reality. The back of one hand swiped over his eyes, and he said, "Well, okay then."

So not what Isaiah wanted to hear, a ten-year-old settling for less than what he deserved. Yeah. Reality sucked.

'Shit,' Isaiah hissed to his partner. 'This kid needs his dad in his life, damn it. Soon.'

Tate nodded once, his gaze on Kitty. 'You don't have to convince me. But do you think she's telling the truth? Do you think she really saw Fillion? What if this is all just a story she made up?'

Isaiah hadn't thought that for a moment. 'Kitty's nothing like Candace.'

'But she is her mother's daughter,' Tate pointed out, 'and kids are loyal to a fault when it comes to their moms and dads. Abused kids will lie to defend the parent who slaps them around. You know that. Like it or not, Candace has been Kitty's role model all her life.'

How well Isaiah knew. 'Hold that thought.'

Kitty never knew she'd been psychically probed; Isaiah was just that quick. 'She's totally honest,' he reported back to Tate once he'd sifted through the young girl's memories. 'Fillion came by the house the one time; that's when she saw him. He had words with her mom. They argued and he left angry.

Darrin wasn't home. He was at Jimmy's like Kitty said, and she hasn't seen Fillion since.'

'Good to know,' Tate replied evenly, his dark gaze riveted on Kitty. *'Tell me. Doesn't she look like Garrett Randall? Just a little?'*

Isaiah rocked Darrin there on the floor of his kitchen while he also compared Kitty's facial feature against the felon's. Both had dark hair. Randall's was wiry and coarse, frizzy, while Kitty's was shimmering silk dripping off her shoulders. Their noses were different, but Randall's had been broken a few times in his past life on the street. Other than their dark eyes and dark hair, there was no significant resemblance to link the two genetically. *'You're barking up the wrong tree. Her father's Bob Bratton. That's who she looks like.'*

'Poor kid,' Tate hissed. *'Never understood men who desert their kids. Wolves don't even do that.'*

BANG! Roxy's empty coffee cup hit the counter.

Isaiah looked up and grinned at the storm clouds in her eyes. Her brows were raised. She tossed an evil eye to Tate and then to Isaiah. She didn't appreciate being left out of their private conversation. *Touché.*

Isaiah cleared his throat and said—out loud, "Anyone up for a good game of—"

"Baseball?" Darrin piped up, the gleam in his sad gray eyes irresistible. He ran a quick hand over his face, the misery in his life forgotten. Right then, Isaiah would've done anything to make Darrin smile again, but baseball? Why couldn't the boy love chess?

He looked to Tate, who for some reason was grinning like *Alice in Wonderland's* Cheshire cat. *'You know much about baseball?'*

'Every red-blooded kid in America knows all there is to know about baseball. Well, except for you,' Tate sent back with a smirk, the mischief in his eyes unmistakable. *'Do you even own a ball, pretty boy? A real ball?'*

Isaiah let the dig slide. It wasn't often Tate turned cocky. *'I think one came home in the car with me after the last team picnic at Tucker's. It's around here somewhere.'*

"Get ready to eat dust," Roxy declared, punching her curled right hand into her left palm. "I play for the Dust Devils, and we are going to... Eat. Your. Lunch."

"The MPD Saturday night women's league? For real?" Tate snickered. "That's you on second base?"

Shifting her backside, Roxy stuck her chin at him. "I see you've heard of me."

Tate pushed his chair back until he towered over her. Isaiah couldn't have been prouder. This was no contest. Tate made five, maybe six, of Roxy, but what a sight.

"All I know is you play ball like a girl," Tate rumbled.

Roxy jumped to her feet, glaring up at him as if he'd insulted her. "Oh, yeah?"

Isaiah didn't get it. Why should that make her angry? She *was* a girl, umm, a woman.

Tate cocked both hands to his hips and peered down at her from beneath thick, dark brows. "You heard me, slugger. G. I. R. L."

Her pointy index finger stabbed his breastbone. "Take it back, Bucko."

"You guys can't be serious. You're squabbling over a ballgame?" Isaiah had to ask.

Darrin giggled. "Course, we're serious, Agent Zaroyin. It's baseball. Come on. Let's play!"

Chapter Twenty-Five

The impromptu morning softball game, which ended up being more toss and catch since Isaiah owned no bats or gloves, turned out to be precisely what Roxy needed to clear her mind. She and the guys had left their weapons on a wooden picnic table near the house in case Isaiah or Tate picked up any bad vibes in the vicinity. Hanging around with a couple psychics had its perks.

Cocking her right hand behind her shoulder, she pitched a fastball into Tate's massive, glove-like hands. The big guy was a good sport, though he'd better not bad-mouth the Devil Dogs again.

He caught her pitch easily and sent it underhand to Darrin, hard enough the boy wouldn't feel babied, but gentle enough that Darrin snagged it out of the air, beaming like any ten-year-old kid who'd done good. Whirling, he called to Isaiah, "Go long!" before he threw a high one.

With his eyes glued on the ball, Isaiah backpedaled to the far edge of his lawn, where it turned from landscaped grass into a stretch of pines. Roxy stuck her knuckles to her hips and watched. The guy was fast, long and lean, built like a racehorse. But he went too long and too deep into the trees.

When the arced throw came up short, Tate yelled, "Scramble or you'll miss it, Zaroyin! You can do it! Run!"

Reversing his momentum, Isaiah charged the ball and plucked it out of midair before it hit the ground.

"You're out!" Kitty called like a referee.

"Are you blind? You can't strike out a catcher," Darrin told her with authority.

"He's not a catcher. 'Sides who cares?" she taunted, shaking her head with attitude in the way of a know-it-all older sister. "If this was a real ballgame, it would've been strike one, right, Agent Higgins?"

Both Tate's hands came forward. "Don't drag me into this. I'm just here to play ball."

Darrin turned his back on his sister, shaking his head. "Girls," he muttered.

"Excuse me?" Roxy teased. "What do you have against girls?"

"Not all girls," Darrin corrected, his eyes bright at being overhead. He aimed a thumb over his shoulder at the one in question. "Just sisters."

Kitty stuck her tongue out behind his back, while Tate yelled at Isaiah. "Whatcha waiting for, princess? Someone to bronze your first fly ball? Toss that rocket. Let's see what you've got."

Isaiah sent a quick pitch back to Darrin, but said to Tate, "It wasn't my first catch, wise guy." Like Darrin, he'd tossed it extra high. The ball slowed as it reached its arc, but in that moment, it seemed as if time had been suspended. The cool spring air smelled extra sweet. The birdsong of some particularly happy sparrow filled her heart. Even the sun shone brighter, more forgiving.

Roxy drew in a breath, caught in one of those perfect, crystal clear moments that a person never forgot. The world between then and now. The window when time stood still.

The camaraderie between both men and even the sibling banter between the kids had combined into one of those heart-stopping fractions of time and space. Darrin's face glowed with hero worship for Isaiah. Kitty beamed with love for her brother. The look on big, burly Tate's face was just as bright.

In that one perfect instant, there was no stalker. No demented mother. No five mil and no worries. Just one perfect—now. The world was good again— until some idiot's big, linebacker body came out of nowhere, and Tucker Chase bellowed, "Got it!"

She burst out laughing. He'd just intercepted Isaiah's toss to Darrin, rolled to one hefty shoulder, and was already back on the balls of his boots—

bouncing and grinning like a kid instead of an FBI director.

"What you've got is grass stains on your knees and your butt, big guy," she taunted as Tucker brushed the grass off his pants and handed the ball to Darrin.

"I was gonna catch that," the boy groused, his thumb and first two fingers on the ball like Tate had shown him, his arm cocked high behind his shoulder, aimed toward Roxy. "Here you go. I'll make it a slow ball."

"Not good enough to pitch a bullet yet, eh?" She egged him on.

Just that fast, Darrin got that competitive look in his eye. His chin came up. He angled his hip, curled one knee in tight, and *wham. The little shit knew how to throw!* It hit center of her left palm, snug in the pocket and stinging like a mother.

"Ouch!" she hissed, shaking her fingers. "You about broke every bone in my hand, Babe. You're a regular deadeye. That one came right to me."

Didn't those words light up Darrin's face? They should. She meant them to.

"Babe? You called me, Babe. Did you mean Babe Ruth, huh? Did you?"

"Of course I did. You've got a good arm on you. I can see it now." She waved a hand across the sky as if seeing an imaginary billboard. "Babe Ruth Bratton. Star pitcher singlehandedly wins the pennant for the..."

"For the Nats!" he squealed even as he skipped like a ten-year-old on his way back to her. "I didn't mean to hurt your hand, though. Sorry if I did."

She waved him off. "You didn't. Your turn. You go long this time. Make it count. No grounders."

"We've had a break in the case," Tucker breathed at her side.

"You got a hit on the note Harley found?" she asked as she delivered a long, straight pitch to the still grinning boy who'd run like the wind to the edge of the trees.

"Damn. You can throw, girl," Tucker muttered under his breath.

"'Course I can throw." She hadn't taken her eyes off Darrin. He'd missed that time, let the ball roll by his feet, but quickly recovered. "And I'm not a girl. I'm a Dust Devil."

Isaiah and Tate had since closed in on their boss. Kitty tagged along behind them, but Roxy didn't want this game to end. Darrin was having the time of his life, and damn it. Days like this were just as important as workdays, maybe more so. Little boys should be able to grow up playing baseball, and their dads should want to play with them. They should teach and coach and spend more than just an allotment of *quality time* with them. Quality time was a myth. Kids needed to smile every day, not just when adult schedules allowed. Life shouldn't be so hard on kids, old people, and animals.

"Here comes a zinger!" Darrin belted out as he, *oomph,* threw his weight behind the ball and sent it flying.

"Isn't that the cutest little guy you've ever seen?" she asked Tucker as she caught the zinger and waved Darrin in. He'd worked up a sweat, but the smile on his reddened face as he ran to her was wide enough it split his cheeks.

"He's not who you think he is," Tucker said softly.

"I know," she said, lowering her voice. "He's got a different father than Kitty. She knows, too. She's seen the guy once. Jack Fillion. Tate says he owns a pub in Boston."

"Do you also know that Fillion's the reason Bob Bratton was in Boston instead of with Randall and his old man robbing the armored car that day? Bob waited until Jack opened his pub that morning, then beat the shit out of him. Broke his jaw. Put him in the hospital. Trashed his business, too."

"Don't tell me. That's when Jack first found out he even had a son," Roxy muttered. Darrin was closing in fast. This conversation had to end. "Do Isaiah and Tate know this?"

But Darrin had come within hearing range. "Hey, tiger," Tucker quipped. "You'll need a Nat's jerseys if you keep pitching like that."

He couldn't have said anything better. Darrin nearly dropped his teeth, his grin was so big. "Gee, thanks, Mister Chase, umm, I mean, Agent Chase. You really think so?"

"I know so." Tucker tugged a red and white jersey from inside his shirt and tossed it at Darrin. "Try this one on for size."

The baseball dropped to the ground between Darrin's feet. "Ohwowohwowohwow! For me?" He couldn't get his head and skinny arms into that jersey fast enough.

"Yes, for you. You're a winner, aren't you?"

Damn this arrogant man. Just when Roxy thought she had him figured out, Tucker Chase went and did something incredibly kind for a kid who needed a father in the worst way. Thoughtful things, like what this brash federal agent just did for this motherless little boy, made her tear up. The jersey was too large for Darrin, but the smile on his face? Heart splittingly beautiful. Beat cops don't cry, but here she was, dragging a fingertip under her eye before anyone caught her looking like a sap.

By then Isaiah, Tate, and Kitty had closed in, and Tucker made it worse. He pulled a folded pink Nats ball cap out of his rear pocket and tossed it to Kitty. "This is for you, princess."

Her shoulders scrunched when she caught it. "For me? Sweet!"

Wasn't that sparkle in her eye when she tugged the brim over her forehead the most adorable thing? And the red glow creeping up her neck? Tucker had just embarrassed her, but he hadn't ignored her, and that was monumental for a young woman who felt ignored and invisible. Guys like him usually didn't pay attention to teenage girls, much less remember they liked presents, too.

Score two for Tucker Chase.

"Thank you," Kitty said shyly, giving the brim another tug and batting her lashes. "I like it."

"Of course you do." He stood there, tall and proud. Beaming. His chest puffed out and so damned sure of himself. "'I knew you would."

"You catch really good, Officer Thurston!" Darrin exclaimed. His gray eyes brimmed with pride, and damn. There it was again, that feeling of—joy—or something that stamped a warm glow in the middle of Roxy's heart.

Fighting the lump in her throat, she reached out and pulled him against her thigh. "And you're a better catcher than Agent Zaroyin," she whispered conspiratorially. "Don't let on, though. He thinks he's better than all of us, but no way."

"I heard that," Isaiah said behind her with a smile in his voice. "You've got news, Boss?"

Tucker's big chest deflated. "Yep. Back to work, boys and girls."

Chapter Twenty-Six

Tucker sure knew how to spoil a good game. Isaiah had sensed him drawing closer long before he'd shown up, but since it was just Tuck and his bright red Dodge Challenger, he hadn't alerted anyone. They'd been having fun. Why spoil a good baseball game?

Before long, everyone was back inside, sweaty, but good. Tucker pulled his sweet ride into Isaiah's secure garage. Kitty left to take a shower. Darrin was back in Isaiah's room with Nugget, while the adults gathered in the living room and—adulted.

"What's up, Boss?" Isaiah asked as he passed tall glasses of ice water around. Roxy'd taken the center of the sofa and held her glass to her sweaty forehead. Watching her interact with the kids had raised Isaiah's awareness of her easy way with children as well as every last feminine curve in her lithe, sexy body. She'd make a terrific mother someday.

Tucker took the chair near the window. Tate sank cross-legged to the floor at Tucker's left. The weapons they'd set aside while playing ball, were back on their hips, ankles, or tucked into shoulder holsters to stay. The reprieve was over.

"Forensics came back with a hit on the note Harley found on the dog," Tucker said. "Garrett Randall's prints were all over it."

"Figures," Roxy hissed.

"Why'd he do it?" Tate asked.

Tucker's shoulders lifted. "Won't know 'til we bring him in, but we do know where he is, and we know where Jack Fillion is, too."

Roxy leaned forward and her elbows hit her kneecaps. "Shit, they're in on this together?"

"No. Ky backtracked Fillion's bank records. I've also got him watching Fillion at the moment. The man's stayed in cheap motels and other dives, all of them within a block or two of each of Randall's last knowns."

"Fillion's following Randall?" Isaiah asked, glad to hear that Ky Winchester was back in town and working the case. He was a good friend and a strong psychic in his own right.

Tucker nodded. "Ky got in yesterday. I know what Randall wants, but Fillion's the wildcard."

"He wants his son, that's why he's here," Isaiah said smoothly. "I say we bring him in and introduce him to Darrin now that Darrin knows everything. What harm could it do?"

Roxy's nod and smile confirmed Isaiah's suggestion. She wanted Darrin's happiness too, but Tucker shook his head. "Not yet. I'd rather keep the kids here until we locate Candace. She's the key to this mess. Once she's behind bars, we'll worry about reconnecting families."

"No sign of her yet?" Tate asked.

"Not yet. She's completely off the grid."

Tate grunted. His nostrils flared. "Every mother bear returns to the same cave to drop her next litter. Bratton's no different. Like everyone else, she's got a safe place where she thinks we can't touch her."

"So, you can track her?" Tucker asked, his gaze gone dark.

Tate nodded. If there was one thing he excelled at, it was tracking wild animals. That those bear-hunting skills translated to tracking humans as easily as they did, amazed Isaiah. Yet over and over again, he'd seen Tate lift his nose to the wind as if he could scent the men and women he was after.

Speaking of which... Isaiah leaned back in his seat by Roxy and stretched his arm on the sofa back behind her. Damn she smelled good.

Ziiiiiipppppppppp. In an instant, he was miles away, peering over the shoulders of a man standing at the locked front entrance of the FBI safe house on Embassy Row.

'That lying bitch,' Jack Fillion hissed as he pounded the massive wooden doors. *'You did it to me again, Bratton! Where's my kid?'* Tears filled his green eyes. His shoulders were tight, his fingers curled into hard fists. He'd come here believing he'd finally get to meet his son, only to find Darrin gone. Again.

Upon those bitter words, Isaiah sank deeper into Jack's mind, needing to know the full story and how he'd gotten onto the secure grounds in the first place. The Bureau maintained the property. The security gate should've been locked. Where was everyone?

Unable to explain the lack of security, he refocused on Jack. Isaiah didn't have to delve far to sense that Candace was behind this. She'd lied to Jack, told him Darrin lived there with her soon-to-be husband, the dashing playboy Isaiah Zaroyin.

Talk about a surprise. No one had ever called Isaiah a dashing playboy before.

The sting of her words still tormented Jack. *'I'm marrying Isaiah Zaroyin, so get over it, asshole. You know, the crazy doctor's son? Yeah, it's true. He's filthy rich. His mom left him a mint when she died, and he plans to adopt Darrin. It's too late for you and you can't do anything about it, Jack, so don't try. Isaiah knows people. He can make Darrin disappear for good this time. But I will do one thing, you know, for old time's sake. If you want to see your kid, be here today, cuz we're leaving the country in the morning, and this is your only chance.'*

Jack's fisted hands told the rest of the story. Frustration. Betrayal. This wasn't the first wild goose chase Candace had sent him on, though this one had been timed to get Fillion off Garrett Randall's back. Most likely because she and Randall were not only working together, but they were close to recovering the five mil.

Damn. Tucker needs to hold that press conference to smoke those two out.

Not smart enough to leave well enough alone, Isaiah allowed his inner sight to delve deeper into Jack's mind. A cloud of rage so thick and black that it nearly sucked the breath from his lungs stopped Isaiah short. Jack Fillion was not only worn out by the lies he'd endured on his quest to find his only child, but a certain mental illness had taken root. It filled him with a depression so dense, Jack Fillion was literally on the verge of going crazy with grief.

He stood there alone and humiliated again at the grand entryway to a one-time monument to wealth and greed. Him, a lowly barkeep from Boston, who'd worked twenty-four-seven every day of his life just to break even. All he wanted was what he couldn't have, the son he'd never seen but loved with his whole heart and soul.

Cathleen, his wife and his childhood sweetheart, wasn't able to have children, yet Isaiah sensed that she craved having Jack's son in her life as much as he did. They both loved the boy they'd never seen. He'd have a good home with them, maybe not everything other boys had, but he'd know genuine love for the first time in his life.

Candace Bratton had Jack by the balls. He had no choice but to dance to her sadistic whims, all in the name of love and sacrifice. Yet even a good man can be broken, and Jack was as low as he'd ever been.

'Just once!' Jack bellowed as his fist hit the massive doors. *'Damn you, God! Just once can't I see him? What the hell did I ever do to deserve this kind of torture? You know I love him. I'd never hurt him. He's mine! Damn you, damn you, damn you!'* Rage against his Maker poured out of Jack's soul, a tangible river of sacrilege and sorrow as he sank to his knees, his fists pressed to his forehead, and sobbed, *'Just once. Please. I'll... I'll do anything.'*

Jack blamed God, and he was about to do something extremely foolish. He was about to give up and blame himself for the rest of his life. *We'll just see about that.*

The man needed a knot in that rope he was hanging onto, so Isaiah intended to send him one. In his hurry on that last nerve-racking night at the mansion, Isaiah had snagged Nugget's ball from the top of the refrigerator on his way out. He'd stuck it in his pants pocket, thinking the toy would give Darrin something to hang onto until he got his dog back. Yet somehow, the ball had gotten lost in the shuffle. It wasn't in Isaiah's pocket when he'd undressed that night, and he'd worried he'd lost one of Darrin's prized possessions.

Yet all things in the cosmic spin of the universe happened for a reason, and Isaiah now knew where that ball was. With one well-placed psychic nudge and a helluva lot of mental concentration, he nudged it out of its hiding place and sent it rolling down the Trex walk that ran along the east side of the estate.

Bounce. Bounce. Bounce. It cleared the three steps between here and there, and with another psychic nudge, it rolled to Jack's feet. And there it stopped. His desperate gaze dropped to the toy that had come out of nowhere. It was nothing but a piece of blue molded rubber that a boy and his dog played with, and yet... It was something that belonged to his boy and Jack knew it.

Jack's shoulders heaved. He swallowed hard and stooped. He brought the ball to his chin, squeezed his teary eyes shut, and he breathed, "Lord, I needed this. Th-thank you."

Isaiah breathed his own thanks.

Jack wasn't crazy and he wasn't a bad man. He just wanted his child in the way that all good fathers everywhere wanted their children. Desperately. He just needed something to hold onto until he could hold onto Darrin and the fluffy yellow dog that came with him.

Isaiah left him standing there with the small token of a boy's love for his dog in his hand.

Sucking in a deep breath, Isaiah withdrew from Jack Fillion's mind and instantly zeroed back to his living room. It always seemed as if he'd ridden some kind of a psychic vortex from there to here, especially when the vision had been as lengthy as this one. Opening his eyes, the spinning room came into focus. He gasped, sure he'd been holding his breath for the duration.

Roxy was on her knees beside him. She had her hands on his chest. Her fingers were warm and fluttering with nerves, but it was Tate who spoke first. "I hate when you do that. You look like you're dead, and I can't tell if you're breathing or dying."

Isaiah drew in a lungful. Then another.

"You scared the hell out of me," Roxy whispered into his face, her dark eyes wild with fright. "Don't ever do that again."

"Sorry." Isaiah nodded so she'd know he was okay, but the after-buzz from this mental probe to the District had been more exhausting than most. Moving objects was not his psychic talent. It took fierce concentration and one helluva ton of psychic energy to motivate even a small rubber ball, but at this distance, it was unheard of.

Rolling his shoulder, he turned to Tucker. "I know where Jack Fillion is, but he's not part of this. Candace is. She's with Randall. There's no time to hold that press conference. We need to move. Now."

Tucker snapped his fingers. "Good. Go with Tate. Find Bratton. Bring her in."

"Me?" Isaiah asked like an idiot, but recovered quickly. "Sure thing, Boss. You'll stay here with the kids?"

"No need," Roxy said, smoothing her palms over her knees. She'd settled her butt to the couch again, but Isaiah had a feeling she would've slapped him if she hadn't had an audience. She still might. "I've got this covered. You guys go and—"

"I'm staying here with Officer Thurston, so report in on the hour." Tucker interrupted. The man had a stare that could crack granite and Isaiah didn't argue.

He did withdraw his arm from the back of the couch, though, his focus on the deadliest sniper in the room. There really was no better protector than Tucker. Isaiah just hadn't planned to be leaving so soon, yet this was the job and a man went where duty called. "I'll pack my bag."

Tucker's big chin hit his chest in one quick nod. "Say your goodbyes. The kids will miss you."

"Copy that," Isaiah replied steadily as he lifted to his feet. Dazed from the vision as much as the sudden shift in assignment, he went to his room, grabbed one of several pre-packed bags from the back of his closet, and told Darrin, "I've got to leave for awhile."

"Aw, you can't do that," the boy said as he climbed to his feet from where he'd been brushing Nugget. He made that Nats jersey look good.

"Sorry, Darrin, but I have work to do that no one else can do." He couldn't tell the boy he was going after Candace, but Isaiah suspected Darrin already knew. As an afterthought, he snagged a leather jacket from his closet in case evenings turned chilly. One never knew with stakeouts. "Don't worry. Roxy's still here and Agent Chase is staying, too. You'll be fine."

Darrin nearly tripped as he barreled into Isaiah. He wrapped his arms around Isaiah's waist, his head flat to his stomach. "But I want you to stay," said the little guy who'd been lied to so much that he fully believed his father had deserted him when the truth was the exact opposite.

Sinking to one knee, he took hold of Darrin's shoulders and told him, "Until I get back, you're the man of the house. Take care of your sister and make sure Nugget doesn't get too tired. He needs plenty of rest. Can you do that for me?"

"I will," Darrin promised, blinking through his tears. "I'll help Roxy, too."

Even the dog seemed to know this was goodbye. Nugget joined the party, his tail wagging. Isaiah disengaged before things got too tender.

"When you coming back, Agent Zaroyin?" Darrin said stoically, one hand on Nugget's neck, the other fisted at his side.

Shit. Was this what fathers went through every time they went off to war? Was this how Tucker felt when he kissed Deuce goodbye, knowing that might be the last time he'd see his son? Could a guy feel any lower? Back to one knee Isaiah went. Just like Jack, Darrin needed something to believe in.

"I know your mother hasn't always been truthful with you, Darrin. I know she tried to hurt Kitty, but you need to also know this. I don't lie. I'm taking you to the first Nats game I can get us into. We'll eat as many hotdogs as we want, and we'll buy a couple of those giant *'We're #1'* foam fingers, and we'll sing *'Take Me Out to the Ballgame'* at halftime, and who knows? Maybe we'll get lucky and catch a fly ball. Trust me, big guy?"

Darrin's brows furrowed deeper. "Um, Agent Zaroyin. Baseball games don't have half times, and everybody sings *'Take Me Out to the Ballgame'* in the seventh inning stretch."

Chagrinned, Isaiah said, "See? I need you to teach me about baseball. Can you trust me?"

Darrin certainly looked like he wanted to trust. His head bobbed, but the poor kid had been lied to so many times before, and Candace had done it so easily. Unclipping the FBI badge from his belt, Isaiah clipped it onto Darrin's waistband. "There. Now it's official. You're my partner and partners never lie to each other. We cover each other's back and we're always straight with one another."

The cutest dimple dented Darrin's right cheek then, and this time his eyes sparkled. His fingers uncurled from their defensive position. "Okay, partner," he said softly. "I gotch'ur back, Agent Zaroyin."

Isaiah gave him a manly knuckle bump to his skinny shoulder. "And I've got yours, Agent Bratton. Now keep the women safe. I won't be gone long."

There was no hug that time, just a brave little man and his faithful dog watching yet another guy leave them behind.

Pressing on, Isaiah knocked at the guest bedroom, but when Kitty didn't answer, he turned the knob and peered in. Apparently, the game had worn her out. She'd fallen asleep on the bedcovers, her hands folded under her cheek, and still wearing her Nats ball cap. The corners of her mouth were curled into the tiniest smile. She looked like an angel. Isaiah didn't have the heart to wake her, just memorized the pretty face of another little girl who thought she had to be tough.

Back in the hallway, he opened his gun safe and quickly geared up. Tate waited at the kitchen door. If he'd been alone with Roxy, there would've been a steamy goodbye kiss, but with his boss watching, Isaiah played it cool.

Goodbye ended up being nothing more than a curt nod in Roxy's direction and a, "Be seeing you around, Officer Thurston. Take good care of our, I mean, the kids."

She nodded back, and that was that. Isaiah drove off with Tate and didn't look back.

Chapter Twenty-Seven

When the FBI moved, they moved like a well-oiled machine traveling a bolt of lightning. Isaiah and Tate were gone before Roxy knew it, but damn. When Isaiah fell into that trance, she'd honestly thought he'd had a heart attack right beside her. He'd all but stopped breathing, and his eyes went scary black, even the whites.

If Tate hadn't murmured, "Easy, Roxy. This is what we've been waiting for," she would've called 911 and started CPR. Instead she'd held her breath until he'd snapped out of it seconds later. So that was a psychic vision. Damned gut wrenching to witness.

This particular FBI group was vastly different from others she'd worked with. Tate was the quiet and steady big man in the shadows, content to play backup to Tucker's superstar routine, or to spend nights on a rooftop standing guard while others slept. The guy could throw. The heel of her palm still smarted from the fastball he'd sent her way. Course, she'd never tell him that.

Tucker was another story, all ego, as evidenced by his dramatic entrance and the showy gifts he'd brought. Yeah, the kids loved the attention, and they deserved to be spoiled. God knew they needed to feel good about themselves for a change. Tucker had certainly done that, but things did not a happy family make, and he seemed to understand that, too. Roxy'd seen the way he'd comforted Darrin back at the safe house. Tucker's heart was bigger than he let on.

But Isaiah? The man was the soul of the game, the willing beginner who hadn't minded a ten-year old teaching him, yet the valiant protector who hadn't taken his eyes off the kids until they were back inside. In only days, Isaiah had become everything. He was Darrin's hero and Kitty's first crush, and he'd gotten under Roxy's skin, too.

Besides the hotter than hot chemistry between them and her appetite for every last inch of his handsome body, something else was happening deep inside. She could feel the change. This was more than a crush driven by the high-octane FBI mission they were on. This was...

No! Roxy gulped, her heart in her throat. She couldn't say it, wouldn't allow herself to think it. Once she admitted a weakness, she eradicated it. It was weakness that had led her into the restroom that night, but it was inner strength that allowed her to walk out with her head held high while Mario Forsythe crawled behind her. Weakness wouldn't be tolerated.

Yet here she was, facing the greatest weakness of them all. One so great she dared not admit it. Only this thing between her and Isaiah hadn't exactly weakened her, had it? If anything, it had made her stronger in ways she hadn't seen coming. Well, except for those times he'd been deep inside of her, and she turned to jelly. She was pretty weak then. Or when he breathed her name with that rumbling come-hither tone and every last cell in her body obeyed. Most men she could take or leave, but Isaiah? Once this joint operation was through, she needed to date him. Exclusively.

But now? She was stuck with Tucker Chase.

The guy had gone through the garage and back outside again. He'd already walked the perimeter three times since Tate and Isaiah left. Because of Isaiah's tight security, it wasn't necessary, but Chase said he needed to know the lay of the land, so off he went. This made number four.

He'd also moved Darrin and Nugget into the same bedroom with Roxy and Kitty. Said he preferred defending one objective rather than two. It made sense, but the cozy feeling in the house was gone. Roxy couldn't shake the niggling sense of impending—something—headed her way. Storm clouds were gathering, She just couldn't see them yet.

So she cleaned her revolver while she waited, methodically broke it down and used the gun cleaning kit she'd found beside the gun safe in Isaiah's hallway closet to ensure her weapon was in proper working order.

A right fine Liberty, the safe boasted steel construction and heavy-duty welds. Mechanical and electric locks. Anti-pry tabs. Spring-loaded external relockers should some savvy thief breach the primary locking mechanisms. Too bad she didn't have the combination to this masterpiece. She was curious to know what Isaiah kept in there besides weapons and ammo.

Personally, she kept all of her valuables in her gun safe. Not like she owned much, but what she valued, she locked up. Her mother's gold wedding band, legal documents, her passport, insurance policies, three rifles, one magnificent AR, two NVGs, a collection of well-used pistols. Enough ammunition to ward off a zombie attack. Important stuff like that.

But Isaiah wasn't the typical federal gunslinger, was he? He seemed—smarter. Less inclined to shoot first. More inclined to ask questions. Always thinking. What kind of guns would a thinker own? How many?

With her revolver cleaned and once more locked and loaded, she tucked it into her hip holster and put the cleaning kit back where she'd found it. The more Roxy thought about Isaiah's safe, the more she wanted to know what was in it. Did he have a secret gun fetish, a collection of weaponry so significant it made hers look weak? This bad boy was a good four feet wide with solid steel doors, and large enough to store an arsenal. She wished she'd gotten a better look inside when he'd geared up, but she hadn't been able to take her eyes off Isaiah then.

She knew the laws of the jungle. The last time you saw your partner might be *the last time.*

Yet again, Tucker entered through the kitchen door, which meant he knew the code into Isaiah's garage and she didn't. Once again Isaiah had neglected to share critical information with Roxy. For a smart man, he certainly was forgetful.

"Grill's warming up," Tucker said on his way to the refrigerator, where he pulled out a hefty package wrapped in white butcher paper.

"What's for dinner?" Roxy asked, pleasantly surprised he'd taken the initiative to fix dinner instead of assuming she'd automatically jump at the chance to cook because of her gender. Although she would have if Isaiah'd been there. Just because she wanted to.

Tucker cocked a brow as if the question surprised him. "Steak. What else? Is there something around here to go with it?"

She waved him out the door and back into the garage. "Go burn the meat. I'll see what I can find."

"Pull over," Isaiah told Tate before they'd gotten more than a mile from his place.

Tate brought the SUV to a full stop. "What's up?"

"You do realize that Tucker just kicked me out of my own house, don't you?"

"So? He's right. We've got work to do."

Isaiah drew in a deep breath. "But we don't need to leave to do it."

"That's not what the boss meant and you know it."

Isaiah cocked an eye at his partner. Tate might be quiet, but still waters ran deep, and with Tate, they grunted a lot. People often underestimated him because of his less than companionable silence, but the man was no idiot. "I know I've been distracted on this operation, but—"

"You think? That little lady's got you turned inside out."

Shit, am I that obvious? Isaiah thought.

That time Tate came through with the grunt Isaiah expected. "Yes," he hissed out loud. "You are that obvious, Isaiah. You can't keep your hands off Thurston, and the mission's suffering because of you, man. You." Tate's meaty fist bumped Isaiah's shoulder. Hard. "This is all on you. Either you pull your big head out of your rear pocket or you're off the case. This is your last chance. Don't you get it?"

Isaiah nodded, surprised Tate had heard what he was fairly sure he hadn't spoken out loud. "Copy that. I've been..."

"Whipped," Tate provided the missing—and perfect—word.

"Yeah, okay. I'm whipped." He stalled. "Your skills are growing, Tate. You can hear me even when I'm blocking you, can't you?"

Tate pursed his lips and nodded. "Animals," he muttered. "I hear a lot of pain from animals. Some nights I can't sleep. Mankind needs to stop what he's doing to them."

Isaiah hadn't expected that. "Like what?"

"Like... Never mind." Tate shook his head. "Not here. Later. After."

Good to know. One unsolvable problem was enough. "The bottom line is... I'm not leaving. We do this right, and we do this now. You're right, Tate. I haven't been on my game since this mission began, but there's no way I'm leaving my home and my woman."

Tate cocked a brow. One eye closed. If Isaiah hadn't known better, he'd have sworn there was mischief in the dark eye now zeroed on him like a sniper's crosshairs. "Your woman? Yeah. You've got it bad. Do what you have to do."

Isaiah hit the down window button on his armrest and drank in the scents of spring and Mother Nature. Now that Tate was aboard with the plan, Isaiah did what he should've done days ago. Closing his eyes, he let his head fall back on the neck rest as he sent his unparalleled psychic talent into the world. And beyond...

It took a specific frame of mind to summon his inner X-Man to the game. That was who he felt like, Charles Francis Xavier of Marvel Comics fame, yet his skill was neither as fantastic nor as far-reaching as that fictitious character's.

Lifting his chin, he drew in another lungful of cool spring air and his journey began. He'd touched Jack Fillion's mind. He knew the man suffered. The evil Candace had caused was unrelenting and fierce. The time had come to get real.

Chapter Twenty-Eight

"So where is he?" Roxy wanted to know. After the kids had eaten dinner and left the kitchen table, she'd poured two mugs of coffee. She and Tucker had things to discuss.

He'd fixed an excellent dinner. Rather, he'd burned half a beef on what had once been Isaiah's shiny steel grill. After one helluva grease fire, which Tucker handled as expertly as if he'd put plenty out before—which Roxy didn't doubt he had—she had to admit that the ginormous rib-eyes were done to perfection. He'd scorched the thick cuts of succulent beef with just enough char, and she couldn't recall ever enjoying a better steak.

Unfortunately, Isaiah's poor grill would never be the same. Tucker had left it as charred as the meat.

Apparently, the higher the flames, the better the steaks. Who knew?

She'd pitched in with smothered baked potatoes, while Kitty put together a pasta salad that was a meal all by itself. Darrin kept Nugget company under the kitchen table, playing quietly, until Tucker stormed in from the garage with a heaping, sizzling platter and bellowed, "Come and get it!"

"If he's smart, he's doing what he should've been doing all along," Tucker replied. "You're a distraction, Officer Thurston. I need him on his A-game. You saw him during that vision. That's what I need him to be, too busy to play around with you."

"He's been working," she pointed out, "and we've been damned busy." Not one of her smartest comebacks. They'd been busy all right, just not enough that they hadn't also gotten *busy* with each other.

Damn. The gleam in Tucker's dark eyes said it all. He knew how much Isaiah meant to her. Roxy didn't bat an eye. "I meant where's Chester Bratton. Where is he? If he's got the money from that armored car robbery, why isn't the Bureau searching for him?"

"And where should we begin looking?" Tucker asked as he lifted his coffee to his mouth and took a sip, his dark eyes on her. "The man's been a ghost since he left town after the heist."

"The FBI has no idea where he went? They can't find a paper trail? No digital footprint?" Roxy nearly snorted. That seemed unlikely, given the Bureau's vast resources and big opinion of itself. "Then how do you know he left town?"

Tucker's gaze narrowed. "I don't. That's why I've got two other psychics combing through the physical evidence from the heist right now. If there's anything to find, they'll do it."

"So tell me about the psychics working for you," Roxy said, glad to get the focus off of her and Isaiah. "How long has the FBI been into all this" —she waved one hand— "paranormal stuff?"

His lip curled as if he didn't like that word. *Paranormal.* "There's more to these agents than meets the eye, Officer Thurston."

She nodded, willing to give him that much. "Are you psychic like Isaiah? Can you read minds?"

Tucker's gaze lowered to the last of the beverage swirling in the bottom of his mug. "They're the smart ones, not me. I'm just muscle. I know how to get things done."

"Like what? Blowing things up?" Why she baited this supreme alpha, Roxy had no idea. The man was just so full of himself.

"If that's what it takes," he said softly. "Isaiah and I have been through hell together. He saved my ass, and I'd like to think I saved his, too. Back then, I never thought the day would come I'd be saying this, but he's a top-rate asset to the Bureau, maybe one of the best we've got." Tucker raked his fingers over his head, ruffling his thick dark hair like a stiff wind on a summer day. "Tate's just as good, though he doesn't believe in his gifts as much as he should. Ky Winchester and his wife, Eden, now there's the real deal. Those two are every bit as good as Isaiah."

"So he's the best?" She needed to know.

Tucker nodded. "Oh, yes. Isaiah and Eden are the only Level Tens in North America. Another two live in Russia. Siberia, the last I heard. Three more in China. One in Tibet."

"There are only eight Level Tens" —whatever that was— "in the world?"

He nodded, a smile tweaking his lip as he lifted the drink back to his mouth. "Bet you wish you knew what a Level Ten was, huh?"

"Hmmpf." Humility was not her favorite flavor. Neither was having her mind read, which it seemed Tucker had just done. "So what is it?"

In the course of the next hour, her head spun while he explained the differences between Clairsensitives, who sensed other psychics in the world; Telekinesists, who moved objects mentally; Telepaths, the real mind readers; Intuitives, who sensed others' emotions instead of their thoughts; and lastly, Precognitors, people who were able to reach out and influence others' decisions. Isaiah, it seemed, possessed most of these psychic talents to some degree. Talk about far-fetched.

Roxy didn't believe. "You mean he could convince a Catholic priest to commit murder?"

Tucker shook his head as he lifted to his feet and took his mug to the counter. "That's not how it works.

A Precognitor's power lies in his ability to accurately decipher another person's aura, then influence decisions they might be faced with, like which flight to take or when to take a vacation. Where to go. What meal to choose at a restaurant. Precognitors can't force people to act against their character, certainly not murder, not unless they tend that way already. But a savvy Precognitor could influence his mark to decide to be in the right place at the right time. He might want a certain person on a specific flight when the plane blows up. Maybe he needs them standing near the president when an assassin strikes. Real life scenarios like that."

Roxy ran her fingers over her lips so her mouth wasn't hanging open. "So, umm, Isaiah's like a police profiler?" *Holy shit. What couldn't the guy do?*

"More like an FBI profiler, but yes. Along those exact lines, only his level of skill is more like a finely honed scalpel in a surgeon's hands. Need another drink?"

Roxy didn't miss Tucker's hoity-toity slam against local profilers. "Only if you put something in it this time," she muttered as she handed her empty mug over. The day had just taken a sharp left turn into LaLa-land, and no, she didn't mean one of Hollywood's latest movies. A good stiff burn would feel good going down about now. "Has he ever planted ideas in your mind?" She had to know.

"As a matter of fact... yes." Tucker sorted through several cabinets until he found the bottle he was looking for. "Ah, here we go. I knew it was here somewhere," he said as he splashed whatever alcohol he'd found into the two mugs before filling them to the brim with coffee.

Back at the table, he pushed her mug across the table with one fingertip. "I was up north in Canada when he first made contact. He had me hearing things. When I came to, I had the migraine from hell." Tucker chuckled to himself as he tipped the cup to his lips and swallowed half of it.

"Like what?" Roxy asked as she took a sip. Ahh, coffee laced with whiskey. Just what she needed. "What'd he say to you?"

Tucker paused, his gaze fixed on the rim of his mug. "He didn't say anything, just messed with my sat phone at first. I thought it was dead, but it wasn't. Eden was there with me. She'd met Isaiah earlier, through some psychic channel, not in person. We didn't know it then, but a couple of his old man's enemies, Senator Bick and his psychotic wife, kidnapped Isaiah. They had him strapped to an autopsy table in a warehouse south of Boston. Cassandra Bick tortured him until he did what she wanted. You've seen his scars? That was her doing."

Suddenly it was hard to breathe. Roxy nodded, her throat gone dry. That was how Isaiah had gotten those scars. There were so many. All over his arms and chest. "That bitch did that?" *I'll kill her if I ever see her.*

Tucker nodded, his gaze still fixed on the mug in his hand. "Yeah. She cut him up pretty bad. Kept him weak. Senator Bick was the power monger of the two, but his wife..." Tucker rolled one shoulder as if he shared those scars. "Cassandra was one twisted bitch. The bastards had some insane notion of ruling the world. They wanted him and Eden for breeding stock. Figured the odds for producing Level Ten offspring would work in their favor. Shitheads."

Isaiah and Eden? Breeding stock? Didn't that trigger the annoying green troll on Roxy's shoulder?

A grumbly growl vibrated deep inside Tucker's broad chest. "Death was too good for those sons-of-bitches. If I had my way, I'd dig Bick and his wife up just to kill them again. After I tortured the shit out of them. After I burned them alive. After I dismembered—"

"I get the picture," Roxy said, her fingers curled around her mug because suddenly, she needed something warm to hold onto. "How'd they die?" She needed the particulars.

"Special Agent Ky Winchester and Mark Houston, one of Stewart's men, tracked Eden. You know Alex Stewart, right?"

She nodded. Everyone knew the former USMC sniper who'd built the elite covert surveillance company known the world over as The TEAM. "Go on."

"Well, anyway, they found her along with Isaiah, his father, and the Bicks, south of Boston in one of

Bick's many warehouses. If I recall the deets correctly, Ky ended the senator on the scene, but Isaiah, even as cut up and weak as he was, still managed to taze that bitch." Roxy saw the glow in Tucker's eyes. He was proud of Isaiah.

"So he messed with your mind and gave you a headache?"

"No. I got the headache when I threatened Eden, and she hit me with a brick of ice. We were still in Canada then." Canting his head, he pointed to three square-cornered scars in a row on the side of his forehead. "She might look like a little girl, but that woman's got a mean right hook. Don't make her mad. She damned near took my head off."

"She hit you?" *I have got to meet her!*

"That she did, but I asked for it. I was ready to kill her, again because of what I thought I'd heard. It was Isaiah who planted that notion in my head, and I—"

"He told you to kill her?"

Tucker shook his head. "No, that's on me, but he did infuse my ego with the need to be a hero. Back then, I was a different guy. I thought Director Strong ordered me to take Dr. Zaroyin down with extreme prejudice. I'm still sure I heard him say *extreme prejudice*, only... he didn't. All he wanted was Eden out of Canada and me to keep her safe. But the way my brain worked then, it automatically kicked into search and destroy mode instead of rescue mode. God, help me, I could've killed her." His voice had grown softer with every word. "I'll never forgive myself for that."

Holy shit. "That was how you knew what Isaiah was capable of?"

"No, that's when I knew for damned sure that I didn't know everything," Tucker admitted. His Adam's apple bobbed as he downed the last of his drink. "Believe it or not, this FBI team is the most powerful team I've ever worked with, and I've worked with the best."

And they were all Navy SEALs, no doubt.

He finally met her gaze. "Freaks you out, all this psychic bullshit, huh? But you do realize that we as a species haven't come anywhere near our full psychic potential, don't you?" He pinched his index finger to his thumb with no space in between. "We use such a small portion of our brains. Maybe there's, for lack of a better word, more to us than meets the eye, Roxy. Scientists once thought the world was flat, remember?"

She stared at the mug in her hands. "You do know we're on duty, right?" she asked, still not sure what to think.

"Don't worry. I didn't put enough in your coffee to water your eyes."

But how much did you put in yours? "So then..." She had no idea what question to ask, other than— *are you guys all crazy?* Yet she believed every last word he'd said because she'd witnessed Isaiah's vision. From the get-go, she'd known he was too good for her, but to realize that he belonged in a loftier sphere than common, ordinary people like her? That was something else entirely. Isaiah really was out of this world.

What on Earth did he see in her? She had no psychic talent. All she'd offered up to this point was distraction. To be all he could be, to truly serve and protect others, Isaiah needed distance. From her.

Tucker huffed through his nose. "Yeah, I couldn't believe it the first time I heard it, either, but trust me. Isaiah's the real deal, and he's the only one who can find Candace Bratton, Chester Bratton, and Garrett Randall. Isaiah just needs to focus. On that. Nothing else."

And no one else. There it was, the truth exposed and her heart along with it. Still fingering the handle of her mug, Roxy swallowed hard at that bitter reality. Tucker was right, but he'd made it sound easy. *Forget about Isaiah. Let him do his job while you do yours. Stop thinking about him, and he'll stop thinking about you.*

She doubted that. Her lashes fell to the black beverage swirling in her mug, the same color of Isaiah's eyes when he'd gone into that trance. There was no sense bluffing Tucker, but there was also no way to stop what her heart told her.

She and Isaiah were linked beyond the chemistry flying between them. This was no one-time affair. The sex was phenomenal, but that wasn't all that connected them. Hell, no. She loved Isaiah, and Tucker knew it. He wasn't dumb. Roxy was.

She'd let Isaiah leave without telling him she loved him. She wished she had, though now Roxy knew she wouldn't have just kissed him. She would've kissed him goodbye.

Chapter Twenty-Nine

Instead of searching after Candace Bratton's nonexistent psychic vibes, Isaiah zeroed in on Garrett Randall's. Neanderthal vibes were easier to locate.

"He's at Bashar's Brazier, seven blocks south of the safe house on Embassy Row," Isaiah murmured. "Back room off the alley. Studio apartment. He's there, but he's alone."

"Guess that'll have to be good enough for now." The vehicle lurched forward as Tate engaged and Isaiah held onto the vision. The stench of cheap booze hit Isaiah's nostrils as if he were in the dingy room with Randall. "He's been drinking and he's waiting for someone."

"Hope it's Bratton," Tate replied as he headed toward the interstate. "Keep talking."

"Not much to tell," Isaiah murmured, his eyes closed and his head against his seatback. "Other than he could use a shower and a breath mint. He's drowsy from drinking all day. This is our chance."

The miles flew by while Isaiah gently probed the sleeping man's mind. So many thinking errors had clouded his judgment over time. So much anger. The man operated on gut instinct that, nine times out of ten, ended in a bare-knuckled fight. Or worse. The blade strapped to his calf belied his mistrust of everything and everyone.

As psychic forays often did, this one ended with Isaiah's mental fingertips sinking deeper into Garrett's unguarded childhood memories of abuse, neglect, and outright torment. A cocaine addict, Luella, his mother offered no protection to any of her four sons. All in turn were pimped out to boyfriends and one night hook-ups, battered and sorely used until Dirk Randall came along and gave them his name. Then things went from bad to worse.

That the Randall boys lived through those ugly times proved Nature's harshest law: survival of the fittest. That their stepfather mysteriously disappeared when Garrett reached the hardened age of thirteen, proved the law of the jungle. The Randall boys were finely honed survivors—and killers—by then.

They'd simply waited until, as usual, Dirk drank himself into oblivion one late afternoon. By morning, the bloody mess of his death struggle had been cleaned, and Mama Randall was none the wiser. Not that she would've heard anything in her coke-induced haze. Not that she would've done anything to intervene. Luella only cared about one thing by then, and it went up her nose. She still lived in the same two-room, dirt-poor shack in the mountains of West Virginia. Garrett kept her supplied with enough coke to keep her quiet. Manageable. And for now—alive.

Isaiah pulled out of his trance just as the afternoon sun dipped below the western horizon behind him. Shadows stretched long and dark. The bright lights of the District glittered ahead. Tate had already crossed the Potomac and now aimed for Embassy Row.

"Take the next right, then an immediate left," Isaiah whispered. Randall hadn't moved since he'd fallen asleep. This part of the op might actually go easy. "You'll pass a pink neon flamingo on the corner to the left. That's Bashar's sign. You can't miss it."

Tate brought the vehicle to a stop in the alley Isaiah had seen in his mind. Two black FBI vans were already parked and waiting.

"You called for back-up?" Isaiah asked, surprised he hadn't heard his partner making that call.

"He's not getting away this time. Two more units are parked out front. Metro's got three a block away in case things go bad. Say when."

Isaiah had to know. "You've got a private link with Tucker, don't you?"

Tate's grunt was answer enough.

"Then let's do this," Isaiah ordered.

Tate flashed his headlights to signal the units ahead, and everything went like clockwork. It took seconds to breach the shabby hollow core door. Without another exit, Randall never stood a chance. Surly as a bear out of hibernation, he charged Tate head-on before Tate delivered a fist to Randall's forehead. Randall dropped flat to his back and that was that.

Tate shook his fist. "Got him," he growled as he dropped one knee to Randall's side, rolled him to his belly, and cuffed him.

Tate helped the dazed man to his knees, and then to his feet while Isaiah read Randall his rights. Randall told them all to go to hell, and Tate showed him to the holding cell in the rear of one of the FBI vans. Isaiah took a deep breath even as he sent Tucker a mental update. *'Garrett Randall is in custody. No sign of Candace Bratton.'*

'Good job,' Tucker sent back. *'You know what to do.'*

'How's things on your end?'

'All's quiet on the western front.' Tucker chuckled. *'Kids are playing some video game in their room. Roxy's cleaning up after dinner. Almost feels like home.'*

The domestic image of Tucker watching Roxy in the kitchen irked Isaiah. The guy hadn't meant anything salacious by his comment, but still. He was there and Isaiah was not.

'*I'll keep you informed.*' Isaiah signed off before Tucker made it worse. It was bad enough that in-processing and questioning Randall would take the rest of the night, maybe most of the next day. He didn't need images of Tucker getting cozy with Roxy in his head while duty dragged on.

"Hey, Zaroyin," one of the other FBI agents called out from the back room. Special Agent Keller Boniface. One of the Bureau's finest. "You need to see this."

Isaiah ducked into the rental's bathroom. There in the tub lay a wooden carton of pasty-white bricks of C-4. Detonators. A spool of det cord. Several burner phones still in their plastic cases. Lead pipes. Duct tape. "No wonder he smells."

"You've got that right," Boniface replied. The man never smiled. "Blond haired, stone-faced and built like Tate, he tugged at his dress slacks when he crouched near the tub, his massive forearms on just as massive thighs. "We should be able to trace all these back to their sellers without much trouble. The C-4's stolen, I can tell you that right now. I recognize the first four digits of those MSNs on the wooden box, the military stock numbers. Looks like Randall's got am Army buddy who's willing to go to jail with him."

Isaiah peered over Boniface's shoulder. He recognized something in the jumbled mess of bomb making materials, too. A red negligee. Had Candace been here with Randall? "Looks like he's got a lady friend."

Producing a mechanical pencil from an inner suit jacket pocket, Boniface maneuvered the silky scrap of fabric from beneath the supplies. "This should give us plenty of DNA evidence."

'No! Stop! Not that!' Isaiah froze as a vision poured over his psychic channel. Someone, a man, screamed through a thick, dark fog. His hands came up. Terror welled in his eyes. *'I can tell you where it is, just don't, God, please don't!'* He angled his shoulder, one hand raised as if deflecting an attacker. *'If you kill me now, you'll never know! God, woman! You're crazy!'*

The frightened warning zeroed in on Isaiah as if he were witnessing one side of the attack. *'I'll never know what?'* Isaiah asked. *'Who's hurting you? Who are you?'*

The man, whoever he was, turned and looked at Isaiah as if they were standing feet apart and side-by-side, as if he'd heard Isaiah and could see him. *'You! Help me! It's Candy! Candy Bratton's going to k—'*

The connection burst like a water balloon splattering on concrete.

"She's killing him," Isaiah told Boniface.

Keller leapt to his feet and spun toward the door, his service weapon instantly in one hand, shielding Isaiah at his rear. "Who, sir? Who's killing who? Where?"

"Stand down," Isaiah replied evenly. The man seemed unusually tight considering his practiced calm just moments ago. "She's not here, but Candace

Bratton is killing someone, a man, right now. I didn't get a good enough look at his face, but I'm almost sure it was Chester Bratton. I just don't know where they are."

An odd shadow shifted over Keller's stern face. With an angry huff, he holstered his pistol. "Sorry, sir. You're the psychic. I should've known you were seeing things that I, umm, c-c-couldn't." He ran a quick hand over his brow. "What n-n-now?"

Had tough-guy Keller just developed a stutter? Tate was back in the room by then, his black eyes ablaze, and Isaiah didn't have time to decipher one more mystery. He let Boniface's strange reaction slide.

"Did you see it, too?" Tate asked Isaiah. "The vision?"

Apparently Chester's scream for help hadn't resonated with just one particular psychic. As adept as Eden was at picking up psychic screams, she'd most likely heard this cry for help as well. "I did, but I'm sure it was Chester Bratton," Isaiah replied. "Did you get any sense of where the murder's going down?"

Instead of replying, Tate's brows narrowed on Boniface. "You saw it, too," he accused. "You know where she is, don't you?"

"I... I..." The man took a full step backward, bumping his calves on the rim of the tub, the room was so small. He lifted a clenched fist to his mouth, disbelieving what Isaiah now knew had happened to him. Fear replaced the cool, calm professional stare. "Oh, my hell, I think I... Damn, I think I know where she is. Umm, I saw her. Shit. It was like I was looking through his eyes." Keller flattened his palms over his gut, his fingers scraping at his shirt. "It was like she was stabbing me. What the fuck's going on?"

"Calm down. You're an empath, Keller. That's all, and you just saw Candace Bratton. Where is she?" Isaiah asked.

It was interesting that Boniface had seen Candace, while Isaiah had only seen Chester. That meant Boniface was an empath, albeit an unwilling one on the verge of a meltdown.

"In... in an abandoned, shit. It's still happening. She's stabbing him again! We've got to stop her. She's at an abandoned service station—"

"North of the Navy Yard?" Isaiah asked. That made sense, Chester and Candace being in her old neighborhood, but wow. Like every other crime related to Candace, Isaiah hadn't seen that coming.

The perplexed agent's head bobbed. His eyes had gone wide and dazed as if he were seeing things he couldn't explain, which he most certainly was. "East Capitol Street Southeast. On the corner. It's a four-way stop. There's a service pit in the abandoned garage there, only water's seeped in over the years. Only a... a... there's a safe in the bottom of that pit, and... Damn!" He thumbed his chin as if he needed to punch something. "What the fuck's wrong with me!"

"That's where the five mil's been all this time," Tate interrupted, unfazed at Keller's spiraling anxiety.

"And where Candace is killing Chester Bratton right now," Isaiah declared. "Keller, calm down. There's nothing wrong with you, but you're coming with Agent Higgins and me. Tell your partners to transport Randall downtown. Be quick about it. We don't have time to waste."

"But... but..." The man stood there shell-shocked, his lips moving, but nothing intelligent coming out of his mouth.

"But nothing. You're with us," Isaiah told him firmly. "Get your gear. Now."

Chapter Thirty

"Go on, go. I'll be fine," Roxy assured Tucker. He'd received some kind of psychic phone call from Isaiah. Garrett Randall was now in custody and they'd also tracked the location of the five million, maybe Candace Bratton and her former father-in-law, Chester Bratton, too. Thank God. This joint operation might end happy after all.

"You're sure?" Tucker asked for the second time. He'd been pacing since his guys contacted him, and Roxy didn't blame him. The man was an all out alpha and anxious to be in the middle of the action, not hanging back in the safe zone, babysitting. He was an FBI director after all, and men like Tucker thrived on the adrenaline punch of a good bust. This was his moment to shine, and shine he should. Recovering five million dollars from a seven-year old heist, as well as apprehending the elusive perpetrators, was the bust of the century. He and his team deserved high fives all around.

Lifting one eyebrow, Roxy leveled her snarkiest glare at Isaiah's boss who had his hand on the doorknob to the garage. "I'm pretty sure I can handle two sleeping kids and a dog, now go. Once the kids get up, I want them to see your smug face on every national news station telling the world how it went down. You meant to hold a press conference anyway. Looks like today's that day."

The man was just like a little kid on Christmas morning. He glowed with the thrill of what his psychic team had accomplished, and didn't that tell Roxy all she needed to know? As deeply as she cared for Isaiah, their being together was not in the best interest of the FBI or the country. He had a far more important mission in life than she did, and he needed to be unencumbered by emotional attachments, so that miraculous psychic skill of his could function to capacity.

It hurt to face the truth, but their time together was over. She had to let him go, and Roxy would do just that. For Isaiah, she'd do anything.

Tucker cocked his head, studying her. "You're sure?" he asked yet again.

She growled instead of repeating herself. Damn, the man was dense.

"Okay, I'll go, but keep the doors locked. Don't let anyone inside. Call if you need me." He tossed a key fob at her, no doubt for the SUV Isaiah had driven home last night.

"Yeah, yeah, yeah," she muttered as she shooed Tucker out of her life and into the garage. "Tell Isaiah and Tate congrats on making a damned good bust when you see them. I'm proud of them."

Enough said. Tucker beat a straight line to the rear garage door and checked—yet again—that it was still secure. Why wouldn't it be? He'd triple-checked it with every perimeter walk he'd made. If nothing else, the big guy was a meticulous guard who took protection seriously. A tiny pinch in her gut told Roxy she might just miss his company once—if—he finally got gone.

He sent her a thumbs-up as he headed to the monster, red Challenger parked in the far stall. "Remember. Doors locked. Ears on," he barked before he dropped into the driver's seat and shut the car door.

She stayed at her post until he raised the garage door, revved that gloriously loud Hemi engine and cleared the driveway. As expected, the car laid rubber when it jumped to his command. She'd expected nothing less. He couldn't wait to get out of there, and she didn't blame him. Any crime scene would be more exciting than babysitting a couple of sleeping kids and their trusty mutt.

When the garage door settled into place and she was sure she was on her own, Roxy cocked her head and waited until the sturdy hydraulic locks hissed into place, signaling that Isaiah's place was once more secure. At last, the end of this joint operation was in sight. What began as an odd pairing of MPD with the Feds had worked. Little by little, justice was prevailing.

Kitty and Darrin could get on with their lives and whatever the future held for them. It had to be better than what Candace Bratton had put them through. Yet even as she thought that well-intentioned lie, Roxy knew better. The kids were headed for foster care, and didn't that suck rocks? The state made a lousy parent. Everyone knew that, and the unfortunate kids who went into the system didn't always end up in the best situations. Too many came out abused and neglected, worse than when they went in. There had to be a better way.

As far as Isaiah? Roxy kicked that heartache down the road, not crossing that bridge until she got there.

Alone at the end of another exhausting, yet interesting day, she double-checked the bedroom where Kitty and Darrin now lay sound asleep, him on his back in the sleeping bag on the floor with Nugget, Kitty on her side facing Roxy and still wearing her ball cap.

It gave Roxy pause to just stand there and watch. To think. Kitty craved a father's love as much as Darrin did, which explained why she'd worn the Nats cap to bed. She couldn't part with it. That silly thing meant something to the fatherless girl the moment Tucker'd tugged it out of his rear pocket and handed it to her. That was when he'd acknowledged that she existed and that she had feelings, that he'd recognized her worthy of a male's attention. Hell, she'd probably crush on Tucker for months, too, and Roxy didn't blame her. He had the makings of a really good dad. Roxy could tell. Tucker really wasn't so bad, once you got past—well, Tucker.

At last, Roxy snagged her duffel and headed for the bathroom. She locked herself in, then unbuckled her holster and hung it on the hook behind the door. It didn't take long to get out of her grimy uniform and into the shower.

After shampooing and conditioning her thick, long mane, she plaited it into a manageable braid down her back. Next she lathered body wash over herself, wishing Isaiah were there to do that. Just the thought of him showering with her, sliding his very capable hands over her shoulders and down her back, set her lady parts to tingling. If he were there, he'd stand behind her and cup her breasts and tell her how lovely she was. He'd nibble at her neck, his nose pressed hard against her skin. They'd kiss—*oh, how they'd kiss.* Before she knew it, he'd have her backed into the tiled corner and...

Roxy groaned at her need for all things Isaiah. It seemed the heart she'd once shielded from outside entanglements now had plenty of room for two kids, their dog, and—him. How had that happened?

Yet this thing with Isaiah was a fling. It had been from the start. He had a greater mission in life than settling down with a wife and two and a half kids, than settling for less. As much as Roxy liked the American dream, she knew the reality that went with it. The man of her fantasies was destined for greatness, and she was just an MPD beat cop through and through. She wouldn't hold him back.

With that reality faced and her decision made, she shaved what needed shaving. She towel dried her dripping wet braid until it was dry enough, then smoothed coconut body lotion over everything. Moisturizer for her face went next, then clean underwear and a bra, only these were cotton and white, nothing so audacious as the underthings she'd worn the day of the bank robbery. Although she had been glad for that leather thong in that broom closet. Recalling the groan that had vibrated out of Isaiah there in the dark still gave her goosebumps. He'd known then that she was no sweet, young thing, but man. What a surprise he'd been.

Don't go there...

Fighting her body's reaction to his memory, Roxy donned a simple pink T-shirt and her oldest, softest jeans, then a clean pair of socks. A cop in pajamas on the job was a fool, and Roxy Thurston was no fool—except where Isaiah was concerned.

She glared at her misty reflection in the fogged mirror. The woman staring back at her looked more like Mama Thurston. Wasn't that a nice surprise, to see her mother's face where once she'd just seen a perpetually angry woman with a gun and a hard job?

"Get a grip, girl," she told herself. "He's the important one, not you. Get back to work and get over him." She blinked back at herself and drew in a deep breath. Yeah. She'd done it before. She could do it again.

It wasn't until she'd strapped her holster back on that she felt more in control. Roxy headed for the living room with her boots, yet with every step, fragments of the dream she'd had upon waking that morning whispered to her, pricking her conscience.

She set her boots beside the couch as sweet remembrances of better days swamped her with the love she'd always felt as a child. They wrapped around her like the soft, warm blanket of her mother's arms. If there was one thing Roxy had that Kitty and Darrin didn't, it was Mama's love, and wasn't it odd to be thinking about that now?

Yet it seemed right. For years Roxy'd planned a hundred torturous ways to end Ritchie Gardner's life. The rat bastard deserved every one of them, and sweet Maria del Rosa Thurston deserved to be avenged for all she'd lost. Only now...

Maria del Rosa Thurston deserved to be remembered for more than just the way she'd died. A revenge killing that would end her only child's life in one way or the other seemed somehow hollow and trite. Roxy swallowed hard at the quandary her heart struggled with. Change was excruciatingly hard, and she faced one mighty course correction.

Pressing her hand to her heart, she let the better memories stored within its chambers wash over her. Her mother's perpetual smile at the end of her own hard workdays. The Spanish feasts she loved preparing for her *familia*. Her mouth-watering tomatillo enchiladas. The sounds Daddy made every single time Mama's homemade mole sauce hit his tongue. The scents of chili peppers roasting on the tiny barbeque grill she kept off the back porch.

Roxy's eyes watered at all those little things, those every day, ordinary things most modern women no longer wanted to bother with, were what had made Mama happy. That all she'd ever needed and wanted was the little cracker box home they'd lived in, the husband she'd adored, and the daughter she'd lived for. Humbling. Heart-wrenchingly humbling.

Roxy bowed her head, awash in the unfamiliar emotion, and so sure that Mama was smiling down at her from heaven, that a single stinging hot tear dripped onto her cheek. Lifting her chin, Roxy whispered to the ceiling, "I get it now. You deserve more than just a revenge killing. You deserve..." *Dare I say it?* "...grandchildren."

Roxy wiped one slender finger under her eye to catch the tears. Resolved, and with a higher purpose, she let her plans for Ritchie Gardner go—the plans she now knew had always been more about her than her mother.

"I miss you, Mama," she said as she scrubbed the hem of her T-shirt over her face. It was time to call home.

Daddy Thurston picked up on the first ring. "Roxy. What's wrong, little girl? Are you in trouble?"

Wasn't that just like him to assume the worst? "Nothing's wrong, Daddy. Just wanted to call and check in. Were you sleeping?"

"Don't lie to me. You've been too busy to call, so you must be on an important case. What's up? Can you talk about it? Is it dangerous?"

There he was, always trying to fix things, including her. "I am on an important case, Daddy, but don't worry. We've made some serious headway today. I hope to be home soon, and then I'll tell you everything I can. You might want to watch TV in case they air an FBI news conference until then."

"You're working with the Feds? How'd you manage that?" He sounded impressed, but that's because he had no idea what a pain in the ass the Feds were to work with.

Roxy smiled at his innocence. "I interrupted a bank robbery, but that's all I can say about it. Sorry I didn't call sooner. It has been a crazy couple of days."

"Don't worry about that, just take care of yourself, and come home to me when you're through."

"How's Toy?" she asked, needing to change the subject. Talking about her cat was safe.

"Ah, she's a lazy thing. We were taking a nap when you called, but she never budged when the phone rang. You know how she is. Fat and lazy as ever."

Roxy nodded as if she were there in her father's living room talking with him. "I love you, Dad."

"Okay, now you've got me worried. What's going on, Roxy? You really okay?"

"Yes, but, umm, I was wondering."

"Oh, oh, here it comes." She could hear the smile crinkling his face. Despite all he'd suffered, Hayden Thurston never stopped looking on the bright side of life.

"What would you think if I adopted a couple kids? A twelve-year-old girl and her ten-year-old brother?" She couldn't give him more specifics. Not yet. What she'd just asked was already a wild breach of MPD protocol, but she needed to hear what he thought.

He came through for her as always. "Sure. The more the merrier. Sounds like you've got two specific kids in mind. I know you can't tell me much, but what are their names?"

That much she could share. "Kitty and Darrin. They're good kids, Dad, but they're going into foster care at the end of this mission, and I can't bear what that means for them. They've already had a tough life, and they deserve better. Would it be too much trouble to bring them into your home? Be honest, because I'm really serious."

"I already told you my answer, Roxy, and I'm always honest, so stop asking. When do I get to meet them?"

"Not until this joint operation's finished, but would you mind getting a few things ready?" Her ears perked up at the sound of a high-powered car engine making the rounds in Isaiah's quiet neighborhood. "They'll both need their own beds eventually, but for now Kitty could sleep in my room with me, and—"

"And Darrin will room with me 'til we figure things out. Heck, baby girl, maybe it's time we pull up stakes and move to nicer, bigger digs. We've been talking about it for years now. This might be the incentive we need to get it done."

Get it done. His favorite saying. Roxy relaxed at the genuine love radiating through the connection with her father. Just like Mama, Hayden Thurston had always understood what was important in life. "Thanks, Dad. You're right. That might be just what we need to do. I'm so glad I called you." She tried to keep the wistfulness out of her tone, but it crept into her final words anyway.

"There's something else going on, and maybe it's this business you're in the middle of, but I can hear it in your voice. Something's bothering you. You know you can always talk to me. If there's anything I can do to help..." He let the invitation hang between them, but now wasn't the time to tell him about Isaiah. It was enough that her father knew her well enough to pick up on that vibe. That was the real reason she'd called, just to hear his calm voice of wisdom and reason and—his love.

"I'm fine," she assured him, "but you're right. There is something else I need to ask. The kids own a big dog. Nugget's some kind of a golden retriever/horse breed, and he'll be coming with them." She cringed at the thought of that four-legged monster in her father's already cramped house. Toy wouldn't be amused, but Nugget needed his boy and Roxy wouldn't leave him behind. Ah-uh. Where Darrin went, Nugget had to follow.

Her dad chuckled. "Like I said, little girl. It's time we find us a bigger place. I'll check out the listings in the paper and I'll start asking around. Sure be good if we could stay in the same neighborhood, though. Think about that and we'll dig in when you're ready."

She huffed a big sigh of relief. "Thanks, Dad. I'll let you know more when I know more. Are you doing okay? Taking your vitamins every day?"

"You sound just like your mom when you say things like that. Sure, I'm taking my vitamins, and I walk every day, too. By the way, a couple of your kids came by yesterday asking about you."

Roxy settled back in the corner of the couch, relaxed and glad she'd called. "Oh, yeah, which ones?" Her *kids* were the young men and women she taught self-defense to at the local community center near Saint Pat's. Most of them were in high school, but some were older college kids. She even taught a few housewives.

"That Vega boy and Valeree. You know the one I mean. The pretty blonde who turns red as a beet when she smiles."

"Jose's with Valeree?" Roxy hadn't seen that coming. Jose was one of five boys in his family. His father had died from a burst appendix when Jose was born, and his mother worked as a housekeeper for wealthy families in the District. Valeree's parents, on the other hand, were out-of-state lobbyists who'd recently moved to Crystal City, Virginia. They'd funded one street project after another to keep the homeless fed and in secure state housing, especially during the frigid winter months. "What'd they want?"

"Just to talk, or so they said, but if you ask me—"

"No," Roxy breathed. "They're in love?"

"Heh, heh, heh," Daddy Thurston purred. "Engaged is more like it if that sparkly ring on her left hand means anything. I told them you'd be home soon, that they needed to come back to tell you their good news in person."

"Aww!" Roxy nearly squealed. These two kids had been eyeballing each other since the day they'd signed up for her self-defense class. Both hard-working seniors with plenty of AP classes under their belts, they'd applied and been accepted by the same community college and planned to start summer quarter. "I'd love to call them. Can you get their numbers for me?"

"Now, Roxy," Daddy Thurston drawled. "There'll be time for socializing when you're home. Finish your job first. It's important, isn't it?"

As always, he was right. "It is. I love you, Daddy," she told him sincerely.

"And I love you, little girl. I'll leave the light on for you."

That was her clue to give him the same answer she'd given him since she'd been a little girl and babysat for the lady down the street. "And I'll be sure to turn it off when I get home. Bye, Dad."

"Bye, kiddo."

The call ended as that annoying high-powered engine roared up the street again. What? Was the pizza man lost? Already dark outside, its headlights glared at the opposite end of the cul-de-sac as if the driver behind the wheel was watching her.

"Jesus H. Christ," she hissed at it. "Do I need to shoot your tires out, so the rest of us can get some sleep tonight? So help me, if you wake my kids..." *My kids?* That made her smile. Yes. Kitty and Darrin might someday be her kids. The thought made her fist clench with the need to fist bump.

As if the driver had heard, the vehicle's engine roared to life. The vehicle never swerved and it never braked. Roxy barely had enough time to scramble off the couch before it jumped the curb and crashed Isaiah's front window and roared into his living room. Shattered glass flew like stinging hornets. She curled sideways to protect herself, while someone exited what she now knew was a monster of a truck. She couldn't see more than a man's shadow coming at her. The truck's headlights were on high beam. He reached out to help her. She thought.

Until everything went dark.

Chapter Thirty-One

"Shit. It's Chester Bratton," Isaiah muttered as he crouched over the bloody body of an adult male, around two hundred pounds, medium build, sprawled on the concrete floor on his back. Out of breath from running from Tate's SUV to the garage, Isaiah offered the obvious cause of death between fast breaths. "No knife present, but he's been stabbed. A lot. This guy suffered. There was no way we could've saved him even if we'd been here when it happened."

Tate leaned over Isaiah's back. "I'll say. She stabbed him at least a dozen times."

"Crime of passion," Keller added from where he paced at the open garage door. The agent was still freaked out that he'd seen the location of the murder in a vision, and that he'd been right. Arriving too late to save the deceased weighed on him. Isaiah didn't blame him. No one wanted to be a hero, not this way.

They'd arrived at the scene along with the army of first responders they'd notified on the short drive over: EMTs, two fire engines and their respective crews, several MPD cruisers. Some insightful officer had already rigged a portable set of spotlights, running off the nearest rig's generator, a smart decision considering the oil slick glistening off the surface of the service pit turned deadly swimming pool. The last thing this operation needed was for someone to fall in that and drown while gathering evidence.

Ky Winchester and his wife Eden had already notified Isaiah that they were in transit to the scene. Isaiah guessed right. Like he and Keller, Eden had heard Chester's distress signal, but the number one player in this mess was nowhere to be found. Candace Bratton.

Tate crouched alongside the body. Crime scene protocol demanded they not do the one thing that could solve this mystery and lead them to the perpetrator once and for all. They couldn't touch Chester's body in hopes of gathering any lingering psychic impression Candace might've left behind. Not that she'd left many impressions in the past, but Isaiah remained hopeful. She was bound to make a mistake one of these days.

So they crouched there under the stark, bright lights, while they studied the agony etched on Chester Bratton's whiskered face.

"He's the one you saw?" Tate asked in a hushed voice. "Are you sure?"

Other responders tended to listen in on the FBI's one and only psychic team's discussions. Isaiah didn't blame them. Psychics were a downright spooky oddity in the very controlled worlds of criminal investigation and forensics. So Isaiah, Tate, and Keller kept their voices low.

Isaiah nodded at Tate, but studied Chester. Had Candace known his whereabouts all this time? It wasn't like many wives were close to their fathers-in-law, were they? Isaiah hadn't a clue, but if Chester had agreed to meet her in the same place he'd hidden the money, had he also planned to share the five mil with her? Was that what this clandestine encounter was initially about?

Chester Bratton hadn't been spotted since he'd supposedly skipped town, but apparently, he'd been here all along. What thief strays too far from five million dollars? But why had he selected a hideout so close to Candace's home? All those questions gave rise to yet another. Did Kitty and Darrin know Chester? Would they recognize him if they saw him again? Had he been to their house? Did they maybe know him by another name? Was Nugget familiar with the deceased? And last, but not least, was the five million dollars really in the safe at the bottom of the pit like Keller had declared?

So yeah, Isaiah had a universe of questions. Just no answers.

Chester Bratton lay flat on his back in a lake of blood and gore. She'd only perforated his gut, and that alone was insightful. She'd wanted him to suffer. He'd been surprised by the attack, but the crime appeared preplanned and well organized. That meant she'd contacted Chester, and set the trap. Isaiah could almost hear the guile in her voice when she'd made that call, and like every other man, Chester came running to her aid.

Judging the viciousness of the wounds, she'd gotten what she'd wanted, namely the location of the five mil. But that conclusion gave Isaiah pause. In the part of the vision he'd seen, Chester had distinctly said, *'I can tell you where it is, just don't, God, please don't...'* followed by, *'If you kill me now, you'll never know!'* Was this murder even about the money?

Isaiah snapped out of it when the side of Tate's boot made definite contact with his shin. *Ouch.*

"Don't zone out on me," the big guy warned quietly. "Folks are watching you. Now, answer me, are you sure Chester Bratton's the man you saw in your vision?"

"Yes, I saw him, but Keller..." Isaiah jerked his head to where Special Agent Boniface still stood, his hands clasped behind his back and rocking on the balls of his work shoes like he'd rather be anywhere else than here with a couple of psychics. Trying to keep his distance, and still undone by what—and who—he'd just realized he was, the man was obviously a stronger clairsensitive than Isaiah. "He might've seen more than he realizes. Get him over here."

"Boniface," Tate called out, waving the frazzled agent closer to the heart of the scene.

Keller obeyed, albeit he moved toward them woodenly. Reluctantly. Judging his ramrod posture and the cut of his hair, Keller was former military, but man, was he rattled. Still at attention and bristling with angst, he met Isaiah's gaze without blinking. "Yes, sir?"

Isaiah curled his index finger, beckoning the man down to his side. "I need your expert opinion."

"You bet." Keller crouched to his haunches at Isaiah's right, his wrists on his knees but his fingers interlocked in what Isaiah recognized for what it was. Denial. Keller didn't want to be a psychic, yet he still asked, "What can I do for you, sir?"

He was no new recruit. Isaiah knew damned well Keller had seen worse things than this dead body in his military career, but what was happening to him now was extraordinarily out of the ordinary. No one expected to wake up a regular guy in the morning and end up a full-blown psychic by nightfall.

"Stop calling me sir, for one thing. Name's Isaiah Zaroyin," Isaiah said as he offered a handshake to seal the deal. He'd no more than touched the agent's fingers when the image of what Keller had seen rolled through him loud and clear, confirming the physical evidence.

Candace hadn't just stabbed Chester. She'd stabbed him with glee, twisting the knife up and into his gut, all but punching the blade into him until his blood dripped off her hands and ran off the knife handle. She hadn't answered his pleas and hadn't hesitated for one second when he'd offered to tell her where the five mil was.

When at last he'd dropped to his knees, she'd knelt with him, but only to deliver more strikes until he was breathing his last. Candace pushed him flat to his back then and spat into his face, "Twelve! Goddamn you, twelve! That's what I owe you, one cut for every year of her worthless life, you fuckin' liar! You promised you'd always be there, but you never visited, not once! How's it feel to be lied to, huh? How's it feel?"

Isaiah dropped Keller's hand. He opened his mouth to report what he'd seen, but Keller beat him to it. "Chester Bratton's Kitty Bratton's father."

Roxy woke up with a rag wrapped tight around her jaw and in her mouth, a bright light burning her throbbing retinas. Closing her eyelids as quickly as she'd opened them, she mumbled past the rag for someone to turn the truck's headlights off. She could see enough. This was the same truck that had crashed into Isaiah's house, and whoever'd done that, now had her restrained.

Awareness came slowly. Seated on a wooden chair, her arms were stretched behind her back. Her wrists were cuffed not zip-tied, and, damn, her ankles were cuffed as well. Stretching her aching back as far as she could brought no relief. She was in trouble and... *Where the hell am I?*

The wicked pain in her neck prevented her from turning to take in the rest of her surroundings. Her throat was drier than dirt and raw as hell. Kitty and Darrin were nowhere in sight. She called out to them, but that ended in muffled growls only. *Where the hell are my kids?*

Whoever'd raced that stupid truck through Isaiah's supposedly secure neighborhood and into his living room was behind this. He had the kids. Maybe Nugget, too, and what about Leonard Sweeny? The driver would have had to get past him first. Was that kindly old gentleman hurt?

"Show yourself," she demanded in her snarkiest tone. The rag in her mouth made it not the least bit threatening, but she thought, *'Coward!'*

A shadow crossed between her and the headlights. "It's about time," a man's voice murmured. He walked to her with a swagger, like he had all the time in the world. "Took you long enough to wake up. Didn't think I hit you that hard."

"You hit me?" she mumbled, lifting her chin in defiance. He approached in a dark blur of shadow, punctuated by the eye-splitting high beams at his rear. "Who are you? Tell me," she ordered. But holding her head up just to keep that all-important, officer-of-the-law eye contact was as difficult as talking through the rag in her mouth.

When the shadowy man crouched at her knee, he placed one hefty palm on the highest part of her thigh as if in warning. *The nerve!* His fingers clenched, triggering the clear-as-the-night-it-happened image of Mario Forsythe to center stage in Roxy's poor battered head. She was back in that restroom, only this time she was restrained and Mario had hold of her. There was no hope of rescue. There was no h-h-hope of anything!

Bet me.

Roxy shook Mario out of her head. Blinking against the glare of those damned headlights, she planned her next move, which wouldn't involve laying down and taking it.

"You're a police officer," he said as he tipped her chin up with his other hand. "Officer Roxy Thurston, huh? It's a good thing you're no man. I might have something to worry about then."

She had plenty to say on that stupid opinion, but settled for a mumbled, "Where are my kids?" It didn't come out snarky like she meant it to, but he got the point.

One upper lip lifted in what started as a smile but ended in a sneer. "*Your* kids? Now they're *your* kids? I don't think so. Candy Bratton only knows how to make bastards, but I'm guessing you already know that seeing as how you're an *officer of the law* and everything." Dropping his hands to his knees, he sat back on his heels, staring at her.

"Who are you?" she asked, squinting to decipher where she'd seen his face before. With the pain in her head and her vision as wonky as it was, she couldn't tell for sure. The guy's facial features blurred in and out of focus. If he'd hold still, maybe she could identify the creep. Turning the bright head lights out would certainly help.

"Bob Bratton at your service, *Officer Roxy Thurston*." He said that with an annoying head swagger. "Sit back and rest while you can. Things are only gonna get better."

Bob Bratton? Candace's ex? "What'd you do to Kitty and Darrin?" she demanded, only it came out more like, "Muh mer meme ma mar." *Damn this crap in my mouth!*

Bob lifted to his feet and took a sideways step away as if he had nothing more to say. But then he stopped short, cocked his right arm back, and... *SLAP!* His palm made stinging contact with the already tender side of her face.

Roxy's poor pounding head bounced off her shoulder. Bright, glittering stars phased in and out at her peripheral. Struggling to stay conscious, she swallowed the blood that welled in her mouth from biting her tongue.

"You're not in charge here, Officer," Bob Bratton declared, "and the sooner you get that straight, the better off you'll be. This is my game and my rules, so shut the fuck up. I'll tell you what's happening next when I'm damned good and ready, but baby…" He stepped back in close to trace an icy finger down her jaw to her neck. Fisting her collar, he tugged her off the chair and into his face.

She refused to shiver in fright. That was precisely what cowards like him wanted. Her shoulders screamed at the contortion of the angle of her body and his hold on her. Her back arched against her will, but one chance—just one!—was all she needed to kick this guy's ass and save her kids.

At last he brought his nose in close enough to make out enough features to identify him in a line-up, if he lived that long. Dishwater-blond buzzcut. Clean-shaven. Rectangular face structure. Angular chin. A scar zigged through his left eyebrow and up his forehead. The man might be termed ruggedly handsome if you got past his penchant for kidnapping and battering women. He had pockmarked cheeks, but plump lips, complete with the perfect Cupid's bow that foolish, infatuated women dreamed of. Not Roxy.

She forced her mind off what might happen in her future and concentrated on breathing as he whispered in her ear, "Trust me, Doll Face. I've been ready for this night for years."

D-D-Doll Face? I should've known. Bob Bratton and Garrett Randall are in this together.

Chapter Thirty-Two

"Say what?" Tucker bellowed over the quiet din of first responders at their work and the noise from their heavy engines idling on the street.

Still crouched with Tate and Keller over Chester Bratton's body, Isaiah caught the wicked death glare from the doorway the second his alpha predator boss arrived. Like the total alpha he was, Tuck's hands were on his hips and his chest was puffed out. Since the medical examiner had arrived within minutes of Tucker, Isaiah and Tate disengaged from the immediate crime scene and crossed the garage to confer with their boss.

Isaiah tagged Keller to join them as the busy MPD men and women stepped aside to clear a path for the FBI team. Amused at the local officers' deference to their federal counterparts, Isaiah led with intros.

"Boss, Special Agent Keller Boniface. Keller, Director Tucker Chase, your new boss."

"Explain," Tucker snapped without batting an eye or acknowledging the latest addition to his psychic team.

Tate jerked his chin at Boniface. "Keller had a vision. He saw Candace Bratton stab Chester Bratton. Mentally. The same way you just heard him say that Chester Bratton was Kitty's father."

A hint of chagrin shifted over Tucker's face at Tate's good catch. There was no way Tucker could've heard what Keller said across the noisy garage. "True that. And?"

"And I saw Candace tell Chester: *'Twelve cuts for every year of her life.'*" Isaiah left the profanity out as his gaze scrolled back to the deceased, now being skillfully maneuvered into a black vinyl body bag by the ME and her male assistant. "Not sure he knew he had a daughter though, are you?" he asked Keller.

"Umm..." Agent Boniface shook his head, but Isaiah got the impression he'd rather have scratched it, but didn't want to make a bad first impression on his new boss. Isaiah also sensed Keller didn't care for Tucker, but who did at first glance? Nobody Isaiah knew.

Still catching his balance, Keller looked Tucker in the eye. "Director Chase, it's good to finally meet you. I'm new at this psychic stuff, but no, sir. I detected nothing to indicate that Chester Bratton was aware he had a child with Candace. All I saw was the insane look on her face when she ended him. She's a cold-blooded killer, sir."

Tucker glared at the newest addition to his band of psychics before he leveled a stern eye at Isaiah. "Then why'd you guys let her go? Where is she?"

"I wish I knew," Isaiah replied evenly, "but she's not transmitting, and stop baiting us, Boss. You know as well as I do that we didn't *let her go*. It was Chester's cry for help that both Keller and I received. That's what brought us here in the first place. Chester probably didn't know it, but he projected tremendous energy into the universe in the last seconds of his life. Like Ky Winchester did the first time he met Eden."

Met, as in psychically found each other across time and thousands of miles of space. At the time, Ky'd been near death, strung by his wrists to an overhead hook in a rat-infested prison cell on the outskirts of Kabul, Afghanistan. It was Eden who'd heard his mental prayer to die. It was her psychically reaching out to him from the East Coast of the United States and all the way to that prison, that got him through what might've been the last night of his life. Coincidentally, another Marine imprisoned in that same death trap did the actual rescuing the very same night. But it was Eden who Ky had resolved to live for. She gave him the strength to hang on. Anyone who saw them together today knew that.

"We just couldn't get here fast enough to save him, sir," Keller offered quietly, his eyes still on

Tucker, his hands at his side. The man was literally standing at attention as if he were still in the military.

That seemed to impress Tucker. "But you did apprehend Randall. That's something," he said.

"Not nearly enough," Tate added. "Candace Bratton's still on the loose, and she's more dangerous than any of the guys in this mess."

"But there *is* a safe below the surface of this murky shit, right, Keller?" Tucker stabbed a finger at the service pit. "Are you absolutely sure?"

For that split second, Isaiah wasn't sure who was trying to impress who, the former SEAL or the former... *Wait for it.* Isaiah skimmed the surface of Keller's memories. *Oh damn. Keller's a former Army Ranger. This can't be good.*

"Yes, sir," Keller said with certainty, pointing to the opposite end of the rectangular pit. "I saw it and it's in that corner. I've already called a hazmat service in to drain the pit, at which point, our men will retrieve the safe and remove it to FBI Headquarters downtown DC before they open it. It's the size of a five-foot locker, made of galvanized metal with rubber seals that haven't corroded. It's sitting on four fist-sized rubber feet. There's a chain around it." Keller looked to the engine hoist at the ceiling. "No doubt that's how Bratton got it down there, and sir." Keller's Adam's apple bobbed. "The money's still dry."

"You mean to tell me that Chester Bratton intentionally hid five million in a water-filled pit?"

Tucker's tone had shifted from snark to honest inquiry.

"Yes, sir, I do. It's the perfect hiding place, and I'll bet ten-to-one Chester Bratton owns this service station, too. It's only vacant because he wanted it that way."

Isaiah watched the two men size each other up as Keller began to settle down and fit in. He'd make a good addition to the team. Isaiah interrupted the staring contest with, "I'll take those odds, Keller, and I'll raise you another ten. Want to bet Chester Bratton also owned Candace Bratton's shitty little place down the road? Want to bet he's kept watch on her all this time, either just because she had custody of his grandkids or—?"

"He knew Kitty was his daughter," Tate interjected. "The bastard's been sitting on money that could've made those kids' lives easier, but instead" — he waved his hands at the glimmering pool of muck in the chilly room— "he settled for that."

By then, Chester Bratton's body was encased in the body bag and laying on the ME's gurney. The FBI's one and only psychic team had nothing to be proud of. Candace Bratton was still on the run. Eventually, the five mil would all go back to First National. None of it would benefit Kitty and Darrin, and Chester Bratton was dead. That Garrett Randall now cooled his heels in an FBI cell seemed a damned small consolation.

"We're missing something, guys," Isaiah murmured. He'd been racking his brain all day at the niggling sensation that all was not accounted for. Knowing that Jack Fillion was Darrin's father, and if Chester Bratton truly was Kitty's father, there seemed to be no loose ends in this robbery scheme besides Candace. Right? How far could a woman drenched in her murdered lover's blood get? Someone had to have seen her coming or going.

"I'll put out an APB for Candace Bratton," Tucker declared, his gaze on Isaiah because he'd had the same thought. "We'll release her picture to the press to get their support locating her. Just wait. You'll see. It's only a matter of time now."

Isaiah shook his head at the canned, politically correct answer that he wasn't buying. Nothing had changed in Candace Bratton's MO since day one. She'd manipulated the robbery scene at the bank the same way she'd manipulated Kitty's asthma attacks. She hadn't been what Isaiah thought he'd seen then, and she wasn't now. There was no damsel in distress behind those innocent gray eyes, and certainly no loving mother. Yet Candace had carried every one of those misdirects off with precision, and he'd fallen for them. All of them. Like a naïve Boy Scout instead of a highly trained federal agent, he'd given her the benefit of the doubt every time.

Well, no more. "We need warrants for all the traffic cams in the immediate area," Isaiah ordered. "And I want four agents sitting outside her house until this thing's done. She might go back home. We need to be prepared if she does. I want more guards for Roxy and the kids, too. Four ought to do it. And bait, Boss…" He turned to his very surprised director, but Isaiah was on a roll and this was important, damn it. "You know as well as I do that Candace wants the five million enough to kill for it. Then let's give it to her. No one but us knows it's at the bottom of that pit, so hold your press conference. Tell the world how the case is going, but dangle that five mil in front of her nose like a carrot. Explain that the money hasn't been recovered. Spin a lie, Boss. I know you can do it. Give her an FBI sob story. Tell her the five mil may never be located. Make her feel safe, Boss. Tempt her to come out in the open. You can do it. Understood?" Isaiah's toes were tapping by the time he finished, but this was the only way forward.

Tucker scrubbed a hand over his chin, and Isaiah was pretty sure he did that to hide that smirky smile of his. "Did you just call Candace Bratton an ass, and" —he glanced at Tate with one brow spiked like the devil— "did you call me a liar, Zaroyin? To my face?"

"So what if I did?" Isaiah shot back at him, even as he blinked at his own audacity that had literally, come out of nowhere. But he wasn't stopping now. He did the one thing Tucker had taught him, and had apparently taught him well. Isaiah didn't back down.

The barest hint of a smile curled the corners of Tucker's big mouth. "You're right, Agent Zaroyin," he said evenly. "I have been thinking about why Candace

Bratton didn't take the cash. Answer seems simple. She couldn't get to it, but are we sure she knows it's down there? There's no sense in broadcasting a lie until we're sure that she does, in fact, know precisely where the five million is, now is there?"

All eyes turned on Keller.

Talk about a deer-in-the-headlights look. "Why are you looking at me?" he asked as his palm came to rest on his stomach again. Empathy worked that way. A true empath suffered from the same physical pains the person transmitting did. Right now Keller's expanded mind was telling him he'd been stabbed and that he needed help, while his very logical brain kept proving the exact opposite. That was why Eden had collapsed on her kitchen floor the evening she'd intercepted Ky's prayer to die. She'd felt every bit of his pain as if she'd been hung by her arms and tortured.

Special Agent Keller would soon have ulcers if he didn't learn how to separate fact from fiction. "All I saw was her stabbing Chester Bratton and grunting when she did it. Seemed all she wanted was for him to die, and she screamed at him for lying to her the last twelve years. I take it I was right. Kitty Bratton's twelve years old and Chester Bratton, not Bob Bratton, was her father."

Isaiah, Tucker, and Tate nodded in unison. At that moment, the ME rolled by with the deceased securely protected within the body bag. Isaiah eyed the puddle of blood left behind. *What if...? Maybe... Just maybe...*

"Guys," he hissed. "Cover me. I need a minute or two." *I hope.*

As a team, Tucker, Tate, and Keller followed Isaiah. When he knelt at ground zero where Chester had died, they stood between him and the remaining MPD officers still at the scene.

Isaiah leaned into the space where Chester's body had been laying. Closing his eyes, Isaiah disregarded the Bureau's stringent protocols as he delved both hands into the remaining puddle of evidence. The blood and gore had gone cold, but a psychic trail lingered.

Chester's aura rose up around his fingers in a murky blue mist that faded to gray then glimmered with blue again. Poor, poor Chester Bratton. At one time, he'd been an honest man. A hard worker. But when his young wife died an untimely death, he'd lost his way. Burdened with a son he couldn't seem to love, he'd turned to petty theft at first, then developed a genuine talent for picking locks and safes. He had, it seemed, a light touch, and he'd left an even lighter trail.

His reputation for safe cracking grew in the dark underbelly of big cities where crime operated as easily as city governments did in the light of day. Yet something was missing in his successful life, and he knew it. Until the day his son brought home his pretty new wife. Enter the new Mrs. Robert Bratton.

Candace. What a breath of fresh air she was. Chester almost began to love his son again. Almost. But he loved Candace more, and she loved him in return. Or so he'd thought.

Isaiah sucked in a breath of the damp, cement smell in the abandoned garage, now mingled with the cloying, coppery scent of blood, and the rancid sting in his nose of leaked stomach acids. Chester hadn't expected to die here tonight. The old fool knew he'd fathered a daughter. That was why he'd bought the abandoned garage, to live in and to hide his treasure, yes, but also to stay close to Candace and her children, yet far enough from them that his sins could never hurt them.

But somehow Bob had found out that Kitty wasn't his flesh and blood, that he'd been betrayed in the worst ways possible—by his father and his wife. After that, the tangled web Chester had carefully spun to protect the woman and child he'd loved unraveled quickly.

With a start, Isaiah jerked his hands from the sticky, icy puddle. The concrete floor materialized first, then the sensation of a wall at his back. His team still stood guard at his rear. His knees ached, and he honestly didn't know how long he'd knelt there. Psychic journeys weren't measureable by time or space.

It was Tucker who offered a hand up, after he carefully encased Isaiah's hands in evidence bags, tugged him into his side and said, "I've got you, son."

And there it was, the link with an older *brother* that Isaiah had forever craved since his mother's death and his father's betrayal, the same type of link that Chester had craved with his daughter. The one he'd never been allowed to experience, first because Bob hated his father on sight; second, because Candace hated and used everyone.

Chester had never held his pretty little girl named Kitty. Not even once. Like Jack Fillion, he'd loved her from afar. Until the day he'd tangled with Garrett Randall and his brothers. Then, unbeknownst to Candace, he'd moved into her neighborhood and he'd settled for the unrequited love of a man wanted by the law.

"He... he... " Isaiah hiccupped in a jolt of frigid air, for a moment dizzy from the journey he'd just taken. "He t-told her where the money is. Candace. She knows. She also knows he loved Kitty. She just... she just didn't care."

"The woman's stark raving crazy," Tucker muttered as he and his team provided a hulking, protective escort for Isaiah from the garage and into Tate's SUV. He reached past Isaiah to secure the seatbelt for him, but by then, the cold had taken over. Isaiah shivered, his breath a smoky cloud. Tate came up with a blanket from somewhere while Agent Keller stood behind Tucker, anxiously waiting to offer a—a hand. For some reason that was damned funny. Isaiah suppressed the urge to laugh out loud. At the moment, he seemed to have plenty of h-h-hands.

"Take him downtown," Tucker ordered Tate, "and keep him warm. I want everything he says recorded, the blood evidence bagged and tagged, and I want him rehydrated and fed by the time I get there. Take good care of him."

"Always do, Boss," Tate replied gruffly.

Isaiah let his head drop to the back of his seat, exhausted to his core. "She knows where the money is, Boss. She knows."

"And now, so do we." Tucker slapped Isaiah's knee like a brother who always—always—had his back, and damn it. Isaiah blinked at that simple, but powerful, tough guy contact. It didn't last more than a couple seconds, but apparently, mind-numbing psychic journeys made him emotional, too. The thing was that Tucker embodied all the honorable traits Isaiah strived to become. Okay, so they came wrapped up in a ton of male testosterone and bullshit, too, but damn. Isaiah ducked his cheek to his shoulder before he made a fool of himself and that tear got away. Men didn't cry. Another Tucker Chase rule.

"You okay, kid?" Tucker asked, his voice gentler now as he ducked low to read the only agent he called *kid*. Even that simple nickname hit Isaiah in the heart. Tucker used a lot of expletives in his daily communications, but damned few nicknames.

Isaiah nodded. "You bet, Boss," he said hoarsely. "D-don't take all night. We've got plans to make."

Tucker nodded, slammed the door, and away Tate and Isaiah went.

"You sure you're okay?" Tate asked once he pulled into traffic. Instead of heading north to hook into Pennsylvania Avenue, he ducked south to I-695, then passed the on ramp to the interstate, and hooked a right onto M Street SW.

Isaiah knew Tate was buying time, taking the long way home, so to speak. Letting Isaiah gather his wits after the emotional deluge from Chester's memories.

"You like this drive," Isaiah deduced correctly. He knew Tate like a brother. Another brother. Damned if that didn't cause more tears at the brim of Isaiah's tired eyes. For an only child to be surrounded by brothers of this mighty caliber was a gift from the universe Isaiah could never have imagined when he'd lost his mom. He thought he'd lost everything that night and the lonely months that followed, yet here he was. Part of a brotherhood like no other.

"I like the waterfront," Tate answered thoughtfully. "You can see the river in a minute."

Sure enough, M Street curved right into Maine Avenue SW, and the Potomac River, with all its watercraft, lights, and wharf-side businesses, sprang into view. Angling left through the heavy late night traffic on Seventh Street SW, Tate dropped into the District's latest and greatest booming enterprise: *The Wharf DC*. Tourists flocked to the nightlife here. Washington's finest patrolled the waterfront, making it a trendy, secure destination any time of the year.

Isaiah sagged into the heated seat, his head turned to the right as he took in the glittering sights. He'd known this part of the Potomac had been renovated into a spectacular sight, but he'd never once eaten at one of the fine restaurants or pubs, much less taken a date here. He'd been too busy with his job as a career FBI psychic and analyst. It hurt to realize that the same thing had also driven Abraham Zaroyin. His job.

His father had never cheated on his mom, yet in a way, he had, simply because he'd chosen to spend his time on a drone project that, in the end, ruined him and got his wife killed. Destroyed his family. Turned his only child into a lonely boy with nowhere to turn and no one to turn to.

At the next corner, a gregarious patrol cop lifted a gloved hand in greeting as Tate drove by. Isaiah waved back, and suddenly his heart ached for Roxy. He'd left her alone with Tucker and the kids, but now, late at night, she was the only one protecting what he knew was the greatest treasure on Earth. The kids. His home. And her.

"Chester Bratton had everything," Tate murmured, apparently lost in the same melancholy. He'd had a tough go when he'd lost his mom, too. His dad had never recovered, just walked out of their cabin in Alaska one day and disappeared. In that tragedy, Isaiah and Tate were the same. They'd been forced to cope with gut-sucking grief and loss alone, and they'd done it as twelve-year old boys. Much like twelve-year old Kitty Bratton would have to do now that her mother might face federal charges and prison time, if Candace were ever apprehended. If she lived.

"I want to go home," Isaiah told his best bud earnestly. "Don't take me downtown, Tate. Take me home." *I want to see Roxy. I need to see her.*

Tate offered the best grunt Isaiah had ever heard—right before he said, "Hell, yeah. Where'd you think we were going?"

Brothers. Nothing like them in the universe.

Roxy had no idea what time it was or how long she'd been out before her rude introduction to Bob Bratton. That she'd awakened somewhere other than Isaiah's house told her she'd suffered a concussion. The throbbing beat in her head didn't contradict her conclusion, but Jesus H. Christ, she was freezing. The flimsy T-shirt she'd changed into after her shower was dirty and wet, from what, she wasn't sure, but she smelled of sweat and—fear.

The last thing she remembered was Bob's truck driving into Isaiah's front room and glass shattering, flying everywhere. She'd scrambled out of the way. Everything went black after that.

She had no idea where she was or if the kids were close by. They had yet to make a sound if they were, and their silence worried her. The kids should be scared and borderline frantic by now—like she was. Her tired brain shifted to worrying about Nugget and Sweeny before it circled back to Kitty and Darrin. *Where are they? Why hurt two little kids and a dog?*

There was no sense calling out to them. The rag around her head not only made conversation impossible, but the coarse fabric continually wicked all excess moisture away from her mouth, tongue, and lips where she desperately needed it. It chafed like a bugger and her lips were already cracked and bleeding. Dying of thirst became a very real possibility. It wouldn't take long as parched as Roxy's throat had become over the last few hours.

That might be what Bob intended. Torture without lifting a finger. It'd certainly make for a slow death. Maybe that was why he hadn't come back. Maybe he'd left the truck running to trick her. No one knew where she was. Only Bob Bratton.

Damn, the wicked thoughts that assailed a woman in the middle of dark and ugly nights.

Twisting her stiff neck, Roxy earnestly tried to locate any landmark that would help her get her bearings, but the glare from those damned high beams made sight impossible.

Dark trees swelled up around her, blocking most of her view of the night sky. A few stars glittered from the midnight blackness, but there was no moon, and the only real light came from the headlights of the truck Bob had left running. *The jerk.*

Diesel fumes drifted her direction. Aching from the chill, she shifted her backside on the hard wooden seat as she strained forward, testing her restraints. Yeah, not going anywhere. There was no way she could lift her arms over the chair back, and the cuffs between her ankles weren't only linked together by a short chain between them, they were also chained to the rung between the chair legs.

But Roxy was one of the District's finest. She'd been in worse situations before. Remember Mario Forsythe? Hawthorne High? The women's restroom in Hawthorne High? First National and a dozen other scenarios stood up for her attention. You're damned right. She was a survivor and Bob Bratton had no idea who he'd messed with.

Stiffening her arms and shoulders, she leaned forward and willed her hands to be smaller, to contract enough to slide out of the metal cuffs. All she needed was one free hand, and she'd be home safe. Criminals did it all the time. If they could break out of handcuffs, she could, too, but—*shit, shit, shit!* All she got for her effort was two scraped raw wrists, a pulled muscle from straining her shoulder so hard, and possibly a cracked tooth from grinding her jaw.

What now? She growled through the annoying and slimy rag between her teeth. *Now you try, try again. And again! You never quit and you bide your time because good old Bob will be back soon, and then... and then...*

Then what? Obviously, Bob Bratton had an ax to grind with Candace, and Roxy completely understood that. She hadn't much use for Candace Bratton, either, but the witch wasn't here, and kidnapping and threatening an officer of the law to get back at an ex-wife made no sense. Whatever Bob planned to do to Roxy surely wouldn't matter to Candace.

Come on, think! Shuddering with anger, Roxy realized her only recourse, and she had to do it before Bob came back. Closing her eyes, she blocked the fear snapping at her heels and she projected her heart and soul into the great beyond, at least, she hoped that was what she was doing. *Not a psychic here, remember? Just an officer of the law who needs an assist in the worst way.*

Swallowing hard to force a modicum of saliva past her parchment dry tongue, she sent her first psychic message to the man she loved. *'I don't know where Kitty and Darrin are, Isaiah, and, okay, yeah, I'm scared. Sure hope you get this message, cuz I can't even tell you where I am, but I trust you. You know I do. Come find me, Mr. Psychic Dude. I love you and I'm sorry I didn't tell you before now, but I do, and I think you've known it for a while. I honest to God love you, Isaiah Zaroyin, and if you asked me to marry you, I'd jump your bones to prove it.'*

A twig snapped to her left and Roxy ended with a frantic, *'Hurry, Isaiah! He's coming back. I need you! N-n-now!'*

Chapter Thirty-Three

Isaiah woke from a bad dream he couldn't remember, but the negative energy it left in its wake niggled at the back of his mind that all wasn't right, that Roxy was angry or tired or—something. It could simply be the residue of Tucker's frustration when he couldn't reach Isaiah psychically. The boss would be plenty angry that his orders had been defied, but some things were worth the pain of reprisal. Seeing Roxy tonight was one of them.

"You're awake," Tate noticed.

"How much farther?" Isaiah squinted into the glare of oncoming freeway traffic to get his bearings.

"ETA in five. Just passed Trucker's Corner." The truck stop.

"You do know you'll have to process my hands in the garage before I can go into my house, don't you?"

"Already thought of that," Tate replied easily. "Stop worrying. I keep a kit in the back. We'll have the evidence bagged and tagged just like Chase wants in no time."

Isaiah cringed. "Has he been in contact with you?"

Tate nodded. "Like I said, stop worrying. I let him know where we were headed an hour ago. He'll be by when he and Keller finish up with Garrett Randall."

"That might take all night. Have they got anything worthwhile out of him yet?"

"Nah. He lawyered up like you thought he would. His aunt's on her way."

"Sylvia Delgado got him off last time. She could do it again."

Tate shot Isaiah a sideways glare. "Am I hearing you right? Maybe you'd better go back to sleep. No way will Randall go free on the charges he's facing this time around. Attempted bank robbery is a federal offense. So's extortion, attempting to bomb anything in DC proper, taking and threatening hostages, to name a few."

"Yeah. You're right. I am beat," Isaiah admitted as Tate veered onto the off ramp. He couldn't wait to see the look on Roxy's face. A hug would have to wait until his hands were free, but when they were...

"Holy shit," Tate hissed as he pulled onto the neatly trimmed lawn between the road in and the pasture fence that lined it.

Isaiah bolted upright, his plastic bag covered fingers gripping his knees. Police cars were everywhere, but the guard shack that Sweeny had religiously occupied until tonight was gone. Obliterated. Broken glass and twisted pieces of lumber littered the expanse now barricaded behind yellow police tape.

"Looks like something exploded," Tate offered.

"Uh-uh. No scorch mark," Isaiah muttered as he wrenched the side door open. He was out of the vehicle before its wheels stopped rolling.

"Wait up," Tate ordered, but the time for waiting was over. Isaiah pulled the plastic off his hands and tucked them into his pockets so he wouldn't alarm anyone.

Tate caught up to him before he made it to the first officer on scene. "Not on my watch, you don't. Back in the SUV, Isaiah. Let me find out what went on here. Then I'll drive you to your house, and you won't end up in the local jail for being the ax murderer you look like."

Isaiah stopped in his tracks. "You might be right."

"I am right. Trust me. I'll be right back."

Isaiah made an about face and climbed back into the SUV to wait. He'd contaminated the evidence Tucker had so carefully preserved, but Isaiah wasn't worried. It wasn't the only blood evidence. The ME had the body.

It didn't take long for Tate to return after talking with three of the officers present. "No explosion," he reported. "Just some wild-assed guy in a souped-up truck who couldn't see to drive straight. The police are still looking for him for a possible DUI."

"What about Sweeny, the old guy who mans the guard shack?"

"Would that be Leonard Sweeny?"

"Yes. Leonard," Isaiah murmured as the bad feelings from his dream slithered up his back again.

"Leonard Sweeny's fine," Tate replied, "and we can drive around this mess if we're careful, but be prepared. One of them said there's been more trouble up ahead. We might have to park and go in on foot if we can't get by the emergency equipment."

"Go," Isaiah breathed, his heart climbing up his throat for no apparent reason. "Go, go, go!" He felt Tate's gaze on him, but he had to see Roxy. Now. Something wasn't right and it had to do with...

"Son-of-a-bitch!" Tate hissed as the SUV jerked to a full stop.

Isaiah took off running. Every last emergency vehicle was parked on his front lawn. Blue, red, and yellow hazard lights flashed everywhere, but Isaiah had to know. Shouldering his way through EMTs with empty gurneys, he stopped the first police officer he ran into. "This is my house. What happened here?"

"You're Isaiah Zaroyin?" the sharp-eyed man asked as his hawk eyes scanned Isaiah's bloody hands before he met his eyes.

Isaiah answered the unspoken question by flashing his FBI badge. "Yes, I'm FBI Special Agent

Isaiah Zaroyin, now what happened? Where is everyone? Roxy and the kids, where are they?"

"Now hold on, son," the officer said as he held both palms forward as if trying to placate a frantic homeowner. "There was no one in the house when we arrived on the scene." He jerked his chin at the hook and ladder straddling the curb. "You can ask Chief Harrington over there. His men made a thorough search after they secured the gas lines. For a while, we thought we might have a fire, but we got lucky. All's well that ends well."

Isaiah ran a quick hand over his head. "Then where are the woman and children who were in this house earlier today?"

The police officer shook his head. "Like I said, the place was empty by the time we rolled on scene. I'll check with dispatch. Maybe they're at one of the neighbors' homes?"

Isaiah knew better. As hard as he tried, he detected no sweet whisper of Roxy's aura in the immediate area. No psychic hint of Kitty's or Darrin's, either. "My security cameras. I need inside to check the footage off my security cameras. That'll tell us both what we need to know."

The man scratched the back of his head, lifting his cap and pushing it over his forehead as if he wasn't sure that was permissible.

"You can have a copy of the footage for evidence when I'm finished," Isaiah offered, ready to do anything to get inside. "Please. I need to know what happened."

Grimacing, the man nodded. "Fine. But I go with you."

"Yeah, sure." Isaiah tripped past the police tape and through the debris of what had once been, he'd thought, the most secure house in town. Guess not.

Yet again, there were no scorch marks to indicate an explosion had taken place here. Had that same idiot who ran over Sweeny's guard shack done this?

Isaiah dropped to his knees amid the wreckage of what had once been his living room. The couch was unrecognizable. Blood splattered the wall behind its broken carcass. One bloody handprint on the wall testified Roxy had been there when everything happened.

"Roxy!" he bellowed, on his feet and running now, needing to see with his own eyes what he couldn't believe his heart was telling him. "No!" he shouted as he kicked aside the chunks of sheetrock and twisted timbers on his way down the hall. "No!"

Frantic, he slammed his palm on the safe room keypad and... "Shit!" The room was empty.

The officer followed as Isaiah checked the rest of his house, yet he found no sign of Roxy or the kids.

"Sir, I need to stop you," the man said at the empty bedroom where Roxy had slept only last night. Darrin and Kitty's things were still there. Nugget's ball lay on Darrin's rumpled sleeping bag, but even the dog was gone.

"The garage," he told the officer. "They must be in the—"

"No, Isaiah," Tate said with authority from the kitchen door that led to the garage. "I've already checked. There's no one out here but first responders. Get the security footage so we know what and who we're looking for."

Breathing hard and unable to focus, Isaiah shouldered past Tate to the fireproof metal cabinet beside the door into the garage. Jerking it open, he flipped open the laptop, keyed in his password, then dropped to one knee so Tate and the officer, whose name he still didn't know because he hadn't yet cared enough to ask, could observe.

Fast-forwarding through scenes of Tucker fixing steaks while Roxy and Kitty chatted in the kitchen calmed Isaiah's angst. His breathing slowed to normal when he saw Kitty and Darrin trail down the hall to their room with Nugget on their six. They were tired and Isaiah could see it in their slumped shoulders and the way their feet dragged. Those poor kids.

He watched Tucker's struggle with indecision at leaving his post after Isaiah had contacted him to tell him they'd caught up with Garrett Randall. Scratching his ear, Isaiah accepted responsibility for that one. If he'd never called his boss, Tucker wouldn't have left Roxy on her own. *This is all my fault.*

"No, it isn't. She's trained and capable. Give her credit," Tate growled as his big hand thumped Isaiah's back. And there it stayed.

"We never should've left," Isaiah worried as he fast-forwarded again. This time he stopped two minutes later, when Roxy stood at Kitty's and Darrin's bedroom door. The most adorable, goofy smile blossomed over her face, and *God, I need her so damned much. Where is she? Please let her be okay.*

'And you'll get her back,' Tate sent him on their private link. *'We'll get her back. Her and the kids. You'll see.'*

Heat swarmed Isaiah's cheeks knowing that Tate could read him so easily, but shit. The time stamp on the footage declared all was well at ten p.m. That was less than three and a half hours ago.

He watched as Roxy made a call from the living room, her boots off and her feet on the couch as if she lived there. Her face lit with a genuine smile and Isaiah knew she was talking with her father. What'd she call him, *Daddy Thurston*?

When the call ended, Roxy looked at peace with herself, and Isaiah wanted to know why. But then she put both feet to the carpet and her shoulders tensed. A bright light blasted the front room. Her left arm came up as if to ward off what she saw coming at her, and...

CRASH! A monster grill breached the front picture window ahead of a black Ford F150 truck. Glass from the window morphed into lethal projectiles that punctured Roxy's left arm like killer bees as she shielded her face and eyes. Shuddering, the truck reversed, then jerked to an abrupt, full stop.

Roxy stood in shock, staring into the headlights while a man walked up to her as if asking something. She blinked, cocked her head, then, out of the blue, he hauled back and... The bastard backhanded her! Roxy dropped into the rubble, and Isaiah saw red. Working fast now, the man looked over his shoulder and inadvertently faced the camera.

Tate hissed. "That's Bob Bratton, Candace's ex."

And he'll die for what he just did to Roxy.

"Come on, come on, come on!" Isaiah begged as he watched Bob dash into the hall and return with a limp Kitty Bratton slung over his shoulder and Darrin trotting at his side. The poor boy was crying. Nugget trailed along in obvious distress, the ridge on his back lifted, but Darrin kept patting his head, and... *Damn it to hell! There's no son-of-a-bitchin' audio to this video!*

Bratton disappeared from view as he most likely placed the kids in his truck, then returned for Roxy. The flaming asshole had the nerve to drag her by her armpits, over the rubble and through the broken glass instead of picking her up. Once again, he disappeared from view. It took a minute before the heavy-duty truck rolled backward. Headlights spotlighted the thoroughly trashed living room as Bob made his getaway, and...

"Son-of-a-bitch!" Isaiah roared, so angry he almost missed Tate saying or asking something that ended with "...know where he is."

"No, I don't know where she is!" Isaiah shrieked. "I'm a psychic, not a damned homing beacon!"

"Man, get a grip. Settle down," Tate hissed, his hand like a vise on Isaiah's wrist. "I said I know where he is."

"You, you, you... What?" Isaiah asked, his heart and soul so overloaded he could barely think straight.

Tate nodded, his dark eyes wide and the whites tinged black, as if he'd just come out of a vision. "I know where he is, brother."

That word again. Brother. Isaiah calmed enough to listen, though every nerve ending in his body throbbed with the need to run find Roxy. "Where who is?"

Tate's tongue slipped over his lower lip. "Nugget. I know where Nugget is. Are you with me?"

"Say again," Isaiah ordered even as he canted his head, confused and heartbroken and not sure he'd heard Tate correctly. "You know where Nugget is?"

"I hear animals." Tate tapped an index finger to the side of his head. "Up here. You know how you can hear most people in the world? Well, I hear four-legged creatures. All of them."

Isaiah knew his mouth was open and his jaw had gone slack, but he honestly didn't care where Nugget was. Only he did. He knew he did. It meant something, and if it was important to Tate, it was critical to locating Roxy and the kids. If only his mind would stop pinging.

Tate tugged Isaiah into an awkward guy-hug. "Nugget's talking to me, man," he whispered in Isaiah's ear. "Trust me. He can lead us to Roxy because he's still tracking his boy. Now, I'll ask you again, but then I've got to move out. Are you with me?"

Isaiah nodded, his brain numb at what he'd just seen, but willing to trust a brother by another mother. And a dog. "Yeah, I'm with you. Let's roll."

Bob was sneaky. After that twig snapping, Roxy hadn't heard so much as one stealthy footstep, but all at once, there he was. Out of the shadow, but only long enough to kill the truck's ignition and headlights. Finally able to see more of her surroundings, Roxy detected the camping trailer parked at an angle behind the truck. A soft, yellowish light emanated from beyond the curtains at the front windows, a rectangular matrix of six panes of glass that opened outward with some type of window winder thingee. Roxy wasn't sure. She just called things the way she saw them since one of those panes was open and the winder thingee was in plain view.

Trees surrounded the clearing he'd parked the rig in. No city lights were visible. There was no noise other than crickets, the whisper of a breeze through the branches, and Roxy's heart clamoring up high in her chest.

He slammed the truck door, then disappeared behind the vehicle. That shiny black pickup had to have cost a bundle. She'd never seen a regular truck that sat so high off the ground before. Telescoping side mirrors extended past the passenger windows like arms on steroids. The damned thing needed steps just to get into the cab.

Bob rounded the back of the trailer next, an electrical cord dangling from one hand, a tool box in the other.

Roxy kept her eye on him. Her heart ripped up her throat when it dawned on her that was no toolbox he carried. It was a camera and a tripod. Her gaze shifted to the row of three red plastic containers by the trailer. *Oh shit. Gasoline.*

Well after midnight, Isaiah left what remained of his home in the secure hands of the local fire department. There wasn't anything he could do, and nothing mattered but getting to Roxy and the kids.

By then, the Winchesters had joined Tucker and Keller at FBI Headquarters back in downtown D.C. Isaiah could barely hold it together while Tate turned his vehicle west and began what seemed like an impossible task of locating Nugget in the dark. Tate kept telling him to relax, but reading animals wasn't one of Isaiah's gifts, and the helplessness of not being in full control of this desperate night, gnawed at him.

Tate left Riverwood behind. He seemed to know where he was going, and that was enough for Isaiah as they headed deeper into rural Virginia.

But a dog, for hell's sake? Roxy's, Kitty's, and Darrin's lives depended on locating a dog in the middle of no-damned-where? Never had Isaiah, one of only two Level Tens in the entire country, felt more worthless than he did now.

He talked to keep his mind from unraveling. "This is what you meant back there when we were leaving the safe house, when you said mankind needs to stop hurting animals. You talk to, umm, animals. Do they talk back to you?"

Tate let loose a soft grunt, so Isaiah pressed his good buddy for details. "Spill. Do you hear all of them at once, or only when they're in pain? How's that work?" *And why can't you drive faster?*

"It's a big world, Isaiah, and just like people, millions of animals suffer every day. They cry out. They scream. It's not easy, but I'm just one guy. I've learned to block most of them."

True that. Isaiah had only recently learned to block the ever-present human clamor in his head, and Tate was the man who'd taught him. But Isaiah had never dreamed Tate heard animals, too.

The extraordinary gifts Isaiah and Tate had been blessed with were often more like double-edged swords that could bury a psychic if they didn't learn to manage the twenty-four-seven bombardment. Eden Winchester didn't have that problem. Her Level Ten gift had always been naturally selective, filtering out all but the most fearful cries sent into the universe.

Take her husband Ky, for instance. He'd been praying to die the night his plea had literally knocked Eden to her knees in the middle of her kitchen floor thousands of miles away. Yet there she'd stayed with her mental gift twined around the fisted fingers of a stranger about to be tortured to death a world away. It was only by the grace of God that another Marine had been in the same prison as Ky that night. He'd physically rescued Ky, but Eden had been the one who'd given Ky the hope he'd needed to hang on in that darkest of dark places.

Now an FBI Special Agent, Eden often used the lingering aura retained in possessions to establish a link with kidnap victims, hostages, and the like, but many times, all she had to do was be still and listen for them. Once she established a link, Eden's green eyes went completely black like Isaiah's did during visions, a common physical reaction when the mind opened itself to the great beyond.

Or when the great beyond reached out and tapped into your puny human mind and changed your life forever. Like Special Agent Keller.

But their biggest difference as Level Tens was the volume of voices Isaiah had been forced to manage after his first vision, that when he was a mere nine-year old. If anyone carried the guilt of surviving like a millstone around his neck, that person was Isaiah. Day after day, he still heard the world's cries for help, but like Tate, Isaiah was just one man.

"Am I losing you?" Tate asked, breaking through Isaiah's mental rant.

"No, just thinking about us psychics. What we do." *What we go through to do what we do.*

Silence reigned again as the SUV ate up the miles. Tate was like that. Quiet. Thoughtful. Probably listening to Nugget right now.

"Where are we going? Do you know?" Isaiah asked after a few minutes.

Tate jerked his chin straight ahead. "There he is."

That brought Isaiah straight up in his seat. The fluffy, gold dog they'd been searching for trotted at the right side of the road in front of the SUV. Nugget glanced over his shoulder and dropped to his butt as if he'd expected them, his tongue hanging.

"He's bleeding," Tate murmured as he shifted into park. Both men climbed out, but Tate was the wiser one. He'd brought not only his jacket, but a bottle of water and a collapsible dog dish. All Isaiah'd brought was anxiety. Yet he dropped to his knee to hug Darrin's very best friend and tell him, "Good, good boy."

"Shit, his pads are worn through." Tate lifted one hefty bloody paw after another for inspection. While Nugget slurped the water Tate had splashed into the bowl, Tate tied leather booties on each of the dog's paws. All four of them. "Sorry, big guy, but this'll have to do for now. How you doing?"

Trailing long strings of drool, Nugget lifted his muzzle to look at Tate, and Isaiah suspected Tate and Nugget were talking behind his back. That suspicion proved true with Tate's next words. "Darrin's close, but he's off the road. We'll go the rest of the way on foot."

Isaiah didn't argue, but Nugget was winded and obviously lagging. He'd walked or run a good twenty miles from Isaiah's place in Riverwood. "Shouldn't we carry him?" Isaiah worried.

To which Nugget let out a mighty bark and Tate grunted, "Of course not. He's a dog."

Isaiah got it then, the uncanny connection Tate shared with all things wild. "You told him to stay to the roads so we could find him, didn't you? He knew we were coming." *That's why he's here. You've been talking with him this whole time.*

Tate never answered, just crushed the empty bottle in one fist, flicked the bowl, collapsing it as he stuffed both inside his jacket, and started walking. With Nugget. Without Isaiah.

Isaiah beat feet back to the SUV, grabbed his leather jacket from the rear seat, locked the vehicle, and called out, "Wait up!"

Chapter Thirty-Four

Isaiah's decision became clearer with every step. The shock had worn off and his rage had kicked in, but this rage was a different kind than the one he'd battled after his mother's murder and his father's betrayal. This was that same sleek beast he'd seen in Roxy's mind, the one she'd groomed and fed and tamed after her mother's murder. Only now, Isaiah understood her need to avenge her mother's murder. He had become that beast. That man-killer.

Until the night he'd lost his mom, Isaiah had been the proverbial good boy. He'd followed the rules, colored inside the lines, and never disappointed his parents or his teachers. But because of his gift, he'd also been the reclusive kid at school. He'd never had many friends, but now? Now he called one of America's most alpha predators friend and boss, and because of that boss, because of Tucker Chase, Isaiah possessed the lethal skills of the highest order. And tonight, he *would* kill Bob Bratton with extreme prejudice.

Tate stopped dead in his tracks at Isaiah's side. His head pivoted as he turned and stared Isaiah down. "It'd be wise to take Bob Bratton in for questioning. Alive," Tate said clearly.

Shit. He's been listening. Isaiah snorted. "Alive's the only way you can question a guy." *But it's not going to happen.*

"We're federal officers of the law, Isaiah. Not vigilantes. American's hold us to a higher ideal."

Says you. Isaiah marched past his buddy, his eyes on Nugget's fluffy tail, but his heart a few miles ahead where Bratton held Roxy, Kitty and Darrin captive. The ass! "That's where you're wrong, Tate. Bob Bratton's mine. Stay out of my way." *And now I sound just like Tucker Chase. Well, hell, I feel like him, too!*

Tate's hand landed on Isaiah's shoulder. "At least have the balls to face me when you go off the reservation."

With both fists clenched, Isaiah did as requested, meeting his buddy's dark scowl. He had no beef with Tate and he didn't want one now. "Let me be clear. You're my friend, Tate, but I'm here for Roxy and the kids, not Bob Bratton. He's just in my way."

Tate cocked his head. "Christ, you sound like your father. Am I in your way, too? Do you even hear yourself?"

That pissed Isaiah off, and suddenly, he was fighting mad and ready to brawl. He'd never believed in revenge or violence, but with Roxy's life on the line, everything had changed. Didn't Tate get it? Everything was upside down and inside out. Backwards. Isaiah was not only glad for the pistol on his hip, but he'd already loosened the buckle for easier access to it—just like he'd been taught at the FBI range. Why waste taxpayer money. He was ready to protect and serve—to do his job—at all cost. His blood flowed hot and thick with the need to end Bratton. Tate needed to back off.

"I'm not my father," Isaiah bit out, cocking his head as the noisy clamor in his brain reached an epic din. He knew precisely how many shots to knock the bastard down. Tate needed to shut up and march. The man was a veritable bear. Thick necked. Thick chested. Taller and wider in every physical aspect, but it wasn't his woman's life on the line, was it?

So why the fuck—?

Bile swept up Isaiah's throat. The bitter sweet scent of pine and burning human flesh inundated his senses. *What the f-f-f...?*

He fell to his knees, sickened at the vision taking him by storm. "Tate," Isaiah rasped, all the bravado of a foolish man gone with the onset of the vision. "Run. We have to run. He means to... to burn them alive."

Tate was out there somewhere, but Isaiah could no longer sense him. Only the vision. Kitty and Darrin were unconscious and strapped back to back on wooden chairs. Trees swelled around them. Pine trees. Kitty's head rested on her shoulder, her long hair draped over her face. Ropes wrapped her chest and arms. Darrin, bound in the same fashion, sat behind her with his head back and his mouth open. They'd been drugged. A dark shadow prowled in ever tightening circles at their peripheral. Had to be Bratton, but there was no sign of Roxy.

Unless...

"Tate," Isaiah breathed even as his FBI brother linked one hefty arm under Isaiah's armpit and pulled him to his feet. "Roxy's projecting what'll happen at daylight if we don't get to them in time. She doesn't know she's doing it, but I can see. Through her eyes, I can see everything."

He swiped at his mouth, surprised when his fingers came away with no blood on them. His lips certainly hurt. They felt swollen and mashed. They should've been bleeding. His throat was suddenly raw and dry and... *Holy shit. He's hurt Roxy. That's what I'm feeling. Her pain. I'm in her mind.*

Both men glanced at the purpling eastern sky as the first rays of the new day stretched westward. There wasn't much time left, and Tate was right. This wasn't about revenge. It couldn't be. These next few moments had to be spent saving lives. All of them.

Maybe even Bob's if the bastard was amenable to not being shot on sight.

"You okay?" Tate asked, his massive hand centered on Isaiah's chest and the only thing keeping him on his feet.

"Yeah. Sorry. I was wrong. Don't know what happened to me."

"A woman happened to you. Forget it."

"Thanks," Isaiah offered, his heart back in the right place. Tucker might've taught him how to kill, but the big guy had also taught Isaiah honorable traits like loyalty to country and brother. Like pride in work well done. Like honesty. Even humility. They welled up inside Isaiah, blocking the darkness that had nearly bested him.

Resolved to not let his brothers down, Isaiah tugged his pistol up off his hip, racked the slide to put one in the chamber and said, "You're right, Tate. No one needs to die today. Let's do this right."

As they marched on Nugget's six, Isaiah reached out for the angry aura of the man he'd seen that night at the safe house after Nugget's wounded body had been ditched over the front gate. Tucker Chase was wrong. Violence wasn't a foregone conclusion. There were options, even now. This rescue required the finesse of a Level Ten who was finally on his game.

'Bob Bratton,' Isaiah projected into the night. *'You're getting sleepy. Very, very sleepy...'*

Bob Bratton had worked up a good head of steam since he'd exited the trailer, which couldn't have been more than ten minutes ago. For nearly an hour before that, he'd made one trip after another into the trees, retrieving armfuls of chopped firewood, which he'd stacked in an organized wall several yards or so in front of Roxy. After that, he'd gone inside the trailer. The kids had yet to make a peep—if they were in there. If they'd only groan or cry or something, she'd know for sure. *Anything! Just give me a sign!*

The trailer light was off now and Bob was back. Prowling. Antsy. Muttering under his breath. Cursing. Talking to himself. "Shoulda known, damn it. Shoulda fuckin' known."

He dodged behind the truck, opening and closing one door after another until he'd circled the vehicle, and, apparently, hadn't found whatever he was looking for. "Have you seen—?" He started to ask Roxy, then waved his hand at her and growled, "Never mind," before he took another lap around the trailer and truck.

Roxy sat still as a frozen stone. Her muscles ached from shivering. The rag in her mouth had dried at the edges, and the corners of her mouth were raw and bleeding.

At last Bob came to a stop at her feet, his hands at his sides and his shoulders slumped. He stifled a yawn and he looked dejected. Roxy couldn't have cared less. Pissed at being helpless when there was so much she wanted to do *to* him, she glared up at the bastard.

He stared down at her, and yawned again, the ass. Interestingly, not once this entire night had his gaze strayed to her breasts. That in itself was a relief, but it wasn't the norm, was it? She would know. Men were salacious pigs. They always—ALWAYS—scoped out a chick's tits and ass, then blamed their aberrant behaviors on their Mommies. Especially crazy guys like Bob. That had to mean something, but for the life of her, Roxy didn't care what at the moment. Something was about to change.

Shifting his weight from one foot to the other, he reached behind her head and untied the rag. *Thank God!* Roxy gulped in one long gulp of fresh air, then licked her poor, chapped lips. A bottle of water'd be nice, but she took what relief she could, while she could. She rolled the strain out of her neck. Roxy was no fool. This night wasn't about mercy, not from Bob Bratton.

Crouching to her level, he looked her in the eye. "You women all think you're so smart."

Well, duh, but Roxy chose discretion instead of the snark dripping off the tip of her tongue. She forced a desperate swallow, her saliva glands still playing catch up. "Wh-what do you mean?" If he wanted to talk, she was willing, anything to keep his attention off the kids.

He slapped a hand to his thigh, startling her. "You all lie! That's what I mean."

He'd made her jump, damn him, but he seemed intent on talking, so she swallowed her panic and put on her calmest, you-can-tell-me-anything face.

"You tell us guys what you think we want to hear, then you talk about us behind our backs with your girlfriends, that's what you do. You plot and you scheme, and—shit!—when we think you're being straight up with us, you're not. You never are, are you? All of you are bitches!"

Roxy diverted that personal challenge. Bob seemed to swing between organized thinking to hysteria. She couldn't let his rant be about her, so she focused on leading him to where she wanted the conversation to go. Away from the kids. If she could only stop shivering. "Candace lied to you, t-t-too?"

"That's what she's best at, isn't it? Every time I turned around, all I got was another story from the bitch, but you already know how she works, don't you?"

Not answering that one, either. "How'd you find out?"

His eyes narrowed to slits then, and she knew she'd hit her target. Bob knew Darrin wasn't his kid. That had to be what triggered this weird trip down memory lane.

He settled his butt to the ground and folded his knees to sit cross-legged at her feet. Without a jacket, he had to be as chilled as she was, but he wanted to chat. How bizarre was that?

Roxy willed her chilled muscles to stop twitching. She wasn't scared, not really, and certainly not for herself, but it was c-c-cold out here and she was pretty sure her arm was bleeding, maybe her cheek and forehead, too.

"Found out when I went in for a check-up," he murmured, his gaze cast over her shoulder and into the trees behind her, like he was looking into his past. "I was tired. Didn't want to do... anything. Thought I had cancer, but Doc said my T levels were low. Really low. He ran some tests. Come to find out, I had no swimmers. I was shooting blanks. It's no wonder I was depressed and tired all the time. You know what I'm talking about, don't you?"

With all the pharmaceutical ads swamping television these days, how could she not know? "You're too young to have low testosterone, Bob." Maybe using his name would create a link and earn her a moment of compassion. It could work. "How long had you been feeling that way?"

"Guess I was born that way." He grunted and tilted forward, cupping his kneecaps, but still not looking at her. "Must've inherited it from my old man."

"So your doctor gave you something to help, didn't he?" Roxy hoped.

"Yeah, but I hate taking pills, so..." *So you know better than a physician and here we are today.* "See, here's the thing. I had plenty of suspicions before that boy in there ever came along." His head jerked in the direction of the trailer.

Good, good, good! Darrin's still alive. Roxy kept her eyes forward as her mind raced for a way to help the kids her heart had already claimed.

"Don't take a genius to see that bastard isn't mine, but the day he was born, she swore he was. 'Course, she swore the girl was mine, too."

What? The girl? Kitty's not yours? Roxy hadn't seen that coming. Surprise must've registered in her eyes, because Bob's far off expression arrowed back to Roxy. "You didn't know, did you?"

"Kitty isn't your daughter? B-b-ut..." *How crazy is that?* "She looks just like you."

"No. No, she doesn't. That little mini-Candy in there doesn't look a thing like me, not if you look close. But she is the spittin' image of my old man."

Chester? Your father? Holy hell and damn, damn—damn! That's the connection I've been missing. Garrett Randall isn't the only one after Candace. He might want her for the five mil, but Bob wants her dead, and where the hell has Chester Bratton been this week? Does he want her dead, too? Doesn't anyone like her?

But what a kick in the gut that betrayal had to have been for Bob. No wonder he was depressed. Thinking fast, Roxy asked, "How can you be sure?"

Genuine hurt shifted over Bob's face, tightening his lips. "DNA, Officer Thurston. D. N. A. I came by one night when Candy was out, who knows where she was that time. But Kitty was glad to see me. She was just six, acting all grown up. That girl…"

He stared at nothing for a moment, lost in the memory before he snapped out of it. "The boy wasn't around. He might've been with Candy, but there my girl was, fixing dinner like a little mother, only she'd cut her finger chopping onions. She was bleeding. I was real careful to collect as much of her blood as I could. She thought I was being nice, but I wasn't. Not really. By then I'd already caught Candy in enough lies. I knew she was using me. Fast as I could, I got out of that house, and I sent the blood off to a lab I'd heard does paternity tests."

'So you betrayed the girl you'd raised as your daughter to get back at your wife,' Roxy thought. *'You're no better than Candace.'*

Bob kept talking. "It took a while. DNA tests don't work fast like they do on all them television shows. No, I waited more than a year for the results, but the morning my bitch wife gave birth to another bastard, I already knew neither of my kids… Ha! *My kids…*" He tossed his head and snorted, his tone edged with anger. "Can't believe I said that. Shit, almost sounds like I care, but I don't. A man with no swimmers can't make babies, not without a lot of medical help, and I'm pretty sure I'd remember that. But there I was, a fool already raising a bastard that wasn't mine, and she wanted me to act like a proud father because she'd screwed around and got knocked up again? Uh-uh. I wasn't having anymore of that shit."

"So you left the little girl who still loves you today, and who truly believes you're her *daddy*—behind," Roxy said softly.

Bob had the grace to look embarrassed, but he asked, "Why should I stay? No man wants to raise another guy's kid."

That's where you're wrong, Bob Bratton. A real man has no trouble loving a fatherless child. You could've been Kitty's and Darrin's hero. You could've been the one to buy Kitty that baseball cap and Darrin that glove, but noooooooooo. You made this all about you.

Instead of voicing the snarky sentiment, Roxy commiserated to keep him talking. "I don't blame you for leaving her, Bob, but do you want to know what she told Darrin when he was old enough to wonder why he has no dad?"

Bob's brows clashed into a slender V like maybe he'd never thought about what happened after he'd left, like maybe he still cared despite what he'd said. Roxy took that as a sign of hope. She tilted forward, but kept her voice pleading instead of letting her snark rule like it very much wanted to. No real man on the face of the Earth would've left a defenseless child behind, not with a woman he knew for certain was a neglectful, abusive liar. "Candy told that innocent little boy that his father, his *Daddy*—you, Bob—took one look at his ugly face the day he was born and couldn't stand the sight of him. Candace told Darrin that was why you left and never came back, and that little boy's been carrying that guilt for all of his life. He thinks he drove you away, that everything is his fault. She broke his heart, Bob. To this day, he thinks no one will ever love him."

"He is ugly! That bastard's still hers, isn't he?" Bob tilted backward, his eyes lit with an odd excitement. "Why the fuck should I care what she told him? Sounds like he asked for it. She shoulda told him to go jump off a bridge for all I care about the little prick."

And then Roxy knew. This conversation was over. She settled her back to the chair. "You stabbed Nugget."

Bob blinked as if he hadn't expected that, and then shrugged. "You could say I learned a lot living with Candy. So, yeah, I lured the kid's dog out of the snooty mansion you guys were hiding in, and once I taped the note to his collar, I stabbed him. Stupid mutt was easy to trick. Like you and your FBI friends."

She canted her head, needing to understand how she'd missed the clues.

Like most criminals, Bob was proud of what he'd accomplished. He needed to brag. "It was easy. Garrett Randall'd already been hanging around Candy for months like flies on shit. He never knew I was always a half-block behind his sorry ass when she'd meet up with him at Mr. G's. Sometimes she had the dog with her, but most times, she went alone. They were up to something, I could tell, so I watched. I waited. At first I didn't know how I'd ever get back at her, but the day she hit the front page, the *poor victim* of an armed bank robbery..." He rubbed his palms together. "I knew I had her."

Bob leaned forward as if dying to share the secret Roxy had suspected from the start. "She and Randall planned the bank robbery, Officer Thurston, and I've got proof. He's the one who bought her that stupid red coat for Valentine's Day, the shithead."

Roxy sucked in a calculated breath. *Talk about shitheads.* Bob still loved Candy. That's what this was really all about.

"So yeah." Bob thumbed his chest. "I took plenty of pictures every time they got together. Then I got hold of a good set of his fingerprints. Figured I could at least make sure he went to jail. Her too, if I could."

That explained Randall's prints on the note Harley'd found on Nugget's collar.

"You sent the *'I can get to you anywhere, anytime'* message?"

A proud smile curled Bob's lips. "Yeah, that was me. See, Candy and Randall trained that dog to obey his command, so I figured, if they could train him, I could, too. The mutt was easy. All you've got to do is give him a treat. He learned real quick to come to a dog whistle. I hadn't decided what I wanted him to take home yet, though. A pipe bomb or dynamite would've been good, but then you guys showed.

Almost thought I'd never get my revenge, but Lady Luck smiled on me the day Randall led me straight to Embassy Row, and" —Bob lifted both shoulders— "there you were."

"But you called me Doll Face, the same name that was on the note."

He cocked his head at her and huffed. "So?"

"So that's what Garrett called Candy in the bank. You couldn't have gotten close enough to them to have heard that."

A sinister smirk twisted his mouth. "She likes being called Doll Face, huh? The bitch. That was my pet name for her when we first married because... because..."

"You still love her."

"No!" he bellowed. "She's the biggest mistake of my life! I don't! Not anymore."

Bet me. Roxy lowered her head and closed her eyes, sucking in a lungful of forest air to keep her cool. She hadn't meant to piss Bob off, but wow. Candace Bratton had ruined everyone's lives.

But Roxy needed the details before the opportunity was gone. She swallowed hard and bought a few more seconds for the kids. "It still doesn't make sense, Bob. Randall slapped her in the bank. He wanted to know where the real money was and she cried when he hurt her. It didn't look phony to me."

Bob huffed through his nose. His nostrils flared. "They had to make it look good, Thurston, especially once you and that FBI agent showed. They knew someone from MPD would show, but the minute the Feds rolled on scene, Randall and Candy had what they'd come for, publicity to smoke my old man out of hiding. It was never about robbing the bank, only that fifteen seconds of fame and limelight and... you gave Candy and Randall exactly what he wanted. Air time."

"Hurting Candy's kids will only get you shot on sight," Roxy told him as calmly as she knew how. Still, it needed to be said. "They're just little kids. They haven't hurt anyone."

"They're *her* kids," he roared, slapping his palms on his kneecaps again. "And they're my dad's kids and that rat bastard up in Boston's kids. Don't you get it? They don't mean nothing to me."

Roxy shook her head, determined to get through to him. "I don't believe that. You're hurt and you're angry, that I understand, but Candy doesn't love them any more than she loves you. You're better than she is, Bob. Please, think about what you're doing. Think about those two children. It sounds like they need a break as badly as you do."

What little light she'd seen in his eyes faded to darkness. "Trust me, Officer Thurston. All I've done is think about what I need to do. First thing in the morning, the whole world will find out what she's done. Then..." He shrugged as if that was as far as his plan went.

"You don't want to hurt innocent children, I know you don't." Roxy'd seen the gasoline cans. "You're better than Candace. Kitty and Darrin are good kids."

"No, they're not. They're just like her. No one wants them."

"I do!" flew out of Roxy's mouth in a rush. "I want them, Bob. I do! Let me loose and you'll never see any of us again!"

Bob huffed at her. "And that's why you're here, Officer Thurston. You actually care about people, and I need a witness. Now shut the fuck up."

Chapter Thirty-Five

Growling with frustration, Roxy bucked against the wood that held her fast, wishing with all her heart she could get at Bob Bratton and rip his throat out before he hurt Kitty and Darrin. He'd already tied the kids back-to-back, then wrapped long ropes around them, binding them together on two wooden chairs. The branches he'd gathered earlier lay stacked against their feet.

Roxy could scarcely catch a full breath at what would surely happen next. The camera he'd been looking for? The dumbass had set it inside the truck bed at some point during the night, and he'd lost track of it. But now it perched on a tripod at Roxy's right. The bastard meant to film her reaction to two kids being burned alive. The moron wanted her to monologue! While children screamed and died! And there wasn't a thing she could do to stop it from happening!

He was inside the trailer now, slamming things, and *God, please let him have cut himself. Please let him bleed out before he hurts anyone else.* Minutes flew by. More banging. More cursing. At last he ducked his head out the trailer door, his eyes wild. "You seen my lighter?"

Like she'd tell him if she had?

"I asked you a question?" he growled.

"No, I haven't seen your lighter," she shot back at him. *You heartless bastard!*

Back into the trailer he went.

"Please, God," Roxy prayed. "I'm out of time down here. Set me free. Help me save my kids. Please."

But no. Bob dropped out of the trailer with a shitty grin on his face and a long-stemmed butane lighter in his hand. "Found it," he said as if reassuring her that he wasn't losing his mind.

Bet me.

Tears flooded Roxy's eyes as he approached, whistling. "Isn't it maddening when you set something down, then can't remember where you put it?"

'Like your brain?' she wanted to snark, but didn't. Riling him now would only hasten the kids' deaths, and damn it to hell! Roxy didn't want to be his unwilling witness to what would be an excruciatingly painful way to die. She'd trained scores of kids in self-defense over the years, and she loved every last one of

them. But these two had gotten into her heart from the start and that heart was breaking.

"Please, Bob, don't hurt them." She begged because begging was all she had left. "I'll do anything. I don't have much, but I know things. I can... I can..."

I can what? Sell out the people I work with? Betray Isaiah and his FBI friends? Go against everything Mama and Daddy taught me? If that's what it takes to keep these kids alive—Yes!

Bob crouched to his haunches between Roxy and the kids. With his back to her, he unscrewed the cap on the one-gallon jug of gasoline at his feet. For now, the lighter stuck up from his rear pocket. He looked to the right and left, then to the sky. The early morning purples had turned to brilliant golds and pinks that Roxy found no joy in.

"Don't do this," she spat even as tears drenched her face and ran down her neck. "They're kids! They never hurt you! God, let me go! I'll take them far away, and you'll never have to see them again!"

Bob glanced over his shoulder. "Be quiet or you'll wake them, and we wouldn't want that, would we? Not until—"

"Fuck!" she hissed, bucking at her restraints, but going nowhere. "Will you shut up and listen to me!"

Pushing up from the ground, he turned to face her, then pulled a remote from his front pants pocket, and aimed it at the camera. A red light flashed above the lens, and shit. This was really going to happen. Her heart stopped even as her stomach twisted in terror. Kitty and Darrin would wake up with their clothes and hair on fire. They'd die screaming and she'd go insane watching them die.

"D-d-don't," she sobbed. "Bob, please don't. I... I love them. Burn me instead. Please. Kill me, not them."

"See? That's why I like you, Thurston. You're absolutely perfect for this part. You're compassionate, and you honestly care about those worthless brats. I'm starting to like you, but first..." The ass pushed to his feet and didn't stop until he stood behind her. He had the nerve to pet the top of her head.

Roxy's heart thumped when he tugged her braid from between her and the chair back, then stretched it tight behind her. This could go so bad, but if it kept the kids alive, she'd play along. If he needed to prove to the world that he was a big man by raping her, she'd suffer through whatever violation he had in mind, just—*Please God. Let the kids live.*

"You're not bad looking for a cop, you know that?" Bob muttered, his voice gone thick with suggestion. "You're perfect. I might have to keep you after all."

He loosened her braid. Tangle by tangle, the coils unraveled until she could barely stand his touch. Her skin crawled as, resigned to endure all he demanded of her until the bitter end, she dropped her chin to her chest and prayed for the same strength that had come to her the night she'd fought Mario. That nightmare alone had proved that miracles happened, and... *God, I need one now.*

Running his fingers through her hair, Bob draped it over her shoulders like a cape. Suddenly warm, Roxy refused to look up at him when he walked around her and took hold of her chin. With his other hand, his cold fingers traced her brow, then brushed several stray strands off her face. Roxy couldn't help it. She shivered.

"Relax. I don't intend to kill you, Officer Thurston," he murmured, his head cocked and his eyes searching hers for what, she didn't care to know. "Wish I'd met you under different circumstances. We could've been friends, but don't worry. This won't take long."

He said that as if he'd done this before, but Roxy was beyond rational thought. Trembling at the awful promise in his words, she lunged forward, leading with her forehead and intent on breaking his nose. But DAMN! He'd ducked just in the nick of time. The deranged smile that stretched his lips turned him into the cold-blooded killer he was. "You can start screaming now," he said as he lifted to his feet and took the lighter from his rear pocket.

"Stop!" she ordered, her tears let loose and her heart in her throat. "Don't hurt them, damn it!"

Bob crouched to the dry branches with the lighter in his right hand. He'd barely extended the black, flexed spout on the nearest gas can when he glanced over his shoulder and said, "Let's get this show on the road, shall we?"

His hand came up. He flicked the lighter. Once. No flame sprang to life at his command. Twice. Still no flame. Then—a growling streak of pure gold roared past Roxy and knocked Bob Bratton on his ass. The lighter flew. *Thank God!*

"Nugget!" she shrieked as the big dog morphed into a vicious lion, tearing and biting Bob's shoulders and neck. Frantic to get into the fight, Roxy struggled to break out of the goddamned cuffs!

Bob bellowed for someone to come save him, to get a gun and end Nugget, but Roxy screamed, "Kill him, Nugget! Rip his fuckin' throat out!"

Bob had curled into a fetal position and covered his face with both arms. His elbows stuck out. He kicked and squirmed, but Nugget gave no quarter. He kept tearing at Bob's ears and fingers, jerking at Bob as if he'd made a righteous kill, which he had. What a sight!

"Jesus Christ!" Roxy screamed at the heavens, as pissed at God as she'd ever been that she couldn't get free and help Darrin's dog. "Can I get some fuckin' help down here?!" Okay, so maybe that wasn't the best prayer she'd ever said. It bordered on blasphemous, but—

"Yes, ma'am," Isaiah's calm voice replied at her right.

"Shit!" Roxy nearly dislocated her neck she'd jerked so quickly aside. He'd done it again, appeared up on her out of nowhere and scared the bejesus out of her. When she was already scared, damnit!

"Isaiah!" she cried, not believing her eyes. "Where'd you...? How'd you...? Never mind. Kitty and Darrin are hurt! Go! Save them, not me!"

"Tate's already got them and Nugget's got the bad guy," Isaiah replied evenly, his tone unruffled and so in charge. "Now hold still, while I save you."

"They are?" Her heart pounded so hard she could barely think. But yeah. Roxy saw Tate then, kneeling with the kids, checking them with gentleness, while Nugget ragged on their would-be murderer. She sagged back in the chair, limp and so damned thankful. There would be no death by fire. The kids were alive.

Gratitude broke out in a sweat over her body. Roxy dropped her quivering chin to her chest and said, "Thank you, Isaiah. Thank you, God. So, so much."

"You're freezing," Isaiah grumbled as he produced an elastic tie out of nowhere and restrained her hair with one deft twist of his wrist. Right then, Roxy could've stared at him forever. He'd knelt at her feet as he picked the locked cuffs at her ankles. His forehead bumped her kneecaps, and she wanted to tug him into her lips and never let him go.

He was the alpha male of her dreams. Broad shouldered and deadly, his pistol rested loose in its holster on his hip, and she honestly couldn't recall seeing it in his hand. But it must've been. He wouldn't have come in here unarmed, would he?

Isaiah moved with the same calm assurance as always, yet something had changed. Power clung to him like a second skin. Maybe it was just the morning light, but the blade of his nose seemed sharper. She hadn't noticed the cleft in his chin or the slash of his mouth before, but she saw them clearly now. This night of terror had changed him as surely as it had changed her.

Once her feet were free, he lingered at her knees, running his palms up the backs of her legs as he stretched them forward. Blood rushed to her cramped calves and thighs and—there. Suddenly, Roxy was caught in a time warp where things moved slowly and deliberately. His soothing palms. His knowing smile. Those oh, so dark eyes. It finally dawned on her.

"You..." she breathed as the passage of time returned to normal. "You had another vision. You saw me, didn't you? That's why your eyes are so black."

He shook his head. "No, Roxy. No vision. This time I saw through your eyes. I saw what you projected me to see. Everything. You finally opened your mind and your heart to me. My eyes might be black, but that's because I tasted your fear, but I also felt your trust and..." He pressed his wide hips between her knees. "I stalled Bratton so we could get here in time and then I prayed like hell."

She could barely speak. "You made him forget where he put the camera and... and the lighter... and..." It was so hard to think. "You made him tired."

Isaiah brushed a hand over his sweaty forehead. "I influenced him to want to talk to you, too. I filled his mind with the need to confess. Hopefully—"

"Get me out of these cuffs," she cried, wriggling forward on the chair to crawl inside Isaiah's arms. "H-hurry."

By then Tate had Bob face down to the ground, his bloody hands cuffed behind his back. Nugget had done a good job. Bob sported claw and bite marks over his head, neck, and upper torso. For now, Nugget fluctuated between whining and licking Darrin's unconscious face, to circling Bratton and growling, the scruff up his back on end and his intentions clear. *Touch my boy again and I'll kill you, I will.*

Suddenly, Roxy was off that awful chair and in Isaiah's arms, and damn. She buried her face in his shirt and cried like a little girl, all at once rescued and so damned thankful that miracles still happened. Her arms were too stiff to lift much less circle his neck, not that she could have once he wrapped his jacket around her, then wrapped her up tight in the steel band of his arms.

"I've got you," he murmured, the scruff on his chin abrading her sweaty temple. Roxy found a uniquely feminine joy in being held by this powerful man. Her man. Here against his heart she'd found trust and safety. She could be weak because he made her strong.

But the anticipation of watching Kitty's and Darrin's deaths had utterly wrecked her. It left her weaker than she'd ever been. They'd come so close to dying. The bravado she'd hid behind for years fled. As happy as her poor heart was at this rescue, it couldn't seem to make the one hundred and eighty degree turn from insanity to reality, from terror to rescue. If not for Isaiah...

When had he learned to be so stealthy? So damned sneaky? So incredibly handsome! Damn, he really was a Special Agent.

"How'd you find us?" she asked between valiant swipes at her face, still dodging tears that insisted on dripping off her jaw and running down into his jacket. "How'd you know where to look?" Had he received the psychic message she'd sent? He must have. She hadn't heard so much as a twig snap, when suddenly, like three ghosts in the night, Nugget was there with Isaiah and Tate on his six.

"Loyalty," he said quietly into the side of her head, "along with a damned good dog and a hearty dose of my big brother's love."

Tate's head jerked up at that softly spoken sentiment. For the space of a heartbeat, something passed between the two men that Roxy couldn't decipher. Tate nodded and the moment was done. She suspected there was more to the story, but details could wait.

Roxy didn't care that she wasn't psychic. She was found. That was all that mattered. "Thank you so much," she murmured into the sweaty hollow of Isaiah's warm neck, a place she never wanted to leave, but would soon have to give up. "If not for you guys... I thought... I thought..."

"My pleasure," Isaiah breathed into the top of her head as dawn broke through the trees. "I will always come for you, Roxy. No matter how far. Always." Cocking his head, he placed a tender kiss to her chapped lips, but she cringed, and he noticed. "He hurt you."

"Yeah, but I'm okay now."

Isaiah's head turned to Bratton. "I should kill him for that alone."

The magnitude of those words coming from her meek and mild warrior caught at Roxy's heart. Killing wasn't Isaiah's calling in life. He might be a trained government agent, but he was meant for better things. After living through this harrowing night that could have ended so, so badly, she wasn't sure it was hers anymore either.

Her shoulders shuddered as if a weight had lifted, as if she had one less burden to carry the rest of her days. And maybe she had. Her kids were alive, and when she and Isaiah parted ways, she could die knowing she'd done her best work here tonight. She'd bought just enough time for her guys to keep Kitty and Darrin alive. Unintentionally, she'd been working with that crazy dog over there, too, the one that left a line of drool and a wake of wiry golden hair everywhere he stepped. Besides, the last thing the world needed was another revenge killer. She would know.

"No more killing. Please. Just hold me," she told her savior and her friend.

When his arms tightened, Roxy pressed her ear to Isaiah's chest, struggling to compose her ragged nerves while she listened to his strong heartbeat. She breathed him in, the mingled scents of manly sweat, leather, and bodywash. Last night was as close as she'd ever come to losing her mind, and all because of the kids she'd fallen in love with. Yes, Kitty and Darrin were another woman's children, but Roxy loved them and she would've gladly traded her life for theirs. They deserved nothing less. And God, she loved Isaiah—enough to let him go. Just. Not. Yet.

Tate passed onto Isaiah that Tucker had two FBI choppers on their way. He turned the video camera off then and secured it as evidence. The kids were still unconscious, but Tate hadn't left their sides after he'd checked their vitals and assured Roxy they'd be fine. He'd spread a blanket from the trailer on the ground, and ever so gently, he transferred them, Kitty first, then Darrin, making sure they didn't bump heads. While the best yellow dog on the planet patrolled the scene, Tate covered the kids with another blanket, then crouched alongside them and glared at Bratton. If looks could kill...

Between the killer energy radiating off Tate and Nugget, Bob didn't stand a snowball's chance in hell of escape or garnering sympathy. He flipped his head to avoid the death glares of two very capable predators.

Roxy took her first deep breath of freedom, and all was right with the world once more. The kids were alive and protected by two of America's best. Isaiah had a good hold of her. There truly was no place she'd rather be.

Nugget made it better when he did what proud dogs everywhere did best. He pranced over to Bratton, lifted his back leg and peed on the man's head. Bob sputtered and spit, thrashed and cried, "Stop him! Get this mutt off me! Police brutality!" Not that in his wretched excuse for a campsite cared.

A genuine smile cracked Tate's normally sourpuss face. His brows lifted, and wow. The tough guy grinned. Isaiah tipped back his head and laughed the most delicious sound ever. It rumbled up his throat and vibrated from deep within his chest. Roxy could've listened to the sound of it forever.

Instead, she cried. Damn it, she didn't know what came over her, but she sobbed like a little girl. The kids were alive and Family Services might approve her fostering them, so why'd it feel like she was losing her whole world?

Because she was. This was the end of the joint operation. She'd file her reports and she'd show for every last court hearing. She'd pass Isaiah in the hall at the courthouse. They'd chat like old friends, but that was all there'd ever be. His was a higher mission in life, and she would only ever be the District's best beat cop. Maybe a stepmom if her prayers were answered.

She choked back another sob when Isaiah's palm smoothed up her back to rest at the nape of her neck. He hadn't let go of her since he'd arrived on scene. "It's okay, Roxy," he whispered. "Everyone's safe now. Trust me."

Afraid she'd give herself away if she tried to speak, she only nodded. *'I do trust you,'* she thought. *'And I'll always love you... enough to let you go.'*

Chapter Thirty-Six

"*You* can't find her?" Eden Winchester asked Isaiah for the second time, referring to Candace Bratton.

For now they were alone in the break room at FBI Headquarters, down the hall from Tucker's office. Roxy had taken a couple days off to stay with Kitty and Darrin at her father's place, though how she'd worked that angle with Family Services, Isaiah had no idea. But she had. To ensure the kids' safety until Candace Bratton was in FBI custody, Special Agents Keller Boniface and Tate Higgins stood guard at her father's home. MPD had posted two units on the street. No one was taking chances.

Bob Bratton hadn't stopped talking since he'd been taken to holding. He didn't want a lawyer or public defender, and he'd already turned over enough evidence to convict Garrett Randall and Candace Bratton ten times over.

Isaiah stowed his cell in his front jeans pocket. He'd texted and phoned Roxy several times since she'd left with the kids, but she hadn't responded, and that wasn't like her. After filing her report on all Bob Bratton had done and confessed, she'd seemed distant and indifferent. Withdrawn.

Isaiah suspected that was due to her tenuous situation with Kitty and Darrin. She seemed to have the cart ahead of the horse as far as her fostering them was concerned, and he couldn't blame her. He wanted the best outcome for Kitty and Darrin, too, but their staying together after this mess was sorted, seemed unlikely. Jack Fillion deserved the opportunity to finally meet his son, and Darrin deserved the same, but Kitty? Her biological father now lay on a slab in the FBI morgue, while the man she'd always known and loved as 'Dad' had chosen self-pity over fatherhood. Poor kid.

"You? The most powerful Level Ten in the world?" Eden made it sound like a bad thing.

Isaiah forced his mind back to business, not embarrassed at all for his lack of psychic acuity in light of what he now knew. He loved Roxy more than he loved his powerful gift/curse. Better yet, he needed her, and if push came to shove, he'd give up the gift and the Bureau for her.

He hadn't told her yet, but his intense feelings for her had limited his psychic focus from their first encounter. It seemed a natural human response, since love clouded most normal people's vision. Wasn't that an unexpected bonus from the universe, to finally be like *most people*, to be *normal* instead of forever being the odd man out?

Some people he couldn't read, and one of them was Candace Bratton. It happened, but now he also knew he could read *through* Roxy. Not that she was psychic. That hadn't changed, but he could see through her eyes, and while it was not a turn-it-on, turn-it-off type of skill, the empathy they shared was a no kidding turn-on. There was joy in the intimate act of seeing through her pretty eyes. Pure. Utter. Joy. The woman he adored made him a better man, and a better psychic. As far as Isaiah was concerned... End. Of. Story.

At least it would've been if they knew where Candace Bratton was. For now it was a game of wait and see if she'd fall for the trap Tucker Chase had cleverly set during the four minute news clip airing on all local television and radio platforms.

Eden cleared her throat. Apparently, she didn't want to wait.

Isaiah growled at her. "You heard me, Eden. I can't read Candace Bratton. Never could. Can you?"

A definite scowl rippled across her brows and most of her forehead. Like him, she'd spent last night and most of the day here at FBI headquarters in downtown D.C. Still dressed in her casual Friday wear, plain blue denims topped off with an extra-large gray FBI sweatshirt, she had to be as tired as he was. Yet the pretty blonde looked as fresh as the proverbial daisy in spring, all sunshiny and perky, while Isaiah'd give his next raise for one uninterrupted night's sleep. With Roxy wrapped up tight in his arms. His nose in her hair. His hands on her sumptuous ass. After a sweaty round of blistering hot sex.

It just wasn't happening with a black widow on the prowl.

Eden cocked her head, her thick blond hair rolling off one shoulder like a golden cascade, and Isaiah loved her. She was the sister he'd never had, and she understood him like no one else, yet as cute as she was—and she was, in a younger sister, annoying kind of way—Eden also had skills and powers beyond his ken. What if...?

"Let's try something," Isaiah said as he flopped one arm across the table, his fingers fluttering for her to take hold. "Now, while it's quiet and everyone else is busy. Think with me, Eden. Project with me. Positivity. Into the universe. Let's link our minds and flood the great unknown with all the good things that money could accomplish in the right hands. All the babies' lives it could save. All the needy children it could feed. The cancer research it could fund. The air it could clean and the trees it could grow. Five million dollars, Eden. That's a lot of money. All we have to do is find it and we can change the world. Come. Think with me."

Eden caught on quickly. She didn't argue that five million wasn't enough to change the world, just sank into the molded plastic seat across the table from Isaiah and stretched her arm to his. They interlocked fingers to wrists, their pulses matched and their psychic powers linked in one last effort to draw the spider out of her web and into theirs.

This mental exercise was not so much about finding Candace Bratton as sending a powerfully focused vibration across the cosmic web that all mankind lived, dreamed, prayed, and died within. The web allowed souls to travel, literally, anywhere. Hence dreams and intuition, empathy, prayers, and, yes, love. A person had only to believe.

But the vibration could also draw out those who disagreed with all that positivity, and that was what Isaiah planned, to seduce Candace with positive energy focused on that five mil. Yeah. That ought to work.

Steadied by his natural gift and armed with his love for Roxy, Isaiah bowed his head and closed his eyes. If anyone were to enter the break room now, they'd think Isaiah and Eden were up to something, and by hell, they were. But this had nothing to do with cheating or romance. This was about the most powerful force in the universe.

If he'd learned one thing during his ordeal, it was that there was a grain of truth to the media's claim of 'like father, like son'. He was no better than Abraham Zaroyin. He was capable of great evil. For a moment there on the road, he'd honestly entertained the rage that favored wiping Bob Bratton from the face of the Earth. What stopped him then was what paved the path forward now. Nations could fight fire with fire until they blew humanity out of existence, but the only power in the universe strong enough to save them all was... love.

Isaiah used that lure now to snare the antithesis of the one true light in the world. Clearing his mind, he pivoted his head from left to right to loosen his neck muscles, rolled his shoulders twelve times—his new magic number—then breathed in and exhaled out just as slowly. He set the images of a brave new world loose in his mind. Future smiles on happy, healthy children's faces, their tummies full and their hearts clean. The pristine surf on a pollution free shore. Seagulls soaring in clear blue skies. Verdant, lush rainforests. A world without hunger. Peace treaties. Simple things like reruns of *"I love Lucy'*, *"Lassie"*, *"It's a Wonderful Life"*, *"The Wizard of Oz"*. All the happily-ever-afters he could conjure, all the best possibilities the five million could provide, Isaiah sent forth like prayers to the universe. Then, because of Tate, he projected images of animals living in peace with mankind. No more slaughterhouses and no more animal testing. No pounds or no-kill shelters. No screaming animals locked in pain, all because of Candace Bratton's five million dollars.

Maintaining their grip and their link, he and Eden kept up with their mental projections for minutes that turned into a half hour, then a full sixty minutes before he felt the first tentative vibration of someone at odds with their idyllic vision. A slow hum radiated up from Eden's fingers on his forearm. She recognized the vibration, too. Someone out there in the universe was not happy. Someone intimately in lust with that five million.

'Work with me, Eden. Think all of your happy feminine thoughts. They're different from mine, but just as powerful. Maybe more powerful. You and she share the same gender. You talk the same language. Crowd Candace's greed out with all the positive could-bees. Challenge her right to be rich at the expense of others. That alone will spur her avarice until it knows no bounds.'

Then... *Bingo*. Isaiah felt Candace's shadowy presence more than he saw her. Her mind lurked in the darkness as indiscernible as ever. But there.

"She isn't happy. It will happen soon," Isaiah murmured. "We'll want to be there when she strikes it rich."

"She's hired a tow truck," Eden answered, obviously clued into Candace in a way Isaiah hadn't been. "You're going to marry Roxy."

Isaiah opened his eyes. "Yes," he admitted, still holding hands with a sister he hadn't realized he'd had until this day. "I love her and I won't live without her. I can't."

"It could change everything." Eden's voice pitched soft and low as if she knew precisely what lay in store for him.

He nodded, pleased to share this confidence. Because of her husband Ky, Eden understood what it meant to finally find the one soul in the universe that gave your soul its reason to exist.

She gave him a final squeeze before she released his hand and lifted to her feet. "This could get messy. Tucker and Ky need to join us."

Isaiah agreed. "Wouldn't have it any other way."

In the end, apprehending Candace Bratton was as anti-climactic as scratching an itch. After their meeting of the minds, Isaiah and Eden hooked up with Tucker and Ky Winchester. Tucker set up a twelve-hour schedule: two agents on, two off, with Isaiah and Eden taking the first shift.

Isaiah fully expected the end of this complex operation would take days, that it'd stretch into tedium long before she showed, but that same evening, a sturdy tow truck rumbled through the gutter and bounced into the lot at the abandoned garage, its yellow lights flashing as if it had a right to be there.

Watching from behind the steering wheel of the twelve-year-old sedan Isaiah had insisted on using for this stakeout, the driver dropped out of the rig and looked around, his hands on his hips. The rig looked legit, but Isaiah called the plate into the FBI switchboard anyway.

Eden leaned forward, peering over the dash. "There's someone else in the cab."

Sure enough. With red hair flouncing off her shoulders like a celebrity, Candace Bratton slid to the ground, her hands stuck deep in the pockets of another trench coat, this one black leather instead of red.

"The lady likes coatsssssssssss," Isaiah hissed.

"Oh, my hell, those boots have got to have six-inch heels, and...." Eden pitched forward in her seat, craning her neck. "Is that a sequined mini-dress under her coat? Seriously? She's wearing thigh-high boots, a leather gangster coat, and a dress that doesn't leave much to the imagination? On another heist? If that doesn't say 'hooker!'" —Eden's dainty fingers fluttered with air quotes— "nothing does."

And see that right there? That was precisely what Isaiah needed, a woman's perspective. It made him smile, was what it did. He hadn't noticed what Eden noticed—yet—because like any guy, he'd focused on the Chevy wrecker/tow truck. The rig's dual wheels and sturdy suspension. The hefty push-bumper up front. The collapsible boom, winch, and metal cables on the raised bed at the rear. The hook at the end of the boom, and the sign below the driver side window that declared *Henry's Tow Service*. The license plate. Important stuff like that.

"Wonder if he's got life insurance," Isaiah offered to prove he'd been OTJ, too.

"Or a tactical vest beneath his shirt." Eden tossed her head. "That's no woman, Isaiah. That's a witch, through and through."

Another smile creased his cheeks. Yeah. Working with women definitely offered insights that working with men didn't, and he loved it.

Without so much as a worry to the left or right to make sure the coast was clear, Candace strode to the office door instead of the garage doors. Once there, she spread her legs like she'd probably seen starlets do in the movies. She tossed that shiny red mane in the breeze, then drew a small weapon from her right coat pocket, and POP! She shot the handle off the office door. The muffled sound of a suppressor barely registered over the traffic noise from the street.

"Damn, she's brazen. I thought you guys left it unlocked?" Eden asked, her attention riveted on the B&E in progress.

"We did," Isaiah replied, wondering how long it would take Candy to use that same weapon on the gentleman friend she'd hooked up with, who even now, reached around her to hold the door. He was the nervous one, looking over his shoulder as he followed her into the work bay and closed the door behind him. "Also had the power company turn on the electricity so she can see what she's doing in there."

Hence the flickering OPEN FOR BUSINESS neon sign now at the front window.

"Wonder if she told him to bring a hazmat suit?" Eden asked as the overhead shop lights in the work bay kicked on.

"Guess we'll find out." What Isaiah wouldn't give to see that guy's face when Candy coaxed him to climb down into that grimy mess. How long would she keep him around once she had the five mil? A month? A week? Or would she leave his dead body behind, face down in the pit, when she drove away in his truck tonight?

On a dead run, the tow truck operator burst out of the garage and beelined to his truck. If he were smart, he'd climb up in that cab and never be seen again, but noooooooooo. In minutes, he'd backed the rig to the garage bay and was busy at the rear boom with cables, levers, and such. The big oaf had fallen under her spell.

Candy must've decided to keep things on the down low. The doublewide doors were still closed, which meant her beefy friend had to drag the hook and cable through the office and into the garage.

"Won't he need to drain the pit to retrieve the safe?"

"It's not that deep," Isaiah assured her. "Not anymore. We left the chain around the safe, too. All he's got to do is anchor that cable over the engine hoist above the pit, hook that chain, and turn on his winch. Shouldn't take long now."

"Good thinking. Tucker's on standby."

"Alert Ky that she's here, too," Isaiah requested.

"And Roxy," Eden added. "She'll want to be in on this bust."

"If you can reach her. She's not answering my calls," Isaiah admitted as shadows played across the narrow row of windows on the doublewide doors. "But it's okay. Tate says she's been busy with her dad and the kids. I'll understand if she can't make it."

Eden cocked a sideways glance in his direction. "Too busy for you?"

Isaiah kept his gaze forward even as he nodded through Eden's disbelief. Candy's accomplice had just cleared the garage again to activate the winch, and things were happening fast, but yeah. Roxy's silence over the last twelve hours—there was that damned number again—rattled Isaiah. He didn't understand what could've happened since they'd parted ways, him to FBI Headquarters, her with the kids to her father's place. Everything between them had been prefect the last time they'd been together. They'd made love in the shower and several more times in his bed at the FBI safe house. Due to the kids they'd had to be more circumspect at his place, but she'd been at his side every minute of this operation, only now... He worried.

The radio sprang to life with DMV details on the tow truck, startling him back to the stake-out. The rig hadn't been reported stolen. Owner was one Henry Oliver. Home address in Silver Spring. Business address in Foggy Bottom. No citations and no criminal record. Not even a parking ticket.

"Copy that," Isaiah replied as he disconnected. "Looks like Henry's branching out."

"Here she comes."

Isaiah stiffened in his seat as Candace ran to the rear of the rig and grabbed the rolled rubber mat tucked alongside the boom. "He must have the safe out of the pit."

"Which means they'll blow it next. Might be what the mat's for. A shield to protect them from the blast."

"Could be," Isaiah mused. "Or she intends to roll her good buddy Henry in it."

Eden growled. "Focus, Isaiah. She can't kill him. She needs him to carry the loot."

"True that," he agreed as an explosion inside the building lit the windows, rattling the garage doors as the shock wave radiated outward. "Shall we?"

Eden grinned. "Tucker and Ky will be here in thirty. Let's have these two in cuffs by then."

And that was precisely what happened. Isaiah and Eden found Candace on her hands and knees with her butt in the air and her face in the locker-style safe. Now out of the pit and on its side, the blast of whatever they'd used had twisted the safe's door enough that she couldn't get it to open. Hence her unladylike position and the expletives pouring out of her mouth at what she now knew was in that safe.

Absolutely nothing.

Did you really think the FBI would have—ever—left five million United States dollars sitting in a safe in an unlocked abandoned garage just to catch a thief?

"Fuck!" she hissed as one now muddy hand swiped at the red tangles hanging in her eyes.

"FBI!" Isaiah proudly announced, his pistol on Candace, and Eden's pistol drawn on Henry. "Candace Bratton and Henry Oliver! Hands over your heads where I can see them. Do it. Now!"

"Isaiah?" Candace asked as she complied, all while blinking her big, gray eyes, a ruse Isaiah knew was not compliance. He was willing to bet that, once again, she had something up her sleeve.

"Candace Bratton, you're under arrest for the murder of your father-in-law, Chester Bratton, and—"

"Ex," she huffed, even as her chin lifted in defiance. "He was my *ex*-father-in-law, Agent Zaroyin. Get it right."

"No, once again you lie. You never divorced Bob. Chester was your father-in-law when you knifed him, Candace Bratton, but he was also your lover and Kitty's real father. Yet you kept stringing Bob along. You couldn't let him go, could you?" Isaiah could feel Eden's sharp eyes on him as that truth settled.

"You still love Bob?" Eden asked.

The cold-blooded murderer morphed into the sultry liar that Candace Bratton truly was. Her shoulder lifted in a coy shrug like she stood a chance of deceiving Eden—a real mother. "Can I help it if men like me?" Man, if she were a psychic, she'd be damned lethal.

"Whatever," Isaiah bit out before Eden answered. "You're under arrest for the murder of Chester Bratton. You have the right to remain silent. Anything you..."

By the time he finished reading her rights, Eden had cuffed and read Mr. Oliver his rights. She'd moved to cuff Candace next, but Isaiah stopped her. "Don't touch her, Eden. Back away. We can wait."

"Oh, come on," Candace complained, her brows furrowed as if she were in pain. "This floor's killing my knees and I'm cold and—"

"And you don't know when to shut up," Isaiah told her evenly, his pistol still trained on her forehead. "You're not going anywhere. Shut. Up."

She huffed through the strands of grimy, red hair hanging in her eyes. "You know where it is, don't you?" She meant the money.

"I do. It's where you can't reach it."

Her teeth clenched. "But it's mine. After what I've been through, I deserve every last penny of it. Do you have any idea what I've had to put up with? How long I've waited?"

That pissed Eden off. "Who cares how long *you* waited? Your kids deserve that money for the hell you've put them through. Did you even think about them? That money should put them through college and buy them a future, not hooker-high heels and a boob job for you!"

Isaiah shot a quick glance at Eden. He'd never seen her so angry. A boob job? Yet another little detail he hadn't picked up on and never would've guessed.

Candace tossed her head, the mud on her pricey leather coat and her knee turning her into a pitiful beggar instead of the rich bitch she'd strived to be. She leaned forward and shrieked, "What would *you* know?"

And the catfight was on. Eden turned downright nasty. "I'll tell you what I know, *Mizz Bratton*. I know good mothers don't use their kids like you've used yours. Good mothers don't lie, and they don't steal, because they want what's best for their kids, first and always. But you..." Eden sucked in a deep breath. "You wouldn't know anything about that, would you?"

'Tone it down, Sis. She's the one on her knees, not you.'

Eden huffed once, message received. *'Did you just call me Sis?'*

Isaiah sent her a cocky grin. *'That's what you are. My sister. My friend. And one bad Mama Bear. I think I love you.'*

That put a satisfied smile on her face, even as she swished her blonde hair over her shoulder, cocked her head and stared Candace down.

Within seconds, Tucker and Ky cleared the door behind Isaiah and Eden. Sure enough, Candace was carrying—a lot. Tucker relieved her of two pistols, one revolver, a switchblade hidden up her sleeve, a cell phone tucked in an inside pocket, and another blade hidden in a boot sheath. She bitched and complained about her knees during the whole search, but at last, Candace Bratton had been apprehended and the mission was done. Almost.

Isaiah holstered his weapon once she was under armed guard and on her way to FBI holding downtown. But damn. He had another long night ahead of him. In processing the suspects. Questioning Henry Oliver. Interrogating Candace. Filing reports and then more reports, and, holy hell, suddenly Isaiah was bone tired. He looked west to where—somewhere out there in the dark—Roxy lay sleeping in her bed in her father's house. He wished he were there with her. Under the covers. Tangled up in the sheets. Kissing her full, lush lips. Loving her.

Eden came into his mind like a whisper. *'Go to her.'*

Isaiah locked eyes with her as Tucker headed for the vehicle he and Ky had arrived in.

'I'll cover for you. Go now before Tucker notices you're gone.'

Isaiah wanted to, but did he dare? Arresting agents had responsibilities, and Isaiah never broke the rules, well except for all those times with Roxy, but—

"Do what the lady says, Agent Zaroyin," Tucker barked over his shoulder. He turned from where he stood at the SUV, a lopsided grin cracking his big chin. "All of you. Go home and get some rest. This op's over for the night. We'll start fresh tomorrow... afternoon. Make it count."

"But Boss...."

Tucker cut Isaiah off. "I said, go. Randall and the Brattons can sure as hell wait. Officer Thurston can't."

Chapter Thirty-Seven

Roxy couldn't sleep. She'd never admit that she had it, but the struggle with Post Traumatic Stress was real. She found herself ready to fight at the silliest things, like when Kitty dropped her fork tonight. They'd ordered pizza and ate in while the kids watched one episode of Sponge Bob after another. Roxy thought she'd finally settled back into a normal zone, but the metallic clink of that single fork when it hit the floor was all it took.

She could no more sit there as if nothing happened than she could swallow one bite of the pizza on her plate. Keller and Tate had no problem eating. Neither did the kids, and for that she was thankful. They'd slept through the terror of their near deaths by fire. But Roxy hadn't.

Fighting the need to get the hell out of there, she shrugged into her shoulder holster and donned Isaiah's leather jacket. Yes, she saw the approval in Tate's covert glance when she zipped up and flipped the collar against her neck, but she ignored it. She caught the question on her father's face, but this was all she had of Isaiah at the moment, and she needed the scent of him in her nose right now, and something that belonged to him wrapped around her, and... and... *Argh! Why am I defending my actions? To me!*

"I'm going for a walk," she said brusquely, then gave Tate and Keller her most business-like nod. If she didn't leave now, she'd scream, so she slipped out the back door and left the tension in her father's place—that apparently no one but her noticed—behind.

Roxy took to the streets, her home away from home. Spring nights in the District were still chilly and damp. Fog from the Potomac had invaded the neighborhood at sunset, and the sidewalks were wet with condensation. She was glad for that, even needed it. The fog offered the muffled sense of privacy and aloneness she needed.

Her boots led her to Saint Pat's. Locked up for the night, its windows were dark as if no one was home. But Roxy knew better. Father Tom Diego might've gone to the rectory, but the person Roxy needed never left.

Careful to not let the sliding hasp clank, she let herself through the side gate onto church grounds.

Instantly concealed in the deep shadow between the cathedral's spires and its sixteen story neighbor to the East, she followed the stone path past the magnificent stained glass windows at her right until at last, she came in stealthy silence to the hidden garden in the corner. This had always been her mother's favorite place, the shrine of the Blessed Virgin.

The lovely white marble statue stood in the hedge of roses that had been here for as long as Roxy could remember. In May, it glowed in warm sunshine with a myriad of pink rose blossoms hugging it, but now Mary stood alone in the dark. Shadowy thorns instead of rose petals stretched around her as if daring anyone to hurt the Virgin they protected.

Roxy let her tired butt sink to the cold surface of the curved stone bench at one side of the shrine. Another bench curved opposite her, with a flat-topped, four-foot stone kneeler between them at Mary's feet, completing the intimate circle of divinity and sinners. *Like me.*

It'd been since her mother's death that she'd sought sanctuary in this simple place, years of following the ways of the world instead of the church. Organized religions had failed her with their various scandals and deceits. God had failed her the night her mother died. Even now, Roxy wasn't certain what she believed, but this was where she felt closest to her mother, and she needed Mama now.

Roxy ducked into the buttery comfort of Isaiah's jacket. Taking a long, full breath, she inhaled the scents of midnight and leather, seeking relief from the throbbing ache in her chest that she couldn't escape. Damn, love hurt.

She bowed her head. She knew the words. The *Memorare*, every traditional Catholic's plea for their Divine Mother's intercession, poured easily from her heart. "*Remember, O most gracious Virgin Mary, that never was it known that anyone who fled to thy protection, implored thy help, or sought thy intercession, was left unaided. Inspired by this confidence, I fly onto thee, O Virgin of virgins, my Mother. Before thee I come, before thee I stand, sinful and sorrowful. O Mother of the Word Incarnate, despise not my petition, but in thy mercy, hear and answer me. Amen.*"

The peace those words had always incited swelled in her soul. Roxy took a deep breath as she became aware that her hands were now clasped at her chest in supplication. Unknowingly, she'd assumed the stance of a true sinner. Wasn't that the truth?

The joint operation had taken its toll on her, and while she knew she should be celebrating Candace Bratton's capture with the rest of her team, she couldn't face them, not with goodbye so imminent. She, the toughest beat cop in the District, was afraid she'd reveal too much of her heart when the time came. And all because...

"I love him," she confessed to the smiling Madonna towering over her with her perfect white palms stretched forth, offering perfect blessings and perfect comforts for perfect believers.

"Which is why I have to let him go. He's bigger and better than me, Mary. He's destined for greater, grander things, and I'm just a millstone around his neck. I'll hold him back, and I can't do that. You know what I mean. It's like when Jesus was twelve and you left Him behind in the temple. Remember? You knew He was different then, that He had more glorious things to accomplish, and that He had to be about his Father's business. That you had to let Him go. That He... that He..."

Tears flowed so fast and so hot, Roxy couldn't speak. Dragging her sleeved arm under her nose, she wiped her lips and cheeks. Her heart shouldn't feel like it had cracked wide open, as if she'd have nothing more to give once Isaiah was out of her life. But it did. It was broken, which was how she knew this love for Isaiah was the real thing. And why she had to set him free. He was no ordinary man, and yeah. He wasn't Jesus H. Christ, but he sure as hell belonged in that same loftier sphere, where miracles happened and angels trod and all that crap.

She wiped her nose again, searching for answers, but seeing nothing more than blurred shadows and looming loss. She'd fallen in love with a man who had visions. He saw things no one else could, and he knew things no one else did, not even his boss.

Isaiah's mission came from God, as did the rest of his team's. That should've given her another reason to celebrate, knowing that a handful of FBI agents with super powers were out there fighting evil in the world. But it only reminded Roxy that her special agent—the one she loved with the breadth and width and depth of her battered warrior's soul—had lost his miraculous gift of sight because of her. She was his Achilles heel and the day might come that she got him killed. Not acceptable. Yeah, they'd made wonderful music together, but she refused to let him fail when he had so much to offer. Still...

"It's not fair," she told Mary as more tears squeezed between her puffy eyelids, "to finally find the one man who lights up my life, only to have to give him back. I don't know how you did it. I don't want to." Her heart crept up her throat, stuck where she could neither breathe through it nor vomit it out. Stuck where it would remain lodged forever.

Bereft of the comfort she'd come for in this secret garden, and in real physical pain at the depth of her love for the unlikely archangel in her life, she begged the Mother of Christ, "Help me. I don't know how to do this. I'm not strong like you are. I don't want to give him up to the world like you had to do with Jesus. I'm selfish, and I want him all to myself, and Mary..." A sob stole her breath. "I love him so much." The anguish tore out of her. "I don't want to lose him. I'm just human and..."

"And I love you, Roxy Thurston."

Startled, she jumped to her feet, her revolver automatically in her hand and aimed at the man who'd spoken from the shadows. Could it be? Shit, yes. Isaiah. And he'd heard every word. "Why the hell are you always sneaking up on me?" she shrilled.

His palms came up as he stepped forward. "I can see through your eyes, Roxy. That's how I knew where you were. I followed you. I didn't mean to scare you."

"Isaiah. You're" —she swallowed hard and lowered the weapon— "here. How... how long have you been there?" *How embarrassing!*

"Long enough." He seemed uncertain, which meant he'd heard everything.

Biting her lip, she turned back to the statue in defeat. "I can't do this," she breathed, though she no longer knew who she was talking to, Mary or—him.

"I'm rich," he said.

That got her attention. "So?" snarked out of her like a whip of lightning. "I don't want your money, you ass. If you think for one second that I care—"

Isaiah had the nerve to grin, and she wanted to smack that handsome face. He took another step forward, his palms still up. "Not once, Roxy. Not once have I thought you cared about money more than people, or you wouldn't be a police officer, right?"

She had to give him that, even as her eyes brimmed. Police officers and other first responders made squat. "Right. So?"

"Answer me this, why do you work so hard at a job that pays so little?"

She didn't know what he was getting at, so she told him what she did know. "Because there are men and women out there who need me." *Duh!* "There are babies and kids who don't have it as good as I do." *Another duh!* "And because I'm stupid. I do believe in truth and justice and the American dream, for everyone, not just the rich dicks who make it big and think the world owes them!"

He took another step forward. "And you have to give back, don't you? It's how you're made and it's who you are, Roxy Thurston."

The gentleness in his voce melted her snark.

"You're just like your mom and dad. You're not a taker; you're a giver." He gestured at the street beyond the churchyard. "You're not one of the entitled masses who wake up offended every day, looking for attention and welfare and something to complain about. You're one of the few and the proud and...Jesus." That same hand raked over his head, ruffling his hair, baiting her fingers with the need to touch it. Her heartbeat swelled like a heavenly chorus in her veins, praising—him. "I'm turning this into an infomercial for the Marines, but what I mean... I-I-I mean..."

Damn, she adored this stuttering, unwilling hero.

"I love you, Roxy. I should've told you before, but I'm telling you now. I love you." His fist settled at his chest—over his heart—just like hers had when she'd been praying. "I love you so much I can't think straight without you."

"That's the problem, moron. You can't think straight with me, either. You lose focus and you can't do your job. You can't read people like you should, and I... I..." There was no other way than to spill her heart. "I make you weak, and that's the last thing you are" —Roxy hated the whine in her voice— "and I need to go because maybe you're weak right now, and that's why you're standing here telling me this, and it's because of me, and...and..." *What the hell am I saying?*

"You're right, Roxy. Everything I am—weak, strong, wrong, or right— is because of you." In one fluttering beat, Isaiah had her in his arms and Roxy clung to him. "I love you. Just you, damn it. Always, you."

"I love you," she cried into the warm, wet cavern of his mouth. "But I'm selfish and—"

His palm came down hard on her butt.

"Ouch!"

"I'm selfish, too," he ground out, "but I'm not giving you up, not for anything or anyone. Marry me, damn it. Tomorrow. Say yes, or I'll bend you over my knee and spank you."

Wowza, the man had a lot of nerve and... she liked it. A blazing glow crept up her spine from what had to be a very fine handprint on the left cheek of her ass, judging by the warm glow on said ass. "You'd do that in front of the Blessed Virgin?" she asked, suddenly coy and tempted to string him along just to see if he meant what he said. "You'd spank me? Out in the open?" Why, oh why did the naughty image of her bent over his knee set her lady parts to watering and tingling?

He never glanced at the statue, just stared down at Roxy without blinking, his eyes dark and aroused, sparkling with the intent of the pure alpha he was. "Try me."

"Home," she ground out against his demanding lips. "Take me home so you can ask my dad and so I can... so I can say yes."

Chapter Thirty-Eight

Isaiah took her home just long enough to have that heart-to-heart with Hayden Thurston and get his permission to marry his only child. While Roxy went to her room and packed an overnight bag, Isaiah chatted with Kitty and Darrin too, so they knew he hadn't forgotten them, and that great things were in store for the both of them. He wasn't sure precisely how he knew, but he did. These kids were not going into foster care.

After high-fives with Tate and Keller for jobs well done, Isaiah was off with the woman of his dreams. Finally alone with Roxy, he drove straight to Crystal City and the Marriott Hotel. Pulling under the grand portico at the entrance, he tossed the keys to Willie, the night valet, and said, "Thank you, William."

Willy replied with a flash of white teeth against his chocolate dark skin. "My pleasure, Mr. Zaroyin."

"How's Leketia?" His wife was working on her final thesis—in nuclear science—at one of the local colleges. While she worked two jobs and raised their three children. Also while Willy ran an Uber service out of their home during the day to make ends meet. These recent immigrants were living every bit of the American Dream and proud of it.

"Only three more weeks," Willy said with a roll of his eyes. "Then I'll be married to a doctor. Can you believe that?"

"Yes, I can. Give her my best and tell her I expect an invitation to her graduation."

Willy gave Isaiah a thumbs-up. "That I will, sir. That I will."

"You *live* here?" Roxy asked Isaiah, her eyes wide as they walked into the lobby of the premier hotel.

"Only when I'm working late and can't make it home," he assured her at the elevator.

"You really are rich."

Isaiah had to stop her right there. "Not really. This is just a room with a bed. Come with me."

Up they went to the fifteenth floor, his *room with a bed*—in the penthouse suite. Roxy'd never believe him at this rate, but he wanted her all to himself tonight, and this place was closest, so there they were. Stepping into the lavish suite, one massive living/dining/kitchen area to his right and a single lonely bedroom to his left, he heard her gasp.

"This way," he said as she dropped her bag and slouched out of his jacket. The poor woman must think him insane to be so blasé about this *room*, but really. None of this was about the money. Not the chilled champagne in the bucket by the gas fireplace. Not the enormous basket of cheeses and grapes waiting on the hearth. Not even the magnificent bouquet of red roses that he'd requested for her. This night was about exposing his true self for the first time in years.

Taking a deep breath, Isaiah led Roxy to the unlimited view the floor-to-ceiling windows offered. He tucked his chin into her neck as they faced the dark stretch of the Potomac River and the wharf beyond. Running lights blinked yellows and blues from various watercraft. As was the norm for this particular stretch of the river, a bevy of dark helicopters, very possibly with the Secret Service aboard, raced westward. A jetliner followed in their wake, no doubt landing at Reagan International as the choppers went onto who knew where.

Isaiah let his chest expand with another deep sigh, inhaling the coconut sweetness of the rest of his life. "The money's not mine," he told her honestly. "Not anymore. It's all in a trust which I oversee."

"It's your dad's?" she asked.

"It was Dad's and Mom's, yes. They left everything to me, but I hated every penny of it and the way I got it, so..." Pursing his lips, he blew out his angst at having deceived Roxy. All along she'd thought he was just another agent. "I put everything in a trust for the foundation I set up in their names. You might have heard of it. One Against Hunger."

Roxy squirmed until she'd turned in his arms to face him, "That's you?"

He nodded, watching her carefully. *One Against Hunger* was his personal pitch into a universe that had ultimately given him back more than he'd invested, expected—or wanted. "So, yeah, in a way I'm rich, but legally, all this..." He tossed his head at the appearance of great wealth behind him. "This is just a room with a bed when I need to escape. I've hired good men and women to run the foundation. I'm only involved when it's time to make decisions or when things go wrong."

Roxy's eyes had gone softer and darker. Her fingertips tapping at his collarbones were the only thing keeping him from tossing her over his shoulder and taking her on the couch.

"So that five million's probably nothing compared to, umm, your net worth."

"It's five million bills, Roxy, that's all it is. It's money. If it was mine, I'd put every last cent to good use instead of drawing interest just to live better than everyone else, and this..." Again he nodded at his suite. "The foundation pays the rent and I work for the foundation. This is just another office. That's all."

But it wasn't all, and he knew it. Roxy knew it, too. He was the mover and shaker behind his foundation. It wouldn't exist without him.

She eased out of his arms. "Does your boss know?" she asked as she tiptoed—how adorable was that?—across the white plush carpet to the fireplace.

"He knows," Isaiah replied, his voice gone hoarse. "Frankly, Tucker's been up here. Remember the drought in Sierra Leon last year? He was the force behind the military operation that took in all those relief supplies. He knows people, and he lined up the Navy, Air Force, and Army." It made the news, Roxy had to have seen it. That was one time the press did good, catching all those smiling faces before they'd turned into emaciated statistics.

"You saved them? You and Tucker? So you're not just FBI agents, you're..."

Her throat worked to swallow or to speak, he wasn't quite certain which. This conversation could go either way, and he wanted to give her room and time to bail if this new development was too much. There were days it was a lot for him, too.

"A lot of people saved them," he corrected. "Tucker's on my board of directors. He keeps his ear to the ground for problems we can fix. Like you, it's important for me to do good."

"You don't want to be remembered for what your dad did."

He nodded. "I'd like to think I'd still be who I am today even if... that had never happened."

She sank cross-legged at the fireplace, facing him with her hands on her knees and a sparkle in her eyes. "You really are Superman."

"No, I'm not," he murmured, but he thought, *'I'm just a man who's head over heels in love with you.'* His blood sizzled at the sight of her sitting there, by his fire—in his home—meek and mild, and so damned seductively hot. But he was just Isaiah, not some super hero. Not a hero at all, but a man who wanted this woman with every fiber of his being.

She crooked a finger at him. "Come here."

He couldn't get to her fast enough. Kneeling at her knees with her olive skin aglow from the fire, her eyes gleaming, and his heart already kicked into overdrive, this—THIS!—was everything he'd ever wanted. This woman. This right here and now. Settling his palms to his thighs, he kept his greedy hands to himself. The next step was on her.

"I'm not Lois Lane," she told him as her fingers trekked up his arms to his shoulders. "I'm more a take charge kind of gal. I'm not inclined to wait for some guy in tights to come save me."

He bobbed his head because he had no idea where she was going with this, only that it would break his heart if she left him now. Cautiously, he extended one finger and traced the sassy lips he loved. "I should've told you about all this sooner," he said, and he meant it.

"I'd like to know when that would have happened. We haven't exactly had much free time lately," she scoffed, right before she tugged his face into hers and licked his lips.

Closing his eyes, Isaiah let the beat begin. "So you don't mind that I live here?" he asked, his blood on fire for this woman. "That we'll live here, I mean, if you want?"

Roxy shrugged, her breath warm and her tongue working delicious magic in his mouth. It was all he could do to focus on where this conversation needed to go, but damn. Like always with Roxy, his control slipped away with every breathy kiss and nibble. When her arms circled his neck, he braced both hands to the floor to avoid crushing her. Still she used her weight against him until, okay, he settled to his forearms and pressed the length of his body against her lush, warm curves.

"You make me crazy," he breathed into her mouth.

She turned her head then, and her chin went up, exposing the long column of her neck. With one long lick, Isaiah was done talking. His hand sought the waistband of her pants, and ziiiiipppp. The denim was out of his way, and her hot body arched into his hips.

She dragged his shirt over his head next, and the race to be skin on skin was over in about five seconds. Not that he counted, not with his hands full of the globes of her sweet, plump breasts. Manna. This woman was manna in his desert, and he dived right in, suckling those pert nipples until she writhed beneath him and begged for, "More," in that sultry, throaty voice he adored.

More, he could do, especially once her hand dipped low to his belly, then to his—*yeah, right there*—cock. The blaze between them roared to life with every pump of her strong, slender fingers. It wouldn't take long if she kept working him like that.

"Stop," he managed to growl, his back stiff as he willed his body to last long enough to please her first. "On your knees. Face the fire. Now."

With a growly giggle, she did what he'd asked, and the sight of her plump round bottom, shaped so much like a heart, so firm and so—*mine*—nearly did him in. Pressing one hand to the small of her back, he bit the right cheek of her ass. Squeezing the left cheek, he curved his other arm around her waist. That was an ass to spank and mark with his handprint, but Isaiah was not that kind of a man. Nibbles and kisses were what he left. Raspberries and goosebumps.

Isaiah took his time, watching how her backside flexed and quivered at his touch. Roxy was ready and anxiously waiting, and her soft mewls were music to his heart, but this was the first time they weren't in a rush. As patiently as he could, Isaiah took in every last expanse of silky smooth skin, her tender curves, and the tuck of her waist. The fullness of her thighs and the proudly arched spine that thrust her rump higher in an invitation he had no intention of denying.

"You're killing me," she whimpered, and with that, he gave her all he had to give, every last piece of his heart and every inch of his sweaty, throbbing body. He took her hard and deep, thrust after thrust until she tensed and pushed into the cradle of his hips and...

"Come for me," he ordered as he found his own release, a might too soon, but just in time.

"Isaiah!" Roxy screamed, shoving back as she matched him every step of the way. Taut muscles gripped his cock just when he thought he was done and—stars. He saw stars as he came again, grinding into her warm, wet heaven to make sure she came with him.

Roxy angled her hips to take more of him into her body, hissing, "Yes, yes, yesssssssssss!"

What a sight, this fiercely passionate woman, giving herself to him and letting him join his body to hers. Letting him worship her. For that's what this was, him on his knees worshipping the body and soul of the woman he adored with every last beat of his heart. She was his goddess and he was just a humble guy who—God willing—meant to serve her every day for the rest of his life.

At peace for the first time in awhile, Isaiah eased her with him to his side. But Roxy had a mind of her own. She wiggled around until she lined up her breasts to his chest and faced him again. Firelight gleamed in her dark eyes, and that right there, the look of love shining from beneath her thick butterfly lashes, was why men fought wars, climbed unreachable mountains, and dreamed impossible dreams. All for the love of a woman.

"Yes," she murmured, her lips swollen and wet from his mouth. "Yes, I'll marry you, but only on one condition."

Isaiah threw an arm over his eyes, needing to hide the emotion welling up in them. "Anything," he breathed, so damned complete that he felt like crying. "Just ask. Your wish is my command."

"Awww," she sighed. "That's so sweet, and I don't mean to be ungrateful, and maybe this isn't the time to bring it up, but...can't you give all that money away? I mean, money's so evil. It changes people and I don't want us to change. I want us to stay like we are right now. Aren't there other charities that already do what you do? Couldn't you give everything to them?"

"Good point," he admitted. "Or I could make you a trustee and let you manage your own charity. You could give it to whatever cause you want."

"I could?" He didn't have to look at Roxy to know she was considering the proposal. "But it's yours, not—"

Without thinking, he gave her ass a solid smack. She yipped with surprise. Good. She needed to know he meant business. "Ours, Roxy. It's ours. There is no mine and yours anymore, just ours."

She pushed him to his back and climbed up his body to straddle his hips. "Oh, well then," she murmured as she dipped low and planted a kiss on his mouth, her palms flat to his pecs and her hair a sensual tease floating over his naked skin. "The community center could use new floor mats. Maybe a new roof. A kitchen."

There she was, thinking about others again. Lifting his arm from his face, Isaiah blinked at the sweet flavor of coconut, lust, and Roxy. "I love you, woman. Marry me. Tomorrow. Right here."

"But my dad—"

"Hayden Thurston already knows and approves," Isaiah finished for her. "In fact, he told me to *get it done*. He'll be here, you can count on it. So will Tate and his wife, Winslow, Tucker and Melissa, Eden and Ky, and... everyone. Invite everyone, Roxy, and stop worrying about money. Just say—"

"Yes," she mumbled, biting his lower lip as she breathed, "Yes, yes, yes, Isaiah. I'll marry you for richer or poorer, in sickness and in health, and... and all those other things."

"Your cat's invited, too."

That got her attention. "You want Toy at our wedding?"

He shrugged. "Sure. I saw her at your dad's. She's your baby, isn't she?"

"Well yeah, but—"

"But nothing. I had a cat when I was a kid. A longhaired Siamese just like yours, only her name was Hot Toi. She had a belly on her. That's how she got her name. After Mom died..." Isaiah paused as the image of his mother sprang to life. He'd give anything if Roxy's and his mothers could be there for this wedding. "Anyway..." He cleared his throat. "I know how much company a cat can be, so yes. Toy is definitely invited."

Roxy settled her chin on her crossed arms at his chest. "Hoi Toi? Seriously? What a coincidence. We nearly gave our cats the same name."

Isaiah smoothed both hands over her shoulders blades on his way to the soft swell of her butt. "There are no coincidences, Roxy. We were always meant to be together. We just had to find each other."

That earned him a smile. "How many kids do you see us having?"

"A houseful. I was an only child. I want more for my kids than that."

"Your favorite color?"

Ah, so she wanted to play sixty questions. Growling, he rolled Roxy to her back and told her, "Red, white, and blue. Yours?"

The prettiest dark chocolate eyes peered up at him. She blinked. Her lips were reddened and swollen, and he was a smitten man. The woman he loved with all of his heart was his. Her favorite color could wait.

This night was just beginning.

Chapter Thirty-Nine

Because of regulations, this had to be done at Family Services instead of in Roxy's home, which she would've preferred. Kitty and Darrin were comfortable there. Nugget, too. After a few tense moments, he and Toy tolerated each other quite well.

She and Isaiah sat on a wooden bench in the waiting room with Kitty and Darrin. Jack Fillion and his wife had been in conference for the last hour with the social worker in charge, a genuinely kind woman Roxy trusted, Naomi Combs. But the waiting drove Roxy nuts. It wasn't good for the kids, either. No matter how many times Roxy and Isaiah had assured them they'd always be welcome in their home, the kids were both subdued and way too quiet.

Finally, Naomi's door opened.

"Relax," Isaiah murmured as he pressed a kiss to her temple. "You look like you're ready to climb the walls."

Swallowing hard, Roxy kissed his mouth—chastely—before she turned to the kids she still thought of as hers. It was difficult, but she went for nonchalance. "Today's the big day."

But neither smiled, and Kitty, damn it, was close to tears. Every last one of his cinnamon freckles showed on Darrin's face. "I had to leave Nugget behind," he squeaked, and that did it.

Roxy gathered him into her arms before she was reduced to tears along with him. "Just for a couple hours. That dog belongs to you, trust me on that one." Yet nothing was definite yet, and she knew she might've just told Darrin a lie. How could she not? Damn, it would break her heart if Family Services split these kids. If either of them had to go into the system. If Jack Fillion didn't want the dog and Nugget ended up in the pound.

Naomi exited the conference room ahead of—

Oh, my hell. That's Darrin's dad? Jack Fillion was Darrin Bratton all over again. Only bigger. Wider. He had the same nose. Same color hair. Same freckles. Wow. He stood a good six feet tall, with the frame and musculature of a boxer. Dressed in a plain white T-shirt that couldn't conceal the plains and angles of his biceps, pecs, or gut, it seemed impossible that anyone could've brought him to his knees. Yet Candace had.

Goosebumps rippled up Roxy's spine when Jack stepped forward with one hand on the waist of the pretty brunette at his side. "Officer Thurston, this is Cathleen, my wife. Cathleen, Officer—"

"Roxy, just Roxy. Please." She could hardly speak by then. "I'm so glad to meet you, Jack and Cathleen." *Only I'm not if you ever hurt either of my kids.*

Isaiah must have sensed her inner turmoil. With one hand cupping her elbow, he reached around her, shook Jack and Cathleen's hands, and introduced himself. They looked like good people. They looked like they cared for each other. *But so help me...*

"It's up to the kids now," Naomi interrupted. "Kitty and Darrin, come closer to meet Jack and Cathleen Fillion. They'd like to adopt you."

Say what? Roxy froze. "B-b-both of them?"

Naomi maintained her cool and nodded, while Isaiah's palm became the only thing holding Roxy upright. She leaned into him. It was either that or fall apart, and the kids didn't need to see her coming undone. Not now. Not when... *Damn, this is really happening. They're leaving and...* Gulp. *I'll never see them again.*

Neither Kitty nor Darrin moved, when Jack crossed the distance between them and crouched at their feet. Kitty reached for Darrin's shoulders, and Darrin took a step back, pressing against his sister. Kitty's chin was up in defiance, but Darrin looked ready to run.

Instead of making direct eye contact, Jack's gaze fell to the floor. The muscle in his throat seemed to be working extra hard, like he couldn't swallow.

Roxy surely couldn't.

Finally Jack said, "You kids don't know me, and I know this isn't easy." He glanced up at Roxy then. "You've already got someone who loves you. I can see that, and I'm glad you've had someone in your corner this last week, but it'd sure be nice if you'd give me a chance, too. I'm not so bad, and I... I..."

It was like watching a giant on his knees, begging for his life. Jack trembled like his heart was breaking, and then Roxy knew. Sight unseen, he truly loved his son. This coming together was the right and only thing to do. Her kids would be okay.

Darrin's sweet little boy voice breathed soft and low. "You're... you're really my dad?"

Jack lifted his chin. Cathleen sniffled. Roxy lifted a hand to her mouth and coughed, while Isaiah's breath hitched. His hold tightened on her. This was so, so hard.

"I am," Jack Fillion replied, blinking fast and his voice rough and hoarse. "And I'd like to be your Kitty's foster dad too if it's okay with her and you and your dog and..." His voice faded.

"I get to keep Nugget?" Darrin asked. Just like any ten-year-old kid, he wasn't worried about keeping his sister.

Jack choked, "Yes, son. You love him, don't you?"

"Ah-huh."

"Th-that's how it works, Darrin. We get to keep the people and things we love." Jack's palm settled over his heart, where he'd been keeping the love for his little boy all these years.

The room stilled. Darrin looked up at Kitty, his eyes bright and his face aglow.

Kitty looked down at him, her lips pinched and tight in that snarky way Roxy loved so much. "I've been so mean to you," she whispered. "You go on and be happy. I'll understand. He's your dad, not mine. I'll be okay."

Shit, shit, shit! It was all Roxy could do not to run to those kids to protect them from this awful, good day. But Darrin was *Jack's* son. Unlike Candace, who'd only wanted wealth, Darrin wasn't about to leave his sister behind. Reaching up, he grabbed onto the hand he loved with all of his little boy heart. "But he wants you, too. Come with me, Kitty. Me and Nugget'll keep you safe. You'll see. You don't hafta be scared no more. It'll be okay."

Teardrops dripped down Kitty's cheeks, when she said, "I love you, brat."

A cinnamon freckled smile split Darrin's face. Releasing her, and with one hesitant step, he flung himself into his father's arms and said, "Okay."

Jack groaned as he tenderly took hold of his son for the first time. Tears ran freely down his cheeks. His fingers straightened, then curled and—

Aw, shit. Roxy couldn't take it.

"And I'll keep you safe," Isaiah whispered in her ear. "You'll see. It'll be okay."

"I know, but... but Kitty's still standing there all by herself." *This was too hard!*

"They're strong kids, Roxy. Give her time."

"I know, but... but..."

But wow. Darrin twisted to beckon Kitty, and just like that, Jack hauled her into his arms. She stood there like a stiff little soldier against his knee, still crying, still holding back, but smiling at her baby brother. It was done. Kitty and Darrin were where they belonged.

Well, shit.

"Well, good," Naomi said, her eyes tender as she nodded to the door, her signal for Roxy and Isaiah to leave. Roxy suppressed her selfish side and focused on breathing and smiling like this was the best thing that ever happened. Which it was, if the pain in her heart was telling her the truth. Poor Cathleen hadn't joined the family huddle. She must've sensed the kids could only handle so much, another sure sign they were in the right place with the right people.

"Bye kids," Isaiah said, his voice as tight as Roxy's heartstrings.

That got Darrin and Kitty's attention. "You're leaving us?" Kitty asked.

"Not leaving," Roxy said, just to be clear while she could still think. "I'll always be just one phone call away, honey, but Jack isn't adopting me and Isaiah.

You kids don't need us hanging around while you get to know your new parents."

"B-b-but..." Kitty's pretty eyes filled as she pushed out of Jack's embrace. "I love you."

Well, damn. Cue the tears all over again.

"And I love you, sweetheart," Roxy said stoically, if blinking like a fool had anything to do with stoicism. Then, because she needed it as much as Kitty, she rushed the kids and pulled them both into her arms. "Be good," she told them as she hugged the stuffing out of them, while Jack and Cathleen looked on. "Give Jack and Cathleen a chance. They already love you. Everyone can see that."

Cathleen sniffed again. Jack cleared his throat. And, yeah, Roxy knew without a doubt they loved these kids as much as she did.

"From now on, it'll be Aunt Roxy and Uncle Isaiah," Isaiah told them hoarsely from Roxy's side. "Can you live with that?"

Kitty burrowed into Roxy's neck while Darrin pressed a little boy kiss to her cheek, and said solemnly, "Bye, Officer Thurston. Me and Nugget are gonna write you everyday, so you don't forget us."

"And I'll never forget you, Aunt Roxy. Never," Kitty breathed, just before she wiped her teary eyes and let Roxy go.

They mugged Isaiah next with kisses and tears. "I'm never gonna forget you, either," Kitty told her first manly crush.

He tugged her against him and placed a kiss to the top of her head as he looked to Jack. "I still owe you kids a baseball game, if your mom and dad don't mind cheering for the Nats with us."

Lifting to his feet, Jack stuck out one hand. "Anytime. We'll make it a family event. But I've got to tell you, Agent Zaroyin, I think we've met before."

"We have. At the hospital. The night Kitty had an asthma attack," Isaiah explained. "You were leaving the chapel as I was going in."

Jack's eyes widened. "Oh. Yeah. That was you. She told me to meet her there, said she wanted to make a deal."

"Candace? A deal?" Roxy asked, her hackles lifting yet again.

With a sideways glance at the kids, Jack lowered his voice. "Is there some place we can talk?"

Naomi nodded to the hall to her right. "You can borrow my office while Cathleen gets acquainted with Kitty and Darrin. Go on. We're not going anywhere."

Once behind closed doors, Jack raked his fingers through his hair. The man had yet to smile. Too much worry had creased his brow and bracketed his mouth, making him look older than his thirty-three years. "She called me to meet her at the hospital. She wanted me to kill her ex-father-in-law, that Chester Bratton fellow, the guy she murdered." Jack's Adam's apple bobbed as if swallowing was difficult. "Do you believe that? She said he was out to kill her, and she knew I'd been watching her, only I wasn't. I was trailing that other guy, the one at the bank with her. I had no idea who she wanted me to kill. I've never met Chester Bratton in my life."

Roxy looked up at Isaiah while she told Jack what she now knew. "Chester Bratton wasn't her ex-father-in-law. She never divorced his son, Bob. But Chester was her lover and he was Kitty's real father. The only reason Candace was at the hospital that night that you saw Isaiah, was because she'd somehow induced an asthma attack in Kitty. Then later, she reached out to Chester the night she killed him, or he reached out to her, we still don't know which. That's when Isaiah finally caught her."

Jack glanced over his shoulder as if he couldn't wait to get back to his family. "That woman cheated on her husband with his father? She... she did that to her own daughter? Damn, she's evil. She told me I could have Darrin once I proved Chester Bratton was dead. I didn't know what to do, I mean, she's had my boy for ten years, damn her, and not once has she let me close enough to... to..." A shudder rattled his chest. "This is the first time I've touched him. He's a good kid, I can tell, but I couldn't murder a guy, not even for my... my son."

Roxy had to know. "How'd you and she ever hook up?"

"Snowstorm hit Boston hard one January night," he said as he hung his head. "I'd just locked up when she pounded on my window. Said her car broke down. I'm stupid, she was good-looking, so I let her in. Thought a cup of coffee couldn't hurt while we waited for the tow truck she'd supposedly called. One thing led to another and…" His hand raked over his head again. "Anyway… after she left I realized she'd taken my deposit for the day. Everything. The money was gone and so was she. Why the hell didn't her husband divorce her? I would have."

"Because he still loves her," Roxy answered, shrugging her shoulders at the stupidity of the situation. Love certainly made the world go around, but it could just as easily knock the planet off its axis and drive a person crazy. Her traitorous eyes lifted automatically to Isaiah. *Like me.*

Isaiah stuck a hand to Jack's shoulder. "Forget about Candace Bratton, Jack. She can't hurt anyone anymore, but if you ever need anything, just ask. Roxy and I are here for you. Now go home with your family."

The big guy brushed a hand over his face, but couldn't seem to look Isaiah in the eye. He stared at the floor, his shoulders heaving. "You have no idea what that means to me. H-h-home. Yeah. I'm taking my kids and…" He looked up through bleary green eyes. "We're finally going home."

And that was that.

While Cathleen and Jack drew the kids' attention, Isaiah steered Roxy out of the building to the FBI SUV waiting in the No-Parking zone at the curb. Damned if Tucker wasn't at the wheel. Hiding behind darker than dark, *"Men in Black"* glasses, it was difficult to get a reading on the big guy. For once he kept his mouth shut when Roxy climbed in the back seat. Isaiah followed, but didn't fasten his seat belt, just tucked her under his arm and asked, "Where to now, Boss?"

"Counterfeit ring over in Arlington. Three suspects. Armed and dangerous. Metro's already on site, but there's a problem."

Swallowing her heart, Roxy forced her eyeballs away from Family Services' front door. She'd never felt more like crying. Those were her kids in there and they had a new home now, but leaving them behind was the hardest thing she'd ever done. She steeled her nerve and faced those dark glasses staring at her in the rear view. "Let me guess. It's risky as hell. Someone might die before we're through, and you need us to save the world."

Tucker's brows cocked above the rim of his glasses. "You might say that, Officer Thurston."

"Just another day in paradise," Isaiah murmured in her ear.

Roxy turned in his arms, and looked up into his steady blue eyes. The bitch inside of her was now broken, its ego tamed and her passionate heart subdued. Tears she tried to hide sprang too easily to the surface. She found herself longing for more than just another day of fighting bad guys and patrolling the streets. In so many ways, she'd been just like her mother, looking for trouble. Finding it.

Things had to change. Roxy wanted to live forever in the paradise she'd found inside Isaiah's arms. She just didn't know how to get there.

All she could tell him now was, "Well, okay then."

Chapter Forty

Isaiah stood in workout pants at his darkened bedroom window looking down on the quiet streets of Crystal City, his arms crossed over his bare chest and the weekend looming ahead. For once, he had two days off in a row. The ordeal at Family Services was three days behind him and things were looking up.

Garrett Randall had lawyered up until his attorney-in-law, Sylvia Delgado, showed. After speaking with her, he'd changed his plea and sang like a lark. Everything out of his mouth confirmed what Bob Bratton had already verbosely declared. Jack Fillion's statement ended up being icing on Candace Bratton's go-straight-to-jail cake.

Kitty and Darrin were finally in a good home. Nugget too. Roxy was now Mrs. Isaiah Zaroyin. He should be happy. But he couldn't sleep.

His lofty home-away-from-home sat high enough above the surrounding office buildings that he could see across the dark expanse of the mighty Potomac to the nation's Capitol. Oftentimes, the view offered more of fog than of the Camelot the District could be. On those days and nights, the outlines of the many monuments barely showed through the mist.

But tonight, the epicenter of the world, the idyllic symbol that millions had died for since mankind crawled out of the primordial ooze, beckoned to brave men and women everywhere like the rare and precious jewel it was. *Freedom.*

Unfortunately, the priceless gift came with the messy business of a republic hard at work, the backstabbing, muckraking, and the burdensome processes of democratic rule. It came with the blood of patriots and right along with it, the disdain for those patriots by Freedom's worst critics. It came with looting and riots when people chose to be offended instead of compromise. Aside from the warmongering dictatorships spread across the globe, democracy had proven to be the world's least ineffective style of government and it appeared doomed to fail. It was sloppy and disorganized, mayhem at its best. Yet it had persevered. More than that, democracy flourished. Still, it challenged the common man to think better. To strive higher. To rise above the grimy, big city alleys rife with poverty and crime. To be all that he—and she—could be.

The ghost of a smile breached Isaiah's lips as he stared at the city he loved. His strange and relentless brain always turned the feelings of his heart into ARMY/NAVY/AF/USMC recruiting slogans.

Be all you can be.

Ready to Lead. Ready to Follow. Never Quit.

The only easy day was yesterday.

Aim High.

The few. The Proud.

His all-time favorite: *Semper Fi. Always faithful.*

He understood why his unique brain translated the emotions of his heart into ideals the way it did. Because this crazy busy, crazy courageous, polarizing land that he loved, had once been his to destroy—or to save.

It all started the day he'd opened the front door of his parents' home to a stranger, the day Cassandra Bick's goons abducted him. His mother had been dead nine years by then. His father was never home. Isaiah had just signed on with a computer software company. The hours were good, the pay reasonable, but the job was brain numbingly stale. It was just him and his cat—until he'd opened the door and let the worst kind of evil in.

Only by the grace of God had he lived through the following months of torture at the diabolical Bicks' hands. It was then he'd first tasted, truly tasted, hungered for and understood Freedom. The universe brought it to him one day with the sweet touch of Eden's delicate fingertips fluttering over his feverish psyche. She'd called him Black Eyes back then, because, well, his eyes were as black as sin during that time in Hell. No hint of white rimmed his pupils. Just the futility of utter despair as he worked the dark commands of a truly wicked woman.

His powerful psychic channels had been forced wide open at the command of Cassandra Bick's rapacious razor blades for too long. Day after day. Week after week. She'd kept him weak and on edge. At first, when his conscience still ruled, he'd appeased her with false information, rather than search out and destroy the individuals she'd ordered him to locate. She was no psychic. She had no way to prove whether he'd lied or not.

But one week into the agony, she'd brought some squared-jawed, bright-eyed, ex-military hulk to the game. McCluskey. A big, broad wall of a man, he'd started simply by questioning Isaiah about those targets he couldn't seem to locate, but he ended beating a younger guy, one who'd avoided sports in lieu of chess most of his life, damned near to death. Oddly, Cassandra stepped in and stopped her trained guard dog before Isaiah passed out. She must've gotten tired sitting on her stool and watching. By then, Isaiah knew. She'd acquired another Level Ten to validate what he told her. There was no choice but to comply.

He swallowed hard remembering those long, hard days, but yeah. A tortured man will do and say anything—ANYTHING—if it garnered even a minute's relief from the razor. By the time Eden arrived, he'd been held captive three days short of five months in the Bicks' concrete warehouse. He'd been starved, beaten, left alone in the cold for days on end, and he'd been forced to do despicable things.

He'd influenced the national budget process in favor of Senator Bick. He'd garnered Congressional support for Senator Bick's election campaign. He'd swayed the movers and the shakers in America to believe in, and to back the conspiracy Senator Bick and his wife touted as sound business practice. But worst of all, and the thing that haunted Isaiah still—he'd hunted Eden, first to California, then onto Hawaii and Alaska. To kill her.

Bile lifted up his throat at how close he'd come to killing her. Everything zeroed back to Abraham Zaroyin and those damnable three Gs: Gain. Glory. Greed.

The Bicks never would've latched onto their insane plan for world domination if Abraham hadn't bragged about his son's unique psychic powers to Senator Bick, and how those powers could be put to good use. A mind like Isaiah's could be used to control soldiers during combat. Think of it! One Level Ten psychic could change the face of war for all time.

But controlling the fog of war wasn't part of their plan. Instead the Bicks set out to control every Level Ten on the planet. They wanted the world. When that wasn't enough for their greedy appetites, they ventured into cryo-technology, thinking that if they bred two Level Tens, they could create their own master race via IVF, Invitro Fertilization, and an army of surrogate mothers. To produce that army, they only needed one male Level Ten, one young enough to milk sperm from for as long as he lived. Level Ten female psychics were throwaway commodities. Unlike male bodies, which replaced sperm indefinitely over a lifetime, females came with a limited number of eggs at birth. There was no need to keep a female alive longer than the time it took to harvest her eggs and cryo-freeze them to be fertilized at a later date.

Isaiah hadn't known it at the time, but by then, Abraham Zaroyin was into the Bicks as deeply as he was. While Isaiah hunted Eden, the elder Zaroyin had also hunted her. After Abraham drove her from the safety of her FBI friends in Alaska, Cassandra had forced Isaiah to synchronize the crash of Eden's Cessna with the arrival of two of his father's FBI drones. He'd killed an innocent FBI Agent, Charles Sweets, in the middle of the bleak Canadian winter. At the time Isaiah didn't know Charlie was an undercover agent monitoring Dr. Zaroyin's laboratory in the middle of Ontario, Canada.

So yeah, some nights, Isaiah couldn't sleep.

Eden could've died in that crash. Ky Winchester and Tate Higgins, Special Agents Sam Becker and Tucker Chase could've died on their mission to rescue her. Yet not once had any of them held Isaiah's crimes against him. They'd simply stormed Bicks' warehouse and rescued him. Eden and Ky gave him a warm place to stay once the hospital released him. They gave him a family and a warm place to lick his wounds. It was Eden's faith in him and her unconditional love for him, that still today maintained a barrier between him and the world that called him a pariah.

Then Tucker Chase adopted him, more or less. Told him *'Things happen, kid. Get over it"* in his brash, Navy SEAL way. Taught him how to flip naysayers off. Gave him the job he'd truly hungered for. Gave him his pride back, too.

Little did Eden know it then, but much like she'd done with Ky on their first encounter, she'd given Isaiah just enough hope to hang onto with her first psychic touch. The closer she'd drawn to him in that morgue of a warehouse that final day, the more hope had flared like a beacon in the night. It was then that Isaiah knew he'd connected with someone who not only cared about him, but who was intent of saving him at all cost.

Eden hadn't known him then. She certainly didn't have to risk her life rescuing him. She could've dismissed him as just the son of a madman. Most of American had. But not Eden. He determined then, because of Eden, to fight Cassandra Bick, simply by taking... One. More. Breath.

In truth, Abraham Zaroyin had come to his son's rescue with Eden that same day. It was his change of heart that had enabled her to subdue McCluskey, and together they'd infiltrated the Bicks' lair, and rescued—*me*.

Isaiah knew for a fact she still visited his father regularly. He'd seen her at the prison during his weekly visits. Abraham Zaroyin wasn't evil in the way of the Bicks. He'd just dreamed a dream that ended up being an out of control nightmare. He'd lost his way and his vision the moment he'd put that dream ahead of his wife and son, the moment he'd sold his soul to the Devil called Glory. The second he'd placed that single call for funding to the conniving Senator Bick.

Because of what he'd been forced to do, Isaiah had vowed never to read any person's mind unless they were in mortal danger or in dire need of his help. Cassandra Bick might have proven how easy it was to influence others, but Isaiah chose to honor his sister and his friend, Ky Winchester's sweet wife. It would never be enough, but it was—something.

Pressing both palms to his biceps, he hugged himself like he used to do in the hospital after his rescue. Eventually, he'd masked the worst of his scars with plastic surgery, but the least of them, he'd let be. They served a purpose Cassandra Bick never could've imagined when she'd started her foul game. In the end, her exquisitely painful methods of enlightenment became a crucible, a furnace of sorts, wherein Isaiah's heart had been purified by blood and fire.

The scars were in no way mementos of her. Oh, hell no. Instead, they were badges of fortitude forged in the worst of times. Each lined welt on his arms, shoulders, thighs, and ribs, proved that his fight had been real and deadly. They proved he'd overcome formidable odds, and that he could do it again if he had to. That good did triumph over evil, and yeah, it might sound corny, but each one of them proved that time heals. They proved the love of a true friend.

Lastly, they proved how desperately mankind craved Freedom. It wasn't simply an inalienable right or a millennial privilege. It certainly wasn't an entitlement. To a man who'd survived his own private holocaust, Freedom was—everything.

The breath he'd been holding escaped, fogging the window. He should've been snuggled against Roxy's warm backside, and yet he lingered where he stood. His greatest adventure, serving the lovely lady wrapped in his sheets, now lay ahead. But that lady's heart was full of sadness and unrealized expectations tonight. She missed her kids.

Roxy'd tried to hide her disappointment. She'd bucked up like the trooper she was at the crime scene in Arlington, which ended up being nothing more than a bunch of teenagers acting out some movie scene about counterfeiting. They'd bragged they had plates to print millions of counterfeit bills, a weak boast to begin with. A real counterfeiter would've known that plates went the way of dinosaurs. Guess someone forgot to tell those kids the movie was a hit long before the digital age.

The guns in their hands made them dangerous and stupid, but once FBI SWAT rolled on scene, they'd morphed into meek little lambs, bleating for their mamas and crying, "Don't shoot!" They had no plates, no paper, and no brains, just an antsy local police force that had erred on the side of public safety when they'd called in the FBI.

Isaiah arched his back and stretched. As a kid, he'd wanted what all kids want, to be rich and famous. Popular. Of course, he'd wanted to be Superman and Ironman, too. His childish dreams were set pretty low back then. Yet from the moment FBI Agent Eden had saved him, he'd known he'd found his niche in life, to use that amazing Level Ten gift to give back to the world. Hence, his new mission: to serve and protect, to please and love the restless woman asleep in the king-sized bed behind him.

The events of the last week had changed Roxy. The gusto she'd lived with had dimmed. Her nerves were frayed, and she'd lost the children she would've gladly given her life for. Roxy had put on her happy face once the operation ended, but Isaiah knew better. At the end of the day, his streetwise, bust-'em-up and knock-'em-down Metro police officer's heart was broken. All because of the love of a child.

The words she'd uttered on the curb that day, the bleakness in her eyes when she'd said "Well, okay then," had very nearly done Isaiah in. Darrin had said the exact same thing when Isaiah'd been forced to leave him behind. The sheer resignation contained in those four syllables cried out a wretched plea for forgiveness that neither Roxy nor Darrin needed. They'd done nothing wrong.

Yet for ten years, Darrin had blamed himself for his father's desertion. Thank God, the little boy's real father had custody of him now. But Roxy? As happy as she was that her kids were where they belonged, she blamed herself for not being good enough to right the wrongs committed against them. She hurt for them—like any good mother would.

What's a man supposed to do with that? Knock her up? It seemed the perfect solution, and they had made love like bunny rabbits in springtime. But she was on birth control, and even if it failed, even if she were with his child right now, it'd still take nine long months to put that baby in her arms. She'd head for the precinct come morning. He'd kiss her goodbye and catch the blue-line into the District and the J. Edgar Hoover building on Pennsylvania Ave. They'd spend their day doing what they were good at until their allotted shifts ended, and they were free to do what they were best at—loving each other.

You'd think a Level Ten would know how to best comfort his woman, but Isaiah simply... Did. Not. So he did what he could. Stealthily, he tugged the big, red Nats bag from beneath his side of the bed. During his lunch break, he'd bought ball caps, baseball shirts, and home game tickets to an upcoming Nats game, but he couldn't wait. She needed to smile now.

Slipping out of his pants, he fastened one cap on his head, then gingerly climbed on hands and knees to where she lay sleeping—in the nude—in the middle of the bed. His blood pooled as he tugged the sheet, baring her satin skin to the ambient light coming through the windows. Moaning, she reached for the quickly escaping sheet, then rolled to her back. Her tummy and the delightful nest of curls at the apex of her thighs came into view.

Isaiah closed his eyes and breathed in the delicious feminine scent of his woman. Part musk, part exotic fruit, but all Roxy. He perched her very own Nats cap on top of her sleepy head and—

"What the hell are you up to?" she asked grumpily, her fingers tugging at the brim.

"We've got tickets behind the Nats' dugout. Wanna come?"

"Just you and me?" Was there hope in her voice?

Isaiah pressed the length of his body over hers, encasing her in his warmth and all of his love. "Would I do that to you?"

She held her breath. Not a good sign. Was she going to cry? He cut that reaction off at the pass with a quick peck on the tip of her nose. "It'll be a party, Roxy. So far your dad's in for a couple corndogs. Tate's bringing Winslow. You'll like her, and Eden and Ky will be there with Kyler, their little boy. He's a doll. Tucker's tied up with some congressional hearing, but his wife, Melissa, will be there. Was there anyone you wanted to invite?"

Roxy cuffed his shoulder, hard enough that it stung. "Stop teasing me. I'm not in the mood—"

With a rush, he rolled her over until she had no choice but to straddle his hips. "I almost forgot. Jack and Cathleen are bringing Kitty and Darrin. Nugget can't come, but—"

"My kids!" Roxy squealed. "Really? They're coming, too? I mean, Jack and Cathleen don't mind? When? Tomorrow? Is there really a game tomorrow?"

Her core bounced against him, starting a fire in his groin. This was the most energy she'd exhibited since they'd left Family Services behind. Isaiah let his fingers roam over her lush assets until they came to rest at the curve of her hips. "The first game I could get decent seats at is next week. Can you wait that long?"

She huffed, her voice tender and close to tears. "Aww... my kids. You did this for me."

He bucked enough for her to get his—point. "I'll do anything for you, Roxy. You know that."

A sad giggle choked from her throat. "But they're not really mine," she whispered, her eyes extra dark and sparkly beneath the brim of her cap. "They never were."

Please don't cry, baby. You're breaking my heart. "Oh, yes, they are. They'll always be your kids. Jack and Cathleen don't mind if we take Kitty and Darrin for an overnighter one of these days, either. They're planning their first family picnic this weekend, and they want us to be there. Your dad, too. You're not just a police officer. You're Aunt Roxy, remember? We're part of their family."

"You called Jack?"

"He called the office before I got in this morning. The switchboard put him through to my cell and..." Isaiah smoothed his palms from her hips to her shoulders. Handfuls of luscious real estate lay in between, but she needed more than just a good time in the sack tonight. "He thanked us for taking care of Kitty and Darrin last week. Guess they haven't stopped talking about us, and Jack said he knows how hard it was to give them up. He knows what it's like to lose a kid." Isaiah shook off the huskiness in his tone. Damn it. He'd grown to love those kids, too, but if Roxy started crying...

She tipped forward until her plump breasts flattened against his chest. It was hard to resist tweaking her nipples or delving into her feminine secrets. Roxy enjoyed a little rough play under the covers, but even as tempting as she was in her birthday suit, this was not the time. To keep his all-male body in line with the fragile feminine creature sitting on him, Isaiah interlocked his fingers behind her back, where they could do no harm.

Roxy removed her ball cap, then his and set them aside. Nose-to-nose and heart-to-heart, she hovered above him. Silky black tendrils bathed him in exquisite luxury, as she closed the distance and planted a quick, wet kiss on his mouth. "I love you so much," she breathed.

"You could be pregnant," he informed her before he lost track of his agenda.

That earned him a grunt. "Not if my doctor knows what's good for her." Roxy tossed her hair to one side, where it fell like a curtain of midnight across his shoulder. "I don't take those pills every day for the fun of it," she said with a hint of the snark he adored.

Turning his nose into the ebony ribbons of her sleek hair, Isaiah drank in the heady fragrance of coconut shampoo as his hips lifted to the lovely lady riding them. All he wanted was for this passionate woman to come back to life in his arms.

"It could still happen, you know. Nothing's foolproof," he murmured, his eyes closed and his lust rising. The enthralling scent of her sex enticed with every breath and wiggle until—

"Oh, no, you don't. Keep your hands where they are," she ordered, just before she sank onto him, luscious and wet, warm and grippingly hot.

"Yes, Officer," he breathed, straining not to grab hold of her ass like he needed to. "You may need to use those cuffs." That ought to get her mind off the kids—for a minute or two.

"Uh-uh," she growled, sinking her teeth into his bottom lip, not enough to break skin, but enough to turn him to steel. "I know what you like and it's not game playing, my love. It's..." she breathed into his open mouth. "...me."

"Yessssssssss." His back arched instinctively, seeking his rhythm with hers, needing to pleasure her as much as she pleasured him. It was all he could do to keep his hands fastened at the back of the alluring goddess rocking him. Filling her. Filling him. "It's always been you, Roxy. It can only be you. Whenever you're ready. If you want to wait, or if you want to stop taking those pills and—Ouch!"

She bit him again! rubbing those soft, warm breasts against his chest as if marking her territory like a cat. "You can touch me now," she purred.

And touch her he did. With his fingers. With his mouth. With his lips.

With every last beat of his heart.

The End

Excerpt

from

Connor, In the Company of Snipers, #5

© 2014 by Irish Winters

"Damn it." USMC Sergeant Isabella Ramos cursed as her ammo clip hit the dirt on the other side of the wall. Sergeant Connor Maher could not help but notice. He didn't write the rules of nature. A real man's always gonna look, and this particular gal's derrière, albeit camouflaged in the uniform of the day and plenty of dust, made for a choice view. What red-blooded, all American male wouldn't?

One minute she was seated all nice and comfortable on that three-foot wall. The next, she was bent over it, damn near ass over teakettles with her boots, legs and butt on display. He glanced away, not wanting to be caught looking—at least not by her.

He and his buddy, Jamie, were part of the United State's military response to the increased violence of the Iraqi insurgency in Fallujah. Both short timers and counting the days, this was their final tour together unless Jamie got another brilliant idea to re-up. With home only a couple months away, Connor was antsy. All he had to do was stay alive. In Iraq. During one of the hottest USMC campaigns of the war. Stolen commercial breaks like this show with Ramos made the grind endurable.

She'd gotten the short end of the stick when their commanding officer decided someone ought to show the two newly arrived non-commissioned officers the lay of the land, and voila. Just like that, they got a snappy tour of U.S. Camp Baharia, and along with it, a floorshow that couldn't be beat.

The good thing about the predominantly USMC camp was the large clear water lake in the center of it. The bad thing was that it was in Iraq. The once-upon-a-time desert resort town was now filled with hard-core military men and women who sometimes forgot how to behave. Like Lance Corporal Jamie Ramos, who by sheer coincidence shared the sergeant's last name, but obviously, not her dedication to the Corps.

Already passed over once for promotion, Jamie was headed for trouble with his CO. He didn't seem to have a problem with his rifle qualification or combat fitness, but his true talents lay in another direction—entertainment. Jamie was a tease to the mathematical power of a gazillion, and that innate need for attention would land him in the brig one of these days.

"You know you want to." He elbowed Connor again, urging him to do the unthinkable. "Just one little smack. It's easy. I've done it a million times. No one else will see you. Just walk over, lay one on her ass and run like hell. She's short. She'll never catch you. Go on. Do it."

"Shut up," Connor muttered out of the corner of his mouth, glancing again at the ass in question and doubting the 'I've done it a million times' line. "You know better than to treat women like that. Knock it off."

"What's she gonna do? You're both the same rank," Jamie persisted. "It'll be fun."

"Cut the crap. She's a lady."

"No, she ain't. She's a jarhead just like us. She's GI. Loosen up, Maher. Walk on the wild side for once in your geeky life."

Connor glanced at the ass in question again. Damn. It was spank-a-licious and hard to keep his eyes off of. This dark-haired and olive-skinned beauty had potential in his book. Lots of potential. He didn't want Jamie's crazy antics to blow his chances before he knew if he had any.

Raised in a house filled with six younger brothers and no sisters, women still perplexed Connor. Sometimes they loved a guy who only two seconds earlier they'd hated. He couldn't keep up. Besides, his mother had taught him early what Jamie's education must have missed. A real man does not disrespect women, even when they cussed like sailors. He'd grown to appreciate Bridgette Maher's wise sayings more now that he was out of her house. Treat a woman like a lady and she'll never turn into a nag.

With a twinkle in his eye, Jamie edged closer to the irritated sergeant's backside, a big cheesy smirk on his trouble-making face. She tipped farther over the wall, the toes of her boots nearly off the ground and still cussing a blue streak. No way was Connor getting close to that action. He shook his head and mouthed a definite, No. Don't do it.

Jamie's eyes brightened with, Are you daring me, man?

Connor didn't know whether to nod or shake his head. Either way spelled trouble.

Jamie's left eyebrow spiked into an incredibly wicked, Here goes. His arm lifted higher.

Connor shook his head, disgusted at himself for letting Jamie take a prank this far. He stepped forward to halt the wise guy before things got more out of hand. Retrieving the clip in question would solve the Sergeant's problem and torpedo Jamie's stand-up comedy once and for all.

"Excuse me, ma'am—"

Jamie's perfectly white teeth flashed a big shitty grin. His flattened hand lifted over the rump in question.

Apparently, Ramos hadn't heard Connor yet, leaning over the wall like she was. He was nearly behind her. "Ma'am, let me get that for—"

The sergeant tipped one booted foot to the sky and exclaimed, "Finally. Got the damned thing."

SMACK!

Crap. Sergeant Ramos came off that wall so fast, she landed in Connor's arms. The deadly scopes of a deadly sniper skewered her one man viewing audience.

Oh, sweet Mother Mary and Joseph.

He gulped and caught a peripheral of his trouble-making buddy. Jamie was on his knees. At the end of wall. Out of sight. Clear out of sight.

Ramos could only see—him.

Those sizzling brown windows to a she-devil's soul were pointed straight up at—him.

Crap. I'll be busted back to private first class.

He should've pushed off. He should've been a gentleman and apologized for the inappropriate contact. He should've done anything, but no. Generations of hopeless romantics from the Emerald Isle had led him to this pivotal moment. His fingers refused to unclench from her biceps. Looking down into two dark pools of what felt like the strongest, bitterest, sweetest coffee, Connor did good just to keep breathing.

Hot damn. If I'm dying, it's gonna hurt, but I'm going to heaven.

Equal rank or not, something about this diminutive spitfire had stomped the hell out of his ego from the first moment he'd seen her. With the meanest reputation in the squad, she could teach the drill sergeant's How to Be an SOB class all by herself. Ramos was a cherry bomb with a short fuse and right now, he was cannon fodder. Nothing but.

"You want to die right here and now, Boston?" she hissed, her shoulders rolling along with her swagger. How could a gal with such sexy brown eyes be so mean and sound so tough? His eyes refused to move off of her, even though her top lip was curled over a wicked Devil Dog bite.

And here he was holding her. Not just holding her, but chest to breast kind of holding her, and either she didn't mind the contact or he was in for one helluva lesson in smack down, hand-to-hand combat. The woman was pure muscle, her biceps as hard as her eyes. Contempt glittered there, and just maybe something else. Mischief?

"Ahh, no, sir – I mean—no, ma'am—I mean—" He dropped his hands and took a full step back to get out of her personal space, stuttering like an idiot.

Jamie still crouched with his hand clamped over his big fat mouth he was laughing so hard. Right then and there, Connor should've handed his buddy over, but real men don't do that either.

Ramos stomped right back under Connor's chin, her eyes dark and deadly, full of the promise of nothing but pain. Maybe death. "You think hitting another soldier's ass is funny, do you?"

"No, ma'am, I do not."

God, she was so damned gorgeous. Yeah, she radiated a certain amount of radioactive hostility, and he was pretty sure he glowed already, but damn. What a package. His nose filled with the lovely whiff of roses and incense. How fitting. The sweetness of flowers mingled with the unmistakable hint of burning ash. He'd been an alter boy. He ought to know.

That drab green T-shirt peeking up from her uniform didn't conceal the rounded landscape beneath from a man of his height, either. Six-foot-three should be the one doing the intimidating instead of peering down a woman's shirt like he was. The thought of peeling her out of those desert cammies tweaked what was left of his common sense. He wanted to touch. Hell, he wanted to fondle, pet, and a whole lot more.

Should I pour on the Maher charm?

Sizzling death glowered up at him, not even blinking once and full on daring him to keep breathing.

Ah, maybe not.

The verbal assault commenced. "I'm gonna make you wish you died during boot camp, you pig-faced, camel-lipped, piece of..."

On and on she went. He took it like a man. Almost. His jaw kept moving, but sound had ceased coming out. Article 128 of the United States Code of Military Justice flashed through his blood-deprived brain.

Question: *Is a slap on the butt considered sexual battery?*

Answer: *Damn straight. Don't touch. Don't tell. And all that stuff.*

Jamie howled, at last overcome by his own hysterics.

Ramos shot a scorching look over her shoulder. "You!"

The instant she looked way, the magic faded. Connor was half-inclined to cup her chin and direct her gaze back to him. Just him. Not Jamie. But Connor was afraid to touch her. She might be too hot for him to handle.

"Why don't you grow up?" Kicking a boot scrape of sand in Jamie's face, she stalked off, which only made him laugh harder. The dumb ass looked like he was having a heart attack the way his face was all screwed up.

Oddly, Connor felt a chill when Sergeant Ramos left. A chill in Iraq? How'd that work? He watched her walk away, her dark brown ponytail twitching side to side in time with her butt, both sassy as hell. Taking one step forward to follow and apologize, he came to his senses and stopped short. Not now. Let her cool off. Mad women were unpredictable.

"You shoulda... You shoulda...." Still laughing his guts out, tears streamed over Jamie's cheeks. "I mean it. You shoulda seen the look on your face!"

"You could get me court-martialed," Connor ground out, even as his gaze returned to the command tent where Ramos had gone. He wasn't so much scared as interested. Maybe it was all those blond brothers he'd grown up with, but dark-eyed girls always caught his attention. Hers seemed darker than most, full of sparks, promise, and a whopping dose of cayenne. The moment he'd seen her, he knew. They would spend time together.

"Oh, hell." Jamie pulled himself onto the wall, dusting his pants off. "Don't worry. She won't do anything. You're safe."

"Yeah, right." Connor huffed out an aggravated sigh. "You ever heard of friendly fire? She was an MP sniper, jerk-off. Now I gotta watch my back the rest of my rotation."

Jamie guffawed through another laughing attack. Connor had half a mind to kick his friend's ass if it'd douse the hysterics, which he doubted. Jamie was a fun-loving, risk-taking Hispanic who could charm the socks off most ladies. Didn't seem to have any effect on the sergeant, though.

Finally, he turned semi-serious. "Don't worry. I've got your six. You know that, Bro."

"Bullshit, you do," Connor shot back at him. "You've got nothing."

"No, really. I've seen how you look at her." Jamie almost sounded sincere. "Listen, Connor. Remember how I told you I'd never seen her before in my life, how lots of us Hispanics got the same last names, only it don't mean we're related? You know, like Martinez, Gonzales, Sanchez, Moreno, Garcia?"

"So what?" Connor could feel it coming. The joke wasn't over yet.

Jamie winked. "I lied. That's Izza. My sister."

Thank you for reading One-Eyed Jack!

If you enjoyed Isaiah and Roxy's story, check out:

Joker, Joker, Deuces Wild Series, Book 2

King of Hearts, Deuces Wild Series, Book 1

Don't forget to visit my sexy ex-military snipers:

In the Company of Snipers.

Coming soon - Seth, #17

Other Irish Winters' books

Angel, An SOBs Novel, #1
Smoke, Hearts and Ashes, #1
Ash, Hearts and Ashes Series, #2

You are the key to this book's success!

Please tell other readers why you liked Isaiah and Roxy's story by leaving an honest review at the retail site where you purchased it.

Recommend it to your friends.

Lend it.

Most of all, enjoy it!

The best way to keep up with my new releases, giveaways, and actionable intel is by signing up for my spam-free newsletter at IrishWinters.com.

About the Author

Irish Winters is an award winning, Amazon best-selling author who, when she isn't writing, dabbles in poetry, grandchildren, and rarely (as in extremely rarely) the kitchen. More prone to be outdoors than in, she grew up the quintessential tomboy on a dairy farm in rural Wisconsin, spent her teenage years in the Pacific Northwest, but calls the Wasatch Mountains of Northern Utah, home. For now.

She believes in making every day count for something, and follows the wise admonition of her mother to, "Look out the window and see something!"

Connect with Irish online:

On Facebook
https://www.facebook.com/IrishWintersAuthor/

On Twitter
https://twitter.com/irishwinters1

www. IrishWinters.com

www.ingramcontent.com/pod-product-compliance
Lightning Source LLC
Chambersburg PA
CBHW030354200726

48286CB00014B/1323